IBEX

I0614139

Jon Schiller, PhD

RISEN

THE SECOND SEAL OF THE KRYPTEIA CONSPIRACY

BY MICHAEL KOOGLER, JED QUINN, & JAREN RILEY

ISBN: 978-1-943519-05-7

Book editing by Elizabeth Humphrey
Bookworm Editing, Littleton, Colorado USA

Book cover art, packaging and design by
Kreative Storm Press, Coralville, Iowa USA

Author Information at:

www.michaelkoogler.net
www.jedquinn.com

IBEX

A fictional novel about a Cold War Iranian Listening Post funded by The Shah with Participation by the US CIA

A Novel authored by Jon Schiller, PhD

Author of Trading Books
Insider's Automatic Options Strategy
Self-Adaptive Options & Currency Trading
The 100% Return Options Trading Strategy
Profit in Index Options Trading Using Decision Charts
Compilation of Jon Schiller's OEX Options Trading Newsletters

Author of Fiction Novels
Masada Never Again
Ultra Taiwan Fighter
Multihulls
Lost in Space

Author of a True Story:
Irrational Indictment & Imprisonment

Jon Schiller, PhD

**BOOKSURGE
CHARLESTON, SC**

2008

WRITTEN BY JON SHILLER, PhD

PUBLISHED BY BOOKSURGE
CHARLESTON, SC 29418
Printed in the United States of America

First Printing
This is a fictional story based on actual actions in Iran witnessed by the Author

ISBN: 978-0-9774305-2-9
BOOKSURGE
ISBN: 0-9774305-2-9
JON SCHILLER SOFTWARE
jonsch1@verizon.net
http://www.jonschilleroptions.com/
http://wwwjonschblogger.blogspot.com/
Lompoc, CA 93436

DEDICATION

The author dedicates this fictional spy novel to the many thousands of men and women of the world who spend their countries' resources spying on each other rather than helping each other.

The author also wishes to acknowledge the contribution of his wife, Emilie, who helped write this novel. Emilie is a combination of Christina, Olga, Fahrina, Heidi, Joanne and Anna, but better than any one or all together. Emilie received the BA in Education from Occidental College and the MA in Education from the University of Southern California

LIST OF CHARACTERS

The complexity of the IBEX story leads inevitably to a large number of characters. Following is a list of characters for the convenience of the reader.

HEADS OF STATE (whose actions and words are fictional)
      President Jimmy Mahoney, USA
      Premier Leonid Ilyich Breznov, USSR
      Shah Pahlano, Shah-an-Shah, Iran
      Prime Minister Anwar Sadim, Egypt

AMERICANS
      Dr. Brad Kelly, project director of IBEX for Associated Aviation Corp., reporting to the president, Dr. Morrell
      Dr. John Morrell, president of Associated Aviation Corporation
      Helen, Dr. Morrell's executive secretary
      Anna Kelly, Dr. Kelly's wife
      Tom Bradley, engineer at Associated Aviation, technical assistant to Dr. Kelly

AMERICANS cont.

Sandy, executive secretary of Associated Aviation, Washington, DC, office

Mr. Thompson, head of Associated Aviation, Washington, DC, office

Jack Johnson, director of Munitions Control Office, US State Department

Robert Hack, director of International Programs, US Defense Dept., Pentagon

Jeannie, executive secretary to Mr. Hack

Colonel Long, aide to Mr. Hack

General John Robertson, head of US MAAG (Military Advisory Assistance Group), Iran

Ralph Hauser, CIA agent, assigned to IBEX

Ambassador Richard Hurd, US ambassador to Iran, close friend of President Mahoney

Colonel Bennett, aide to Ambassador Hurd

Joanne Curtis, executive secretary to Ambassador Hurd

Bob Anderson, Associated Aviation pilot

Jerri, Associated Aviation receptionist

Bill Wilson, Associated Aviation engineer

Dr. John Vries, Associated Aviation engineer

David Elliott, Associated Aviation engineer

Jack Nishamoto, Associated Aviation engineer

Bob Thompson, Associated Aviation engineer

Jim Smith, Associated Aviation engineer

Captain Bradock, USAF C-130 copilot

Major Wells, USAF C-130 pilot

Elizabeth, executive secretary to President Mahoney

Bob Jones, Associated Aviation corporate attorney

SWEDES

Christina Rimsen, blonde, resident of Tel Aviv and travels widely

Olga Sonnensohn, redhead, resident of Tel Aviv and travels widely

ISRAELIS

General Shlomo Izhack, Director General, Israeli Ministry of Defense

General Rafi Yidron, head of Mossad, Israeli intelligence agency

Colonel Joseph Ladrun, electronics officer assigned to IBEX, reports to General Izhack

Amnon Milchbucher, member of Mossad, trusted agent of General Yidron

Ilona Ladrun, wife of Colonel Ladrun

Yossi, bodyguard from Israeli embassy, Washington, DC

IRANIANS

General Hatami, Chief of the Royal Iranian Air Force

Mr. Abfol Mahi, armament agent, reputedly bastard brother of the Shah, owner of Iran Software, Ltd.

Shaheen Mouhoud, member of Savak, the Iranian intelligence agency, trusted agent of the Shah

General Doshenshah, Deputy to General Hatami

Colonel Abdul (Abe) Fahi, director of the IBEX project, reports to General Hatami

Fahrina Mahi, daughter of Abfol Mahi, PhD in computer science, director of software development, Iran Software, Ltd.

Salim (Bob) Mena, head of Associated Aviation in Iran

Shahan, bodyguard of Mahi family

SWISS

Professor Doctor Rudolf Halter, professor of mathematics, specialist in cryptology, Federal Institute of Technology (ETH), Zürich

Dr. Heidi Zehnzeit, PhD in mathematics, assistant to Prof. Dr. Halter

Dr. Peter Dichter, technical director of Cryptomatik, AG, Zürich

Herr Maler, president of Cryptomatik

Herr Rediess, project manager, Cryptomatik

Dr. Ochsner, marketing director, Cryptomatik

TABLE OF CONTENTS

PROLOGUE

The IBEX project was a direct result of the perceived need of one nation to clandestinely collect information about other nations for reasons of national security. The two superpowers, the United States and the Soviet Union (when it existed) each spent billions of dollars each year spying on each other. The news media was filled with stories about spies on one side or the other defecting, or spies being prosecuted, convicted, and sent to prison. These stories in the news media usually deal with the human side of intelligence gathering, referred to as HUMINT by the intelligence communities (CIA of the US, SAVAK of Iran, of the old Soviet KGB, and MOSSAD of Israel.) IBEX represent a much larger enterprise than just HUMINT. This is electronic intelligence gathering, referred to as ELINT.

IBEX is a fictional story of the people involved in developing, installing, and using an ELINT system during the Shah's reign in Iran. Although the actual titles of world leaders are used, the words and actions of these leaders are purely fictional. The story of IBEX portrays what impact electronic spying can have on world events and how world leaders might react to information so collected.

AUTHOR BACKGROUND

Jon Schiller received the BS in physics from Caltech and the doctorate from the University of Southern California. He served as an executive in aerospace companies for over 20 years. One assignment while employed by a large aerospace company was to obtain business in the Mideast in the countries of Iran and Israel. It was during this assignment that gave him the background to create this fictional novel.

Dr. Jon Schiller

Chapter 1.

Discovery

Dr. Bradford Kelly rubbed his eyes, trying to wake up, after the pilot of Lufthansa flight 807 announced they would be landing in a few minutes at Ben Gurion Airport. Looking out the window on his left at the blue Mediterranean Sea below, Kelly could just barely make out the white beaches and high rise buildings of Tel Aviv in the distance. As the 747 continued its descent, Kelly felt a growing tumescence in his groin as he anticipated the upcoming Shabbat *afternoon delight* with Christina and Olga in his Tel Aviv Hilton suite. He wouldn't have to bother checking into the hotel - already the girls would have taken care of all the formalities and would have the key to his suite.

On a more serious note, Kelly didn't look forward to his meeting with General Shlomo Izhack tomorrow, Sunday morning. He wondered how he would explain the Associated Aviation Corporation board of directors had ordered him to halt the Associated Aviation joint venture with Israeli Aircraft Industries. The AAC board had been disappointed the AAC/IAI joint venture's sales were projected to be only fifty million dollars a year for the next five years. The AAC chairman had stated, "We are looking for one billion dollar bales of hay to feed this elephant - not fifty million dollar grass patches." His summary comment had been, "The Israelis have brains and diligence, but not oil! Concentrate on Iran. The Shah has oil and that means money and he wants to spend it on US armaments. Go to Tel Aviv and meet with General Izhack. Say whatever you have to, but dissolve the AAC/IAI joint venture."

As the Lufthansa 747 taxied to a parking spot on a remote section of the Ben Gurion airport, the chief cabin attendant warned the passengers, "Remain seated after the aircraft comes to a stop." Kelly knew what that meant, *there would be a security check.* The cabin door swung open and four husky Israeli soldiers with Uzi submachine guns boarded the plane. They proceeded down the aisles, carefully looking at each passenger in turn. About five rows behind Kelly, they came to an Arabic-looking man who seemed to fit the profile of their search. He was led off the plane to an army truck parked on the tarmac. Kelly watched through his window as the Israelis seemed to be questioning their suspect. The soldiers inside the airplane continued on down the aisles.

Finally, all the passengers were allowed to deplane and board the busses which would take them to the terminal for passport checking and luggage retrieval. The crush of humanity forced Kelly into the center of the throng, and so he was slow getting out of the bus. He ended up behind a long line of passengers at the passport checking queue. Just as he sighed with resignation, *It's going to take me at least thirty minutes to get through this line*, someone tapped him on the shoulder. He looked around into the smiling face of Amnon Milchbucher. Amnon was an aide to General Rafi Yidron and had been a key help in getting the AAC/IAI joint venture set up. Amnon always seemed to know the right people to talk to when the Israeli bureaucracy slowed or stopped progress on their plans. Amnon gave Kelly a bear hug and led him to the front of the Crew Line in Passport Control. The passport control officer looked up, recognized Amnon, and waived Kelly on through.

Kelly never checked any luggage; he used a carry-on bag only. He was proud he didn't have to face the confusion at the luggage carousel. Today, as usual, he was the first passenger out of the terminal and he and Amnon threaded their way through the large crowd waiting to greet the other passengers. Kelly's excitement surged as he caught sight of two tall beautiful girls, one blonde and one redheaded, waving at him from the end of the exit passageway.

Christina and Olga were two Swedish girls in their mid-twenties who lived in the sunshine of Israel. The pair had often met Kelly at international airports during his frequent travels. They were always fashionably dressed and had plenty of spending money, although they didn't seem to have jobs. He was somewhat puzzled that they always seemed to know his travel plans, but the sexual pleasures they provided stifled his curiosity.

Amnon led Kelly, Christina and Olga to his Mercedes convertible parked illegally at the curb next to the Hertz and Avis rental car booths. The airport policemen were busily giving out tickets to other cars parked there, but Amnon's car seemed immune. Even though it was December 21, 1975, the Israeli sun was bright and the weather warm - in the mid-70's - so they drove toward Tel Aviv with the top down. It was a delightful drive except for the terrible odor from the smoldering Tel Aviv garbage dumps along the side of the highway.

Kelly sometimes wondered how a $500 a month civil servant like Amnon Milchbucher could afford to drive a Mercedes convertible which cost almost $50,000 in Israel. He assumed Amnon's family helped with such expenses. Amnon was a fourth generation Israeli whose father owned an enormous citrus orchard in Renovate, a suburb of Tel Aviv, and had donated the land for the Weizmann Institute.

As they left the green countryside and entered the crowded metropolitan area of Tel Aviv, Amnon headed down Arlozoroff Street which led right up the driveway of the Tel Aviv Hilton. The tall, friendly Hilton doorman, dressed in a smart red uniform, greeted Dr. Kelly by name and with a loud *Shalom!* While the trio of passengers climbed out of the car, Amnon took the opportunity to remind Kelly he had a dinner date that evening with General Shlomo Izhack, "Get some rest. I'll pick you up in the lobby for dinner at 9:30."

As Kelly, Christina and Olga walked though the sumptuous Hilton lobby, the 3pm Shabbat crowds in the large sitting area were having drinks, coffee and pastries with loud conversations all around in a multitude of languages, but mainly in Hebrew and English.

They were lucky - they didn't have to wait for an elevator. The Lufthansa crew had just checked in and were filing into an elevator so Kelly and his friends chose the same one. Christina pushed the 15th floor button. Kelly smiled in recognition to the blonde Viking stewardess who had been on duty in first class on his flight from Frankfurt today. She had served him a glass of champagne immediately after he settled into his 747 seat. He had to run to catch the Tel Aviv flight since his flight from Los

Angeles to Frankfurt had been almost an hour late.   The champagne had been a welcome relaxant.   The stewardess got off on the 15th floor also.

Christina led Kelly, followed by Olga to suite 1501 at the west end of the hotel.   The view from their combination sitting room was magnificent - the long line of beach bordering the sparkling blue Mediterranean stretched southward toward the Old City of Jaffa and northward toward Herzylia.   The coffee table was almost groaning under the large basket of fruit and a bouquet of roses plus a cold bottle of Mumm's, compliments of the Hilton manager, with a personal note of welcome to Dr. Kelly.

The balcony of the adjoining bedroom overlooked the hotel swimming pool.   A large Bar Mitzvah reception was underway. Guests gorged themselves at a long table loaded with delicacies. They were wearing formal clothes, in sharp contrast to the bikini clad crowd on the beach outside the west window.

Kelly unpacked his things and climbed into the shower, while the girls disappeared into the other bathroom. *Which one will I get this afternoon?* Kelly wondered, stretching out on his back on the huge bed.   He didn't have to wait long to find out – Olga slid in beside him and kissed him warmly.   He wrapped his arms around her and a few minutes later they sank into a deep slumber.

Kelly awoke at 9 to find the bed empty.   The girls had heard Amnon tell Kelly about dinner plans.   *Will the girls realize they are not invited?*   He glanced into the sitting room and saw Christina and Olga drinking the champagne, eating some of the fruit and engrossed in a TV movie, completely oblivious to Kelly. He quietly closed the sitting room door, decided the girls wouldn't miss dinner at all.

Taking a quick sitz bath, Kelly washed away the evidence of his earlier pleasures, using the great advance to civilization contributed by the French - the bidet.   He finished dressing, left the suite through the bedroom door and walked down the hall toward the elevator.   As he passed by room 1508, *his* Lufthansa stewardess was welcoming inside a tall, handsome Israeli.

Kelly hurried toward the revolving lobby door, just in time to see Amnon and General Izhack driving up in the Mercedes.   The top was now up and there was a chilly north wind blowing, making the canvas front of the hotel awning whip back and forth noisily. General Izhack opened the right car door and climbed out, "Dr. Kelly, as our honored guest, I insist you take the guest seat. I will sit in the back."

Kelly laughed, "Thank you, sir, but in the US we call the right front seat the *death seat* because the passengers in that seat suffer the highest fatality rate."

General Izhack laughed heartily and settled into the back seat, "Don't worry, Dr. Kelly. We Israelis are much better drivers than you Americans."

Amnon carefully pulled out of the long Hilton entrance road and turned left on Hayarkon, heading north toward Herzylia. General Izhack leaned forward, "Dr. Kelly, remember, no business discussions this evening. We will save business until tomorrow morning. Tonight we will hear about your sailing in California and you will hear about my skin diving in the clear waters of the Gulf of Eilat."

At that moment, Amnon pulled up to the Casbah Restaurant on Yesha'avahu Street. Standing beside the door was a large, heavy-set Israeli whom Kelly guessed was a security guard, judging from the bulge of a weapon on his left side. Surprisingly, on this crowded street, there was an available parking space right next to the front door so Amnon parked the Mercedes there. Next to them was a late 1950's Plymouth with white Venetian blinds covering the back window.

General Izhack remarked, "I see Moshe is having dinner at the Casbah, too; that's his special Plymouth."

Entering the restaurant, they were greeted by the owner, Abraham, dressed in a tuxedo with a black tie, "General Izhack, I have reserved the second best table for you. General Dyan has the best table."

"Don't worry, Abraham, Moshe deserves the best. But we don't come here for your tables. We come for the fantastic food."

With a *thank you*, Abraham led the trio to their table, passing by the first booth against the wall. Kelly noted a very beautiful woman sitting in the booth, facing the front door. Just as they passed the booth, the lady's hidden companion shouted, "Shalom, Chich!"

Kelly turned to see General Moshe Dyan emerging from the booth, his face dominated by a big grin and highlighted by the black patch over his right eye.

General Izhack responded, "I knew you were here, Moshe, when I saw your Plymouth with Danni guarding it. I would like you to meet Dr. Kelly, our guest from America. You already know Amnon, of course."

General Dyan replied, "Shalom, Dr. Kelly. Welcome to Israel. We are always glad to have our American friends visit our country. Please meet my lady, Dvora." The beautiful woman with reddish blonde hair and brilliant blue eyes greeted the trio graciously.

They proceeded to their table in the back of the restaurant in an area raised above the main dining room floor. Amnon ordered two bottles of Israeli wine, one red and one white, from the Carmel vineyard on the road to Jerusalem. After giving the group time to taste the wine, which had a young, but excellent flavor, the waiter returned to ask for their dinner orders. General Izhack explained, "Dr. Kelly, I insist you order the duckling! Abraham prepares the finest duckling in the world; it is served crisp with a delicious orange sauce and wild rice."

"Sounds great," was Kelly's answer.

The waiter disappeared and reappeared shortly with their salad, a Casbah house special: fresh spinach with piquant mustard-honey dressing.

Next the waiter served the main courses. He served half the duckling divided between General Izhack and Kelly and placed the other half in a covered dish on a flame heater to keep the seconds warm. Amnon had a filet mignon covered with béarnaise sauce and accompanied by mushrooms sautéed in butter. "This food isn't exactly kosher," observed Kelly.

Amnon replied, "Only the hotels serve kosher food. Visiting American Jews love to eat kosher food in the Hilton, since they can't do that at the New York or Los Angeles Hiltons."

Over dessert and Turkish coffee, General Izhack asked, "Now, Dr. Kelly, tell us about your latest sailing adventures."

Well, I've been very busy this year but I did find time to sail a chartered 39 foot Erickson on the Los Angeles to Honolulu TransPac Race this last July."

General Izhack asked, "Who'd you have for crew?"

"My wife and five children plus the owner of the boat, who served as navigator - this way he waived the charter fee."

"How'd you do?"

"Fairly well. We were second in class and third overall. The big boats were clobbered by a hurricane that destroyed the Pacific High for two days. It's the High that generates the trade winds which make it a fast crossing. Anyway, we completed the race in 14 days and 15 hours, finishing at midnight off Waikiki. "

"Good for you," exclaimed General Izhack. "I was talking to our Israeli 470 champion the other day and he said you son is a contender for the Olympics in the Tornado class sailboat."

Kelly responded proudly, "That's right, he might make it to the 1976 Olympics but his main goal is the 1980 Olympics in Tallinn, Russia, in the North Sea. Now, General, what about your skin diving in Eilat?"

General Izhack's blue eyes gleamed from his deeply suntanned face. "December is a glorious time for skin diving off the reefs south of Eilat. But now that Israel controls the Sinai, we can go diving off Sharm Al Sheik at the tip of the Sinai. The water is unbelievably clear. I just returned from there. In just 2 days I speared enough fish and langouste to fill the freezer. And you should see the girls on the beaches! This time of year, European tourists trade the winter snow at home for the Israeli sun. And they bring their topless sun bathing tradition with them. So far, our religious parties haven't stopped it. I believe that proves we Jews have a benevolent and understanding God."

Amnon broke in, "Gentlemen, your sporting adventures sound fantastic, but it is after midnight and you two have an 8am business meeting Sunday morning. If you don't mind, we shall leave now."

As they left the table the restaurant owner thanked them for coming, "Shalom, Dr. Kelly. Welcome to Israel and you are always welcome at the Casbah."

Walking out of the restaurant, Kelly noticed Moshe Dyan going from table to table, chatting briefly with the guests, shaking hands, and smiling happily. General Dyan was a true folk hero of the Israeli people.

Amnon picked up Kelly at 7:30am at the Hilton and they drove through the Tel Aviv morning rush hour traffic to the Ministry of Defense complex on a hill in the center of Tel Aviv, west of the corner of Haifa Road, the main coastal highway from Tel Aviv to the port city of Haifa, and Sha'ul Ha-melekh Street.

Amnon pulled up to the Ha-melekh gate, attended by two Israeli soldiers with Uzis. The guards recognized Amnon and waved his Mercedes through the gate. This use of personal recognition for security was quite a contrast to the elaborate picture badges used by the security facilities in the US. Kelly thought, *Probably more secure, too!*

The Ministry of Defense complex was a crowded jumble of ugly buildings. Amnon led Kelly into a large grey building. A young, mini skirted Israeli girl soldier guarding the lobby waved Amnon and Kelly on down a hall to General Izhack's office. Kelly was always surprised at the small size of Israeli official's offices. General Izhack was the director general of the Ministry of Defense, the number two man reporting directly to the minister himself. The equivalent job in the Pentagon ranked an office four times the size of General Izhack's and was filled with overstuffed red leather chairs and couches. By contrast, this office seemed austere, with only a desk and its chair plus four non-upholstered guest chairs.

"Shalom," General Izhack greeted Kelly. A trim Israeli girl appeared and offered them drinks, coffee and soft drinks. Kelly chose coffee and was served Turkish coffee with *hell* in a small cup with a round seed floating in it. Kelly had learned on previous trips *hell* is Hebrew for the spice cardamom, which added a distinct flavor to the coffee.

General Izhack began the meeting, "Now, Dr. Kelly, tell me why your trip was so urgent that you are going to be away from home on Christmas Day? Christmas is just another work day here in Israel - except, of course, in Bethlehem where there is a big Christian celebration."

Kelly answered, "My wife was quite upset when Dr. Morrell told me I had to come to Israel at this time of year to meet with you. I offered to bring her but she didn't want to leave the children and the rest of our family at Christmas, so I came alone." *This was it! He couldn't avoid revealing his message any longer.* "I have bad news. The Associated Aviation Corporation board of directors decided our AAC/IAI joint venture is too small for AAC. The board is looking for bigger hunks of business. They ordered the joint venture be dissolved."

With a surprising lack of dismay, general Izhack responded, "But, we promised that for the first year the Israeli Ministry of Defense would give the joint venture ten million dollars worth of business and that this would grow to fifty million dollars per year in five years."

"Yes, I know, but our board is only interested in one *billion* dollar projects. Also, I know one of the division presidents complained they may lose a five hundred million dollar project with Algeria if the Arabs learn about AAC's Israeli joint venture."

Appearing totally calm, General Izhack answered, "OK, Dr. Kelly, I accept your board's position that the joint venture must be dissolved. I understand their concern about losing Arab business, even though I know of no case where this has actually happened. The Arabs are good at making noise about American companies doing business with Israel, but they rarely do anything about it. It so happens, our intelligence agency, Mossad, has just learned from their Iranian colleagues of a one billion dollar project the Shah wants. Perhaps we can work with AAC on this project by having IAI, the Israeli Aircraft Industry, acting as a subcontractor. Under these circumstances, we would be pleased to let AAC *off the hook* on the joint venture. I am sure you and your corporate lawyers realize we could probably sue AAC for canceling that contract. We both know we Israelis would be entitled to a great deal of money for damages if we did sue."

Kelly took a deep breath and carefully avoided commenting about the possibility of a law suit. "From its size, the Iranian project sounds very interesting. As a matter of fact, the board did suggest we should try to get a large project in Iran using some of the Shah's oil money. I'm sure the board would go along with IAI being subcontractor to AAC, providing the relationship is low profile and the word doesn't leak out to the Algerians." Kelly took a sip of his coffee, stalling for time to decide on his next step. "First, tell me about this Iranian project. Is it something AAC could do?"

"Dr. Kelly, I am not the one to tell you about this project. It has to be conducted at the highest level of security. I believe you Americans call it SCI or compartmentalized security. There are two people who can give you those details. First, you must meet General Rafi Yidron, Amnon's boss. He is just down the hall from here and I have already alerted him to expect you and Amnon after our meeting is over."

Kelly's eyes widened in surprise.

The general answered his unspoken question, "As you may know, we have good connections on your board. I already knew what you came to tell me." He went on, "The second person you must meet is Colonel Joseph Ladrun, who is my special assistant for the Iranian project. He'll be waiting to meet with you at 2pm, just after lunch today. He just returned from Tehran last Friday, so he can give you the latest details on the project."

Kelly was surprised each time he ran into a situation involving the close but covert relationship between the Shah's government and the Israelis. The Arabs were well aware of their Moslem brother's dealings with the Israelis, but they never did anything to sever the relationship. The Shah needed the Israelis' technical know-how, a commodity in short supply in the Mid East, more than he needed the Arabs' advice on whom his friends should be.

Kelly and the general shook hands, exchanged warm *Shaloms* and Amnon led Kelly out of the office and to the opposite end of the hall to a corner office guarded by a blonde Israeli girl soldier/receptionist, with very large breasts and the traditional mini-skirt. But it was something else that caught Kelly's eye: she kept a mean-looking Uzi on her desk next to the typewriter. Looking up from her typing, she greeted them, "Shalom, Amnon. Welcome to Israel, Dr. Kelly. General Yidron is expecting you. What would you like to drink?" They both picked Orangiata, an Israeli orange soda, and she motioned them on into her supervisor's office. It was about twice the size of General Izhack's office. There were two large red leather chairs and a red leather couch reminiscent of the Pentagon furniture. The bright Israeli sun lit up the large executive desk in the corner of the cheerful office. Kelly thought to himself, *The size of General Yidron's office reflects the importance the Israelis place on the intelligence function of their government.*

General Yidron met Kelly and Amnon with the traditional *Shalom* and directed them to the red couch while he sat in the chair closest to Kelly. The blonde soldier girl appeared with Orangiata for each and placed an assorted tray of cookies on the large coffee table in front of the men. General Yidron motioned for Kelly to help himself to the cookies and then started the meeting, "I see Amnon is taking good care of you. He is my eyes and ears. I get a lot of intelligence reports from a lot of sources, but I always trust the ones I get from Amnon. I am sometimes skeptical of some of the others. The intelligence business is a tough business. I've been head of Mossad for eighteen months now and I'm grateful to Amnon for bringing me up to speed quickly.

Kelly replied, "I know intelligence is a tough business, General Yidron. I've been exposed to the intelligence community from time to time in my technical assignments at AAC. Also I met two of your predecessors, Vivian Herzog and Meir Amit. I was enormously impressed with the knowledge and intelligence of both of them."

"Yes, of course I know them both, too. Vivian is a big time expensive lawyer in Tel Aviv now and Meir is chairman of Koor Industries, the largest company in Israel."

"I met them when we were setting up the joint venture between the Associated Aviation Corporation I work for and Israeli Aircraft Industries. Vivian was AAC's corporate attorney in Israel and we talked to General Amit about a joint venture with Koor before we decided on IAI as a partner."

General Yidron interrupted, "Dr. Kelly, I understand you are interested in Iranian business."

"Yes, AAC would like to get back some of the Shah's oil money. As you know, our airline division uses a lot of Iranian oil refined into jet fuel. Our board of directors believes there are opportunities now in Iran to get the kind of billion dollar project that AAC needs. General Izhack tells me you know about such a project."

"First, I must warn you about the severe security our government and the Shah's government have placed on this project. Everything about it is top secret. Also, I must ask you to sign this non-disclosure agreement." General Yidron held out a one page legal agreement which Kelly read carefully, noticing it was a fairly standard *boiler plate* agreement, very similar to the one he had signed with IAI during the formation of the joint venture. He noted the project was named IBEX. He signed the paper and handed it back to General Yidron, who then asked Amnon to sign as witness. Amnon signed with a flourish which was unreadable.

Kelly asked, "General Yidron, what is IBEX?"

"An ibex is a wild mountain goat found in the mountainous areas of Iran as well as in Iraq and Afghanistan."

"But what does the acronym, IBEX, stand for?"

"Dr. Kelly, we have learned many things from you Americans, including how to create names for projects from acronyms. However, in the Israeli intelligence community, we never use acronyms for projects; we pick some Hebrew word to name each one. But in this case, we didn't pick the name. The Shah is so interested in this project that he picked the name IBEX himself. So far as we can tell, he chose that name because he loves to hunt ibexes in the Iranian mountains. IBEX is his favorite project. Shooting ibexes is his favorite sport - not counting the sport of young girls. He often has General Hatami, the Iranian Air Force Chief, fly him to the mountains in an air force helicopter to hunt ibexes."

"Then what is IBEX all about?"

"I can give you a thumbnail sketch, but you're meeting Colonel Ladrun after lunch, so he'll be giving you the details. First of all, the Iranians, and the Shah in particular, are paranoid about their neighbors....."

Kelly interrupted, "You mean the Soviets?"

"No, as a matter of fact. The Shah is smart enough to know he can't beat the Soviets, so he buys enough armaments from them to keep them happy and to keep them from being a threat. The Shah is worried about the Iraqis, the Afghanis, the Saudis and the Pakistanis. As a result, he wants to put up an *electronic fence* around all the Iranian borders, except the Iranian/Soviet one. He wants this *electronic fence* to include electronic interception receiver systems, or *eavesdropping systems* to listen in on Iran's neighbors to the east, west, and south. The Shah has budgeted one billion dollars for the entire package and wants a large US multinational company to be the prime contractor. That's where AAC comes in. We Israelis want a piece of the action to keep our electronics industry busy and to bring in hard currency."

"That sure sounds like the size of project AAC would like to have and its in a technical business area where AAC has a lot of expertise."

That was what General Yidron wanted to hear. "Dr. Kelly, the Israeli government is depending on you to convince AAC that IAI should be your subcontractor. It is the *least* you can do, considering you are breaking the joint venture agreement AAC has with IAI."

"But, General Yidron, I'm not the one breaking the agreement - it is the AAC board of directors."

"Yes, yes. But we think of you, Dr. Kelly, as AAC, since you have been the spark plug for the joint venture all along."

"I'll do what I can, but AAC is such a huge corporation that its hard to guess the outcome."

"Dr. Kelly, we trust you will be successful. Now it's time to break for lunch. There is an excellent oriental-style restaurant a short walk from the MOD, over on Carlebach Street. Will you be my guest?"

Kelly quickly accepted and he walked with General Yidron and Amnon west on Sha'ul Ha-melekh to Ibn Givrol where they went south until Ibn Givrol became Carlebach and they turned into the restaurant. The owner, Dov, greeted them, "Shalom, General Yidron, welcome to the Kadish," and he led them to a table set with white linen, crystal and Israeli flowers. They settled themselves around the table and the waiter immediately served a full array of oriental appetizers including sliced eggplant in olive oil, hummus with tehina (ground sesame seed dip), and sarma (rice wrapped in grape leaves).

The waiter asked, "And what will you have to drink?" General Yidron ordered a glass each of Carmel Avdat Vin Blanc and Vin Rouge from the Negev winery for all three.

After the appetizers were attacked by the hungry trio, the waiter returned, "And what do you wish for the main course? Our specialty of the day is charcoal broiled lamb entrecote." All three ordered the lamb, which was served with rice pilaf. It was delicious. An hour and a half after arriving at the restaurant, the trio was ready for dessert and coffee. They were served creme caramel and Turkish coffee with hell.

As Kelly was finishing his coffee, General Yidron looked at his watch, "We must get back to the MOD now. You have a meeting at 2pm with Colonel Ladrun. I know he is eager to fill you in on the technical details of the project." The three walked back the short distance to the MOD. Kelly couldn't help thinking to himself, *I can't imagine a three star general from the Pentagon walking to lunch. There, the general would have a major as a chauffeur and a government furnished limousine.*

Chapter 2.

Ibex Details

Kelly and Amnon left General Yidron as soon as they passed through the security gate of the Ministry of Defense and headed for Colonel Ladrun's office in a drab, three story building an hundred yards from the building housing General Yidron and General Izhack's offices. Amnon led Kelly up the stairs to the top floor and down the hall to a small corner office with a large reception area crowded with four desks, one occupied by a beautiful oriental soldier girl with an Uzi on the desk next to her typewriter. The other three desks were occupied by two captains and one major. Kelly had learned to recognize the shoulder emblems that denoted the Israeli military rank. The soldier girl receptionist looked up, greeted Amnon and Kelly with a *Shalom* and continued, "Dr. Kelly, please go right in. Colonel Ladrun is expecting you."

Then she said something in Hebrew to Amnon that Kelly couldn't understand. However, from the way she spoke the words and smiled at Amnon, Kelly was sure they knew each other very well.

Kelly and Amnon entered Colonel Ladrun's small office and he motioned them to be seated on the two hard chairs facing his modest-sized desk. The colonel was a tall, grey haired man, about 47 years old, wearing a full colonel's insignia on his shoulder emblems. He had blue eyes in a tan face and a generally athletic appearance. He started the meeting, "Dr. Kelly, I expect you and I are going to be seeing a lot of each other during the next several months. Please call me Joseph and I'll call you Brad, if you don't mind."

"That's fine with me, Joseph. You understand, of course, I must get approval from the AAC management before we can officially agree to work together on IBEX."

"Oh, bah! Brad. I know how large US companies work. AAC's management isn't going to turn down a one billion dollar project. There is no doubt in my mind that you'll be given the green light. Otherwise, I would be talking to your counterpart from Boeing or Lockheed."

Kelly laughed. "OK, Joseph, you are probably right. But, how do you know the Iranians will let us take on an Israeli company as a subcontractor on a project as sensitive as IBEX?"

"I was just in Iran. General Hatami told me it was OK."

"But what if the Shah over-rules General Hatami?"

"Don't worry. The Shah always gives General Hatami what he wants. Remember when the Shah returned to Iran from exile in 1952?"

"Well, no. My knowledge of Iranian history doesn't go back that far."

"That's surprising! Persian history goes back 4000 years and we're only talking about the last 25. Anyway, General Hatami flew the Shah out of Iran when he left for exile and flew him back when he returned in 1952. Your CIA handed out a truck load of rials to the people lining the street to make sure the Shah was welcomed and not killed by the population. The CIA didn't like his leftist predecessor whose supporters had urged the people to kill the Shah when he came back."

"Now that you mention it, I do remember reading in a book that it was Kermit Roosevelt who directed the CIA distribution of rials."

Amnon got to his feet, "Joseph, I have another meeting now. Besides, I've already heard about IBEX," and hurried out of the room.

Nodding agreement to Amnon, Joseph continued, "OK, Brad, now let me tell you about IBEX. This project will be an *intelligence collection system* to collect intelligence information about the Shah's foreign enemies: the Iraqis, the Afghanis, the Pakistanis, and the Saudis plus all the other countries ringing Iran.

Kelly interrupted, "I thought the Shah was worried about Saudi Arabia, not Oman, the United Arab Emirates and Qatar."

"Brad, the Shah is worried about all the Arab states in the Persian Gulf area. He thinks they're all threats to the shipping of oil from Iran through the Strait of Hormuz. Remember, oil is the lifeblood of Iran!"   Rightly or wrongly, the Shah is concerned about the military threat from these countries and he wants to know their intentions."

"How?"

By using what the intelligence community refers to as **ELINT**: **EL**ectronic **INT**elligence.   And more particularly, **COMINT**: **COM**munications **INT**elligence, and **SIGINT**: **SIG**nal **INT**elligence from their radars."

"I should think any intelligence communications from these surrounding countries would be in code."

"Of course. Any communications that might reveal their plans to carry out secret attacks will be coded, actually encrypted. Whenever anyone sends encrypted messages rather than communicating in the open it's a warning they want to hide some really important information. Your National Science Agency and our Ministry of Communications can decode almost any encrypted message. We just put our decoding computers to work. We can usually do it within two hours.   Probably your NSA super computers are even faster."

"You mentioned radar signals, What can you tell from radar signals?"

"Radar SIGINT tells us the level of alert of the airplanes at an airbase. And the readiness condition of anti-aircraft missiles. And so forth."

"I have another question - why does General Hatami want you Israelis involved in such a sensitive project?"

"Two reasons: first, we Israelis helped General Hatami equip Karg Island, the Iranian oil terminal in the Persian Gulf, with sophisticated communications and air defense systems in the early 1970's. We did a good job and he knows it. Second, we Israelis have another intelligence tool, **HUMINT**: **HUM**an **INT**elligence. Mossad has penetrated the inner circles of the governments, military organizations, and terrorist organizations of all of the Shah's enemies. And Savak has told both General Hatami and the Shah."

"Savak? I never heard of that."

"Savak is the Shah's intelligence agency - his secret police. They eliminate the Shah's enemies within Iran in a most brutal but efficient way.   So all he needs to worry about are his external enemies."

"Has a schedule been set up for IBEX?"

"Sure thing, Brad.   General Hatami wants a budgetary proposal for IBEX by Saturday the 25th of January.   That's only about four weeks away.   General Hatami expects a briefing with nice, colorful charts so he and his officers can understand what is being proposed."

"But, Joseph, the week between Christmas and New Years is an AAC holiday week.   We can't get a major proposal ready in such a short time.   Not even a budgetary proposal."

"I'm sure General Hatami won't go along with any delay.   He has a French company, Marcel Aviation, waiting in the wings, in case Associated Aviation doesn't come through."

"I thought the French wouldn't work with Israelis ever since it came out in the open that the Mossad stole the drawings for the French *Mirage* fighter plane and Israel Aircraft Industries built their *Kfir* fighter from those plans."

"The French would work with the devil for a one billion dollar project!   You can be sure Marcel Aviation is a legitimate threat to AAC's getting the IBEX business if you can't meet that schedule."

Kelly frowned, studied his hands for a few minutes.   "I'll have to get a lot of corporate approval signatures.   It won't be easy but I think we can do it."

"Good.   Now I need to fill you in with some of the technical details.   There will be five surveillance sites on top of the highest peaks overlooking all the Shah's enemies.   Just like a real ibex likes to climb the highest peak and survey the area for his enemy, the mountain lion, the IBEX project will do the same thing for the Shah.   He'll be able to watch his enemies' activities using electronic eyes and ears."

"What kind of electronics will these surveillance sites include?"

"First, they will have multi-band antennas capable of intercepting all communications and radar signals coming from the enemy countries and their military forces

"Second, these antennas will be connected to sophisticated wide-band radio receivers.

"Third, the receivers will be connected to computers all set up to decode any encrypted messages and to interpret the meaning of the radar signals."

"Fourth, the five mountain sites will be connected through microwave relays to a central processing station at General Hatami's headquarters at Doshen Toeppeh Air Force Base in Tehran."

"Joseph, It looks to me like these microwave relays represent a weakness in the system. Can't the Shah's enemies intercept these signals and then they'd know what Iran is doing?"

Colonel Ladrun smiled, "Good for you, Brad. I was just about to mention one of the most important attributes of the system: **COMSEC**, or **COM**munications **SEC**urity. One of the main reasons the Shah wants to use a US multi-national company like AAC is that he knows they'll give him the very latest **COMSEC** technology, like spread spectrum and hard cryptology."

"Well, I don't know much about these technologies but I do know there's a small group working in this area on a CIA project at AAC. These guys are the best in the business."

"We knew that. That's one of the main reason's we wanted AAC to do this job. I'm sure that special group will have in their *threat library* the details on the type of radar and communications signals we need to be able to intercept."

Colonel Ladrun spread a large relief map on his desk. "Here are the mountain tops where the equipment will go. There are no roads up there so everything has to go in by helicopters.

"I can't understand why the Shah would care about what goes on in either Pakistan or Afghanistan."

"I told you the Shah was paranoid about his neighbors. And probably rightly so. Pakistan has a large population and is very poor. They need room to live and they need oil. Afghanistan is also very poor and they are fierce fighters. The mountains ringing Iran have given it natural protection in the past, but near Zahedan there is a low pass from the Afghani and Pakistani plains that leads into the great central deserts of Iran – Dasht-e Lut and Dasht-e Kavir. And those deserts lead directly northwest to Tehran."

"You are quite an expert on Iranian geography and threats."

"Listen, Brad, we Israelis need some of the Shah's oil money, too. But we think the way to get it is by helping him with our technology, not by fighting a war with him. Anyway, the last or fifth site is on a 3019 meter high peak overlooking eastern Afghanistan and, incidentally, could also have a view toward the Soviet Republic of Turkmen, if the antennas were turned."

"But General Yidron said the Shah wasn't interested in looking at the Soviet Union."

"He isn't, but I'm sure your CIA is! The Mossad tells me the CIA will certainly be interested in IBEX. The CIA and the Shah's Savak work very closely, you know."

"No, I didn't know, but thanks for warning me. I'm sure the Pentagon will get the CIA involved when I go to get approval for IBEX in connection with the export license this project will need."

"I hope I've given you enough details so you and your team can put together a good proposal for IBEX.

"Joseph, I need to know how Israel fits into the picture so our proposal will dovetail with your plans."

"I'm glad you asked. I would have told you anyway. You know we Israelis are not coy when it comes to getting what we want."

"Yes, I noticed how you took the Sinai from the Egyptians in the Yom Kippur War. And you took the West Bank from the Jordanians and the Golan Heights from the Syrians in the 1967 War."

"That's the price the Arabs must pay for attacking Israel. General Sharon would have taken Cairo as well in the Yom Kippur War if your President Nixon hadn't stopped us. I'm glad we didn't take Cairo, though. I don't know how we could have fed the more than ten million people living there. Sadim has a difficult time doing that.

"Getting back to what Israel would like from IBEX. IAI has an electronics division called ELTA that makes just the type of antennas needed at the sites. We have installed such antennas ringing Israel to provide surveillance of our Arab neighbors -- who are not always friendly toward us.

"If your antennas are so good, Joseph, how did the Egyptians surprise you during the Yom Kippur War and shoot down so many Israeli aircraft?"

"*Before* the war the Egyptians never transmitted on the frequencies they used during the war.   That's the weakness of electronic intelligence.   We Israelis also depend on human intelligence.   Unfortunately, however, the Egyptians wiped out our human agents in Egypt several months before the Yom Kippur War, so we were terribly surprised."

"So you want to supply the antennas for IBEX?"

"AND, we would like the installation subcontract.   We could use Iranian labor to do the site preparation, to pour the concrete, and so forth.   We don't think an American firm could do this."

"What not?"

We learned a lot working with the Iranian Moslem labor during our Karg Island installation.   The workers must bless each work site before beginning construction.   That means we had to fly a Mullah and sacrificial lambs to the site by C-130 and helicopter to perform the ceremony.   Or else nothing gets done."

"I see.   We'll be glad to give you the Iranian labor tasks.   Now, for the 64 million dollar question.   How much will it cost?"

"Brad, you know we are very good at financial matters. I have here a firm, fixed price proposal complete with installation drawings, specifications, and a work statement.   The fixed price is two hundred million dollars.   A bit more than your 64 million dollar question.   That should be about 20% of the total one billion dollar IBEX project price."

"Very good, Joseph. I can work your offer into our proposal."

"I'm looking forward to working with you. I'll pick you up at the Mehrabad Airport in Tehran on Friday, January 24, 1976, at 5:30pm."

"How could you be so sure about when I'd arrive?"

"I assumed you'd take TWA flight 760 from Los Angeles to London, arriving there at 10:30am.   Since I understand from Amnon that you never check any baggage, you will be able to catch the Iranair flight 176 leaving non-stop from London to Tehran and arriving at 5:30pm."

"Simple! I hope the flights won't be late."

"When doing business with the Moslems, Allah arranges for airplanes to be on time."

Colonel Ladrun declared, "Brad, now that our business meeting is finished, I would like to invite you to dinner at the Alhambra in Old Jaffa tonight, if you are free."

Kelly replied, "Why, thank you, Joseph. I would love that. I do have a problem, though."

"What's your problem?"

"Well, I have two friends – Christina and Olga. Last night I left them alone in the hotel room while I had dinner with Amnon and General Izhack. I'm sure they would not appreciate that treatment two nights in a row."

"Brad, that's no problem at all. Christina and Olga are invited. I'll reserve a table for four. I'll pick you up at the Hilton at 9:30. Dinner's at 10."

"Great! See you then. Thanks for the info about IBEX."

Amnon was waiting in the reception office and talking to the girl soldier, but he cut the conversation short when Kelly appeared. The two climbed into Amnon's speedy Mercedes, and Kelly was soon walking into the Hilton entrance.

He was greeted by Christina and Olga, dressed in brightly colored, floor length Hawaiian "muumuus" which showed off the girls' luscious and ample breasts. *Those two must be clairvoyant, the way they always seem to know when I'll return.* "Hello, Girls, we're all invited to dinner at the Alhambra this evening. Colonel Ladrun will pick us up at 9:30."

Olga smiles, "That's great. I was afraid we might get another evening without dinner tonight."

"You didn't need to worry about that. Since it's only 4:30 now, let's go swimming."

Christina answered this time, "Olga and I are already ahead of you. Here's your swimsuit; we have ours on under our muumuus."

"Great, let's go. It's too bad the Hilton doesn't have the same topless tradition as the beaches at Eilat."

"Don't worry, Brad," consoled Christina, Olga and I will give you a private topless and bottomless show when we get back to our room."

"I'll buy that."

While walking through the lobby, the trio noticed a Luftansa crew checking in. Kelly was sure they were from flight 840, the same flight number Kelly arrived on yesterday. The three friends continued down the staircase to the swimming pool level where the girls stopped to admire the silver and turquoise jewelry in the shop at the bottom of the stairs. The King Solomon restaurant just across from the shop was for the hotel tourists who didn't know about places like the Casbah and the Alhambra.

Olga pointed to a ring, necklace and earring set, "Brad, you really should buy these for your wife."

"I already bought her a set almost exactly like that on my last trip. The shop on Yafo Street in Jerusalem charged half as much. What I really need to buy her this time is a big diamond to make up for being away on Christmas. Especially since the sixth of January is our 25th wedding anniversary."

Christina remarked, "Israel is the right place to buy diamonds. Amnon has a friend in the Diamond Exchange, over in the Ramat Gan area. He'll sell you a diamond at the best possible price."

"That would be great. I have a free morning tomorrow, before General Izhack takes me to Jerusalem to meet someone in the afternoon. You and Olga can help me select the diamond; I know you have *diamond taste*."

They picked three lounge chairs on the right hand side of the pool. While Kelly headed for the changing room to get out of his somber business suit and into his swimsuit, the girls spread towels on the chairs and slipped off their muumuus. Christina's minimal sized bikini was bright yellow and Olga's was bright red, to go with their hair colors.

The three dove into the dark, blue pool filled with salt water from the Mediterranean, which the Hilton pool crew changed daily. Kelly raced the girls two laps of the pool the long way. Then they floated on the water relaxing from their physical exertion for a while before climbing out and spreading themselves on their west facing lounge chairs. They had about an hour to sun themselves before the sun slipped below the sea horizon.

Olga motioned for one of the pool boys to bring her a poolside phone. She dialed a number and spoke a few, short sentences in Hebrew, and then said, "Amnon says he will arrange a meeting for us with his friend, Danni, in the morning at 10. He's on the 20th floor of the Diamond Exchange Building."

Kelly looked surprised, "I didn't know you spoke Hebrew."

Olga responded, "I speak seven languages besides my native Swedish - not counting the language of love. When you have lived in Europe and the Middle East all your life like I have, you pick up languages. You know, of course, all the European languages, with the exception of Basque, Finish and Hungarian, are considered Indo-European languages. Once you master one of them, the others come easily. The Middle Eastern languages are quite different however, but the same rule holds: once you learn one, the others are similar."

After gathering the last rays of the December Israeli sun, the three collected their belongings and headed for their room. In the hall, they passed the Lufthansa stewardess's room. The same tall handsome Israeli they had seen yesterday was coming out the door. Kelly thought, *The stewardess has just finished her afternoon delight and will probably sleep straight through until 3am when she will have to get up for the Luftansa flight 841 that departs at 7am.*

Kelly and Christina followed the stewardess' example: after their own *afternoon delight*, Kelly fell into a thoroughly relaxed sleep, relying on his mental alarm clock to get him up at 9. On awakening, he glanced at his digital watch. It was reading 21:00:46. His mental alarm was still accurate. He heard the girls in the next room dressing for dinner. He quickly showered and put on his dark blue *funeral director's suit*, the aerospace executive's uniform.

Christina and Olga were in the living area, sipping a split of champagne from the hotel refrigerator bar.

The phone rang. Olga picked it up and said something in Hebrew, then turned toward Kelly and Christina, "That was Colonel Ladrun, already in the lobby. I told him we would be down right away."

Chapter 3.

Meeting in Jerusalem

The three rushed to the elevator and were happily surprised when one came right away. They hurried inside and rode it down to the lobby. Heading toward the front revolving door, they quickly spotted Colonel Ladrun. Kelly introduced the girls and invited them all to a drink in the hotel lounge.

"No, thanks," the Colonel responded. "Our reservation at the Alhambra is for 10pm. By the time we fight the evening traffic along the way to Old Jaffa and find a parking space, we'll just make it. The owners don't like to hold tables for late arrivals. That's the peak of the evening dinner crowd."

The doorman opened the doors of Colonel Ladrun's car for the girls to climb in the back seat and for Kelly to get in the guest's seat, front-right. Kelly slipped US money into the doorman's hand, who wished them goodbye with a loud *Shalom.*

Colonel Ladrun drove out the Hilton driveway and turned right onto Hayarkon to head toward Old Yafo (or Jaffa). The lights of the old city were slightly to the right and in the distance as they followed the road hugging the beach. Evening strollers in the cool sea breeze filled the walkway along the beach. On the other side of the road away from the beach, the sidewalk tables at the many fish cafes had no space available.

The traffic lightened as their car continued south, and they were able to go faster. "We're making good time" remarked Ladrun. "Would you like to take a quick tour of Old Jaffa?" He reached the corner of Raziel Eilat and drove up the hill on Yefet Street, where he turned right through the artists' quarter. The cobblestone road wound through restaurants and artists' shops on both sides. At the top of the hill near St. Pierre's Church, they luckily found a parking space and everyone climbed out. The Colonel said, "Come this way, I want to show you something."

The quartet walked to a path overlooking the Mediterranean. To the right, the bright lights of Tel Aviv glittered to the north. Ladrun directed their attention to some rocks sticking out of the water a few yards offshore.

Brad nodded, "I see them. They're a reef, aren't they?"

"Well, yes. But they have historical significance. This is the place where tradition says Jonah was spit out by the whale."

"I remember that Bible story from my Sunday School days. Thanks for pointing it out."

"Now, quickly, everybody back to the car!"

Ladrun drove down the hill and turned right on Yerusalayim, a very dark street. He pulled up to a dark building and parked. "We're lucky to find a space so close."

The front door opened onto a small room filled with original paintings by local artists. Climbing a narrow stairway to the second floor, they were greeted by the owners, Jacques and his beautiful wife, Bridgette. She used to be a French fashion model and met Jacques while appearing in a fashion show at the Hilton. "Shalom, Joseph, and welcome to the Alhambra. We have a special table in a private alcove for you and your guests." Bridgette led the four their table and after they settled themselves, she began to recite the menu from memory.

Ladrun interrupted her recital in mid-sentence, "We'll have the *Symphonie des Crevettes* with two bottles of Moet champagne."

Brad asked, "I know what Moet is, but what is *Symphony of Shrimp?*"

Bridgette replied, "It's our house specialty - shrimp prepared five different ways: shrimp cocktail with piquant sauce to begin. Then shrimp deep fried, shrimp sautéed in garlic butter, shrimp béarnaise with wild rice, and finally shrimp curry with Indian chutney. There are *beaucoup* shrimp!"

"That sounds fantastic. I suppose you serve shrimp for dessert?"

"*Non, non!* We have fresh Israeli strawberries with heavy cream."

Ladrun inserted, "We'll have the best green salad you've ever eaten after the shrimp cocktail. And that rounds out our menu."

Bridgette personally served each course. Kelly found the shrimp even better than he expected. The strawberries were huge and the cream was thick and sweet with the consistency of sour cream.

As the four were finishing their after dinner coffee, Colonel Ladrun remarked, "Brad, I understand from General Izhack that you are meeting a very famous person tomorrow."

"He told me we were going to Jerusalem tomorrow, but he didn't say who we would see. I assumed it was someone interested in IBEX. It isn't Moshe Dyan, is it? I already met him last Sunday night."

"No, it's not, but it is someone of the same stature. You'll just have to wait and see -- I won't spoil your surprise."

The group left the crowded restaurant just after midnight. Brad noticed when Colonel Ladrun paid the bill, it was for 2,500 Israeli pounds or over $200 at the official exchange rate of 12 IL to the dollar. Brad wondered how the restaurant could be so crowded with Israelis paying $50 per person for dinner when the typical Israeli executive took home $500 a month after taxes. Then Brad realized Israel had become an expense account society, just like the US. These people were not paying their bills personally. Their companies or their government agencies were covering the costs.

Kelly, Olga and Christina met Amnon in the Hilton lobby at 9:30am for their visit to the Diamond Exchange in the Tel Aviv suburb of Ramat Gan, a short drive from the Hilton. Amnon headed his Mercedes through the late morning traffic up Jabotinski, continuing onto Haifa Road, cutting over to Petah Tiqua where he pointed to a black, high-rise building.

Brad exclaimed, "You mean that building is full of diamond merchants?"

"Right. Israel is second only to Amsterdam in the diamond trade. Most of our diamond traders were trained in Amsterdam."

In the foyer of the Diamond Exchange, Kelly found the tightest security he had ever seen. Each of them had to have a numbered badge based on their passports, and the passports were held by the reception guards until they returned to the lobby at the end of their visit. Even with the badge, they were not allowed to go through the barred doorway into the inner waiting room on their own. They had to wait until Danni's girl assistant came down to personally escort them inside the security entrance and to stay with them on their elevator ride to the 20th floor. Among the people in the packed elevator there were several Hassidic Jews with their black hats and suits and long side hair curls: all in the diamond trade.

Danni's office had a spectacular view of the beach, stretching northward toward Herzylia, which could be barely seen through the dense Tel Aviv smog. Danni greeted Amnon with a hug, shook Kelly's hand and gave him a welcoming, "Shalom, Dr. Kelly. You were wise to bring Christina and Olga. They both have excellent, if expensive, taste in diamonds," and motioned everyone to be seated.

Danni took his place behind his large desk and moved a small pile of shimmering diamonds he had been sorting to one side. He pulled out a desk drawer full of small white paper packets. Choosing three, he dumped out their contents on a black velvet cloth.

"I could show you many more, but I understand you want a good diamond for your wife in a size a little over one carat."

Danni arranged the three diamonds in a row on the velvet. "The middle diamond is 1.1 carats and the price to you is $1,800. Ordinarily, it would be $2,200, but you are a friend of Amnon's. The large diamond on the left is two carats and its price is $1,500."

Kelly interrupted, "Why is that big diamond cheaper than the smaller one?"

"Dr. Kelly, pricing diamonds is a complex art. Briefly, four factors determine the value of a diamond: size in carats, the cut, the color, and the lack or presence of defects. Here, look at the big one through this loop."

Holding the jeweler's eye piece in front of one eye, Kelly examined the larger stone. There was a fracture and a cloudy black shape inside the diamond, and it was a distinctly yellowish color. "Now I see why this one is cheaper."

Danni continued, "The third diamond is 1.25 carats and its price to you is $1,200. I advise you to buy the middle diamond. It's the best buy. Look at these two with the loop."

Through the eyepiece, Kelly found the middle diamond was clear and bright. The third diamond had a slight yellowish tinge and a tiny crack. "What do you girls think?"

Olga and Christina checked all three diamonds with the loop. They were unanimous in choosing the clear diamond. Christina exclaimed, "That middle stone is one of the best one carat diamonds I've ever seen, and I've seen many."

Kelly faced Danni, "I'll take it. May I write you a check?"

"If you don't mind, I'll need cash. If you pay by check the price is considerably more."

Kelly shrugged and counted out three 500 dollar bills and three 100 dollar bills and handed them to Danni, who picked up the central diamond, wrapped it in a white paper and handed it to his assistant, Esther. He then brought out a tray of rings ready to have stones set in them.

"Dr. Kelly, I recommend you chose one of these settings for your diamond and we'll set it for you. This way, you can legally avoid about $500 in custom charges when you arrive in the US."

"Thanks for the advice." Kelly bent over the tray and chose a gold ring.   "I think my wife would like this one and if she doesn't, she can have it reset at home. If it fits my little finger, I know it will fit her ring finger."

"The ring will be $100. You can pay Esther when she delivers the ring with the diamond set in it to your hotel tonight around 7pm."

Danni stood and extended his hand to indicate the meeting was over. Kelly happily shook hands and left with Amnon, Christina and Olga, escorted, of course, by Esther to the elevator and down to the security entrance. One of the guards collected the badges they had been wearing, handed over their passports and then unlocked the iron door to let them out of the tall, black glass Diamond Exchange building into the bright sunlight.

Driving rapidly, Amnon announced they were a little behind schedule. "We can't be late for your 1:30 meeting!" He dropped off the girls at the Hilton entrance and rushed on to pick up General Izhack for their trip to Jerusalem.

The Mercedes stopped next to the Ministry of Defense gate on Sha'ul Ha-melekh Street. General Izhack was there waiting for them, dressed in civilian clothes. "Glad you're on time," he remarked, settling in his seat.

Amnon immediately headed east, out of the city, towards Jerusalem. They passed the turn-off to Ben Gurion Airport at Lod, and then what was once the *Green Line*, the boundary between the Israeli territory and the Arab holdings before the 1967 War. Now the green line was fading. The Israelis had cleared the rocks from the old Arab fields and were turning them green. As they passed Fort Ladrun, guarding the entrance to the narrow valley leading to Jerusalem, General Ladrun declared, "Here at Ladrun we fought one of the bloodiest battles in the 1948 War of Independence. At great loss of life, we took the fort from the Arabs. At an earlier time, this is where the Biblical battle took place when God commanded the sun and moon to stand still so the Israelis could overcome their enemies."

Kelly replied, "You Israelis all seem to have a fantastic understanding of history, both recent and ancient."

"Dr. Kelly, we Israelis live in an historical place. We absorb history the way you Californians absorb sun."

The Mercedes continued into the canyon leading up the mountain to Jerusalem, some 2,000 feet above the coastal plain. Scattered along both sides of the roads were relics of armored vehicles from the 1948 war, kept in place as a monument to the War of Independence. General Izhack reminisced, "Those wrecks bring back memories. I met my wife during the battles for this canyon. I was a young lieutenant in the infantry and she was a private in my platoon. She could shoot better than I could. We lost many good soldiers during those battles for this valley. But we did open it and keep it open to supply Jerusalem during the War of Independence. Those old armored cars led the supply missions."

"It's amazing you could get through, with all the Arabs lining the hills on both sides of the road."

"When your President Truman officially recognized our new State of Israel it really raised our spirits. America was the first country to recognize us."

Kelly broke in, "Who are we meeting in Jerusalem. Amnon wouldn't tell me, said it would spoil the surprise."

"You're going to meet a man who was considered a criminal by the British before the 1948 war. He was the leader of the Irgun, a Jewish underground group fighting for Jewish rights. The British called the Irgun *Jewish terrorists.*

"You must mean Prime Minister Begin."

"That's right. Mr. Begin is very much interested in IBEX. He expects to collect intelligence information about what our more distant Arab neighbors are planning."

"How are you going to get intelligence information by doing the installation on the Iranian antennas?"

"We expect to supply the operators at each site. The Iranians have a shortage of competent electronics people. General Hatami has already asked Colonel Ladrun to write up a proposal for post-installation support of the sites."

Amnon's Mercedes reached the top of the hill on the outskirts of Jerusalem and made an easy right turn onto Weizmann Street and passed the Jerusalem Hilton on the left. They continued along Herzl to the sweeping Ruppin Avenue which circled the Israeli government office buildings and stopped at the guard gate of the parking lot near the Prime Minister's office. The guard waved Amnon inside.

In the building they rode the elevator to the top floor, and arrived at Mr. Begin's reception room at 2:20, some ten minutes early.

The prime minister's male secretary recognized General Izhack and said, "Just a moment, General Izhack. The Prime Minister is on the phone. Just as soon as he finishes you may go in." A light on the secretary's console went off and the secretary motioned for the group to enter.

The Prime Minister of Israel had a large, sunny, well furnished office and with a wave of his hand, he motioned his visitors to the corner where two large leather couches and three leather chairs were arranged. He greeted the trio with a hearty, "Shalom," and continued, "Shlomo, it's so good to see you. It brings back memories of earlier times. Amnon, are you keeping your boss, Rafi Yidron, under control?"

Amnon grinned. "Well, I try, but as you know, he isn't easy to control!"

The Prime Minister answered, "Yes, I remember very well. Rafi was my head of intelligence in the Irgun. I couldn't control him then either." Turning toward Kelly, he continued, "Dr. Kelly, you'll have to forgive us. We Israelis love to reminisce about our past struggles. But we also have to worry about today's and tomorrow's conflicts. That's why I asked General Izhack to bring you here today."

The visitors settled into the comfortable couches and Mr. Begin sat in one of the overstuffed chairs facing them. He started the meeting, "Dr. Kelly, I want to get straight to the point. You already know the IBEX program is urgent for Israel because we expect to get more useful intelligence about our enemies than the Shah will get about his. Also, you need to know our ambassador in Washington met with your CIA director last week and briefed him on the project. So don't be surprised when you visit the Pentagon and you are asked to include a sixth site for IBEX on the Caspian Sea so your government can look at the USSR. Electronic intelligence from IBEX is as important for your government as it is for ours."

Kelly tried to hide his surprise. This intelligence gathering project was getting more complicated all the time. "But, Sir, what can I do?"

"That's easy. We want Israeli Aircraft Industry to be your subcontractor for the antennas and site preparation and installation."

"I know that, but my company doesn't even have the contract. In fact, our management doesn't even know about the project, yet. They won't know until I get home to tell them."

"Well, that's quite true, but your probability of getting the contract is very high. Also, I met your board chairman. He isn't the kind of man who is going to pass up a one billion dollar project. We are depending on you, Dr. Kelly, to be sure we get all the official approvals needed from the various departments of your government for a secret project of this size and complexity."

"Thank you, Sir, I'll do my best. This will be an extremely important project for the US if a USSR surveillance site is part of the plan."

"Thank you for coming, Dr. Kelly. Shlomo and Amnon, it's good to see you both again. Now, I must get over to the Knesset for a late afternoon session. I'm supposed to give a speech."

During the trip back to the Tel Aviv Hilton, General Izhack mentioned to Kelly, "I know Wednesday is Christmas to you, but it is a working day for us. I need to meet with you and Colonel Ladrun to hear about your plans to visit General Hatami in Tehran next month. Please be in my office at 9am. Colonel Ladrun will pick you up at 8:30."

"OK, General Izhack. I'll see you then."

Exactly at 8pm Tel Aviv time, Kelly dialed the 213 area number directly from his hotel room. The Israelis may have been isolated from their Arab neighbors but their convenient direct dial system let them reach anywhere in the world in a few seconds. Kelly needed to talk to Dr. Morrell, his boss and the president of Associated Aviation Corporation (AAC) in Los Angeles where it was 10am local time, the day before Christmas. Kelly knew AAC would be closed the whole week between Christmas Eve and New Year's Day, which meant if he didn't get hold of Dr. Morrell before lunch, he'd miss him. No one returned to work after lunch on Christmas Eve!

Dr. Morrell's secretary answered the phone with a cheery, "Merry Christmas, Dr. Morrell's office." When Kelly heard the *Merry Christmas* a picture of his family around the gaily decorated tree danced in front of him and a wave of homesickness covered him. He vowed to find time to phone home in spite of his busy schedule tomorrow.

"Hello, Helen, Merry Christmas. May I speak to the boss? This is Brad."

"How's Israel, Dr. Kelly? It's raining here in L.A."

"It's been sunny and warm, but I'd rather be home even in the rain at this time of year."

"Your wife just called and said she would meet you at the LAX airport. Are you still returning on the afternoon of the 27th on Air France?"

"That's right. I wouldn't change my return home for anything."

" I'll tell her. Here's Dr. Morrell."

"Brad! Good to hear from you. How's it going?" Did you have any trouble with General Izhack when you told him we were going to cut off the joint venture?"

"Quite the contrary, John. Would you might getting your phone scrambler on?"

"No, just a minute."

Brad took his phone scrambler out of its case and placed the hotel phone receiver in the acoustic coupler cradle and flipped the switch of the speaker. Dr. Morrell did the same at his end of the line, and said, "Brad, can you hear me now?"

"Yeah, it's a little distorted but we have privacy now."

"I can hear you, too, What's up?"

"I broke the bad news about the dissolution of the joint venture to General Izhack. I got the impression he was expecting it, as though the Israelis had intelligence sources even on the AAC board. Anyway, instead of being upset, he started talking about a new project with the codeword IBEX. It's an electronic surveillance system for Iran with a one billion dollar budget. He says we can get the project sole source, but there's a slight hitch."

"One billion dollars! We sure can use a project like that. What's the hitch?"

"The Israelis insist we give them a $200 million subcontract for the antennas and site preparation and installation. They gave me a firm, fixed price proposal complete with technical descriptions."

"So that's why they didn't fuss about the cancellation of the joint venture. They want a piece of the pie on this new project. I don't see any problem as long as we can keep their involvement covert. Our other division presidents would be afraid of losing their Arab business if our division had a high profile tie-in with the Israelis, even on a subcontractor basis."

"We can probably manage that since the whole project will be labeled Compartmentalized Security. Only a few people at AAC should know the details of the program."

"You've come up with a great opportunity. You really earned your Christmas bonus! Let's get together right after January first to go over the details."

"That's why I called you today. I'm afraid it can't wait until after the first. I need to meet with the technical team on the 28th of December to put together a briefing for the folks in the Pentagon and in the Munitions Control Office. I have to have clearance from both of them for a briefing and budgetary proposal I'm scheduled to give to the Iranians during the last week of January. That was the latest date I could get. You know how slow the Pentagon and State Department are about giving such approvals."

"Wow, Brad, you're a real slave driver! It'll take some doing to get people to come in during their Christmas vacations, but I'll get your team collected in the Red Room at 1pm on the 28th. I'll be there at 10am to hear all the details from you and I'll stay to kick off the afternoon meeting. I'll have to have the company Sabreliner fly me there from Snow Valley that morning and back that afternoon. My wife will be furious that I'll miss a day of skiing with her."

"One other thing, I would appreciate it if you could get Ralph Hauser at the meeting, too. Bringing him on board in the beginning will get the CIA on our side. They can help *push* on the Pentagon and State Department for those approvals.

"OK, It's done. He'd asked me to call him after you checked in, anyway. Those *spooks* really keep tabs on everything we do here!"

"That's for sure! I have a Christmas morning meeting with General Izhack to discuss the January Iranian trip. He'll send Colonel Ladrun to accompany me to the meetings. He knows the territory. Merry Christmas, John."

"Sorry about your Christmas meeting, but I understand Christmas is just another work day in Israel. All the best."

"All the best, and goodbye." Kelly removed the phone from the scrambler and locked it in its case. Christina and Olga had left Kelly a note saying they had to leave and would see him later.

Kelly tried to order a hamburger and a milk shake from room service, but he couldn't because of the kosher rules forbidding meat and dairy at the same meal. He had to settle for just the hamburger plus an orange soda from the room refrigerator for his *festive* Christmas Eve dinner and went to bed, alone, early.

Christmas Day dawned bright and sunny in Tel Aviv. Kelly rushed through the Hilton lobby toward the front entrance just as Colonel Ladrun came in the front revolving door. Exchanging *Shalom*s, they climbed into Ladrun's car parked right outside the door and headed out into the workday morning traffic toward the Ministry of Defense. Parking on the street, the two were waved through the security gate by the guard and headed for the ugly building housing General Izhack's office. In his outer office, the girl soldier with the Uzi on her desk recognized them, buzzed General Izhack and then motioned them to go in.

General Izhack stood up to greet them. "Merry Christmas, Dr. Kelly. Thanks for coming in today. Shalom, Joseph."

"Kelly relied, "Shalom, General Izhack. Thanks for the greeting. It's easy to forget it's Christmas in Israel."

"If you were in Bethlehem this morning you would know it! There are always several thousand people jamming Manger Square outside the Church of the Nativity. And the Israeli security police will be busy trying to prevent any terrorist acts against those crowds. Our terrorist enemies like to prey on innocent people who have no connection with the Israeli-Arab conflicts."

"I've read about the Christmas crowds. I visited Bethlehem when I was here at a different time of year."

"Now, let's go over the details of your briefing in Tehran next month. It's very important that your briefing to General Hatami must be well prepared. It shouldn't be too technical and should include lots of easy to understand pictures and diagrams."

"I've briefed a lot of generals in the Pentagon and I know the material must be kept on a basic level. They can't understand a lot of technical details and they get bored."

"That's right. Now, we must discuss another important point. You must find a good agent in Iran. Without an agent, General

Hatami and his staff will listen to your briefing and they will all smile and shake your hand. But afterwards, nothing will happen."

"Why do we need an agent? I thought you said we were sure to get this project."

"The agent makes things happen. *Baksheesh* is the oil that makes Moslem bureaucracies run smoothly. Your agent will know where to apply the oil of *Baksheesh* to the bureaucratic machinery."

"But we have a new anti-corruption law in the US. We can't bribe Iranian officials. It's illegal."

"We know that, Dr. Kelly. You or your company are not going to *bribe* anyone. Your company will pay a negotiated commission to your agent for sales services rendered. You can not control or even know what he does with his commission. It is his money. Your agent will furnish you with a signed statement that he is not making payments to any Iranian officials, just as your law requires."

"Well, then we should have no problems."

General Izhack brought up the next subject, "Joseph, please outline the agenda for the Tehran meeting with General Hatami."

"Yes, Chich. General Hatami's aide Colonel Abdul (Abe) Fahi told me the meeting has been set up for 0900 Sunday the 29th of January."

Kelly interrupted, "That will be right after Jimmy Mahoney is inaugurated as our new president."

"All US presidents treat Israel well. They need the Jewish-American votes."

Colonel Ladrun continued, "OK, Brad. You should arrive in Tehran on the afternoon of Friday the 24th of January, 1976. I'll meet you at Mehrabad Airport. Let me know what flight you'll be coming in on. I recommend you fly to Tehran on Iranair from Europe. It's safer than on US or European airlines."

"Joseph, I got a telex from my company just this morning. I'm leaving Los Angeles via TWA to London and then continuing on a non-stop Iranair flight from London to Tehran, arriving at Mehrabad at 4:30pm."

"Brad, was it a telex to your hotel?"

"Yes, why?"

"For your own personal safety I strongly suggest you change the reservations. Our Arab friends intercept all open telexes to Israel. Their terrorist organizations now know your travel plans to Tehran. Change them!"

"OK, thanks for the advice. I had checked the connections to Tehran so I know there are several other ways to get to Tehran on that Friday afternoon. I'll take one of those. Now, I'll need the first working day to meet with the US ambassador and with our company's marketing man in Tehran. I'll ask him to help find the right Iranian agent for our business there."

Colonel Ladrun apologized, "Look, Brad, I don't want to tell you how to conduct your business, but I strongly recommend you consider Mr. Abfol Mahi. He's well connected at the top of the Iranian government."

"You mean with the Shah?"

"Well, Abfol is reputed to be the Shah's bastard brother. They look a lot alike."

"I'll look into that possibility. Now, how about the agenda for the meeting?"

"Our meeting will be with General Hatami in his office with his Chief-of-staff, General Doshenshah, present. First, I will introduce you as a top official from the US firm of Associated Aviation Corporation and then you will give your presentation. If your briefing passes his screening, you will be invited to present the plan later to a larger audience. If you don't get the invitation to give a second briefing, you might as well pack your bags and go home. You flunked the test. We'll contact Boeing or Lockheed then."

"That sounds a lot like my PhD screening exam."

"But you didn't have a one billion dollar prize riding on the PhD exam."

"Joseph, it sounds like I'd better have a good briefing."

General Izhack broke his silence to interject, "No, Dr. Kelly! You had better have the right agent!"

"OK, I get the picture."

Joseph continued, "More advice, Brad. I recommend you stay at the Tehran Hilton. It's full of American aerospace executives and you won't be conspicuous there at all. I'll stay at the

Intercontinental. I feel more comfortable in an European oriented hotel."

Joseph filled Brad in with more details about the meeting. Then General Izhack straightened up in his chair, "Gentlemen, I suggest we break up now. I've got a meeting at the Defense Minister's office in a few minutes. Good luck on IBEX to you both."

Kelly staggered groggily out of bed at 4am on Thursday, the 26th of December and splashed water on his face trying to wake up. His Air France flight would leave at 7am for Paris. With the extremely elaborate security procedures at Ben Gurion Airport, passengers were required to begin check-in at least two hours before their flight's scheduled departure. As he showered and dressed and packed his small carry-on bag, he felt lonely in the room without Christina and Olga. He wished he could have said goodbye to them.

During busy times of day, Kelly had trouble getting one of the jammed elevators down to the lobby to stop, but at this hour hardly anyone else wanted to use them. There were only a few people trying to check-out at the cashier's counter in the lobby, probably passengers on other early morning flights. Kelly paid his bill which came to a huge sum in Israeli pounds. *That's a lot of pounds, but it's about the same in dollars as the New York Hilton would have been.*

The doorman just outside the revolving door hailed a taxi for Kelly from the line-up. Kelly slipped him a US dollar and scrambled in. They drove rapidly through the deserted early morning streets of Tel Aviv toward the airport, arriving just before 5am. Kelly paid the driver, threw his carry-on bag on his back, and strode into the jammed terminal.

He got in one of the lines at the crowded Air France counter to check in for his flight. Each passenger had to be checked by Israeli security guards before presenting his ticket to the Air France agents. The guards were mainly young girls who spent a lot of time poking through all the suitcases, requesting the passengers to open gift packages, and asking a lot of questions, like:

'Did anyone give you a package to carry on the plane with you?'

'Whom did you visit in Israel?'

'Did you go to any Arab areas?'

Etc.

As he submitted to the inspections and grilling, Kelly thought, *I guess it's worth it all for security. I'd hate for my aircraft to be high jacked by terrorists. They would be sure to find my scrambler and the proposal from IAI for IBEX. As an American, I would be in deep trouble.*

After this baggage inspection, Kelly passed through the ticket check-in, a passport check by customs, and a final body search by another security officer. The whole procedure took well over an hour. Finally, he was allowed to go into the International Departure Lounge where he picked up his seat assignment and exchanged his remaining Israeli pounds back into dollars. Then he was glad to drop into a chair in one of the coffee shops where he ordered a coffee and a sweet roll while he waited for the boarding call for Air France flight 841. *What a crazy turn of events! I come over to terminate a joint venture which would have brought the company fifty million dollars a year within five years and I learn about a one billion dollar project. The aerospace business is wild.*

Kelly's flight was announced in Hebrew, French and finally English. He crowded down the stairs to the airport bus which carried him and his fellow travelers to the Air France 747 parked in a remote site on the airport, guarded by Israeli soldiers with Uzi machine guns.

On board, he sank into his first class seat and fastened his safety belt. A beautiful, blonde stewardess immediately poured him a glass of Moet champagne. "Merci beaucoup!" he answered and raised his crystal goblet in a silent toast and then sipped the bubbling liquid. *What a strange time to drink champagne – before 7 in the morning. Well, it's 9 at night in California on Christmas Day, so I guess it's OK.* The big aircraft took off and climbed to cruise altitude. Kelly received his sumptuous breakfast of eggs Benedict while the Boeing 747 passed over the Greek Isles. Afterward, Kelly leaned his seat back into an almost horizontal position and slipped into a deep slumber.

Four hours later the announcement that they were landing at Charles De Gaulle Airport filtered through his consciousness. He glanced at his watch, which he had set on Paris time before take off, and it was just after 12 noon. He straightened his tie, smoothed his hair, and pulled his carry on bag a little way out from under the seat in front of him, ready to be one of the first passengers out of the plane and through the flexible "snake" tunnel from the plane to the terminal.. Inside, he headed down the long tunnel with its moving sidewalk to Passport Control. He took the escalator to Customs, went out through the Nothing to Declare line and headed for the exit.

Christina and Olga greeted him with hugs and kisses. Kelly gasped, "What are you two doing here? I thought you were in Tel Aviv."

Christina, as usual, spoke first, "We flew to Paris yesterday on the early morning TWA flight to help Amnon pick out his new apartment."

Olga broke in, "We found a nice two bedroom place on Kleber Avenue near the Baltimore Hotel."

"Why does Amnon need a Paris apartment?" wondered Brad.

This time, Olga answered, "You can ask him. He's in his Mercedes waiting for us just outside the terminal entrance."

A few more steps and the trio saw the car. The girls chose the back seat with Kelly's bag between them while he settled into the right front seat. Amnon immediately headed out of the airport and took the autobahn toward Paris.

Brad greeted Amnon, "What a surprise to see you here. The girls say you found an apartment in the city. Are you moving from Tel Aviv?"

"No, Brad," Amnon laughs. "It's just that my *company* has a lot of activity in Europe, centered in Paris. Our Arab *friends* are also very active here. I spend about a third of my time in Paris since it's a good listening post to learn about terrorists plans against the Israelis in Europe. Besides, the apartment is cheaper than a hotel, only $400 a month. The Baltimore where I usually stay is over a hundred US dollars a night."

"I like to make a rest stop in Paris on my way home to California. It's possible to fly back to Los Angeles from Tel Aviv in one day, because of the ten hours I gain by flying west. But I prefer to stop for a *cultural readjustment* before going home. I'll catch the noon Air France non-stop to Los Angeles and be home by 4 tomorrow afternoon."

"How about you and the girls joining me at the Taillevent Restaurant near my apartment. That should help with your *cultural readjustment*."

"Great!" the three chorused and Christina added, "Providing we can get back to Brad's Paris Hilton room by midnight. We want to be sure he sleeps well tonight."

Brad grinned, "Based on past performance, that should be easy."

Amnon steered off the freeway and headed for the *centrum*. "You Americans always stay at the Hilton. You should try the Baltimore next time. It's a three star hotel in the finest European tradition." Amnon headed the Mercedes toward the Eiffel Tower and turned off toward the Hilton in the shadow of the famous Paris monument. Pulling up in front of the lobby entrance, he added, "I'll pick you up at 2100 for dinner. Our reservations are for 9:30."

The two girls and Brad piled out of the car, calling "Au revoir," to Amnon. Christina held out a plastic card, "Here's your room key, Brad. We've already checked in for you."

"How did you know where I was staying?"

"Amnon knew your complete itinerary. His *company* keeps track of their friends as well as their enemies."

Suddenly Brad caught on - This was Mossad's way of protecting one of their *valuable assets* – him!

In the Hilton lobby, they took the elevator to the seventh floor, and went into a two room suite at the end of the hall, with a fabulous view of the Eiffel Tower and the Seine River. Brad quickly unpacked, then said, "Instead of an *afternoon delight* lets do a little sight seeing in Paris. It's not 2 yet and I had a long nap on the Tel Aviv flight."

With the help of the Paris Metro, the three toured the avenues, shops and parks of Paris and even found time for a late afternoon trip on a sightseeing boat that cruised up and down the Seine announcing points of interest on either bank. They hurried back to the hotel with just enough time to dress for dinner.

Heading back down to the lobby to wait for Amnon, they found the area was full of Japanese, Arabs, Indians, and Iranians, as well as the usual American tourists and businessmen, who liked to schedule their travels so their work agenda finished just as a holiday began, so they could enjoy an exotic stay without using any of their vacation time.

Amnon, as always, was right on time. They drove toward the Champs Elysées, turned onto Avenue George V and passed the Crazy Horse Saloon on the right. They turned left between the crowds on the Champs Elysées and headed toward the traffic circle around the Arc de Triomphe where they entered the Parisian *Roulette Game* of circling the famous arch without being hit by the driver on the right who had the right-of-way. Amnon chose one of the spokes sticking out from The Etoille (the star traffic circle) and headed down Kleber Avenue, where he parked in the garage of his newly acquired home. Walking the few steps to the Taillevent restaurant, they arrived just before their reservation time. Inside, the owner, Georges, greeted them, "Welcome to Taillevent, Messier Milchbucher. And Mademoiselles Christina and Olga!"

Amnon introduced Kelly, and Georges added, with a French flourish, "Welcome to Taillevent, Dr. Kelly. We have some special surprises for you this evening. We're going to treat you to a tasting of new wines, on the house. Messier Milchbucher is one of our best customers and his guests are always welcome here at the Taillevent!"

As soon as they are settled at a choice corner table overlooking the small but elegant dining room with every table taken, the wine steward appeared pushing a cart loaded with twelve different wine bottles. Georges told me to let you taste these new wines at your leisure. Make your choices, and you will be given a full bottle of each when you leave." Brad decided not to follow the American custom of a cocktail before dinner and joined his friends tasting the multitude of wines in turn, using small pieces of French bread to remove the taste of one before trying the next. Kelly found two of the wines especially appealing: one red and one white. He told the wine steward who brought

Kelly the two bottles wrapped in a Christmas package. Amnon asked for four bottles of his single choice and the girls each followed Kelly's plan of one white and one red.

The quartet dined on a sumptuous meal of wild Cornish game hens on a bed of wild rice, with Bordelaise sauce and a variety of vegetables. The fresh green salad came after the main course, in the French fashion. A soufflé Grand Marnier topped off the meal.

Amnon drove the three back to the Hilton and told Brad, "I'll pick you up at 10:30 in the morning. That should be in plenty of time for your noon flight to Los Angeles."

Kelly, Christina, and Olga hurried through the lobby to the elevators up to their suite. After washing in the bidet, Brad and Olga climbed into the queen size bed after Christina lost the flip of a coin. She watched TV a while and then smoothly slid into bed on Brad's other side, opposite from Olga. The trio slipped off into a deeply relaxed sleep.

In the morning, the three had a leisurely breakfast in the bright and sunny Hilton breakfast room, choosing from an expansive array of dishes at the buffet. When he checked out, Kelly noticed the bill for the one night, with breakfast, snacks and splits of champagne in the room came to just over 250 US dollars. Amnon arrived right at 10:30, drove Kelly and the two girls to the Charles De Gaulle Airport, where they dropped Kelly off at the Air France terminal with ample time to check in and catch his flight.

Kelly stretched out in his large first class sleeper seat on the Air France 747 after finishing a feast of filet mignon and several glasses of champagne. Being a seasoned traveler, he had no trouble falling asleep as the huge plane flew over the polar route from Paris to Los Angeles. With the winter headwinds, the flight took a full thirteen hours and arrived in LAX as scheduled at 4pm on Friday, December 27, 1975.

Chapter 4.

Ibex Team Set Up

Kelly felt the Boeing 747 begin its long descent to the Los Angeles Airport. Out his window, the snow on the San Gabriel Mountains north of the Los Angeles basin sparkled in the sunlight. Through the window to the left, he saw Catalina Island and recognized some of the coves where he often anchored his racing sailboat. The weather was crystal clear. Not a sign of the usual Los Angeles smog.

The huge airplane continued to slide down the glide slope and landed smoothly on runway 25, then taxied up to the International Arrivals Terminal. Kelly rushed to be first off the plane with his carry on bag so he would be near the front of the passport control line to get his passport stamped. Then on to the Customs area where the agent waved him through, making him the first passenger out into the crowd waiting to meet the incoming passengers.

His beautiful blonde wife and his five children, three sons and two daughters, were happily waving to him. Kelly handed his bag to his oldest son and threw his arms around his wife and kissed her warmly. Then he hugged each of the children in turn, starting with the 23 year old and ending with the 13 year old. Reaching into the outside pocket of his bag, Kelly took out two packages.

He held the smaller one out to his wife, "Darling, here is a belated Christmas present or an early Anniversary gift, whichever you want to call it."

Anna quickly tore the wrappings off the little package. When she saw the diamond, her beautiful smile lit up her whole face. A tear sparkled in her eyes, "Oh, Brad! It's beautiful. What a wonderful surprise!" She kissed him again.

Then Kelly handed the larger package to his oldest son, "Chris, since you are the only one over 21, I guess you get this. Don't drop it."

Christopher squeezed the present, tore off the paper, "Wow! Real French wine. My girl friend and I thank you for this."

Kelly reached down into his bag again and pulled out the four small sacks holding the gifts he had picked out in the Israeli and French airport duty free shops and he passed them out to the other four children. They made excited noises of appreciation as the group headed out of the crowded International Terminal and across the street to one of the multi storied parking buildings.

Anna exclaimed, "Darling, it's so nice to have you back again. Christmas was lonely without you. I hope you can stay home for awhile."

"I can't promise that, but I don't have to go overseas again until the end of January. I uncovered a new project."

"What is it?"

"I can't tell you much about it, but I can say I'll be going to Iran frequently over the next several months."

"I'll be so glad when you finish all this secret work so I can know what it is you do at work. I feel so foolish at my bridge club when all the other wives talk about their husbands' jobs. I can't tell them what you do."

Anna dug in her purse for the car keys and handed Brad his set so he could unlock the doors of their Buick station wagon for everyone to get in. Kelly followed the ramps down to the ground floor and out onto the road that made a big circle from one terminal to the next until he came out on Century Boulevard. He drove east to the San Diego freeway where he could turn north toward their suburban home in the hills on the north side of the San Fernando Valley. They were a convenient twenty minutes away from the huge Associated Aviation aerospace complex located just off the San Diego Freeway on the Van Nuys Airport.

Kelly lived in a large two-story house with six bedrooms, four baths, and a large patio with a kidney shaped swimming pool and a landscaped garden full of tropical plants and trees. The house sat at the end of a cul-de-sac on a hillside looking south across the whole San Fernando Valley and over the tops of the Hollywood Hills to the city of Los Angeles. On a super clear day like this one, they could even see Santa Catalina Island in the distance. By the time they got home, the snow capped peaks of the San Gabriel

Mountains to the east looked pink in the last bits of light from the setting sun.

Halfway around the world and back in less than a week. I'm sure glad I took that rest stop in Paris. I feel like I'm back on LA time already. I'm sure ready to get started on IBEX.

The next morning, Kelly had an early breakfast and scanned the Los Angeles Times to catch up on the news he missed during his trip. He apologized to his wife, "Honey, I'm sorry this new project means I have to work during all the rest of my Christmas vacation. I'll be home early today, by 4:30 at the latest. How would you like to go out to a champagne and steak dinner at the Stockman's tonight, on my AAC expense account, of course."

"Great! I'll wear my new Christmas dress and this!" She flashed the new diamond ring from Israel. "You'll be happy to notice Christopher washed your car and filled it with gas in honor of your home coming."

Kelly kissed her goodbye and backed his MG convertible out of the garage, pushing the automatic door closing switch as he backed down the driveway. He wound down the road leading to the San Diego Freeway where he headed south to the Van Nuys Airport turn off. The freeway exit took him almost to the entrance of the Associated Aviation parking lot where he pulled into the space marked Dr. B. R. Kelly. He glanced toward the giant AAC hanger full of production and experimental aircraft as he walked toward his office building. He showed his picture badge to Jerri, the receptionist in the large lobby. She pushed the button opening the security door entrance. Kelly took the elevator to the fourth floor and hurried to his corner office, overlooking the airport ramp. The company Sabreliner was taxiing up to its parking space. *There's Dr. Morrell, back from Snow Valley for our meeting already. I won't be able to read much of my mail.*

His two in-baskets were full. The Priority basket was overflowing and the Routine basket was stacked almost twelve inches high. The tackled the Priority basket first and sifted through the stack to see what urgent items needed his attention. His intercom buzzed and Dr, Morrell's voice announced, "Brad, come on down and tell me about IBEX. We got here a bit early.

At 43,000 feet we had a 150 knot tail wind. These winter winds aloft really blow."

"Good, Sir. I'll be right there." Kelly walked quickly to the opposite side of the Executive Headquarters Building to Dr. Morrell's corner office. It looked huge after the Israeli offices, and had a reception lobby of its own, which was larger than his office. Helen, Dr. Morrell's secretary, smiled at him, "Good morning, Dr. Kelly. How was your trip to Israel? Did they give you a hard time for dissolving the joint venture?"

"Helen, the trip was fine and it turned out to be a friendly meeting. In fact, the Israelis told me about a new project. But, first, here's something for you." Kelly took a small package from his briefcase and handed it to Helen.

"Oh, how beautiful. Malachite earrings," she exclaimed.

"I got them in Israel. They are supposed to be from King Solomon's mines."

"I love them. Thanks for remembering me, Dr. Kelly. You go right on in, Dr. Morrell's waiting for you."

Dr. Morrell's office looked south toward the Hollywood Hills and west toward Van Nuys Airport and the rocky hills beyond it, separating the San Fernando Valley from the Malibu area of the Pacific coastline. The white Sabreliner that brought Dr. Morrell was still parked on the ramp, waiting to fly him back later that afternoon to his interrupted skiing at Snow Valley.

Dr. Morrell waved Kelly to the couch in the corner of the room where there were several overstuffed chairs and another couch, all in matching brown leather. "Welcome back, Brad. I called the AAC Board Chairman about this new project after I talked to you on the scrambler. He gave us the green light to go ahead on IBEX. In fact, his exact words were, 'Pull out all the stops! Let's get this one. You've got a budget of $250,000 from the board's discretionary funds for the proposal.' Your technical team knows that so you don't have to tell them in the meeting. It's all set up in the big conference room at 1pm."

"That's good news, John. This project must be an SCI or compartmented security project. The Israeli participation is particularly sensitive."

"I assumed that from our scrambled phone conversation. Don't worry, our board doesn't want the Israeli involvement known either. The Director of Security is already busy setting up the SCI procedures for IBEX, and has already briefed your team on what the rules are for this kind of project. You can concentrate on the technical details."

Kelly gave Dr. Morrell a thumbnail sketch of the project, describing the five sites ringing Iran and the central processing center at the Doshen Toeppeh Air Force Base in Tehran. Then he asked if Ralph Hauser would be at the meeting at 1 o'clock.

Dr. Morrell explained, "I invited him, but he's on Molokai for his Christmas holiday. He wants to see you as early in January as possible after he gets back from Hawaii. He wants to hear about your trip. I got the impression the CIA wants to find out more about IBEX. Perhaps you can have a briefing ready by then."

"I'll start laying-out the briefing this afternoon after I finish the kick-off meeting. I think a first cut version should be ready in about a week."

"Good. I want to see it before you present it to anyone outside AAC."

"Of course. But I need to tell you one more thing. The five IBEX sites I mentioned don't include one for surveillance of the USSR. The Shah isn't worried about Russia, but only about his Moslem brothers. However, Prime Minister Begin personally warned me that when the Israeli ambassador briefed the CIA Director about IBEX, the director asked for a site near the Caspian Sea, looking at the Soviets. So that would be a sixth site!"

Dr. Morrell nodded, "Now I know why that CIA agent wanted to talk to you about your trip! OK, include a sixth location in your proposal and briefings. Break out the costs for site six separately so we can see how much it affects the overall cost of IBEX. My guess is the increase will only be a few percent."

"I think you're right, John. I've already picked out a place for the sixth site. It's a 4,819 meter peak called Takht-I-Suleyman in the Elburz Mountains near Rashit on the Caspian Sea. Here it is on this map of Iran."

"That looks like a fine choice. I has a clear view of the southern part of Russia across the Caspian Sea."

Kelly appreciated his boss's decisiveness. His technical background allowed him to quickly grasp the key technical factors in complex situations. Both Morrell and Kelly had PhD's from the California Institute of technology (Caltech) in Pasadena, California. Kelly had been a beginning graduate student in 1952 when Dr. Morrell received his doctorate. Kelly finished his PhD in 1956 and went to work at Associated Aviation in the research department under Dr. Morrell, who was a section manager at the time. Dr. Morrell was promoted through a succession of positions until he was made president of this section in 1972 and he pulled Kelly along with him. Kelly was now a vice president of technology, a special staff position reporting directly to the president. Kelly became a technical trouble shooter who headed up special projects on an ad hoc basis. After a new project got moving in the right direction, it was turned over to the regular line management for execution and completion.

Dr. Morrell went on, "I think you've brought me up to speed now on IBEX. It's almost noon now. Let's go to the 29th Squadron for lunch."

"You talked me into it." responded Brad and the two left the private office and headed out through the reception area where Brad handed Helen some papers he had written during the morning meeting. "Helen, please make viewgraphs from these notes for the afternoon meeting."

She smiled, "OK, I'll bring them to you in the conference room."

The two men rode the elevator down to the lobby where Bob Anderson, the pilot for the AAC Sabreliner, was talking to the receptionist, Jerri. Dr. Morrell invited him to join them for lunch adding "You can drive."

"Great, let's go," was his immediate response. The three climbed into Bob Anderson's Pontiac for the very short drive to the restaurant which had been built to look like the World War I French farmhouse used as the headquarters for the 29th Squadron of the French Air Force. It overlooked the Van Nuys Airport runways and most of the patrons were private pilots who flew their small airplanes into Van Nuys for lunch.

The three men ordered steak sandwiches and green salads with Roquefort dressing, preceeded by dry martinis on-the-rocks. Except the pilot Bob Anderson who passed on the drinks since he had to fly the Sabreliner back to Snow Valley that afternoon. He had a Virgin Mary (Bloody Mary without vodka) while Kelly and Dr. Morrell enjoyed their martinis.

During lunch, Kelly ventured, "I suspect the engineers on my team won't be very happy to be at work during their Christmas week vacation."

John agreed, "No, probably not. You tell them the jobs they're saving are their own. Look, Brad, I'll fix it so they get paid overtime for their work this week. That should cheer them up."

"Thanks, John. I'm sure they'll like that. They know that, as salaried employees, they usually don't get any overtime pay. It'll really increase their enthusiasm for IBEX."

After coffee, Bob Anderson picked up the check and paid for it with his company credit card. Another executive perquisite at Associated Aviation.

Bob Anderson stayed in the lobby to resume his conversation with Jerri, the blonde receptionist, who had the reputation of sleeping with all the company pilots (and also, some of the top executives!).

Drs. Morrell and Kelly took the elevator up to the large conference room which the executive staff used as the corporate office control center for project reviews, business reviews, and financial reviews. There was a huge mahogany conference table in the center of the room. At one end there was a large white *blackboard* and at the other a screen to be used with the viewgraph projector sitting on the conference table. Along one wall schedule charts kept track of AAC's current major projects. On the remaining wall were financial charts showing sales, bookings and billings for the major projects of the entire corporation.

As Dr. Morrell walked in, the eight engineers who were to be the core of Kelly's IBEX team all rose. They tried to hide their hostility with varying degrees of success. Dr. Morrell said, "Please, be seated, gentlemen. Thanks for coming in during the holiday week. I know its a personal sacrifice for you and your families for you to be here. You have been chosen to be an important part of the IBEX proposal team, a project which is expected to bring in a billion dollars worth of business to AAC over the next 12 months. You know that's a significant factor in our overall business. It will provide stable employment for the next several years."

The antagonism on the engineers' faces began to dissipate after those opening comments. Kelly spoke up, "Also, gentlemen, Dr. Morrell has authorized overtime pay for this week to compensate you and your families for the intrusion on your holiday." The faces of the eight engineers broke out into broad grins at this unexpected good news. Paying engineers overtime at AAC was an unusual event, indeed. The top management expected the engineers to spend many long hours of uncompensated overtime, particularly when working on a major proposal such as IBEX.

Helen came into the conference room with a stack of viewgraphs for Dr. Kelly. "I hope I read your handwriting correctly."

Kelly flipped through the colored plastic sheets, "These are beautiful. Thanks."

Helen continued, "The new Wang word processor made typing your notes into these charts easy."

Dr. Morrell broke in, "Gentlemen, thanks again for coming in. Dr. Kelly will take charge now," and headed for the door.

Kelly called after him, "Thanks for the opening comments. Have a good flight." He headed for the projector and projected the first viewgraph on the screen. It said, "IBEX – SCI."

Kelly explained, "Gentlemen, Dr. Morrell said you have already been briefed by the AAC Security Director about the need for tight security for IBEX. I want to emphasize -- Don't discuss IBEX with anybody, not your wife, not your friends at AAC. Nobody!" He frowned at his audience, scanning their faces to see if they took him seriously. They did.

One by one, Kelly flashed the other viewgraphs on the screen and described the six sites and the central processing site in Tehran. He added his preliminary thoughts on the overall system concepts. "Tomorrow morning, you can pick up an outline for the

Pentagon briefing, with a suggested list of 45 briefing charts we'll need. With nine of us preparing them, that's an average of five charts apiece. Any questions?"

Tom, a tall man with an Oklahoma drawl, asked, "Jes' when do we need to finish this here briefing?"

"By working all this weekend I hope we can get the first cut of the report ready to give to the graphics department early Thursday morning, the day after New Years."

"Does that mean we'll have to work on New Years Day?"

"I don't think so. I hope we'll finish by 5 Monday afternoon. Then we can all take off Tuesday and Wednesday for New Years. Be sure you turn in time cards for these three days. You'll get triple pay because they're holidays."

An engineer in the back piped up, "Don't worry about the time cards, Brad. We'll get 'em in for sure. I need the overtime check to help pay for the Christmas bills. For the rest of the fellows, I'd like to say *thanks* for the overtime pay. We certainly didn't expect it when we came in today."

"I know. I could tell by the looks on your faces. Tom, could you stay and help me outline the briefing. See the rest of you at 8am sharp in the morning."

A voice from the back called out, "Aw, Brad, can't we make it 9, being a holiday and all?"

"OK, 9 it is. See you all then."

Tom and Kelly outlined the briefing charts on the white blackboard, erasing here and adding there to come up with the 45 charts. Then he called Helen on the intercom to come to copy it down so they could erase the board.

"I sure hope you can read our scribbles. You can either type it up now or in the morning before the team gets here at 9. Maybe that new Wang word processor will make short work of it. Make ten copies, keep one for Dr. Morrell. Remember, destroy your written notes and put the copies in the Top Secret vault when you finish. We're sorry to keep you so late. Come on, Tom, let's get home to our wives."

As Kelly drove up the winding road to his home, he was happy to discover that, for once, his children had remembered to park their cars off to the side of the huge driveway, rather than blocking the garage door. He pressed the garage door opener, the door yawned open, and he drove in. "Honey, I'm home," he called as walked from the garage into the house.

"I'm almost ready," called his wife from upstairs so Kelly walked on into the family room where his kids were watching the *boob tube*. During his few free minutes, they were glad to give their Dad a quick run down of what everyone had given everyone else for Christmas.

Kelly and Anna drove away from the house in his sports car just before 8. It was already dark and the elaborate Christmas light decorations on the Kellys' house and on all the neighbors' houses gave off a joyful glow. In the spectacularly clear Los Angeles weather the lights on the floor of the San Fernando Valley sparkled in continuous flickering dots, with the lights of the Hollywood Hills in the background. It took only twenty five minutes to reach the expensive Stockman's Restaurant on Ventura Boulevard. The Los Angeles freeway system made it easy to cover a long distance in a short time.

Kelly pulled up to the restaurant entrance and was greeted by a red coated doorman, who took the MG and parked it in the valet parking lot.

The Kellys had a typical California restaurant dinner. They started off with two martinis, then had avocado salads with Roquefort dressing. Champagne and garlic bread were served with the salad. Large filet mignon steaks with onion rings, baked potatoes with sour cream topping, and asparagus spears constituted the main course. They had cheese cake for dessert with Kahlua coffee.

Kelly's tolerance for alcohol had built up over the years as an executive at AAC. Aerospace executives were expected to drink a lot. They did!

Kelly paid for the dinner with a company credit card. As Kelly and Anna came out of the restaurant, the doorman recognized him and sent the valet parking attendant to fetch the MG. Soon the convertible pulled up, the parking attendant opened the doors and stood by the driver's door waiting for his tip. Kelly slipped him two dollars. The couple drove down Ventura

Boulevard toward the San Diego freeway and retraced their steps home. Kelly didn't feel a bit tipsy in spite of all the alcohol he had consumed.

Kelly pulled the MG into the garage and he and Anna headed for their large bedroom overlooking their swimming pool and the carpet of lights from the valley floor beyond.

They both undressed rapidly and jumped into their king sized water bed. Anna turned on the Hi-Fi. Kelly kissed her and whispered, "Darling, I miss you on these long overseas trips. I'm so eager to have you tonight." Anna nodded in agreement, her eyes sparkling. The pair dissolved into a frenzy of lovemaking, aided in intensity by the martinis and champagne from dinner.

Kelly left home at 8:30 Sunday morning and arrived in his office about ten minutes before the meeting scheduled at 9am. He opened his Top Secret vault and found his copy of the IBEX briefing outline. Helen had done a beautiful job. She left a note that said,

> 28 Dec 75
> Dr. Kelly,
> Here is your copy of the briefing outline. I hope I read
> Your writing correctly. I'll be in at 11 on Sunday.
> Dr. Morrell asked me to support you and your team
> this weekend with the word processor. I'm the
> only secretary cleared for IBEX.
>   Helen

Kelly took out his other notes on IBEX, locked the vault and strode over to the conference room. Helen had arranged for security to bring coffee and donuts to the conference room. Kelly mused, *Helen thinks of everything.* The other team members were already reading their copies of the briefing outline and planning the layout of the briefing charts assigned to each of them.

Kelly strode to one end of the conference table and announced, "Now for some ground rules: first, you may seek technical support from other members of the engineering staff, but under no circumstances will you disclose the IBEX concept or details to them. This will require that you break down your task into sub-tasks which can be carried out by engineers not familiar with IBEX.

"Second, you must coordinate your subsystem designs closely with me so I can be sure they meet the overall IBEX objectives, some of which I am not free to disclose to you.

"Third, we are going to have to meet some very tight time schedules. There will be trips to Washington DC and to Tehran in the near future. You must be prepared to work whatever hours of uncompensated overtime that are necessary to meet these schedules. Please remember how important Dr. Morrell said IBEX was to AAC's financial future."

One of the engineers asked, "Brad, when will you leave on your first trip to Washington?"

"I hope to have a complete project schedule laid out by the end of the day. It looks like I'll have to carry the briefing to Washington the week after January first. The folks in the Pentagon and in Munitions Control must be briefed to smooth the way for the necessary approvals and export licenses. We are talking about some sensitive technology. The last administration gave the Shah everything he wanted. I expect President Mahoney's people to do the same after his inauguration in a few weeks."

Kelly walked over to the blackboard and sketched an organization chart, "Gentlemen, you've been selected to work on IBEX because of your expertise in the technical disciplines required. The team will be broken down into areas with one or two people assigned to each of the functional areas:

Dr. Kelly, Tom Bradley - IBEX System Concept
Bill Wilson, Bob Thompson - Communication Systems
Dr. John Vries - Encryption Algorithms
David Elliott, Jim Smith - Computer Hardware and Software
Jack Nishamoto - System Interface and Electrical Power Subsystems

"You will note I've assigned the briefing charts consistent with this organization."

Tom broke in with his Oklahoma drawl, "It looks like you've forgotten an important area. How about the antennas?"

"Thanks for reminding me, Tom. The electronic division of Israel Aircraft Industries (IAI) will handle the antennas. They will also take care of the site preparation and installation. I have a detailed technical description of the IAI antenna subsystems including a firm fixed price proposal from them. Their proposal will be on the table here during working hours for your reference."

One of the engineers asked, "With all this super secret security, who will type up the viewgraphs and do the drawings?"

"Helen will be in later this morning and tomorrow. She's been cleared to prepare the viewgraphs on her word processor. Tom will do the block diagrams. Then after New Years, we'll turn our efforts over to the graphics department for clean up. Their artists can turn your sketches into works of art. We want to present a first class briefing to the Pentagon."

The team worked hard all day Sunday and Monday. Late Monday afternoon, Kelly carried the typed up first cut into the conference room. "Congratulations! We've met our first milestone. There's obviously a lot of detailed thinking and knowledge behind each chart. You've done a really professional job. Now go on home and enjoy what's left of your Christmas vacation."

Kelly celebrated New Year's Day 1976 by taking his whole family to the Caltech Athenaeum (faculty club) for breakfast. Kelly pointed out the upstairs room where Albert Einstein had lived when he was teaching there. His family nodded in appreciation, although Kelly had shared this piece of information with them many times before. Later, they walked up to Colorado Boulevard with a large group of Caltech Alumni and spent about two hours watching the colorful Rose Parade from reserved seats in one of the many grandstands alongside the street. Back to the Athenaeum for a buffet lunch before they climbed on board a bus full of Caltech Alumni for the short ride, at a snail's pace because of the intense traffic, to the Rose Bowl. There they watched the University of Southern California football team trounce the Iowa State team. Kelly remembered his football playing days. Caltech wasn't in the same league as a team like USC, since there were only about 1500 students, counting both graduates and undergraduates. They tried hard, but won only one game during his four years of playing. Their coach had been fired from USC because he lost one game in the season before Caltech hired him. The Caltech Trustees and Alumni loved that coach because he came from the *Big League*. His job was assured until retirement as long as his team won a game about every four or five years.

Kelly went in to work extra early on the day after New Years hoping to plow through his stacks of accumulated mail. But it was not to be. His intercom buzzer went off.

Helen announced, "The boss wants to have a dry run of the IBEX briefing at 10:30 this morning."

Kelly sighed, "I'll be there. Please tell the other IBEX team members so they can hear Dr. Morrell's comments first hand."

He opened his safe and removed the briefing, then quickly leafed through the sheets of paper to prepare mentally what to say.

The team gathered in the conference room on time, leaving a place at the head of the conference table for Dr. Morrell. He strode in about five minutes late, "Gentlemen, sorry to be late for my own meeting but I just got a call from the board chairman asking about IBEX. That shows how important this project is. I told him you all had worked through the Christmas vacation. He said I should offer you his appreciation. Now let's get started. I have to finish before lunch. The company *chopper* is scheduled to pick me up at 11:50 to fly me to a meeting over at our computer division in Orange County."

Kelly started the briefing. Dr. Morrell stopped him frequently, asking a number of detailed questions. Kelly had to call on some of the team members for answers to some of the questions. Kelly thought, *These questions are a lot more detailed than those the colonels in the Pentagon will ask. But, then, they don't have PhDs from Caltech.*

At the end of the briefing, Dr. Morrell rose and declared, "Gentlemen, I appreciate how hard you've worked to put this briefing together, but, frankly, it's lousy! I want to see Associated Aviation's innovativeness coming out more clearly. I want a major re-do. Let's get more technical detail into it. I'll see you here on Friday, same time." He headed out of the conference room to catch his helicopter flight.

Kelly sighed dejectedly, "Well, fellows, it was a good try but I guess it's back to the drawing boards."

Oklahoma Tom broke in, "Aw, Hell, don't worry, Brad. If the ole man didn't have something critical to say, he wouldn't think he was doing his job as president. I made detailed notes on his comments and I think it'll be easy to fix."

"Thanks for the cheering up, Tom. Let's see your notes."

Kelly read the notes aloud

and the team members stuck in items they'd noticed during the presentation. They all worked together to come with modifications for the existing charts and with ideas for additional charts. The tasks were assigned to the various team members before lunch. The team agreed they'd have to get these revisions to the graphics department by late in the afternoon. Kelly observed, "I'll have to see about getting authorization for Graphics to work all night if necessary to get these edits finished before tomorrow morning. We'll have to get together early tomorrow morning to go over them to make any last minute changes before our 10:30 meeting with Dr. Morrell."

The group gathered in the conference room at 7am on Friday morning. The graphics department had turned the engineering sketches into beautiful multi-colored drawings. There were lots of block diagrams and schematics showing the surveillance coverage from the six Iranian IBEX sites. The antennas from Israel were included. A master schedule chart showed the interlocking events needed to build and install the system in Iran. Kelly had time to go through a complete dry run in front of the team. They interrupted with helpful comments on how to present the information that each individual had prepared. By 10:30, Kelly was ready for the boss!

This time the briefing went better. Dr. Morrell made comments like, *That's more like it*, and he asked very few questions. At the end he said, "You're ready for the Pentagon, now."

"Thanks, Sir. I have an appointment with Mr. Robert Hack, Director of International Programs in the Pentagon at 10am next Tuesday. He promised he'd have all the right colonels there for the briefing. They'll have all the right security clearances, too."

"I recommend you brief Ralph Hauser, our in-house CIA type, as soon as possible. And you should brief General John Robertson in the Pentagon. He has just been tagged by President Mahoney to be the head of the US Military Assistance Advisory Group (MAAG) in Tehran. He'll be a key player for IBEX."

"OK, John. I have a meeting set up with Ralph this afternoon. I didn't know about General Robertson's new assignment. I'll try to schedule a meeting with him while I'm in Washington. I do have a meeting arranged with Mr. Jack Johnson, Director of Munitions Control, before the Pentagon meeting."

Good for you, Brad. It looks like you have all the Washington players covered. But I want to warn you to get *all* the necessary US Government approvals for IBEX. There could be severe trouble if you miss some required signature. The Washington bureaucrats can get nasty if you make a mistake dealing with critical technology like IBEX."

Ralph Hauser walked into Kelly's office at 2pm sharp. "How was your trip to Israel, Brad? Did you learn anything my *company* might find interesting?"

"Yes, Ralph. Dr. Morrell suggested I give you the same briefing I'm going to give in the Pentagon next Tuesday." Kelly laid the hard copy of the IBEX briefing on the desk in front of Houser.

Ralph leafed through the report, "My director sent me a message you were going to work with the Israelis on this IBEX project. Would you please drop by the *company* at Langley while you're in Washington and brief the director about IBEX? He's heard a little from the Israeli ambassador, but he'd like more details."

Kelly looked at his trip schedule. "I could be out at Langley by 2pm Tuesday afternoon, after I finish at the Pentagon."

"Fine. Can I use your phone to call the director?"

"Sure. Dial 91, the access code to get the Wats line."

Hauser called CIA Headquarters and set up the meeting. He hung up and turned to Brad, "Everything's set. One of our *company* men will pick you up on the steps of the River Entrance to the Pentagon at 1:30. You'll recognize him. He'll be dressed in a dark blue suit with a striped tie, the Harvard uniform. He'll be driving an old grey Chevrolet."

"OK, good. What's his name?"

"Brad! You know our agent's names are classified. Just call him Joe."

"Thanks for setting up the meeting with the director, Ralph. We want to cover all the bases for IBEX. We need the approval for the export license to go through quickly. I know the right word from your director will help a lot."

Kelly went through the briefing thoroughly.

Hauser remarked, "I'm glad to see there's a sixth site. The director was a little upset when the Israeli ambassador said he didn't think there would be a surveillance site over the Soviet Union."

Kelly explained what Colonel Ladrun had said about the Shah not considering the Russians as a threat.

Hauser replied, "That's wishful thinking on the Shah's part: to think buying a few anti-aircraft guns and such from the USSR would satisfy them. The only thing that's keeping them out of the Shah's territory now is the US military presence there. Before we came along, it was the British keeping the Soviets out. In fact, the Shah wouldn't be back in Iran at all if it wasn't for the CIA's help in the early 50s when he returned from exile."

"You're probably right about the Russians. That's all I can tell you about IBEX now."

"Thanks for the briefing. There is one other thing. You know the *company* is always interested in how the leaders of other countries think, even our friends. Could you summarize your meetings with the various key people there on your last trip? I understand you even met the prime minister."

Kelly was not surprised at this request. He had given oral reports like this to the CIA after his previous overseas trips. He reviewed his meetings with Generals Izhack and Yidron and his short meeting with Mr. Begin. He included highlights of their conversations and his impressions of the men.   Hauser took copious notes, thanked Kelly and left.

Kelly shook his head, *I wonder what the CIA does with information like I just gave Hauser. I can't imagine he learned anything they don't already know. Maybe it just gives someone like Hauser something to do. Being a CIA employee may not be as exciting as it sounds in the spy novels.*

Kelly packed his briefcase with the briefing and other papers he would need in Washington.

Helen came in with his airline tickets and five hundred dollars trip cash. "I put you up in the Roslyn Marriott. I didn't reserve a rental car for you, since I thought you usually took the Metro in Washington. The company chopper will be waiting for you on the pad on our roof at 7:45 Monday morning . The pilot knows you're on American flight 2 at 9am."

"As usual, you took care of everything, Helen. Thanks."

Kelly added the tickets to the items in his briefcase, and locked the whole works in his safe, ready to be picked up early Monday morning. Now he was free for the weekend. As he walked to his car he planned, *There's a race in Los Angeles Harbor this weekend. I'll have to get the family organized to go on it.*

Kelly and his family were avid sailboat racers. With his wife and five children, he had a built in crew. Many of his competitors had to scramble for a crew for each race. That was one of his secrets for winning: having the same crew each time, so each person knew exactly what to do and when to do it.

Chapter 5.

The Pentagon Visit

Kelly hurried into his office at 7:30 Monday morning to get his briefcase out of his safe. He signed the official security receipt certifying he was carrying classified papers to Washington and dashed up the stairs to the roof. He waved recognition to the pilot of the Bell turbine powered helicopter idling on the pad. It was Bill Anderson again, who doubled as a chopper pilot when he was not flying the company Sabreliner. Kelly ducked under the whirring blades and climbed in, settling into the seat next to the pilot. He was the only passenger today. Bill immediately revved up the engine, pulled the collective pitch, the chopper lifted off smartly and headed for LAX.

They landed at the American Airlines finger at 8:10 and Kelly walked straight into the building from the tarmac and continued on to the American Airlines' Admirals Club to pick up his first class seat assignment and boarding card. To fill in the wait until departure time, he ordered a Bloody Mary and then phoned his wife to tell her goodbye again and to remind her to pick him up on his return at 2 Wednesday afternoon on TWA flight 841. At the first boarding call he headed down to the gate with his briefcase and small carry on suitcase and strode through the tunnel onto the DC-10 non-stop flight for Washington. As soon as he was settled in his seat the stewardess poured him a glass of champagne. A thought surfaced in Kelly's mind, *I've done this so many times, it's becoming boring, almost like riding a commuter bus.*

After a steak and eggs brunch, he started to watch the in-flight movie, but soon fell asleep. He didn't wake up until the captain announced the seat belt warning for their landing at Dulles Airport. It was a short flight. With the help of the 150 knot winter jet stream, the flying time from Los Angeles was just under four hours.

Climbing out of the transporter that brought the passengers from the airplane to the terminal, Kelly was surprised to see Christina and Olga waiting for him. He asked them, "How in the world did you know I would be on this flight?"

Christina, as usual, spoke first, "Amnon told us. You can ask him how he knew. He's waiting for us outside." They headed out through the Dulles terminal and took the escalator down through the baggage claim area. Since Kelly had no checked luggage, they walked straight out of the tunnel to the lined up cabs and airport buses. Among them was a black limousine with diplomatic plates with Amnon sitting behind the wheel.

The two girls got in the back seat and Kelly climbed into the guest seat next to the driver. A man who had been walking behind them in the terminal got in the back seat next to the girls.

Amnon introduced him, "Brad, meet Yossi. He's been watching over you. We don't want anything happening to you."

Kelly looked at the husky Israeli security guard in the back seat. *Probably a member of Mossad*, he thought as he noticed a bulge under the guard's coat, large enough to be an Uzi.

Yossi said, "Don't worry, Dr. Kelly. I made sure no terrorist could get you as you got off your plane in Washington." He patted the bulge.

Yossi, I didn't even think about terrorists here in Washington," responded Kelly.

Yossi answered, "They're everywhere. They have unlimited travel budgets and safe passports. We're sure they already know about your involvement with IBEX. You're on their list. You must take steps to protect yourself against this very real threat. We'll help during this trip, but we can't always be with you."

Kelly said, fervently, "Thanks, Yossi." Then he asked Amnon where he got the limousine.

"I borrowed it from the Israeli Embassy. I'm your chauffeur because the ambassador's budget doesn't include one. Anyway, we Israelis are too democratic to use chauffeurs, even if we could afford one."

Then Kelly asked how Amnon knew Kelly was coming.

"Listen, Brad, you're a valuable resource to Israel. There're 200 million dollars riding on your success with this project. Mossad checked the airline reservations computer."

Amnon drove out of the airport and headed for the Dulles Parkway and Washington DC. When he reached the Beltway, he headed toward Baltimore to the first turn off, which was the George Washington Parkway that would carry them to Roslyn and the Marriott Hotel, just off the parkway.

Traveling along the tree lined GW Parkway they passed Langley, the CIA Headquarters where Kelly had a meeting the next day. He thought, *I wonder if the CIA will give me the same protection as Mossad? Probably not. Besides, who would do it? The FBI or the CIA? One's responsible inside the US and the other outside the US. No, no one is going to protect me but myself.*

Amnon pulled into the Marriott driveway and Kelly and the two girls climbed out. Kelly thanked Amnon for the ride and Yossi for the protection and the three waved goodbye. Then Christina said, "Here's the key to your suite. We've already checked you in. We're in 616-618."

One of their sixth floor corner rooms overlooked the Potomac River as it paralleled the George Washington Parkway. The other room had a view of the city of Washington. The white Watergate complex, made famous by Nixon and his assistants, gleamed in the setting sun. The city lights were already coming on this late winter afternoon.

Kelly slipped his briefcase under the bed for safekeeping while the girls were in the sitting room opening three splits of champagne from the room refrigerator. He unpacked his bag and stowed it in the closet. Walking back into the sitting room, he was surprised to see Christina sitting topless by the table, sipping champagne. She was only wearing tiny red bikini panties that clearly showed her blonde pubic hair around the edges. He exclaimed, "You're way ahead of me."

She answered, "Well, go catch up. I'll save your champagne."

Kelly went back to his room, undressed and hung his clothes in the closet. He returned to the sitting room completely nude.

He noticed Christina matched him. The red bikini underpants were now missing.

She handed Kelly his glass of champagne and said, "Here's a toast to the success of your new project, whatever it is."

"Cheers," the others responded.

Olga warned, "Brad, in the car we couldn't help but hear Yossi's comments about terrorists. We don't know what you're involved in, but be careful!"

Christina added, "Here's another toast. To Brad's health and safety!"

"I'll drink to that. Don't worry. I've got the message. I'm going to be damn careful from now on!"

They finished the last of the champagne with this toast. Christina moved over closer to Kelly and kissed him passionately on the lips.

Kelly gasped for breath, "It must be late. Let's skip dinner and go right to bed."

Christina immediately agreed, "That's a great idea! I like bed better than eating anyway."

Olga remarked, "We had a big lunch. Since it's Christine's turn I plan to stay here in the sitting room and watch TV."

Christine and Brad climbed into the large queen sized bed. They made love as the bright lights of Washington DC bathed the room with a soft glow through the picture window. Afterwards Kelly melted into a deep sleep full of dreams about Moslem terrorists.

The two girls were still sleeping when Kelly got up at 7:30. He dressed quietly and retrieved his briefcase from under the bed, then went down to the hotel café for a quick breakfast from the buffet. He walked the short block and a half to the State Department's Office of Munitions Control (OMC) in Roslyn and took the elevator to the fifth floor. In the OMC reception area he told the girl behind the glass window who he was and asked if he could go in for his meeting with the OMC director, Jack Johnson.

She replied, "Let me see if he has finished his staff meeting," and she buzzed Mr. Johnson's secretary on the intercom to let her know Dr. Kelly was waiting. Then she turned to Kelly and said, "The staff meeting has just broken up. You may go to his office now. Do you know the way?"

"Yes. I've been there before," answered Kelly as the receptionist opened the access door for him. Kelly walked down the hall, turned right and continued to the end of the hall. As he walked into Mr. Johnson's corner office, he noticed the view from Johnson's window was the same as from his Marriott room, a view of Washington DC with the Watergate, Washington Monument and the Capital Building all clearly visible on this chilly, winter day.

Johnson motioned Kelly to the large dark brown leather couch against the back wall. "Dr. Kelly, have a seat and tell me what you're up to now?"

"Mr. Johnson, I've just come back from a business trip to Israel and we've found a new project for Associated Aviation in Iran. It's a big one. We expect the contract to run a billion dollars."

"That should help our balance of payments. Besides, the Shah has a lot of money from the oil we're buying from him. But, what have the Israelis to do with it?"

"General Hatami, Chief of the Iranian Air Force, told the Israelis about it. General Hatami wants a large US aerospace firm as the prime contractor, but, according to the Israelis, he wants them to be a subcontractor."

"I know General Hatami, I met him on my trip to Iran last year. He's really close to the Shah. The Israelis are probably right. They have a close, but covert, relationship with the Iranians. I remember one of our intelligence reports said the Israelis helped the Iranians plan and build the defenses and communications on Karg Island, their oil terminal in the Persian Gulf."

"That fits with what the Israelis told me during this trip. I'm working with their Colonel Ladrun, special assistant to General Izhack, Director General of the Israeli Ministry of Defense."

"Good. I met General Izhack during my trip to Israel last year. He's a straight shooter. Now tell me about the project."

"Mr. Johnson, first I must warn you we are treating this project with the highest security: SCI, compartmentalized clearance."

"I understand the sensitivity, but your information is secure here. We'll handle your export license application with special care."

Kelly described the highlights of his IBEX briefing using a hard copy of the view graphs, which he agreed to leave with Johnson.

After the briefing, Johnson cautioned, "Don't forget, if you're planning to carry this briefing to Iran, you will need an export license for the technical data in it."

Kelly was surprised. "I didn't realize that. Can I get the license in time for my trip scheduled for the 24th of January?"

"Well, it normally takes two months. It depends on how quickly they *staff* it over in the Pentagon."

"I have a meeting with Bob Hack, Director of International Programs, at the Pentagon later this morning."

"I know him well. He's the right one to push the colonels who *staff* the license applications over there. Be sure you tell him about the short time frame."

"I will," responded Kelly as he started closing his briefcase to leave.

Johnson added, "Dr. Kelly, it looks like you've got a live one here. Good luck! Remember, you're talking about some sensitive technology. Before you get an export license for the hardware, a lot of people are going to have to say *yes*. Be sure to cover all the bases."

" I certainly plan to. I don't want to miss anyone."

Kelly shook hands with Johnson and left for his next meeting. This time he walked the short block to the Roslyn Metro Station and caught the next Metro heading towards Washington National Airport. While the train waited at the first stop, the Arlington Cemetery, Kelly reflected on the many US servicemen buried here and remembered the eternal flame marking the resting place of the young, assassinated President Kennedy. Arlington was indeed a special place for all Americans!

Kelly got off at the Pentagon Metro Station, the second stop, and took the long escalator up to the Pentagon Concourse. This was a large shopping center on the ground floor for the vast working population in the Pentagon. It had banks, laundry and cleaning services, theater ticket sales, bakeries, bookstores, and a travel bureau. Kelly showed his Pentagon pass to the guard, walked up the ramp to the second floor, took the stairs up to the fourth floor, and walked around the inside or 'A' ring to corridor '10'. He strode out corridor '10' passing several other rings until he came to the 'E' ring where he turned right and headed past a few offices to Bob Hack's office, number 4E1018. It was easy for Kelly now, but it had taken him a while to learn the Pentagon coordinate system. Once he tried to find an 'E' office by walking around the 'E' ring, the outside ring of this huge five sided building. The walk took thirty minutes. He learned to find the correct corridor by walking along the 'A' ring, the inside ring, until he came to the proper corridor or 'spoke.'

Kelly went into the inner reception office at 4E1018 and was greeted by Jeannie, Bob Hack's beautiful brunette secretary. Jeannie went with the office. The Director of International Programs typically served for two to four years. Jeannie had gone through four directors so far. It was rumored she had slept with all four of them.

Jeannie welcomed him, "Happy New Year, Dr. Kelly. Mr. Hack's on the phone with Colonel Brown in our Embassy in Singapore. He'll see you just as soon as he hangs up. Have a coffee and a left over Christmas cookie while you're waiting."

"Thanks, Jeannie. I don't mind if I do."

Soon Jeannie saw the light go out on the phone line Hack was using. She rang Hack on the intercom and then said, "Dr. Kelly, you may go right in."

Hack's office had a view of the Potomac River and Jefferson's Memorial. Hack motioned Kelly to sit at the round conference table in one corner and said, "Brad, it's great to see you. Hope you had a merry Christmas and a happy New Year."

"I had a great New Year's. We had seats for the Rose Parade and for the Rose Bowl game. But I spent Christmas in Israel, working!"

"Yeah, I know. Christmas is just another work day in Israel. I was there at Christmas a year ago. If you don't mind, I'll call my aide, Colonel Long, in for the meeting. If there's any follow up, he can take care of the details." Hack rang Jeannie to call Colonel Long.

Hack continued, "While we're waiting, summarize the business picture for this new project. I mean, how big is it and who will be your suppliers and subcontractors?"

Kelly answered, "Bob, we haven't picked our suppliers yet, but we plan to issue a subcontract for twenty percent of the total to the electronic division, ELTA, of Israeli Aircraft Industries. The total contract is expected to be one billion."

"Wow! That means the Israelis will get 200 million dollars. Brad, I should warn you, I don't trust the Israelis. Be careful."

Kelly had known Bob Hack for a long time. Hack's original name had been Rashid Haddad, but his family had Americanized their names when they immigrated from Lebanon when Hack was only nine. Kelly assumed a Christian Arab like Hack would naturally be suspicious of the Israelis, and replied, "I'll be careful of the Israelis, but they are going to play a key role in our new project."

Colonel Long walked into the office and Hack introduced him to Kelly. Long said, "Pleased to meet you, Sir."

Kelly was always impressed when the senior officers in the Pentagon called him *Sir*. Kelly was a member of the Secretary of Defense's Science Advisory Council. As such, he had a protocol rank of a three star general. The contacts he made while belonging to the SAC were a help to Associated Aviation and his consultation to the Secretary of Defense was a real service to the Defense Department. It made Kelly feel at home in the Pentagon, a member of the *inner circle*.

Kelly started off his talk by warning Hack and Long about the high security level of the IBEX project.

Hack responded, "As you know, I have all the right clearances, and Colonel Long has more than I have. Don't worry about security here in this office."

Kelly used Hack's viewgraph projector and screen to show the IBEX briefing. He was interrupted from time to time by Hack with clarifying questions.

At the end, Hack said, "That's quite a system. I should point out it's going to be tough to get approval to release all that sensitive technology to the Iranians. Right now, it looks like the Shah will be ruler forever. But what if he should be overthrown and the Iranian Communist *Tudah* party takes over? We here in the Pentagon have to worry about such contingencies."

"Here's an idea: we could control the most sensitive part of the technology, the cryptographic part, by having an American present at each site to keep tabs on the software tape with the cryptographic algorithms on it. There could be a red button that will erase the sensitive cryptographic formulas it there's trouble."

"Good idea. That would put a lot of people's minds at rest. I suggest you add that feature to your briefing before presenting it to General Robertson."

"I know he's going to be the new Chief of our US MAAG in Tehran but I've never met him. Can you introduce me?"

"I'll do better than that. I'll have Colonel Long set up a briefing meeting, and also he'll invite all the colonels in the Pentagon who'll be responsible for approving your export license. You can kill all the birds with one stone!"

"That's great, Bob. Thanks. Another thing, I'm going to need an export license for the technical data in this briefing. I have a trip planned to Tehran the end of the month."

"No problem! I'll call Jack Johnson over in OMC and tell him to issue the license in a hurry."

"Thanks. That's a big load off my mind."

"Brad, can you meet with General Robertson tomorrow morning, if he's free then?"

"I'm free in the morning but I'd hoped to catch the noon TWA non-stop to LAX tomorrow."

"I'd recommend you take a later flight. This is a key meeting and there'll be lots of questions afterwards, particularly from the colonels after the general leaves. You can only keep his attention about an hour."

Hack sent Long to the phone to set up the meeting for tomorrow morning, if possible.

Brad agreed to change his flight. Then invited Hack to dinner that evening, saying, "I've got a couple of friends in town. We'll let them decide whether you get the blonde or the red head."

"Sure, Brad. You know I'm foot loose and fancy free since my latest divorce. I'll pick you up at your hotel. Knowing you, you don't have a car."

OK, Bob, I'm at the Marriott in Roslyn, room 618. Make it 7pm and we'll have a cocktail before leaving for dinner. I'll make reservations at the Flagship."

Colonel Long came back from the phone, "Sirs, the meeting between Dr. Kelly and General Robertson is set up at 0900 tomorrow morning. I'll go to my office now to round up all the right colonels. They'll want to hear General Robertson's reaction to your briefing, Sir. Goodbye, Sir." He saluted and left.

Hack went on, "There's one other meeting you must have while you're here, the CIA. They'll be very interested in the *product* from IBEX, particularly site six."

"Bob, our in-house *spook* at AAC has already set up a meeting with the director at Langley at 2 this afternoon. I'm to meet *Joe* on the River Entrance steps at 1:30."

"You're way ahead of me. It's about noon now. How about lunch with me in the Secretary's Executive Dining Room? You'll love the food and the price is right."

"Thanks, I'd like to. I've never eaten in the Secretary of Defense's dining room. It'll be a new experience."

The two strolled over to the Executive Dining Room on the 'D' ring. Hack nudged Kelly every time they passed a girl in the halls who had large breasts or who was wearing tight pants or a very short skirt or who had some other noteworthy physical attribute. Kelly thought, *Hack seems to need Olga tonight. I'll settle for Christina after dinner.*

In the Executive Dining Room, the waitress recognized Hack and showed them to a two place table with elaborate linen, crystal and silverware settings. There were several three and four star generals and their naval admiral equivalents spread around the room. The Secretary of Defense was at a large table in the back corner of the room, lunching with some foreign visitors. Kelly knew the Pentagon had a large scale business going that made the annual sales of Associated Aviation look like peanuts. It was called Foreign Military Sales or *FMS* in *Pentagonese*. It amounted to many billions of dollars per year. The Pentagon put a service charge of 15% on top of the defense contractors' selling prices, which helped pay for the Pentagon's huge overhead expenses. Few people understood the economics of Foreign Military Sales, but both Hack and Kelly understood it well. That was their business: Hack on the government's side and Kelly on the defense contractors' side. Foreign Military Sales were on a *government to government* basis. But the defense contractors helped the Pentagon with the marketing job. They created the demand. The Pentagon satisfied the demand with FMS sales. IBEX would not be an FMS project, however. Kelly would have to do the marketing for IBEX. The colonels and generals could help, though, if they thought the system was in the US national interest. With the sixth site overlooking the Russian threat, Kelly was sure they would think the project was good for the US.

The two finished their lunch. Hack signed both checks. Kelly's would be free since he was the guest of an executive. Hack's would be deducted from his bi-weekly paycheck.

Kelly took the stairs near the 'E' ring leading down to the River Entrance and out the elaborate mahogany doors used by the Secretary of Defense and the high brass of the Chief of Staff of the military. It was 1:25. He immediately spotted a young man in his late 20's or early 30's wearing a dark blue suit and a striped tie, standing by an older model grey Chevrolet. Kelly walked up to him and said, "You must be Joe."

The CIA agent laughed and said, Yes, Dr. Kelly, my name's *Joe*. Get in, the Director's waiting."

Joe left the Pentagon parking area and drove onto the George Washington Parkway heading northwest towards Langley, Virginia. Langley's main business was housing the CIA headquarters. They reached the headquarters building in twenty minutes in the light afternoon traffic. Joe escorted Kelly inside and cleared him through security, where he was given a red badge, showing he had a Top Secret clearance.

The two then strode down the hall and into the Director's office where *Joe* said, "I'll be back to pick you up in about an hour and drop you off at your hotel."

The Director motioned for Kelly to sit on the couch in the large corner office.   It wasn't as big as the top Pentagon executive's offices, but the furniture was sleek and modern so it looked more like that of a top executive in industry, rather than a government office. Kelly found himself thinking, *The CIA is big business.*

The Director said, "I understand Associated Aviation is going after the Shah's IBEX program, Dr. Kelly."

"Yes, that's right.   We plan to use the Israelis as subcontractors for the antennas and the site preparation and installation."

"I figured that would happen. The Israeli ambassador briefed me on IBEX recently. He said they were trying to line up a US aerospace company to be the prime contractor. They just wanted 20% of the action. Is that about how it worked out?"

"That's exactly how it is working out. They even gave me a firm fixed price proposal for 200 million dollars while I was in Israel during Christmas week."

"Those Israelis are good businessmen. Their Mossad is a hell-of-an-intelligence service as well! Their ambassador didn't have many details to give me. He didn't even know where the sites would be. Fill me it."

Kelly presented a formal, stand-up briefing using the viewgraph projector on the Director's conference table.   The Director asked a number of questions about the *product* Kelly expected to generate from the six sites.

At the end, the Director stated bluntly, "Dr. Kelly, either we have a CIA agent at each of those sites and at the central processing station at all times or you're not going to get an export license. I'm not the only voter, but, if I vote *NO*, your export license application will be rejected."

"I see no problem with your request. I understand from Colonel Ladrun that the Iranians will need technical help running the sites."

"Yes, that's true, but these third world countries like Iran can come up to speed quickly.   Then they want to get rid of all foreigners. You've got to get an iron-clad clause in your contract to assure the right of US personnel in those sites at all times."

"I understand. I'll get our corporate attorneys working on the contractual words after I get back to California tomorrow."

"And, after your company attorneys get the words drafted, my *company's* attorneys must review them to be sure that iron-clad guarantee is there. Now for another matter, I believe you will become a prime target for terrorists when the word gets around that you're the key man on IBEX."

"I'll try to be careful, but, isn't there some way the US government can help protect me?"

"Dr. Kelly, that's very complicated for a private citizen like you. The CIA could be responsible overseas and the FBI in the US, but neither is responsible in both places. When you get back to LA, call your local police department and they'll give you a number to call if anything happens."

"But, if anything *happens*, I'll be dead."

"Yeah. But that's the risk you private businessmen have to take when you deal in these international projects. The US government doesn't have the resources to protect all the citizens who travel overseas on business."

"Thank you for your time and advice. I'll let Ralph Hauser know when the contract clause is ready for your attorneys."

"Thank you for the briefing, Dr. Kelly. Good luck."

As if by magic, *Joe* re-entered the Director's office and led Kelly back to the security area, where Kelly turned in his red badge. They climbed into *Joe's* grey Chevrolet and headed back on the George Washington Parkway to Roslyn. When he dropped Kelly off at the Marriott entrance *Joe* again wished him, "Good luck!"

Walking into his room, Kelly found Christina and Olga watching an 'R' rated movie on the Marriott's video system. They were wearing Paris fashion type evening clothes.

Kelly grinned, "It looks like you already know this evening's plans."

Olga answered, "It's because Mr. Hack's secretary called a while ago. She said Mr. Hack would arrive about 6pm rather than seven. And she had already made reservations for four at the Flagship for 7pm. So we assumed we were the other two! That's why we're dressed instead of our usual hotel room garb – nude."

"You're way ahead of me. By the way, would one of you take care of Bob tonight? I should warn you, he's real horny!"

Again Olga answered, "As a matter of fact, Christina and I flipped coins after the phone call. Christina won you, so I'll take Bob."

"You two *are* way ahead of me!"

Christina pours three glasses of Mumm's champagne from the room refrigerator. "We might as well relax and watch the end of this sexy movie. It'll be over before Bob gets her at six."

"That's fine, girls. Let me propose a toast: *to a lovely night of love*."

The girls chorus, "I'll drink to that."

Shortly after the movie ended, they heard a knock on the door. Olga answered it and Bob Hack said, "You must be Olga. Hello, Darling!" and he gave her a big kiss right at the door.

Kelly introduced Christina and Hack kissed her, too. Christina laughed and said, "Mr. Hack, what would you like to drink? We have quite a collection in the Fridge."

"Christina, call me Bob. I'll have a double gin on the rocks."

"Any vermouth?"

"No, it's poison to me."

Christina poured the double gin and handed it to Olga, who led Hack to the couch, where she set the drink down on the coffee table. Hack grabbed Olga and gave her a passionate kiss as they sank onto the couch. Christina refilled the three champagne glasses.

Hack asked, "And where are you two dolls from and why haven't I met you before?"

Olga answered, "Christina and I share an apartment in Tel Aviv across from the Hilton, next to the British Embassy."

"I know exactly where it is. I always stay at the Hilton when in Tel Aviv. I get there about four times a year. The Israelis are one of our best customers."

Christina asked, "And what business are you in, Bob?"

"Defense, I guess you would say. I'm in the Pentagon. We sell the Israelis over a billion dollars a year in military equipment, mostly aircraft like the F-15 and F-16 fighters."

"What do you mean, 'we'? Aren't those planes sold by McDonnell Douglas and General Dynamics?"

"Yeah, McDAC and GD make them, but we in the Pentagon sell them on an FMS basis."

Kelly added, "FMS is *Pentagonese* for Foreign Military Sales. They speak in acronyms over there."

Hack broke in, "Enough of this business talk. I propose a toast to this evening. *May we all make merry tonight*."

Kelly responded, "I don't know about *Mary* but I'll try Christina. You can try Olga!" They all laughed and finished their drinks in a background of chatter. Hack listed all his favorite restaurants in Israel and the girls gave their views of the best dishes at each. When he noticed it was twenty minutes until their reservation time, he warned them to put on their winter coats, "It's down to 15 degrees out there."

They stepped out of the elevator into a packed lobby, full of aerospace and defense contractors checking in, getting ready for their busy three day week in Washington. They would all be on the Friday afternoon airliners returning to California, Texas, Florida and the other aerospace centers. In the meantime, they would be jamming all the expensive Washington restaurants and 'watering holes' with their expense account spending. After his inauguration later in January, President Mahoney would try to stomp out the three martini lunch. He would not be able to. This expense account spending was such a big business that the lobbyists of the restaurant and entertainment business, allied with those of the aerospace-defense business, would kill the new president's tax reform bill. The people in these circles knew that it was this business luncheon and dinner environment that provided the informal atmosphere for making the *big deals*.

Kelly would do more during his evening of *entertainment* toward convincing Hack to approve the IBEX project than his beautifully colored viewgraphs did in the morning. Hack would have to pay his share of the dinner bill, however. It would be illegal for Kelly to pay for it. The players in the big aerospace/defense business never violated this rule in public restaurants. Hack, of course, wouldn't get a bill for his gin or later 'fun-and-games' in the hotel room. That would be considered repayment for Kelly's free lunch.

The quartet hurried across the parking lot to Hack's car. Olga sat in front with Hack and Christina in back with Kelly. Hack maneuvered around the traffic circle in front of the Marriott and back onto the George Washington Parkway again, this time heading for National Airport. Hack branched onto the parkway that crossed the 14th Street Bridge and left the freeway at Dupont Plaza. He wound through the city streets to the Flagship Restaurant on the Potomac River. Kelly liked eating the fantastic East Coast sea food found in Washington. He couldn't seem to find that kind of food in California. Hack let Brad and the two girls out in front of the restaurant and they hurried into the warm lobby. Hack luckily found a parking space just across the street and joined them in only a few minutes.

The maitre d' showed them to their reserved table next to a window with a gorgeous river view. They all ordered crab cocktail to start and then Maine lobsters. The waitress immediately brought them a loaf of hot bread with honey to spread on it and large green salads. The bread was almost a meal in itself. Before bringing the broiled lobsters, the waitress ceremoniously placed a large paper bib with a picture of a lobster on it around each of the diner's necks.

Over after dinner coffee, Kelly asked Hack, "Bob, about the export license for the technical data needed for my trip to Iran at the end of the month, how can you help to make sure the license is approved in time?"

"First, have you submitted the license application?"

"No, but I'm meeting our AAC Washington rep for breakfast in the morning. His office will type it up and he'll hand carry it over later in the morning. But we have to come up with a non-classified description of the project to go on the license application."

"Brad, is the technical data for the Iranians included in the briefing you gave me this morning?"

Brad nodded.

"Many people without clearances will see that application. I advise you to simply put your company's briefing report number on the paperwork."

"That simplifies things. Then what?"

Tomorrow afternoon I'll phone Johnny Johnson at OMC and tell him the Defense Department approves the release of the IBEX technical data to the Iranians. He will tell one of his licensing officers we have coordinated it between *State* and *Defense*. With a little luck, the approved license should go in the mail to you by Friday."

"That's great! I was afraid the approval could hold up my trip."

"Considering the information the US government is going to get from IBEX, that project is worth more to us than it is to AAC. By the way, your 10am meeting tomorrow with General Robertson is in conference room 3D982. Jeannie said to be sure to tell you."

Hack signaled the waitress for the bill and said as he signed the credit card voucher, "Tonight's dinner is on me. I don't want anyone to get the idea you're *influencing* me with a dinner and night on the town. This way, I can prove I paid for you."

Kelly and the two girls waited in the warm lobby for Hack to retrieve his car, then they headed for suite 616/618 at the Marriott. Hack and Olga took the sitting room with its double bed that unfolded from the couch. They undressed and climbed into bed where they spent an hour of interesting activities until they fell asleep.

Meanwhile, Kelly and Christina had a similar session in the bedroom. Soon they also dropped into a deep sleep.

Hack got up early enough to give himself time to drive home to his suburban Virginia condominium. He didn't want to wear the same clothes to the office. It might make his warm and cooperative secretary, Jeannie, jealous if she suspected he spent the night away from his condo.

Kelly got up just in time to get to his 8:30 breakfast meeting. He kissed both Christina and Olga goodbye and told them he'd see them *next time, whenever that might be.*

The AAC Washington representative, Mr. Thompson, was waiting in the Marriott breakfast café when Kelly walked in. Kelly relayed the instructions Hack had given him for the license applications for the technical data for IBEX and handed Thompson a double wrapped package containing the required three copies of the IBEX briefing to go along with the license application. He carefully instructed Thompson to personally carry the whole application to Mr. Johnson in the Office of Munitions Control before noon. Thompson signed a receipt for the classified data Kelly gave him, promised to take care of everything and left to have his secretary type out the application.

Kelly went to the front desk and paid his bill, using his company credit card, and told the clerk his room would be vacated by noon. He hurried through the chill early morning wind to catch the Metro for the Pentagon. He arrived at 9:40, walked up to the third floor, then down the 'A' ring to the 10ᵗʰ corridor. Walking down the 10ᵗʰ corridor toward the 'D' ring, he realized he wouldn't be through with his meeting in time to catch the noon non-stop to LAX. He had forgotten his promise to Bob Hack to change his flight plans. It was only 6:45am in Los Angeles, but he decided to call his wife now, before the meeting, when he knew she would be home rather than to phone her later and risk missing her. He remembered the warnings from the Israelis and the CIA Director and thought, *If the terrorists are after me, the worst thing I can do is have my name in the airline reservation computer, listing the flight I'm going to take. I'd better go standby. That way, they can't track me. I'd better be careful talking to my wife, too. They may have tapped my home phone. Boy, I'm really beginning to sound paranoid.*"

Kelly found a pay phone in the corridor and woke up his wife. After exchanging *good morning, darlings* he said, "Honey, don't go to the airport until I phone you. My plane may be late with winter weather and all."

Anna replied, "OK, Darling. I'll wait for your call. I'll still be able to meet you since it takes you longer to fly here than it takes me to drive to the airport."

"Also, I might want you to meet me at the same terminal where you met me the last time I went to Washington."

"You mean......"

Kelly interrupted her and warned, "Don't say the name on the phone. I'll tell you why when I get home."

"I don't know why you're being so mysterious, but, yes, I know where you mean."

They exchanged *goodbye, darlings* and hung up.

Kelly arrived at conference room 3D982 a few minutes before ten. The room was already filled with senior Pentagon colonels and one US Navy captain. There was a one star general as well. An empty place had been left at the head of the long conference table, marked with two star General John Robertson's name plate.

Colonel Long from Hack's office greeted Kelly at the door, "I've got all the right colonels here and they all have the right clearances, so don't worry about that. I'll introduce you as soon as General Robertson gets here and then the show's all yours."

Thanks, Colonel Long. Can I get someone to flip the viewgraphs on the projector for me?"

"Yes, Sir. I'll do it."

General Robertson strode into the room. Immediately, everyone sprang to their feet. General Robertson declared, "Good morning, Gentlemen, and welcome, Dr. Kelly. I'm looking forward to hearing your briefing on IBEX." Only after Robertson said, "Please be seated, Gentleman," did every sit down again.

Colonel Long introduced Kelly to the General and added Kelly would head up the IBEX project for Associated Aviation.

The General announced, "Well, Dr. Kelly, I might as well warn you. If we don't get a site near the Caspian Sea overlooking the Soviet Union, there won't be an IBEX system. Not from the USA anyway."

Kelly immediately responded, "General Robertson, thanks for raising that point in the beginning. As a matter of fact, Associated Aviation has included a sixth site overlooking Russia. Also, Sir, while we are discussing sensitive points, I assured the Director over at the *agency* in Langley yesterday that we would include an iron clad clause in the contract with the Iranians saying US personnel have the right to be at all IBEX sites around the clock."

"Good, Dr. Kelly. I'm glad we understand each other. As head of the US Military in Tehran, I'll see the clause you refer to is enforced. Now, please proceed with your briefing."

Kelly gave the briefing. He was interrupted frequently by the colonels who asked questions that would make them seem knowledgeable in front of the general. General Robertson also asked a few key questions. Kelly noticed the colonels took careful notes of the general's questions and of Kelly's answers.

At the end, the general said, "Dr. Kelly, thank you for an excellent and detailed briefing on IBEX. I can see this system will be a benefit to the security of the United States."

"Thank you, General Robertson. I'll be giving this briefing to General Hatami in Tehran at the end of this month."

"Very good. I may see you there. I'm leaving for my new post in Iran next week. And as the new chief of the MAAG in Tehran, I will insist this project be approved."

A murmur went from colonel to colonel. These were the men who would *staff* the hardware license when the application reached the Pentagon. Now IBEX was sure to pass.

Colonel Long handed the viewgraphs back to Kelly as the meeting broke up, saying, "I think we have a program. I'll report the general's closing remarks to Mr. Hack. And Mr. Hack told me this morning he'll support IBEX. I think you have all the votes you need."

It was half past 12. Kelly used a pay phone in the corridor to call the AAC Washington Representative. He got his secretary who reported Mr. Thompson was out to lunch, but said she had typed the IBEX technical data export license and she knew Mr. Thompson had delivered it to Mr. Johnson's office at the OMC, Office of Munitions Control, at about 11:30.

Kelly was elated about how smoothly the approval process for IBEX was moving. He didn't realize there were other *voters* he hadn't met who could still block IBEX.

Heading for the rows of taxis outside the Pentagon Concourse, Kelly took the first taxi in the *Virginia* line and put his overnight bag with his briefcase inside on the back seat next to him and directed the driver to Dulles Airport.

Unfortunately, Kelly had missed his noon flight and all the remaining non-stop flights to LAX left after 5pm. None of the flights with intermediate stops landed in Los Angeles any earlier. Kelly decided to try to get on the United Airlines non-stop to LAX since it was the first to leave, at 5:15. There was probably plenty of time to get on standby for that flight. If not, he could try American or TWA, which left later. Suddenly Kelly realized he had forgotten to tell TWA he wouldn't be going on the noon flight. *Well, some lucky guy on standby for that flight got my plushy first class seat by the window in row 2. He'll thank me for being a no-show.*

Kelly paid the cab driver twenty five dollars for the fare and tip and strode up to the United counter, where he asked for a one way ticket to Los Angeles. The ticket agent told him the flight was full but that there were always a lot of no shows on Wednesday. He was sure Kelly would make it onto the plane, especially since the standby ticket was for first class. Kelly paid with his company credit card and went to the United Red Carpet Club, downstairs from the departure gates. He pushed the button and the door opened. He showed his membership card to the elderly blonde at the desk, signed in, and showed her his standby ticket, "I hope you can get me a seat."

"Just a moment," she entered the flight number on her computer terminal. "You're in luck. Is seat 2A OK? It's a window seat."

"That's fine. In fact, that's the same seat number I had on the noon TWA flight that I missed today."

Pushing the boarding pass into his jacket pocket, Kelly sat down by one of the credit card phones on the circular tables and dialed his wife, using his company phone credit card number. Anna answered, and Kelly told her he was on a different flight, "The same one I took last time. Do you remember the arrival time?"

"Yes. I see you're still being mysterious."

"I'll explain when I get home." They exchanged *goodbye darlings* and hung up.

Kelly had missed lunch but he made up for it by having three martinis and lots of cheese dip while he caught up on his magazine reading. Before he realized it, the desk attendant tapped him on the shoulder and said, "Dr. Kelly, your flight is ready for boarding. I wouldn't want you to miss our flight, too."

As Kelly hurried out of the United lounge, he caught a glimpse of a news bulletin on the TV. Something about an airliner making an emergency landing in Albuquerque. He didn't have time to hear more. He rode the up escalator and turned right to Gate 2, ran his bag through the x-ray machine at security and handed his boarding pass to the United attendant. Then he boarded the mobile lounge which took him to the United DC-10.

Kelly settled into seat 2A and the pretty blonde stewardess poured him a glass of champagne and gave him lounging slippers to wear during the five hour flight. With the three hour time difference, he would arrive at 7:15. After dinner, he started to watch the in-flight movie. He discovered it was the same one he and the girls watched last night at the Marriott. *Between the hotel movies and the airplane movies, I see every film 3 or 4 times. Hollywood must have a shortage of movies.* Kelly fell asleep and didn't wake up until the captain announced the seat belt sign for landing and reported it was a *chilly* 60 degrees at LAX. That sounded warm to Kelly after the fifteen degree weather in Washington.

As usual, Kelly was the first off the plane and was greeted by Anna with a big hug and kiss as he stepped into the Los Angeles arrival lounge. She could hardly wait to tell him, "Darling, you were smart not to take that noon TWA flight. I heard on the news while driving to the airport that it had to make an emergency landing in Albuquerque. There was an explosion. They were lucky, though. Only one fatality. The man in seat 2A was blown out the window by the decompression."

"I'm the lucky one! That was my seat."

Chapter 6.

Iranian Intrigues

When Kelly reported the good progress he made on paving the way for the approval of the export license for IBEX, Dr. Morrell congratulated him for his good work.

Kelly spent the next two and a half weeks directing the technical team writing specifications for IBEX, selecting suppliers for the hardware, picking the necessary computers and software, and preparing a budgetary cost proposal for the total program. The bottom line price was $1.2 billion, some $200 million higher than the amount the Iranians wanted to pay for the project. Kelly and Dr. Morrell agreed the difference in their budgetary price and the Iranians' budget was because of adding the sixth site. It was also quite clear from the Washington meetings that *no sixth site, no IBEX program.*

Dr. Morrell emphasized, "Brad, it'll be up to you to sell the Iranians on the higher price."

"I'll do my best. Colonel Ladrun warned me, though, the Iranians are tough negotiators."

"You'll just have to hang tough. Explain the facts-of-life to them," explained Dr. Morrell.

In December, Dr. Morrell's secretary had made Kelly's reservations from LA to London and on to Tehran, leaving at noon Thursday, January 23rd and arriving in Tehran at 6pm on Friday the 24th. After his near miss on the return trip from Washington, Kelly vowed to take special precautions this time. Without saying anything to his office about his plans, Kelly went to the airport on Thursday the 23rd in time to catch his reserved flight. However, he walked over to the Lufthansa desk and bought a standby ticket on a first class, non-stop to Frankfurt, West Germany, with the possibility of catching an Iranair flight that arrived in Tehran at 6:30pm. Kelly almost phoned Colonel Ladrun to tell him the new arrival time, but then decided if he wasn't on the original flight, Ladrun would wait to see if he came in on the next Iranair flight from London which arrived at 6:40pm.

Boarding the plane just before 1:30pm, Kelly sank into his first class seat by a window. A pretty auburn haired stewardess poured him a glass of champagne and handed him the menu for the sumptuous dinner to be served in flight. It took eleven hours to fly from Los Angeles to Frankfurt. With the nine hour time difference, the flight arrived just before 10 am, Friday the 24th of January. Kelly took his carry on bag and the briefcase with the IBEX briefing and budgetary cost proposal and walked briskly to the first class ticket counter of Iranair, where he was third in line. When his turn arrived, he said to the ticket agent, "I'd like a first class ticket for your 11am flight to Tehran."

"I'm sorry, sir, but that flight is completely filled."

"It's very important for me to make this flight. Please put me on standby." Kelly handed the clerk his company credit card with a hundred dollar bill folded behind it.

The ticket agent looked at the credit card, slipped the $100 in his pocket, and pressed a few keys on the computer terminal He smiled and announced, "Why, Dr. Kelly, you're in luck. A first class seat has just opened up. I can confirm you on our Iranair flight 160, first class, leaving Frankfurt at 1100, gate 31. It arrives in Tehran at 1830."

Kelly picked up his ticket and boarding pass and walked to gate 31. There, an Iranian security guard went through Kelly's carry on bag looking at the contents very carefully and passed it as OK, putting a red tag on it. Then he started on Kelly's briefcase. He pointed to the IBEX briefing, which had been double wrapped as required by US security rules for classified documents. The guard said, "Please open this package. I must examine its contents."

"I'm sorry, but I can't open the package." Kelly surreptitiously put a hundred dollar bill in the briefcase so the guard could see it. The guard looked at the bill, looked at Kelly, and held up five fingers. Kelly dutifully pealed off four more one hundred dollar bills and placed them in the open briefcase.

The guard carefully picked up the five hundred dollar bills, rolled them up tightly, and slipped them into his shirt pocket, making certain none of his colleagues saw him. He then said, "Your carry on items are safe, sir. Have a good flight," as he closed the briefcase and sealed it with a red tag.

Kelly wondered how many hundred dollar bills it would have cost if he had a gun in there. *Some security, but it's worth the five hundred to avoid any hassle.*

After the hand luggage check, the passengers boarded a bus to take them to the ramp where the 737 was parked on the Frankfurt-Main Airport ramp. All of the checked baggage was sitting beside the aircraft boarding stairs. Each passenger who had checked any luggage had to identify his or her baggage before it could be loaded on the airplane.

At first Kelly thought these steps slowed down the loading procedure. Then he realized it was to avoid a terrorist checking a suitcase with a bomb in it and then not taking the flight. It was a good, prudent procedure, except in the case of a *suicide bomber.*

Iran under the Shah had very restrictive travel regulations for Iranian citizens. Each trip required a visit, before hand, to the police station to submit the travel itinerary and have it approved. Normally, businessmen were not permitted to take their wives on trips and were limited in the amount of currency they could take out of the country. The government preferred to hold the businessman's family and wealth hostage while he was out of the country. These regulations made the businessman less likely to leave permanently and also made it difficult for him to move assets to a safe haven in Switzerland or elsewhere.

Kelly boarded the 737 and settled into his window seat in the small first class section. There were only eight first class seats and the one in the front on the left was occupied by an Iranian wearing a dark suit, white shirt and dark tie with a large bulge under his coat. Kelly thought, *That must be the Iranian idea of the man riding shotgun on the old American stagecoaches.* As the passengers came on board, the *shotgun* eyed each one carefully. During the flight, he turned around and examined with searching eyes each passenger who left his seat to go to the toilet. He appeared to expect every passenger to be a possible hijacker.

En route to Tehran, Kelly was served his customary martini and then champagne with the exquisite French cuisine. The main course was chateaubriand, which the exotic Persian stewardess served from a cart, slicing Kelly's large portion of meat to his individual specification.

Even though Iran was a Moslem country in which alcoholic beverages were theoretically banished, under the Shah, alcohol was freely available in Iran and also on the national airline, Iranair.

There was a two and a half hour time difference between Frankfurt and Iran. Tehran was one of those major cities that were on a half hour basis relative to Greenwich Mean Time; others included New Delhi, Rangoon, and Singapore. That time difference explained why a five hour flight leaving at 11am Frankfurt time arrived in Tehran at 6:30pm.

After dinner, Kelly peered out the window to see where they were. Since shortly after passing the Swiss Alps there had been a heavy cloud cover, but now the clouds were breaking up and Kelly could see Athens in the late afternoon sun with the blue Aegean Sea beyond to the east. The captain had announced earlier the route of flight would be over Athens, Crete, Cypress, then over Adana in southern Turkey, Tabriz in Iran, and finally to their destination. Tehran, the huge capital city of Iran, contained almost twenty percent of the total population of the country. The Iranair flight carefully avoided over-flying any part of Iraq, because of the eternal border skirmishes between the Iranians and Iraqis in the areas peopled by the Kurds, who defied both governments. In spite of these border conflicts, the two countries maintained diplomatic relations, and Iraq, one of the countries in the Shah's surveillance plans, had a full embassy in Tehran.

Kelly fell asleep as the orange sun dipped into the Aegean Sea. His body would be confused for several days in Tehran by the eleven and a half hour time change from Los Angeles and the nap would help him begin the difficult adjustment. He woke up when he felt the 737 start its long descent into the Mehrabad Airport. Gazing out the window into the black emptiness of the early evening he made out the lights of a few villages northwest of Tehran. The cabin announcements were given first in Farsi, then in French and finally in English. The passengers were advised to fill out their immigration entry cards as they were about 25 minutes from landing. Kelly double-checked the visa stamp in his passport. The aircraft made a straight-in approach from the north heading for the huge glowing city area stretching out ahead.

When the airliner landed it taxied to a remote area on the tarmac. Kelly was one of the first off the plane and into the airport bus. Heading for the terminal, Kelly barely made out a row of F-14 aircraft dimly outlined against the sky. He nodded, knowingly, *The Pentagon FMS salesmen moved a couple of billion dollars worth of aircraft on that deal. The very latest radar and air-to-air missiles went with those planes. If these front line US aircraft fell into unfriendly hands it would compromise the US's latest military technology. Well, I'm sure the US would never allow a revolution in Iran; we would have too much to lose.*

A Japan Airlines 747 had landed just ahead of Kelly's plane and hundreds of Japanese tourists and businessmen were jamming the passport control lines in the terminal. When Kelly finally got to the window, the passport control officer said something in Farsi and pointed to the visa in Kelly's passport. The date was written in Farsi numbers which Kelly could not yet read. Apparently the Iranian consulate in San Francisco put the wrong date on the visa and it wasn't valid. By now, Kelly was beginning to understand Persian culture. He picked up his passport and slipped a hundred dollar bill into the page with the Iranian visa. The officer held up three fingers and Kelly pealed off another two bills and put them in the passport. The officer scribbled something in Farsi on the visa, handed the passport back, and waved Kelly on.

Kelly exited through the green customs gate marked Nothing to Declare and walked outside and found himself almost engulfed in the large crowd greeting the arriving passengers. Apparently, it was one of the Iranians' favorite pastimes to meet relatives on incoming flights. From the edge of the crowd, he heard someone call his name. Christina and Olga! And Colonel Ladrun standing near them. Fighting his way through the jam, he hugged each in turn.

Colonel Ladrun said, "Are we ever relieved to see you!"
Christina continued, "We were afraid you were killed!"
"What do you mean?"

Ladrun answered, "There were news reports out of London this afternoon that a Moslem terrorist shot and killed an American getting off the non-stop TWA flight from Los Angeles. He also killed an airport policeman before he was killed himself by the airport security guards. The description of the American resembled you."

"I'm surprised you didn't give up waiting for me, then."

"I had the Israeli embassy check with TWA in London and discovered the dead man was not you."

Olga interrupted, "We checked the 5:30 Iranair flight from London you had said you would take and when you weren't on it, we got worried again."

Ladrun broke in, "I tried to reassure the girls you would probably be on one of the later flights from any city except London. I assumed you would take the advice I gave you in December and come through Frankfurt."

Christina added, "Amnon told us you had a close call returning to LA from Washington. It's a good thing you changed your flight that day."

Ladrun replied, "Mossad has intelligence information that one of the radical Moslem terrorist groups from Iran is after you."

With a wry grin Brad said, "I've been trying my best to be careful. I want to make it as difficult as possible for them. Let's get away from here."

"We have an Israeli embassy car with a trusted Israeli driver," explained Ladrun pointing to a nearby black Buick limousine with diplomatic plates.

Brad climbed in the back seat between Christina and Olga, who each kissed him passionately, while Ladrun got in front. The driver, who, of course, turned out to be Amnon, headed out of the terminal onto Eisenhower Boulevard. When Brad remarked about the name of the street, Ladrun filled him in, "The Shah's not taking any chances with US politics. He named one street after a republican president and another one, Roosevelt Boulevard, after a democratic one. He needs American support to keep his regime propped up. He's under pressure from the communist Tudah party, which he outlawed, and from the fundamentalist Moslem group."

"I've heard about the Tudah party before, Joseph, but I'd never heard about a Moslem fundamentalist group in Iran."

"That's because your government believes the Shah will be in power forever. They ignore the other political forces in Iran, except the communists. The US hates communists wherever they are and keeps careful track of them."

Amnon broke in, "I keep telling your CIA not to worry about the Tudah party. The Shah's secret police, the Savak, have effectively decapitated the Tudah by executing all its leaders. Even the Russians couldn't help them." He turned onto Shimron Road, the freeway from the airport to the wealthy northern section of Tehran. Since it was Friday evening, the Moslem Sabbath, the traffic was light. Tomorrow, Saturday, was the first day of the Moslem workweek. The Iranian weekend was Thursday and Friday. Friday was quiet except at the hotels like the Hilton, Sheraton, and Intercontinental, which catered to American and European businessmen.

Kelly glanced out the rear window, "I think someone's following us!"

Amnon grinned, "Don't worry, Brad, that's Shaheen Mouhoud of Savak. He's been assigned to protect you while you're in Iran. I'll introduce you when we get to the Hilton - in your room, not in the lobby!"

"That's a relief. I hope the Hilton hasn't lost my reservation."

Christina broke in, "Don't worry about your reservation. You're already checked in to the presidential suite on the twentieth floor. It has a spectacular view in every direction. Here's your key."

"Hey, girls, my expense account won't cover the presidential suite."

"Olga took care of that last night. She gave the Hilton manager some special personal services. He gave you the suite at the regular room rates."

"Iranians are lousy lovers. I hope you appreciate the discount, Brad," Olga added.

Amnon parked the embassy limousine near the Hilton entrance and got out with his passengers, while Joseph slid over to the driver's seat, "Joseph, you go on over to your hotel. I'll ride back there with Shaheen later. Brad, you and the girls go on up to your suite. I'll bring Shaheen up to meet you as soon as he gets here."

Brad and the two girls nodded agreement and walked into the Hilton lobby, packed with foreign businessmen as well as Iranians enjoying the Friday holiday evening. In the center of the lobby a huge man dressed in a red and black Russian Cossack costume was handing out small piles of caviar for *only* twelve dollars a serving while the lobby waiters served Mumm's champagne at fifty dollars a bottle.

As they stepped into the elevator for their ride to the twentieth floor, Christina suggested, "Let's stop in the lobby after your business meeting and have some caviar and champagne. It's fantastic."

Kelly replied, "That sounds great. And where shall we have dinner? You and Olga seem to know your way around already."

"All the good restaurants in the downtown area closed on Friday night, so we'll have to settle for the Hilton dining room. It's good, though."

Olga added, "We can go dancing after dinner in the disco downstairs."

Kelly replied, "Great idea. That fills out the agenda for my first evening in Tehran."

Christina laughed, "Not quite, Brad. The best entertainment will come later when we get back to the presidential suite."

"I'm glad to hear that. A session with you should help get my internal clock synchronized with local time."

Inside the presidential suite, Olga remarked, "Amnon said this is where President Ford stayed when he visited Tehran. Aren't you glad I got the discount for you?"

"Olga, this is the most lavish hotel room I've ever seen. Thanks to you. I'm sure you earned it."

"I think the manager got his money's worth OK!"

To the north Kelly gazed on the snow capped peaks of the Elburz mountains dimly lit by the January moonlight. To the east, the broad tree-lined, brightly lit Avenue Pahlano stretched from the downtown section in the south up to the palatial estates of the wealthy in the north. A carpet of lights ran down the slope from the Hilton to the downtown area, and further beyond to the Bazaar. During his long flight, he had poured over the Tehran city map Helen, Dr. Morrell's secretary, had thoughtfully placed in his travel folder.

Off to the west of his hotel room, many high rise condominium apartments were homes for the rapidly expanding Iranian middle class. As a direct result of the Shah's lavish spending on armaments, many educated Iranians were needed to man the management and technical jobs in the new industrial and service companies that grew up in the first half of the 70's. Many Iranians had escaped the poverty and unemployment of the 60's in their country by earning PhDs in Europe and the US and then staying in those places. When they found they could make more in Iran than in those foreign lands, they returned home in droves. Many expatriate Americans and Europeans also came to take the new high paying positions. The IBEX program would provide additional sources of employment for these *technocrats.*

When the suite doorbell rang, Olga hurried to open the door for Amnon and Shaheen. Amnon introduced Shaheen to everyone. Shaheen greeted Kelly with a warm, *Selamat,* the Moslem equivalent of *Shalom.* Shaheen had gone to the University of Paris for eight years, so he greeted the girls by kissing their hands in the French fashion. He had returned to Iran in 1964 and was now an agent in the Iranian intelligence service, Savak. Since Shaheen was also a nephew of the Shah, he provided *family* supervision of the director of Savak. The Savak director secretly resented this surveillance, but he was savvy enough not to let Shaheen detect that annoyance. It wasn't healthy not to treat the Shah's family members with respect. The power of the Peacock Throne was solidly behind them.

Kelly responded, "Mr. Mouhoud, I am amazed at how big and modern Tehran seems."

"Dr. Kelly, please call me Shaheen. We're going to be seeing a lot of each other during your visit. You'll find Tehran is a city of contrasts. The modern and the ancient. The advanced technology of our computer centers and aerospace company. And the backwardness of our people."

"Shaheen, please call me Brad. I was glad to hear you're going to guard me while I'm here."

"I heard about the two recent threats on your life because you're in charge of the IBEX project. The Savak knows the group that's after you. Don't worry. We'll protect you. You're an extremely valuable resource."

"Thanks for those comforting words."

"About tomorrow, Brad, I'll pick you up at 8am and take you to your meeting with Colonel Ladrun at the Israeli embassy. I advise you not to ride around in cars with diplomatic plates while you're here. I understand Ralph Houser from your CIA will pick you up at the Israeli embassy and take you to meet the American ambassador, Mr. Hurds. I have assigned a man to accompany Ralph Houser, since he also needs protection. The terrorists know who most of the CIA agents in Tehran are. Now, goodbye until tomorrow," and Shaheen left with Amnon.

Immediately, Kelly gave each of the girls a *hello* kiss to show how glad he was to see them here in this foreign land. "Give me a few minutes to unpack and shower away the grime from my trip. Then let's go down and have some of that Russian caviar."

"That caviar in the lobby is Iranian caviar from the Caspian Sea. The Iranians produce almost as much caviar as the Russians."

"I stand corrected. But the man serving it had on a Russian Cossack uniform."

"I know but that's just Hilton Hotel *showmanship*."

In a few minutes the trio took the elevator down to the lobby and found an available couch. Immediately one of the waiters came over and Olga ordered in Farsi.

Kelly was surprised, "This is the Hilton, why didn't you order in English?"

"Christina and I have already discovered that if we don't order in Farsi, there's no telling what we may get. This morning, we both ordered poached eggs on toast in English and I got scrambled eggs and Christina got French toast."

Christina added, "It's part of the Persian culture. If an Iranian doesn't understand, he'll never admit it by asking a question. He'll smile and then do or say what he thinks you asked for."

Kelly responded, "I'll have to keep that in mind in my business dealings here. I wasn't aware of that quirk in their way of life."

The waiter returned with three small plates of Iranian caviar and a bottle of Mumm's champagne. He handed Kelly the check which was for 6,842.50 rials. Kelly exclaimed, "Isn't that a fantastic amount for a little caviar and champagne!"

Olga looked at the bill, "That's only 684 tomans."

"What's a toman? I thought their currency was rials."

"It is, but there are ten rials to a toman. It's an unofficial monetary unit the Iranians use. It's like a guinea in England, 22 shillings to the guinea."

"How many rials to the dollar?"

"Right now, 68 rials to the dollar."

"That means our caviar and champagne cost over a hundred dollars."

"Christina responded, "Caviar is very expensive and, of course, champagne purchased in a hotel is three or four times the liquor store price. Unfortunately, there are no liquor stores in Iran, since it's a Moslem country. You can only get liquor in the hotels and restaurants that cater to foreigners."

"I didn't have time at the airport to change any dollars into rials. I guess I should get some local currency at the hotel desk."

Olga shook her head, "Pay for this by writing your room number on the bill. It would be better to get your dollars changed in a bank tomorrow or Sunday. The hotel only gives 60 rials to the dollar. Tomorrow, you're going to the US embassy on Shahrazah Avenue. There's a bank just a half a block away on the same street."

"Christina, you and Olga appear to be old hands on Iranian matters."

"Olga and I have been coming to Iran a few times a year for the last several years. It's a good place to shop. It's only a two and a half hour flight from Tel Aviv. It's one of the few countries surrounding Israel where an Israeli resident can go."

"I though you and Olga were from Sweden. Can't you go to the Arab countries with your Swedish passports?"

"Theoretically we could. But with the Israeli entrance stamps and resident visa in our passports, it wouldn't be wise."

"Since you two know Tehran so well, where can I buy my wife some typically Persian jewelry?"

"There's a nice jewelry store right across the street from the US embassy. They specialize in gold and turquoise rings."

Olga added, "There are some nice jewelry stores in the old Bazaar near Topaneh Square."

"How much are these things?"

Olga answered, "That depends on how well you bargain. The shopkeepers in the Bazaar are insulted if you accept their first offering. It's always ridiculously high. They expect you to bargain them down to about half their original price."

"If I can find time to go shopping tomorrow, can you two go with me? Can you meet me at the Associated Aviation Corporation office? It's on Pahlano Avenue, between the Israeli embassy and the Iraqi embassy."

"I know that office building? Yes, we'll take a taxi down from the Hilton. What time?"

"Well, I'm having lunch with our AAC representative, Salim Mena, right after my meeting with Ambassador Hurd. How about 2pm?"

"OK, we'll be there. It should take about an hour and a half to go to both the jewelry store on Shahrazah and the ones in the Bazaar. I'm hungry now. Let's go to dinner."

They walked across the lobby toward the dining room on the west side of the Hilton and had no trouble getting a table. The maitre d' handed them menus written in French and Farsi. He also sent a waiter to their table who explained in English with a French accent the day's specials. Kelly decided to have charbroiled lamb with Iranian rice pilaf. Christina and Olga both chose charbroiled sturgeon from the Caspian Sea, also with rice pilaf. They all wanted French onion soup and green salad before the main course.

When the main course came, Kelly was surprised at the hard crust of heavily toasted rice included with his pilaf.

"Olga explained, "That's the browned rice from the bottom of the pan. It's considered a Persian delicacy and is always served to the honored guest. That's why you got it and we didn't."

"Well, it tastes OK but it's a little hard on the teeth."

"You must eat it. Otherwise its an insult to the host."

"OK, but I hope they have good dentists here. And, by the way, I'm the host tonight!"

"Yes, but you may be invited to an Iranian home and you must practice."

Kelly looked around the sumptuously decorated room. His eye fell on a beautiful girl sitting at a table nearby. Her companion or husband was wearing an Iranian Air Force uniform. She had blonde hair and blue-green eyes. Kelly remarked, "That girl over there must be European, with her coloring."

Christina laughed, "No, Brad, she is Persian. In fact, that is Fahrina Mahi, the daughter of one of the wealthiest businessmen in Iran. Persians are Caucasians, with many blue eyed blondes among them. The Persian culture is very old."

Olga replied, "You may remember Esther from the Bible story was from Persia. There is still a large Jewish population in Iran. That's one reason why the Israelis are accepted here."

Christina added, "A few years back, the Shah held an elaborate celebration complete with Persian tents and feasts in Isfahan, south of Tehran. It was to celebrate the four thousandth year of Persian civilization."

"I'm impressed with your knowledge. Now, since we've finished dinner, let's head for the discotheque and learn about today's Persian culture."

Kelly motioned for the bill. The dinner and drinks came to 9,792 rials, including the 15% service charge. Almost $150. He was glad he had an unlimited expense account. He mentally figured Olga and Christina would be listed as 'General Hatami' on his expense account voucher."

Walking across the lobby to catch the elevator down to the disco, Kelly thought, *The Hilton Hotels do a terrific job of creating a pseudo-atmosphere of the country where they're located.* Kelly had learned this in Tel Aviv. At first he thought the Hilton Hotel restaurants represented true Israeli food. But when he sampled the *real* restaurants around Tel Aviv, he learned the truly diverse culture and food of Israel. He warned himself the true Persian culture wouldn't be found in this Hilton either.

It was eleven when they walked into the disco and the place was almost deserted. The pretty Iranian hostess showed them to a good table near the dance floor and took their drink orders. Kelly remarked; "I would have expected this place to be packed on a Friday night."

Christina replied, "Wednesday night is the big night. Then this place is jammed by eleven pm. But tonight the crowds will arrive just before midnight."

The music was pure American. The lights were flashing and created the hypnotic effect of all discotheques. A small group on the dance floor undulated to the rhythms. Kelly, Christina and Olga joined the dancers. No one seemed to notice there were two girls and one man. No one on the floor danced close to his partner as they all went through sensual body motions.

The crowd indeed arrived at midnight. It became difficult to find space on the floor to undulate. Kelly suggested, "Girls, let's retire to the next activity."

They chorused a resounding affirmative.

Kelly quickly paid the bill and the trio took the elevator up to their luxurious presidential suite where they had a quick discussion and agreed it was Olga's turn this time. She immediately undressed and crawled into the queen sized bed. They melted into an exotic tangle of passion and fell into a deep, relaxed sleep.

Kelly's mental alarm clock woke him up at 7:30am. He slid out of bed very quietly without disturbing the girls, who were still fast asleep. He dressed and went down to the breakfast room on the east side of the lobby. He ordered fried eggs and got poached eggs on toast. He ordered orange juice by pointing to the item on the menu and got a grapefruit.

He went to the center section of the lobby to wait for Shaheen Mouhoud to take him to his 9am meeting at the Israeli embassy. 8:30 came and went. Kelly took advantage of the extra minutes to read the International Herald Tribune, the overseas American newspaper, and catch up on the news and the Friday Wall Street closing numbers. He always worried about the fluctuations in his stock portfolio.

Shaheen finally arrived at ten to nine. Kelly would learn on this trip that Iranians, unlike Israelis, were never punctual. A time like 8:30 meant somewhere between 8:45 and 9:15. So, in the Iranian time frame, Shaheen was fairly early for his 8:30 appointment.

Shaheen greeted Kelly with a happy *Selamat* and led him to his black Chrysler parked just outside the lobby door. Kelly noticed the Hilton rule of *don't leave unattended vehicles at the lobby entrance* didn't apply to Shaheen. There were a lot of advantages to being the Shah's nephew.

Shaheen drove quickly down the Hilton driveway and turned right on Shimron Road. He headed at high speed down the divided street until he reached Avenue Pahlano, a broad, tree lined, four lane highway running north and south. Tehran sprawled on the fairly steep slope of the alluvial fan from the Elburz mountains to the north. A meter wide, open, concrete channel ran along each side of the road. This waterway, called *jupa* in Iranian, carried rain water, snow run off, and sewage down the sides of all the major north-south streets of Tehran.

Shaheen careened right on Pahlano and continued to drive at high speed, When a car got in his way, he merely crossed over the double center line, forcing the on-coming traffic to swerve. But he got by the slow pokes!

Half a block off Pahlano to the west, Shaheen pulled up to the Israeli embassy entrance at one minute after nine and remarked, "Here we are, right on time. Let's get in. The Israelis don't like people to be late, you know. I'm going to sit in on your meeting with Colonel Ladrun."

By embassy standards, the Israeli embassy was a modest sized building, less than half the size of the Iraqi embassy a bit farther down south on Pahlano.

They walked into the lobby and Shaheen addressed the pretty, dark haired Iranian Jewess at the reception desk in Farsi. She replied in unaccented English, "Dr. Kelly and Mr. Mouhoud, Colonel Ladrun is expecting you. I'll ring him to come pick you up. If you would be seated, please."

Ladrun arrived in the entrance area shortly and led Shaheen and Kelly down some stairs to a tiny cluttered office. There were two visitor's chairs that would barely fit into the space in front of the desk piled with papers.

Ladrun said, "Brad, I've been busy setting up the meetings with General Hatami. I had hoped to have you brief the general this afternoon, but Saturday afternoon is his day for staff meetings after the two day weekend. At any rate, we are all set to meet with the general at 10am Sunday morning at the Doshen Toeppeh Air Force Base."

"Where's that?"

"It's south east of the city center, about five kilometers from here. You better leave the Hilton no later than 8:45. The traffic in the southern part of the city is horrendous."

Shaheen broke in, "Brad, I'll pick you up at nine. We can make it easily."

Kelly grinned, "I'm sure you'll get us there quickly. Now, Joseph, what's the plan for this meeting?"

"After your briefing of General Hatami, he will probably want you to meet with his technical staff to go into more details. Colonel Abdul Fahi is the director of the IBEX program. He'll have a lot of questions. General Doshenshah, General Hatami's chief of staff, will also be in both meetings. He never asks many questions. He leaves that up to the more technically oriented officers. He's an old fashioned general - just worries about protocol mostly, not technology."

"Joseph, I brought a budgetary price proposal. Who do we talk to about that?"

Shaheen broke in, "Discuss financial matters with Colonel Fahi. He's responsible for both the technical and financial aspects of IBEX. As for General Hatami, he has a budget of one billion dollars and as long as the price is within the budget, he'll be happy."

Kelly said, "Shaheen, we have a problem with the budget. We added a sixth site overlooking the Soviet Union near the Caspian Sea, and that put us about twenty percent over the budget."

Shaheen frowned, "That is a problem We don't need to look at the Soviets. The Shah doesn't believe the Russians are a threat to Iran."

"I must be blunt, Shaheen. *No Soviet surveillance site, no IBEX*. That's my government's position."

"I see. This is a very delicate matter. Who is your agent?"

"We don't have one yet. That's something I must do during this trip."

It was Shaheen's turn to be blunt. "Brad, I don't want to tell you how to conduct your business, but I would strongly recommend you retain Abfol Mahi as your agent. He has a close *family* relationship to the Shah-an-shah. General Hatami will need an increase in his budget. Only the Shah himself can raise his budget. Mahi can convince the Shah to raise the budget, if he's your agent."

"I'll probably take your advice, Shaheen, but I need to know what this *family relationship* is."

"Well, this is a family secret and you should be very discrete who you tell about it. My grandfather, the Shah's father, was a lusty man. During a period of indiscretion, he made love to a beautiful village girl from Tabriz, who became pregnant and gave birth to a son. So you see, the Shah has a bastard brother, Abfol Mahi, who took his mother's family name. The Shah pledged to his father he would take care of Abfol, and he does. Mr. Mahi is the agent for about 70% of Iran's armament business, which is about five billion dollars a year. An agent's fee is five percent."

"That's about 250 million dollars a year!"

"Abfol doesn't get to keep it all. He rebates 60% to the Shah's personnel treasury and distributes about 20% to his buddies in the armed services, such a General Hatami."

"That still leaves fifty million dollars a year."

"Abfol has a large office staff and other overhead items, including a personal jet aircraft, expenses that have to come out of his part of the fee."

"I would guess that would be, at most, 25 million dollars a year."

Shaheen agreed, "That's about right. Abfol's net worth is more than one billion dollars."

"I'll bet he has it in Swiss banks."

"I would think so. That's where the Shah keeps his personal wealth. That's why he spends a month each winter with his family skiing at St. Moritz. He wants to be near his money."

"Now, Shaheen, for the 64 million dollar question. How do I meet Mr. Mahi?"

"That's easy. I'll take you to his home this evening and introduce you."

"Great. What time?"

I'll pick you up at 7 and you should be finished by 8. Abfol can conclude a billion dollar deal very quickly. He lives about fifteen minutes north of the Hilton.

Kelly almost blurted out, *Fifteen minutes the way you drive is quite a distance*, but he managed to keep his face blank.

Amnon and Ralph Hauser appeared in the doorway. Amnon announced, "I brought Ralph here to go with you for your meeting with Ambassador Hurd. You better leave soon."

Colonel Ladrun spoke up, "Brad, we're about finished here. By the way, that was good advice from Shaheen about Mr. Mahi. Frankly, General Izhack was hoping you'd choose him for your agent."

Kelly thought, *Here in this tiny room are agents from three of the world's intelligence agencies: the CIA, Mossad, and Savak. They're working together and seem to like each other. I'm sure glad to have their help on IBEX!*

Shaheen jumped to his feet, "OK, let's go, Brad. I'll drive you and Ralph to the US embassy for your meeting. Don't worry, we'll be there before 11."

Shaheen, Kelly, and Hauser left the Israeli embassy and climbed into Shaheen's car. He pulled out the entrance gate and turned south on Avenue Pahlano. This broad avenue carried the family name of the Shah. Many places and avenues and people's names reflected the Shah's family name or some form of Shah, such as Shaheen or Shahad. A short distance down Pahlano, Shaheen pointed out Mr. Mahi's high rise office building as they sped by. About a kilometer farther, they turned right on Shahrazah Avenue, a major east-west street in the center. On the north side of the street, a little farther on, they came to the huge American compound. Shaheen swung the big black Chrysler through the gateway, Hauser showed the US Marine guard his pass, and they were waved inside. Shaheen drove up to the main building housing the US Ambassador's office and let Kelly and Hauser out, saying, "I'll meet you in the entrance lobby after your meeting. Then I'll take you to your luncheon meeting with your Rep, Bob Mena. In the meantime, after I park the car, I'll visit with the embassy receptionist. She's a dear friend of mine."

In the lobby, Kelly and Hauser were greeted by a beautiful Iranian receptionist with reddish brown hair and brilliant green eyes. She was wearing a tight, white sweater that showed off her ample breasts, and a tight, black leather mini-skirt and knee-high leather boots.

In perfect American-style English she said, "Mr. Hauser, the ambassador is expecting you and Dr. Kelly. You may go on up to his office on the third floor. I've already alerted his secretary that you are here."

Kelly glanced back as the two stepped into the elevator. Shaheen was conversing intently with the receptionist in Farsi. He was oblivious to Hauser and Kelly.

Their path led out of the elevator and down to the end of the wide hall. They walked into the ambassador's outer office and his efficient secretary Joanne said, "Gentlemen, Ambassador Hurd is expecting you but he just received a phone call from the assistant Secretary of State. He won't be too long, I hope. In the meantime, would you like a cup of coffee or tea?"

Kelly answered, "Why, thank you. I could use a strong cup of black coffee. My body thinks it's late in the evening."

"I guess that's a problem for you, coming from California. It's 10:30 at night in Los Angeles, isn't it?"

Kelly checked his world time watch and said, "Yes, that's right. No wonder my eyes keep trying to close."

Soon the coffee was in their hands, and shortly afterwards the ambassador's phone light went out. Joanne spoke into the intercom and then announced, "You may go in now."

The ambassador rose from behind his desk and waved the two to the couch. The office was huge, with a plate glass window behind the desk facing the snow capped peaks to the north. They could barely be seen in the morning smog. *Worse than our famous Los Angeles smog* thought Kelly.

Ambassador Richard Hurd said, "Welcome to Tehran, Dr. Kelly. I'm looking forward to hearing all about IBEX. Ralph has told me a little about it and the CIA director alerted me when I was home for Christmas last month that the project was moving. We here in the embassy have a hard time digging out of the Iranians what IBEX is all about."

"Mr. Ambassador, I've brought a viewgraph briefing which takes about an hour, or I can cover the Executive Summary in about fifteen minutes."

"Let's hear the Executive Summary, Dr. Kelly. It's after 11 now and I have a 1 o'clock lunch at the Palace with the Shah. I can only spend thirty minutes with you."

Kelly pulled the necessary viewgraphs from his large pile and said, "Fine, Mr. Ambassador, You will get the important points from the summary. Ralph, would you mind running the projector for me?" He handed the viewgraphs to Hauser, who walked over to the projector, put on the first plastic sheet and projected it on the screen directly across the room from where the ambassador was sitting.

Kelly went through the briefing charts, carefully explaining the planned six surveillance locations plus the central processing site. The ambassador asked a few clarifying questions during the presentation. At the end, he said, "IBEX is quite an undertaking. It should give the Shah the surveillance of his Arab neighbors that he wants. More importantly, it will give the US another key surveillance site to keep track of the Soviets."

"That's right, Mr. Ambassador, and I should point out that the CIA Director insisted we have an iron-clad contractual clause giving the US rights for US personnel to be in the collection sites and processing center at all times."

"That's good, but who's going to enforce the clause? Our embassy staff is too thin to take on such a task."

"Mr. Ambassador, I'm glad you asked. When I gave this IBEX briefing to General Robertson in the Pentagon, the general said the MAAG, Military Advisory Assistance Group, here would enforce the clause."

"Yes, that should work. He certainly has a large enough staff. He got here last week. It's important for the US ambassador and the head of the US MAAG to work well together. Mrs. Hurd and I have already had General Robertson and his charming wife over to the embassy for a dinner."

"I'm giving the briefing to General Hatami tomorrow morning at 10."

"Good. General Hatami is a key factor in the Iranian military. His importance supersedes his military rank because of his close personal relationship with the Shah. When the Shah was forced into exile, General Hatami flew him out. When the US government provided the proper *environment* for the Shah to return, General Hatami flew him back. The Shah is still grateful to both the US government and to General Hatami."

"Mr. Ambassador, thank you for your time and for your helpful comments and suggestions." They shook hands and the visitors went back down to the lobby where Hauser left for his office in the embassy.

Shaheen was still conversing happily with the beautiful receptionist who didn't seem to have much in the way of official duties to keep her busy. She smiled and said something in Farsi to Shaheen as they left. Walking to the car, Shaheen confirmed he had a date with her for that evening.

The Shah had liberalized the position of women in his country. There was quite a contrast between Iran and other Moslem countries where the women had to wear shroud-like clothing that completely covered them. In Tehran, the women wore the latest western fashions, including mini-skirts and tight fitting jeans in the city and bikinis at the beaches of the Caspian Sea and the many other large lakes. The embassy's receptionist was a leader in the strong women's liberation movement. Driving Kelly to his next meeting, Shaheen related what the receptionist had just told him about the latest victory in the women's lib campaign. The women soldiers went on strike for their fellow married women soldiers. They were seeking the right of the married soldiers to sleep at home with their husbands instead of in the army barracks alone since male soldiers already had that right. The ladies won.

The Associated Aviation Corporation office was just north of the Iraqi embassy. Shaheen parked just off Avenue Pahlano beside the six story office building. They searched for Salim Mena's name mounted on the wall of the lobby, with a sign saying, *room 610, on the top floor.* The small elevator carried them up to the sixth floor where they found 610, a three-office suite with large windows overlooking the city.

The receptionist said, "You must be Dr. Kelly. You may go right in. Mr. Mena is expecting you."

She then said a few words in Farsi to Shaheen and smiled happily at his response. To Kelly it seemed all the receptionists in town were in love with Shaheen.

Mr. Mena introduced himself as *Bob* Mena. He explained to Kelly that although he was born in Tehran, he went to the US to go to the University of Southern California where he earned a BS in electrical engineering. Then he got a *green card* and a job with Associated Aviation and, later, his US citizenship. He had never expected to return to Iran but when AAC needed someone to head up the Tehran office, he applied for the job. He was being paid a higher salary than in the US plus a generous living allowance. He bought a three bedroom condominium for $300,000 in one of the high rise buildings sprouting up around Tehran. His living allowance and lower income taxes gave him enough extra spendable income to afford such expensive living quarters.

Then Mena said to Kelly, "I must point out to you there is no chance of AAC getting a contract here unless we have a local agent."

Kelly laughed, "Bob, you're the third person today to tell me that. As a matter of fact, Shaheen has already set up a meeting for me with Mr. Abfol Mahi this evening at 7. I plan to offer Mr. Mahi a contract to be our sales agent for IBEX in Tehran, subject of course to our corporate legal staff's approval."

"Excellent. He's the best. Now I'm sure you'll get the contract."

"I'm glad to hear you agree he's the right one. The next step is to telex Dr. Morrell and ask him to have Mr. Mahi's background checked."

"I'll get the telex off this afternoon."

"By the way, Bob, I have two friends who are meeting me here in your office at two. Their names are Christina and Olga. Would you ask your secretary to make them a home if we're late getting back from lunch?"

"No problem. I'm sure we'll be back by two easily. We're going to the Shaherazade, just around the corner."

While Mena called the receptionist on the intercom and told her in Farsi about Kelly's friends, Shaheen took Kelly aside. "Brad, if you don't mind, I'll let you go to lunch with Mena alone. I'll be taking his receptionist to lunch. I promise to have her back by 1:30 though. Then I'll drive you and your friends wherever you want to go."

"OK, have fun. See you before two!"

Kelly and Mena walked the short distance to the Shaherazade Restaurant. They had a typical Iranian lunch with lamb and rice for the main course and creme caramel and Iranian tea for dessert. Mena explained some of the logistics problems Kelly could expect during installation and later during site operations in Iran. Mena was sure he could find living quarters for all the AAC employees who would be on assignment in Iran. Kelly paid for the restaurant bill with his company credit card and the two walked back to Mena's office, arriving just before two. Christina and Olga were already waiting. Shaheen and the receptionist, whose hair-do no longer had its beauty shop look, were talking animatedly in Farsi.

On the way to the car, Kelly explained the afternoon shopping mission to Shaheen, who agreed the girls had chosen the right places to buy gifts for Kelly's wife. First they went to the jewelry store across from the US embassy. All four went in and helped Kelly pick out a gold and turquoise 'princess' ring with exquisite delicate coiled cable details. The carefully matched stones were a strong turquoise color with no flaws. The store owner asked 15,000 rials for the ring, over $200. After an animated negotiation in Farsi, with much finger pointing by Shaheen, and hand wringing by the store operator, a price of 6000 rials, less than $100, was agreed upon. As they left with the beautiful ring in a small box, everyone was happy with the deal.

Back in the car, Shaheen turned south on Abadan Street and headed for the huge Tehran Bazaar. Driving the few kilometers, the neighborhoods became poorer and poorer, with more and more population density. They reached Topaneh Square, across a wide street from the Bazaar. Shaheen bribed a young boy to guard his car. The boy immediately began cleaning and polishing the black Chrysler with a large chamois he pulled out of his jacket pocket.

The Bazaar was covered by a roof of filthy panes of glass. Many narrow alleys led to a conglomeration of shops spread over a multi-acre area. The group wandered through quite a few of the alleyways so Kelly could get the flavor of the fantastic array of goods. Pungent odors emanated from the shops. They saw stores offering the expensive jewelry they wanted, plus sumptuous carpets, exotic spices, glittering brassware; in fact, every conceivable commodity from sheepskins to T shirts.

Soon Christina and Olga led Kelly into a medium sized jewelry store containing a dazzling array of gold and turquoise jewelry in elaborate show cases. Sensing a foreigner with money to spend on expensive women, the shop owner quickly took charge of the sale from the pretty clerk who first approached the group. Christina explained they were looking for gold earrings and a necklace to go with a ring they had already bought. Kelly showed the ring. The store owner immediately led them to a case with earrings and necklaces of the same general style. He picked four sets of earrings and four necklaces and spread them on the counter. Christina and Olga sorted through the options still in the case and picked out two more of each. The girls examined all this jewelry carefully and agreed on the ones Kelly should buy for his wife. Kelly looked at their selections and agreed they had picked the right ones.

This time Shaheen argued and cajoled in Farsi for almost ten minutes. He finally arrived at a number about 40% of the original stated price. Kelly counted out a stack of thousand rial notes to pay the owner the 9000 rials. He also bought a set of earrings for Helen, Dr. Morrell's secretary.

The four shoppers headed back through the alleyways to the entrance and across to Shaheen's car. The young boy had Shaheen's black Chrysler gleaming. Shaheen handed the lad a hundred rial note for his efforts and he grinned happily at them as they drove off.

It was after 4pm and the Tehran traffic was reaching a peak. The streets were jammed. The drivers were fearless. The four turned north onto Avenue Pahlano to start the long incline up to the Hilton. Approaching the first intersection, Shaheen suddenly jammed on the brakes. A car coming south on Pahlano had suddenly pulled left in front of the on coming traffic at the intersection and stopped. This was a signal for all the other cars behind it who wanted to turn left to do so. They used the stopped car as a shield and poured left behind it. Shaheen explained this was standard practice in Tehran traffic. Surprisingly, few accidents happened. When one did, the Iranian police had an unique method of resolving liability. The blame for the accident was established immediately at the scene. The driver at fault was required to come up with payment for damages on the spot, or else he was hauled off to jail until payment was made. The procedure avoided lengthy court liability battles with their accompanying high lawyer fees.

When Shaheen let his passengers out at the Hilton just before 5pm he said, "Brad, I'll pick you up at twenty minutes to six. Mr. Mahi wanted to move the meeting up to 6 since his board of directors meeting started early today. He wants to be finished by 7 so he'll have a free evening.

"OK, Shaheen, that's fine. I'll meet you in the lobby."

Kelly and the girls enjoyed a bottle of Mumm's champagne, cheese dip, and potatoes chips from the elaborately stocked refrigerator in their suite. The girls told Kelly the bad news; they had to leave for Tel Aviv Monday morning. Kelly would have to sleep alone in the big presidential suite Monday night before his departure Tuesday morning. Kelly decided he'd make up for that night of deprivation tonight and Sunday night.

Chapter 7.

The Arms Agent's Daughter

Shaheen was only 5 minutes late to pick up Kelly. *Mr. Mahi must be really be important for Shaheen to be so punctual.*

Soon they were hurrying north along Avenue Pahlano. The road began wandering eastward between many enormous, palatial estates. This was where the truly wealthy Iranians lived. An armed guard let them through an iron gate where a circular driveway led up to Mr. Mahi's home. In front of the massive entrance door, a short, plump, two star Iranian Air Force general got into a staff car chauffeured by a young major and drove away as Shaheen pulled up. The luxuriantly landscaped front area with its extensive rose garden reminded Kelly of the movie stars' homes in Beverly Hills.

A blonde woman with blue-green eyes greeted them at the door. Kelly recognized her as the beautiful woman in the Hilton restaurant last night, but she did not seem to remember him. She greeted them in American English, "Dr. Kelly, I'm Fahrina. My father is expecting you. He's in his study. Please follow me."

As they turned right, into the hall leading to the study, Kelly noticed a magnificent marble fireplace sitting in the corner but obviously not installed, not ready for making fires. He asked Fahrina, "What is that for?"

"I'm so pleased you asked. Last month I was on a business trip with my father to Florence. While my father was busy, I found this antique Italian fireplace in a little shop and fell in love with it. I thought it would look perfect here. The shop was asking the Italian equivalent of $100,000 for it, but my father is a good negotiator. He bought it for only $75,000."

"I think it's beautiful. Do you know how old it is?"

"It was built in 1570 and came from the Duke of Montua's palace. He was the unscrupulous duke in the opera 'Rigoletto'."

Fahrina escorted Kelly and Shaheen down the hall and opened the study door. Mr. Mahi was sitting behind an uncluttered 16th century marble-topped desk with beautifully carved walnut legs. He stood up and greeted them, "Welcome to Iran and to my humble home, Dr. Kelly." He motioned them to an elegant couch of the same vintage as the desk and seated himself in a facing throne-like chair with a black marble coffee table between them. Kelly estimated the room was about 20 by 28 feet. The floor was covered with a shimmering light turquoise silk Persian carpet. The ceiling was gilded in thick gold leaf. The light from the large crystal chandelier reflected off the gold leaf giving a warm golden glow throughout the room - a warm ambiance that made business discussions seem natural and friendly. Knowing an ounce of gold cost about $300 and was about 2 cm by 2 cm by 4 mm thick, and assuming the gold leaf was one millimeter thick, Kelly mentally estimated the gold in the ceiling was worth roughly ten million dollars.

Mr. Mahi opened the discussion, "Shaheen tells me you are interested in retaining my services to help on a new project in my country."

"Yes, Mr. Mahi, the IBEX project is considered very sensitive by your country."

Shaheen interrupted, "Dr. Kelly, Mr. Mahi has the highest clearances with the Iranian government, so you can discuss your project freely here."

Mr. Mahi added, "I'm not interest in discussing any classified or technical details, but I am interested in the scope of the project and your budgetary estimate. Then I can decide whether my firm will accept an agreement to represent you on IBEX."

"The project involves installing devices on six mountain tops ringing the borders of Iran plus a central processing site with mainframe computers and software. It is a large program."

"What's the primary purpose of this system?"

"It's an *electronic fence* to look at your enemies or potential enemies. It can detect electronic signals that indicate whether or not a threat to Iran's security exists."

"With Iran's great oil wealth, there are many forces that would like to get their hands on our oil. Can IBEX identify a security threat like this?"

"Yes, Sir, it can. The surveillance sites will be able to intercept both radar signals and communication signals. The electronics will include special cryptographic equipment to decode hostile encrypted messages as well."

"Then it's really a big electronic spy system, isn't it?"

"Yes, you could call it that."

"And what is your budget? I should warn you, our fees are high, but reasonable for the services we provide. For small projects under one hundred million dollars, our fee is ten percent. For large projects up to five billion dollars, our fee is reduced to only five percent, with a sliding scale in between."

"Mr. Mahi, the bottom line for our budgetary price proposal came to one billion two hundred million dollars. So there is a problem. We understand General Hatami has been allocated only one billion dollars for the project."

"What caused the over-run?"

"General Hatami's original concept only included five remote sites. My government insisted on a sixth site overlooking the Soviet Union. They said the project wouldn't get an export license without the sixth site."

"In other words, your government wants to spy on Russia and have the Iranian government pay for the spy site. Isn't that so?"

"That's stating it rather bluntly, but I guess that's about right."

"Dr. Kelly, our defense budget is about five billion dollars a year, so your over-run amounts to about four percent. If General Hatami isn't given the extra money, there won't be a project and we're wasting each other's time. There's only one person who can authorize an over-run of that magnitude. Will you excuse me for a minute?"

Mr. Mahi walked over to his desk, picked up the phone and dialed a number. He spoke heatedly in Farsi to someone. After about three minutes he returned to his chair, "Don't worry, General Hatami will get the extra two hundred million. That was the Shah. He wasn't very happy to pay for a spy site for the Americans to spy on the Russians. But he's a realist. He wants to spy on *his enemies* and now he understands he won't get the system from the US without the sixth site. He knows he could go to Europe but he want the latest US technology."

"That's fantastic news! That removes the last road block for IBEX."

"All but one. You need an agreement with me. My fee will be one hundred million dollars payable as you receive progress payments."

"But we only had fifty million in the budget for sales commissions."

"There may be a solution. What kind of mainframe computers are you going to use?"

We haven't made the final decision, but it will probably be IBM. We need about 25 million dollars worth."

"Good. My company, Iran Software, Ltd., is the exclusive distributor for IBM mainframes in Iran. Include a 75 million dollar fixed price subcontract for Iran Software, Ltd., in IBEX and that will make up the difference."

"But that's fifty million more than we expected to pay for the computers."

"Then we'll include both standard and custom software in that price."

"That does it then. We had 75 million included for the software."

"Then it's a deal!"

"I'll try my best but you must realize I can't commit the Big Brass at Associated Aviation will go along with this change."

"I know how big corporations work. But they'll have to accept your recommendations. They don't have any other choice if they want the IBEX contract."

Kelly and Mr. Mahi shook hands. As if by magic, a servant dressed like an English butler arrived with a bottle of champagne in a silver bucket and three glasses. A maid followed behind with an enormous silver tray completely covered with an array of hors d'oeuvres. The butler poured the three men glasses of champagne.

Mr. Mahi raised his glass, "Here's to a successful and profitable IBEX program." The three drank the toast.

Reaching for an hors d'oeuvre Kelly said, "Mr. Mahi, it would help the approval process at Associated Aviation if you could visit Los Angeles next month. You and our corporate legal staff could execute your agreement then."

"As a matter of fact, I plan to be in Los Angeles for three days beginning the tenth of February. I can meet you for an hour then. I'll be at the Beverly Hills Hotel. Call me there."

Mr. Mahi walked to the front door with Kelly and Shaheen and wished them goodbye with a hearty, "All the best, Dr. Kelly. I look forward to doing business with you."

Shaheen dropped Kelly off at the Hilton and left with the reminder, "I'll pick you up at 9 tomorrow, Sunday, for your meeting with General Hatami."

Kelly walked into the presidential suite to find the girls watching x-rated movies on the TV. Both were topless with bikini panties. Christina's were bright green and Olga's were bright red.

Kelly said, "I'm exhausted after all the meetings today. I'm having trouble adjusting to the time difference. But guess who I met?"

The girls chorused, "Who?"

Kelly told about meeting Fahrina Mahi and her father, about the beautiful marble fireplace and about the unbelievable gold leaf ceiling in Mr. Mahi's study."

Olga commented, "I understand land parcels in Mr. Mahi's neighborhood cost in the range of three to five million dollars. I'll bet the market value of his house is ten or twelve million dollars."

Kelly replied, "I think you're a bit low. I computed the value of just the gold leaf in the ceiling is about ten million dollars."

Christina added, "Yes, Brad, but if Mr. Mahi ever has to leave Iran, that gold will go with him. That's instant liquidity to add to his assets in his Swiss bank."

Olga suggested, "Brad, if you're tired, let's have dinner up here and watch sexy movies."

"That's a good idea, but let's go to bed early."

Christina had an idea, "We can watch the movies in bed. That way you can try the positions shown on the screen."

Olga ordered steak and champagne from room service. After dinner and refreshing showers, the girls played three 'goes' of 'Rock, Paper, Scissors' to decide who would get Brad tonight with the loser to get him the next night. The couple piled into the king sized bed and replayed the sex scenes from the two x-rated films on the Hilton video.

Shaheen picked up Kelly at the Hilton at ten minutes after nine, Sunday morning and headed south down Pahlano. The Sunday workday traffic was heavy and wild because of the undisciplined Iranian drivers. At the city center, Shaheen worked his way southeast through the crowded streets to a broad avenue where he turned east. When they passed a large military installation on the left, Shaheen explained that was an army training school and the Doshen Toeppeh Air Force Base was just a little farther along the avenue.

Soon Shaheen turned left into the main gate of the base, showed his identification papers to the two machine gun armed guards, and they waved him inside. He parked at a small building just inside the gate on the left side. The small security office was jammed with Iranian workers lined up to get day passes to work on the base. Kelly quickly found Colonel Ladrun, waiting with his pass in hand. Shaheen pushed through to the duty officer, showed his I.D. and waved for Kelly to come to the desk. The officer motioned for him to sign in and asked for his passport in Farsi, which Shaheen translated. Kelly traded his passport for a red badge. Shaheen explained Kelly would get his passport back when he returned the badge.

Kelly, Shaheen and Ladrun walked back to Shaheen's car and he drove on the main base road to the Royal Iranian Air Force Headquarters building where they left the car. They walked in the main entrance and took the elevator to the top floor where Shaheen led them to General Hatami's office. A four-star general, he was the chief of staff of the Royal Iranian Air Force and the personal pilot of the Shah.

General Hatami's executive officer, a colonel, greeted them with, "General Hatami will be with you shortly. He's on the phone speaking to the Shah-an-shah." He introduced the man standing next to him, "This is General Doshenshah, deputy to General Hatami. He'll take you into the general's office soon."

Kelly recognized General Doshenshah as the Iranian officer who left Mr. Mahi's house just as Kelly arrived. *Maybe Doshenshah is on Mahi's board of directors.*

When the executive officer announced General Hatami was off the phone, General Doshenshah led Kelly, Ladrun, and Shaheen into the office and announced, while he pointed to each individual in turn so there was no chance the general could get confused, "General Hatami, this is Dr. Kelly from the United States who will present you a briefing on IBEX. Mr. Shaheen Mouhoud is Dr. Kelly's escort while he is in our country. And you have previously met Colonel Ladrun."

"I am very pleased to have you visit Iran, Dr. Kelly. I'm most anxious to hear your briefing. Colonel Ladrun, it is good to see you again."

Kelly nodded, "Thank you, General Hatami. My complete briefing takes over an hour, but the executive summary takes fifteen minutes."

"Please present the complete briefing, Dr. Kelly. IBEX is our most urgent project."

Kelly handed the briefing viewgraphs to Colonel Ladrun and asked him to project them. The screen and projector had been set up so the general could see the projected images from his large brown leather overstuffed chair. The others settled themselves on two brown leather couches which also viewed the screen and General Doshenshah left the room. Kelly began the briefing and in about ten minutes he came to the part describing the six surveillance sites.

General Hatami interrupted, "Dr. Kelly, why do you have a sixth site overlooking the Soviet Union? Our requirements given to Colonel Ladrun clearly stated my government doesn't consider the Russians a threat. We don't need a sixth site."

Kelly explained the official American position about the sixth site, "The US government will be releasing some very sensitive technology to your government. It's a simple trade. You get the technology, we get vital electronic intelligence information about the Russians."

"When you put it that way, it seems fair. We Iranians understand how to trade and bargain. How about the price?"

"Sir, here is a copy of our budgetary price proposal. The bottom line is one point two billion dollars."

"Well, the price is no problem. The Shah-an-shah has informed me today my budget has been increased to that amount. The Shah-an-shah said this increase reflects his belief in the importance of IBEX to our nation's security."

General Hatami picked up his phone and said something in Farsi. General Doshenshah immediately re-entered the office and General Hatami addressed him in English, "Please arrange a briefing for all interested parties at 1pm in our special IBEX building. We are going to go with Dr. Kelly's concept for IBEX."

Then he turned to Kelly, "Please excuse me but I've heard enough of your presentation. I now want Colonel Abdul Fahi, who is my IBEX project manager, to hear your complete briefing and to delve into all technical details he may be concerned about. General Doshenshah will also invite certain other interested parties."

Colonel Ladrun picked up the viewgraphs and handed them to Kelly. The visitors shook hands with the General and were led out of the office by General Doshenshah to the outer reception office. General Doshenshah suggested, "Dr. Kelly, perhaps you and Colonel Ladrun would like to go down to our officers' dining room and have tea and cookies while I am notifying everyone about your 1pm briefing. Shaheen knows where it is. I'll meet you there about 11:30 and we can have lunch together."

"That will be fine, General Doshenshah. We'll see you in about an hour then."

The dining room reserved for the general officers of the Royal Iranian Air Force was empty except for two uniformed waiters who quickly brought the three tea and cookies after a brief request in Farsi by Shaheen.

Kelly finally had the chance to ask Shaheen about the officer they had seen leaving Mr. Mahi's home.

Shaheen answered, "Yes, it was General Doshenshah. Since Mr. Mahi is a representative for almost all the Iranian Air Force purchases, those two must meet frequently to discuss air force business matters."

"But, isn't it unusual for an air force officer to meet in the businessman's home?"

"Mr. Mahi's much too busy to travel all the way down to Doshen Toeppeh Air Force Base to meet with General Doshenshah. So it is convenient to have meetings at his home. Besides, the general only lives about a kilometer away from Mr. Mahi's."

"I see, but isn't the real estate in that neighborhood awfully expensive for someone in the military, even a two star general?"

"General Doshenshah is independently wealthy. He has done very well in his investments. So has General Hatami."

Kelly looked down into his teacup and stirred vigorously so the others wouldn't read his thoughts from his facial expression, *Mr. Mahi probably had something to do with the generals' success in investments.*

After a short time, General Doshenshah came into the dining room with the news, "The briefing is all arranged. There will be a staff car waiting at the entrance at 12:50 to take us to the conference room. Let's have lunch now."

It took almost an hour and a half to get through the sumptuous noon meal with multiple courses and then it was time to get in the staff car, which took them to a concrete building on a remote site on the base. The conference room was set up like a theater. The general directed Kelly to the speaker's podium and handed his viewgraphs to a projectionist behind a large screen. Almost immediately the first briefing chart was projected onto the theater type screen and the general made the introductions, "Gentlemen, this is Dr. Kelly from the United States. He will present the Iranian concept for project IBEX. General Hatami has already approved the concept in total."

Kelly looked out into the audience and was surprised to see several Americans as well as about ten Iranian Air Force officers. The Americans included General John Robertson, the newly arrived head of the Military Advisory Assistance Group in Tehran, a US Air Force colonel, who appeared to be the general's executive officer, Ralph Hauser of the CIA, and another civilian wearing the *Harvard uniform*. It was the CIA agent *Joe* who picked Kelly up at the Pentagon and drove him to meet the CIA Director.

General Doshenshah continued, "Dr. Kelly, please begin your briefing."

The lights dimmed and Kelly went through his viewgraphs, explaining carefully the overall concepts of the projects as well as the details of implementation. There were no questions interrupting his talk. At the end, General Robertson asked, "How soon do you expect to collect the first electronic intelligence about the Soviet Union from site six?"

"Sir, that should happen in October 1976, by the fifteenth at the latest."

"Excellent. Thank you, Dr. Kelly for a fine briefing on IBEX."

An Iranian officer stood up, "Dr. Kelly, I'm Colonel Abdul Fahi, the IBEX project manager. I also congratulate you on your thorough briefing. However, I would like to make sure you understand what we Iranians would like to get from sites one through five. I assume your friends in the CIA have already explained what the US expects to get from site six." He went on to explain he was looking for information about radar sites, missile sites, troop movements, and so forth. He also wanted to know about his neighbors' hostile intentions vis-à-vis Iran. He wanted to get this information by decoding encrypted massages which might contain such sensitive data. He asked, "Dr. Kelly, will your concept of IBEX give Iran this needed information?"

"Yes, Colonel Fahi, I assure you we are including the technical capabilities to intercept all those different kinds of information, even the *hostile intent* information you asked about."

"Good. Then I concur with General Hatami that your concept meets our requirements."

The group adjourned to a coffee and tea bar down the hall. Kelly was quickly surrounded by some members of the audience who asked him about several points. The tenor of their questions and his reception by the group around him indicated the briefing was well accepted. The AAC project was now sold to the Iranian *decision makers* and to the American *approvers*.

Joe, the CIA agent, commented, "Site six should give the US some excellent information about Soviet capabilities. It seems to me site five could also look at the Russians, but you only talked about north Afghanistan. What would it take to collect Soviet intelligence from site five?"

"About five minutes. Just change the direction of the collection antennas."

"Good. I may ask you to do that from time to time after site five is operational."

"We could do it on a routine basis. We'll probably get more intelligence from the Soviets than from the Afghanis."

The staff car took Kelly, Colonel Ladrun and Shaheen back to where their car was parked and Ladrun decided to ride back into town with them. Once in the car he commented, "Brad, I think you sold IBEX today."

"Yes, everything went really smoothly."

Shaheen added, "You may still have problems. Our Persian culture is such that we never make criticisms in public. You will hear about any dissatisfaction in private, probably from Colonel Fahi."

Shaheen dropped Colonel Ladrun off at the Israeli embassy and continued to the Hilton. He left Kelly there saying, "Mr. Mahi would like to meet with you at 10 tomorrow morning. He wants to hear first hand how your briefings went today. I'll pick you up at 9:30."

"OK, Shaheen. I'll see you in the morning," agreed Kelly.

As Kelly walked into the presidential suite, Olga was talking to someone on the phone in Farsi. She turned to Kelly, "This is Colonel Abdul Fahi. He seems quite agitated about something and wants to see you right away. Here, you talk to him.'"

"Colonel Fahi, this is Brad Kelly. Can I help you?"

"Yes, Dr. Kelly. We have a real problem. Can I meet with you at 5 this evening in your room to discuss it?"

"Of course, Colonel Fahi. That would be fine. Just come up to the presidential suite on the top floor. Selamat!"

"Selamat, see you then."

Kelly and the two girls had time to shower and drink a bottle of Mumm's Cordon Rouge champagne with caviar from room service while waiting for Colonel Fahi. He arrived at 5:30, dressed in civilian clothes. Brad introduced Olga and Christina, then said, "Colonel Fahi, would you like to have dinner with me and the two ladies this evening?"

"First, Dr. Kelly, my American friends call me Abe."

"OK, Abe, and my friends call me Brad."

"Brad, I would be pleased to have dinner with you but I have two problems: first, I'm married and would not like to be seen in public with a young lady, and second, it would not look good for us to be seen together at this stage in the IBEX negotiations."

"Well, Abe, that's easy. We'll have dinner in the suite. There's almost a complete dining room here."

"That would be fine. But first, I have a serious problem I must discuss with you, privately."

"OK. Girls, would you take our dinner orders and go into the other room to call room service? We'll call you when we are finished with our discussion."

Kelly and Fahi gave their dinner choices from the room service menu and the two girls left the room. Brad asked, "OK, now. What's the problem?"

Fahi explained, "You have chosen Israelis as a major subcontractor on this project, but General Hatami doesn't trust them and wants them off the program."

"That is a problem! But why this sudden change in attitude toward the Israelis? I thought the Iranians were grateful to the Israelis for their help with the Karg Island installations."

"They did give us good technical support but we paid them very well. General Hatami is very sensitive to the ground swell in Iran of the fundamentalist Moslems. The fundamentalists don't want the Israelis in Iran."

"What has a religious movement got to do with the Iranian Air Force?"

"The day-to-day operations of the air force are run by the Homofahrs, the non-commissioned officers. They service the airplanes, perform the construction, serve in the dining rooms, etcetera. General Hatami listens to their spokesmen and they are very displeased with any Israeli presence in Iran. And they don't want Israelis involved in IBEX."

"I though IBEX was a super secret program. I'm surprised the Homofahrs know about the project at this stage."

"It's difficult to keep secrets from the Homofahrs. They have their hands in everything going on in the air force."

"The non-commissioned officers are pretty influential in the US armed services also, but I don't think the US Air Force Chief of Staff would let them influence policy."

"You don't have the threat of a revolution in the US. We do!"

"I've never read anything about a revolution in the newspapers. And no one I've met in the US government has mentioned the risk either."

"Your government relies almost entirely on the word of the Shah. He's paranoid about the external danger from the countries surrounding us. He can't believe there's an internal menace. He believes all Iranians love him. That's because he is so isolated from the people."

"Abe, I'll do what I can about General Hatami's worries. It would be difficult to drop the Israelis at this stage. The cost of the project would probably increase, since they were in charge of a big chunk of the action for a fixed price of $200 million. If a US firm did the same job the cost would be higher because of the much greater labor cost of Americans compared with Israelis."

"We'll face that problem when it comes. You said in your briefing the price was 1.2 billion. That's what we expect now."

"But I said that was the *budgetary* price. Our firm price proposal might be higher if we have to make changes like you're requesting."

"We Iranians never hear the qualifications on statements. We heard $1.2 billion."

"OK. Abe. I heard your problem. Now I'll have to work on it."

"Brad, I think we'll be able to work well together on IBEX. You know, I lived in California for two years. The air force sent me to the University of Southern California for my master's degree in electrical engineering."

"USC has a good engineering school. I'm looking forward to working with you, too, Abe. Let me assure you, Associated Aviation and its team of suppliers and subcontractors will do a great job on this project."

"I'm sure they will. Now, let's relax and have dinner."

"Do you like to dance?"

"I love to dance to American disco music."

"In that case, I'll ask Olga and Christina to set up the hi fi for disco after dinner." And Kelly went into the next room to get the girls.

With a hint of command in his voice he said to Olga, "I would appreciate it if you would take care of Colonel Fahi. It would help IBEX."

"Oh, no! Not another lousy Iranian lover. OK! Anything for your project," she moaned.

The quartet had an exquisite dinner in the room, followed by disco dancing. When the music switched to a slower tempo, Fahi danced very close to Olga and Kelly danced very close to Christina. After a while, Olga led Colonel Fahi into bed in one bedroom and Kelly and Christina slipped into bed in the second bedroom. All four had a wild evening of sex until they fell asleep, spent.

About 4am, Colonel Fahi dressed and left.

The next morning, Shaheen picked up Kelly in the lobby and they left for Mr. Mahi's home. On the way, Kelly asked, "Doesn't Mr. Mahi ever go to his office on Pahlano?"

Shaheen answered, "He goes there about once a week or so to check up on his managers. He finds it more relaxing to work at home."

Mr. Mahi's butler welcomed them into the entry hall. Kelly had a clear view of Fahrina lying topless in a bikini beside a glass enclosed swimming pool, toasting in the bright January sun. She had a lovely uniform suntan on her large breasts and exposed body.

In the study, Mr. Mahi greeted them and immediately asked how the briefings went.

Kelly was happy to reply, "The briefings went very well. Your call to the Shah took care of the budget problem." But then he went on, "However, now we have another problem. General Hatami wants to drop the Israelis from the project because of objections from the Homofahrs. And if we change from the Israelis, the costs will go up because the Israelis had agreed to do their work for a fixed price of $200 million!"

"How much more?"

"The price of the installation and antenna segment could more than double because of the higher American labor costs. Also, the schedule might have to be extended by several months."

"So we're looking at an additional $200 million."

"That's about it, Sir!"

"The Shah won't be sympathetic to the Homofahrs' feeling, and he certainly won't be willing to dig up another two hundred million."

Mr. Mahi excused himself, strode to his desk, picked up his phone and dialed. He spoke for several minutes to someone in Farsi. He returned to the sitting area where Kelly and Shaheen were waiting and announced, "I have just spoken to the Shah-an-shah. He said it was General Hatami who runs the air force, not the Homofahrs, and he will explain that to the general. The Shah pointed out we need the Israeli's help. They did a good job on Karg Island and they'll do a good job on IBEX."

Kelly responded, "I'm surprised the Shah supported the Israelis so strongly. Doesn't he worry about his Arab neighbor's hatred of Israelis?"

Shaheen interrupted, "Brad, let me tell you about an interchange I overheard between the Shah and Prince Sultan of Saudi Arabia when the prince was visiting Iran. I was in the security force helping to protect the Shah when he met the prince on his arrival at Mehrabad Airport.

"The prince, seeing an El Al airliner on the tarmac when he stepped out of his royal 747, said to the Shah, 'When are you going to stop the infidel Israelis from flying El AL to Iran?

"The Shah replied calmly, You must be mistaken, Prince Sultan. El Al doesn't fly to Iran."

They all laughed as Mr. Mahi led them back toward the entrance. Fahrina was still sunning by the pool. Kelly said, "Mr. Mahi, thank you very much for solving my latest problem."

"Dr. Kelly, it takes a Persian to understand a Persian problem. That's why you need a knowledgeable Iranian like me when trying to do business in our country. Thank you for bringing me up to date. Remember to phone me at the Beverly Hills Hotel about 10am on the tenth of February so we can set up a meeting time with your corporate attorneys."

Shaheen dropped Kelly at the Hilton and arranged to pick him up at 6 the next morning to take him to the airport. Kelly found the girls had already left. Without them his presidential suite seemed enormous and lonely and empty. The phone rang, shattering the oppressive silence.

"Dr. Kelly, this is Fahrina Mahi. I wonder if I might come to visit you this afternoon?"

"I'm glad you called. I'd love to see you. Can you stay for dinner?"

"Thank you, I'd love that. I must confess I'm having problems adjusting to life in Iran after being away at school for eight years. I'm eager to talk to a technically educated American like you."

"I'm flattered, Fahrina. Come as soon as you like. That meeting with your father was my last appointment before I fly back to Los Angeles in the morning."

"In that case, I'll be over very soon. I have to get out of my bikini and into more suitable clothing for the Hilton."

"Then we can have lunch together, too."

"Great! I'd love that, too."

Fahrina arrived at Kelly's suite just before 1, wearing an afternoon dress that looked like the latest Paris style. The blue-green silk matched her eyes. Kelly greeted her with a handshake.

She smiled, "Why are you being so formal?" She grabbed Kelly, hugged him and kissed him passionately.

Kelly said, "But, you're the daughter of the man my company expects to use as our agent here in Iran."

"Of course. I'm also a member of my father's firm. I'm better educated than any of his other employees. My father has his ways of doing business and I have mine." She kissed Kelly again.

Kelly grinned, "Fahrina, I promised you lunch. We have the rest of the afternoon for lovemaking."

Fahrina corrected him, "No, we have the rest of the afternoon *and* the night for lovemaking. Where shall I put my overnight bag?"

Kelly led her to the large bedroom closet that Christina and Olga had emptied when they left, "You may hang your things here. While you're getting ready, I'll order lunch. What do you want?"

"Champagne and lobster. I don't like anything heavy for lunch."

Kelly ordered from room service and the waiter quickly brought the lobster and champagne plus a green salad.

Fahrina waited in the bedroom until the waiter finished setting up the repast in the dining area. Then she walked back into the sitting room. Her suntanned breasts and nipples showed clearly through the short, white, transparent gown and her blonde pubic hair curled around the tiny, black bikini panties. She proposed a toast by raising her glass, "To the success of IBEX!"

"I'll drink to that. And to the success of your father's company's participation."

"Did you know I'll be working on IBEX here in Tehran?"

"No. For the air force?"

"No, I'm the Director of software development at Iran Software, Ltd. You do remember you agreed to a 75 million dollar subcontract to ISL, don't you?"

"Well, I wouldn't say I agreed, but I plan to propose this to my company's top management."

"Brad, let's be frank. *No subcontract to ISL, no contract to Associated Aviation.* It's that simple. This is how things work in Iran."

"OK, I understand that. Assuming your father's company does get the subcontract, what is your technical background to do the work?"

"I went to MIT in Boston for my BS in electrical engineering and then spent four years in Zürich at the Eidenossishe Technische

Hochschule where I received my PhD in mathematics with a minor in electrical engineering. At ETH-Zürich, sometimes called in English the Federal Institute of Technology, my PhD dissertation was on the *Mathematics of Cryptology*. Working under Professor Dr. Rudolph Halter, I developed some new mathematical rules, or algorithms, for encryption and decryption of messages. Professor Halter thought they were so good that ETH-Z offered them under license to a Swiss industrial firm called Cryptomatik, in the Oerlikon area of Zürich. They've used my algorithms in a new, microprocessor based, cryptographic machine that can take words spoken into a telephone, or typed into a telex machine, and turn them into a secret code that can only be understood by someone with a matching machine at the other end."

"Wow, Fahrina, I'm impressed. We plan to use that type of equipment in IBEX, but, of course, we'll get it from an American firm, probably Datamatic in Dallas, Texas. We feel American cryptographic equipment is best."

"Maybe it was at one time. But I think the Swiss equipment is best now. Cryptographic technology in Switzerland is driven by the secrecy needs of Swiss banks. American cryptology is driven by national security. In Switzerland, bank security and national security are two aspects of the same thing. Without the secrecy of their banks Switzerland doesn't have a viable economy."

"Fahrina, I'll keep that in mind, but right now the plans call for American equipment. By the way, if your cryptographic algorithms are so secret, how did you publish them in a PhD dissertation which can be obtained by the public?"

"I used the so-called *public key* concept. In other words, with the public key, anyone can encrypt a message, but without the matching secret key, no one can decode it."

"I think I read something about public key cryptology in the *Scientific American* magazine."

"Yes, I read that recent article, but my idea goes far beyond that."

By this time, Kelly and Fahrina had finished their lunch and were feeling the effects of the champagne. Kelly suggested, "Enough of this business talk, let's dance." He tuned in some soft, sweet music on the hi fi.

Fahrina threw off her flimsy top for the dancing, which didn't last long. They soon tumbled into bed. Fahrina showed Kelly some Persian lovemaking techniques he hadn't realized existed. Their lovemaking continued on throughout the afternoon and evening with occasional two hour naps to recover their vigor. Neither remembered dinner.

Kelly's internal alarm woke him up at 5am. He gave Fahrina a goodbye kiss. She mumbled a goodbye to him before she rolled over and went back to sleep.

Amazingly, Shaheen was on time to pick up Kelly in the Hilton lobby. As they drove towards Mehrabad Airport, Shaheen warned Kelly again that Savat knew the Fundamentalist Moslem terrorists were after him and any other American working on IBEX. "Savak can protect you while you're here, but you're on your own when you leave."

"Thanks for the warning, Shaheen. I'll try to be careful. In the US, unfortunately, I can't expect the protection you've given me here."

"I understand. Your FBI is too busy chasing white collar criminals and the Mafia to protect US citizens from foreign terrorists."

As Kelly got out of the car at the airport entrance, Shaheen added, "You'll be watched by one of the Savak members to see that you are safe until your departure."

Kelly scanned the departure board listing and found a British Airways flight leaving non-stop for London at 7:30. At the ticket counter, which was operated by Iranair, even for the foreign airlines, he asked the ticket agent for a first class ticket on the London flight.

The agent responded, "I'm sorry, Sir, that flight is sold out."

With a wry smile, Kelly handed over his passport with a one hundred dollar bill sticking out and said, "But I must get on that flight. Can't you check on your computer terminal to see if there are any cancellations?"

The ticket agent took the hundred dollar bill and held up two fingers. Kelly peeled off two more hundred dollar bills and handed them to the agent along with his company credit card.

The agent smiled and said, "Why, how lucky. There is one first class seat available. That will be $637. Shall I put it on your credit card?"

"Yes, and thank you very much."

"We are always glad to accommodate American travelers."

Kelly went to the departure lounge, passing through passport control on the way. There was no place to sit in the crowded room. However, there was a duty free shop so he browsed through it. As soon as his flight was called, he boarded the jammed transporter bus for the ride to his plane sitting on the tarmac close to a row of Iranian F-14s. He noticed anti-aircraft gun installations spread around the airport.

Pushed along by the wave of humanity, all with the same purpose, he was propelled out of the bus and up the stairs into the British Airways L-1011 wide-body jet where he found his first class seat 2A, next to the window. The efficient stewardess poured him a glass of champagne and served black Iranian caviar. Kelly thought, *It's a bit early for champagne and caviar, but it is a long flight*. He finished his glass and the caviar while the aircraft taxied to the south end of the long north-south runway. The pilot shoved the throttles forward on the Lockheed Tri-jet and the take-off acceleration pushed Kelly back against his seat. As the aircraft took off, he looked out toward Tehran and felt an unexplainable relief to be leaving this strange country.

Chapter 8.

The Corporate Gods

Kelly woke up to hear the British Airways captain announce the approach to Heathrow Airport. Looking out the window he was treated to a rare sight: London with a crystal clear sky, so clear it seemed almost unreal. He could even see the British Channel off to the east. A large high pressure system had cleared out the London fog and smog.

The L-1011 taxied to the arrival finger at Terminal 2 and, as usual, Kelly was the first off the aircraft. He walked swiftly down the long corridor and took the escalator down to passport control. He queued up in the short line and showed his passport. Happy to have his carry on bag already in hand, he strode through the baggage claim area to the customs area and exited through the green Nothing to Declare gate. He was astounded to see Christina and Olga waiting there.

He hugged them both and asked, "How in the world did you know I was coming into London? I did everything I could think of so nobody would know."

Christina said, "Well, Brad, you can ask Amnon. He's out in the car waiting for us."

Kelly stopped to exchange $200 into British pounds as they walked through the terminal and out to the curb where they found Amnon arguing with an airport policeman who was determined to give him a ticket for loitering. When Kelly and the girls climbed into the car, the policeman gave up and waved them on their way.

Kelly asked Amnon, "OK, tell me, how did you know I was on this flight?"

"Easy. Savak sent an encrypted telex to the Mossad station in Paris. They phoned me at my apartment and, by pre-arranged code, said *Your friend is arriving in London at 0900.* That was 0500 Paris time. The girls and I caught the 0800 flight to London, arriving here at 8am, since London's an hour earlier than Paris. We had time to rent a car while waiting for you."

"Why'd you go to all this trouble?"

"To protect you from the terrorists. Where are you staying?"

"I don't have a room. I planned to go to the Hilton and take my chances."

Christina interrupted, "We assumed that. We've phoned and reserved a large suite in Amnon's name."

"As usual, you're way ahead of me. All three of you."

Amnon drove into London on M4 and followed Cromwell Road into Knightsbridge and turned left onto Park Lane to the Hilton. He turned the car over to the doorman and the quartet walked up to the crowded desk. It took Amnon a while to get checked in but as soon as he got the keys they all went up to the suite on the eighth floor. Two of the rooms faced Hyde Park and the third faced Green Park, across from Buckingham Palace.

"I'll spend the night here in your suite, if you don't mind, Brad," Amnon asked. "Mossad will pick up the tab. I assume you're flying on to LA tomorrow after your rest stop here, right?"

"Of course you can stay here, Amnon. It's in your name anyway. I'm planning to take a standby flight to LAX about noon tomorrow, either TWA 761 or the Pan Am non-stop. I haven't told anyone which flight I might take."

"That's a good plan. It definitely increases your chances of survival."

"After the close calls I've had, I'm a fast learner. Girls, where do you want to go for dinner?"

Olga responded, "Simpson's on the Strand. I love their roast beef and Yorkshire pudding!"

"Good idea. I'm tired of Hilton Hotel food. Is that OK with you, Christina and Amnon?"

They chorused, "Great!"

Kelly continued, "I want to buy some crystal for my wife. Do you girls know a good shop?"

Christina answered, "Yes! There's a great one just a short walk from the Hilton, one or two blocks."

"Good, let's go crystal shopping. Would you like to help me pick out some?"

The girls chorused, "We'd be glad to."

Amnon declined, "I'll wait here. I've some business matters to take care of on the phone. You should be safe, since no one knows you're here."

Walking through Mayfair, Christina led Olga and Kelly through the exclusive shops to one with many examples of fine crystal and headed for the Stuart's Irish crystal display. Kelly had no trouble finding the pattern he preferred. Helical lines spiraled down the stems and the deeply cut diamond pattern on the container sparkled brightly in the store lights. The girls liked it too. He ordered a dozen each of champagne glasses, water goblets, and wine glasses in two different shapes. The clerk promised to air express them to Kelly's home within a week.

They decided to have lunch in Holburn and then try to buy theater tickets for this evening. They caught one of the famous big, black London cabs to Cambridge Circus and then walked until they found a small restaurant just off Longacre. After lunch of spinach salad, trout, and white wine, they wandered through the crooked streets of the Holburn area until they found the Theatre Market. After much discussion, they decided to buy four tickets for *Man from La Mancha*, the musical version of Don Quixote. They strolled through Covent Gardens until about 5 when they took a cab back to the Hilton.

Amnon was glad to hear their plans for the evening. Since the show started at 8, they decided to have dinner early, at 6. Amnon suggested they take the London Metro instead of trying to find a parking space for the rental car. Dressed for dinner and a gala evening at the theater, they followed Amnon to the nearest Metro station, about one and a half blocks from the Hilton. They rode down the long escalator and took the next train headed towards Charing Cross Station. Once there, they walked the short block to the Strand, turned right, and continued on the short distance to Simpson's Restaurant. They climbed the stairs to the second floor and checked their coats with the costumed coat check lady.

The headwaiter, dressed in white tie and tails, led them to their four place table. The tuxedoed waiter took their order for an Italian red wine, La Savanella 1972. The *carvery cart* loaded with *joints* rolled up to their table and they ordered a mixture of roast beef and lamb carvings. Kelly had his favorite, an end cut of roast beef, which was served with a large piece of fluffy Yorkshire pudding and a heap of horseradish sauce. As they were finishing their dessert coffee, Kelly motioned to the waiter for the check and paid with his company credit card.

The quartet retrieved their coats and walked the short distance to the theater. They were all delighted with the excellent performance of *Man from La Mancha*. They hummed snatches of *Dulcinea* and *The Impossible Dream* as they rode back to the Hilton in a cab.

Once in their suite, they agreed to leave for Heathrow Airport at 9:30 in the morning to give Kelly plenty of time to get a standby ticket for one of the Los Angeles flights. Amnon and Christina headed for one bedroom, Kelly and Olga for the second. They dissolved into a twisting mass of lovemaking before dissolving into a deep, satisfied sleep.

Amnon, Christina and Olga dropped him off at Heathrow's Terminal 3 just after 10am and Kelly headed straight to the TWA Ambassador first class ticket counter where he asked for a standby seat on flight 761, non-stop to Los Angeles. He handed the pretty, young ticket agent his company credit card.

She typed a few keys on her computer and said, "Dr. Kelly, I can confirm you have a seat in first class on flight 761. The ticket is $780, standby fare. It leaves at 11:30 am this morning, arriving in Los Angeles at 3:30 this afternoon. Window or aisle?"

"I'll take a window, please."

She handed him a ticket and boarding pass and thanked him for the business. Kelly went upstairs to the TWA Ambassador lounge. After signing in, he ordered a glass of champagne and phoned his wife.

She answered groggily, "Brad, do you have any idea what time it is here?"

"Yes, Darling. It must be 2:40 am there because it's 10:40 am here.

"Well, anyway, it's nice to hear from you. How was your trip?"

"The trip was fine. I have some nice presents for you."

"That's lovely for you to remember me on these busy trips overseas."

"I want you to pick me up at LAX today. I'm on the same flight you and I came back on from Europe last October. Remember?"

"You mean......"

"Don't say it. Just be there."

"Oh, you're still being mysterious. But I know you have a good reason. I read about the London incident! I'll be there. Love you."

"See you then. I love you, too."

Kelly looked out of the Boeing 747 as it descended into the Los Angeles basin on a brilliantly clear January day. The visibility was more than one hundred miles! He could see San Clemente Island out beyond Catalina. There was a mild Santa Ana wind condition which brought warm weather to Los Angeles in the middle of winter. The captain announced the temperature on the ground was 85 degrees Fahrenheit or 29 degrees Celsius. A murmur of approval spread through the passengers. Although clear, it had been a bone chilling 20 degrees Fahrenheit or minus 7 degrees Celsius when they left London. Fifteen minutes later the huge plane was on the ground and taxiing up to the International Arrivals Terminal at the Los Angeles International Airport.

Kelly was first off the airplane and walked quickly through Passport Control and, with his carry on bag, beat the 747 horde through customs. He was met by his beautiful wife, Anna, and their five children. He hugged each in turn, then reached into his bag, pulled out their gifts, and passed them out. He kissed Anna and handed her three small gift packages from Tehran.

She opened the presents, one by one and exclaimed, "How lovely the ring is. The matching earrings are beautiful. I just love the necklace. You know my favorite color is turquoise." She put them on and added, "The girls in my bridge club will be so envious. Their husbands never go to the exotic places you do."

The children opened their gifts which Kelly had purchased at the Tehran, Paris, and/or Heathrow Airport gift shops. They added their thanks to their dad.

When they reached the family station wagon in the parking lot, Kelly let his middle son, who had just passed his driving test, drive home.   The other children scattered themselves on the remaining seats while Kelly and Anna climbed into the back seat. There Kelly handed Anna an envelope with the sales voucher from the crystal shop. "Here's another gift. They're shipping it from London by air express. It should get here next week."

Anna read the description of the crystal. She exclaimed, "I just love Irish crystal. But you must have paid a small fortune for them. They're at least $30 each in Buffum's."

Kelly grinned and replied, "They were only $11 each in London. See, there are some advantages to my being gone all the time."

"That's a small advantage. I'd much rather have you home all the time like my friends' husbands."

Kelly learned close to Anna and whispered, "I'll try to make up for my absence when we get to bed," and blew in her ear.

She whispered back, "You better! I missed you so much!" and kissed him on his ear.

One of the kids turned around and teased, "Cut out all that smooching back there."

Kelly and Anna just grinned happily.

Kelly had been gone for one week and had traveled about 22,000 miles, almost as far as around the world. When he went into his office early Thursday morning, his office mail had piled up and the letter tray was overflowing. He had just picked up the first letter when his phone buzzed.

Helen, Dr. Morrell's secretary said, "Welcome back, Dr. Kelly. Dr. Morrell wants to hear the results of your trip. Can you come over here right away?"

"OK, I'm on my way."

Kelly stuffed his small notebook holding his diary of notes from his trip into his briefcase and strode over to Morrell's office. As he walked up to Helen's desk, he called out, "Here's a small gift from Persia."

Helen pulled the turquoise earrings out of the package and exclaimed over their beauty.

Kelly replied, jokingly, "Helen, you're going to earn your gift. Here are my expenses. There are 68 rials to the dollar and $1.95 to the pound. Please make out my expense report." He handed Helen a thick envelope of used and unused airline tickets, hotel bills, restaurant receipts, and left over trip cash.

He added, "Please make me come out even. I had to do a lot of entertaining."

Helen groaned. "I'll do my best, Dr. Kelly. Now go on in. Dr. Morrell is expecting you."

"Welcome back, World Traveler. How'd it go?" said Dr. Morrell as he motioned Kelly to the large leather couch in his office.

"Well, I've got some good news and some bad news."

"Please! Start with the good news."

"The Shah approved increasing the budget to $1.2 billion. Our extra costs for site six are covered now and the Iranians accepted our rationale for making a sixth site."

"What's the bad news?"

"We're going to have to give Iran Software, Limited, a subcontract for the mainframe computers and standard software."

"For how much? And who the devil is Iran Software?"

"It's a company owned by Mr. Mahi, our new agent."

"Now, Brad, you know very well you can't commit Associated Aviation to the services of an agent. Our corporate legal staff and the board of directors have to approve all agent agreements now with the new Foreign Corrupt Practices Act."

"I explained that to Mr. Mahi. His response was, *You retain my firm's services and give Iran Software the subcontract, or else no IBEX for Associated Aviation!* His sales fee will be $50 million. That's the amount we had in the cost estimate. The subcontract will be $75 million. That's $25 million less than we had in the cost estimate."

"That's good that you're saving $25 million. And I'm glad you made it crystal clear you needed corporate approvals before he is officially our agent. He's probably right that we need him to get the contract. Our Washington staff did a background research on him and their report says he's the bastard brother of the Shah and that he handles all the big armament and aerospace sales in Iran. He'll be a good member of our team."

"Mr. Mahi will be in the Beverly Hills Hotel the middle of next month. He suggested we could all sign the agent's agreement then."

"Great. I'll be in town that week. Our attorneys will have to get all the t's crossed and i's dotted for his agreement. Then the board of directors will rubber stamp their formal approval. I'll tell them what Mr. Mahi said. They'll approve!"

"John, the next step is to re-write the paperwork I took to Iran and make it into a completed firm proposal that Tehran can use to give us a firm order. We need the firm order before we can apply to the US government for the export license."

Brad, get your team humping so the firm proposal will be ready to hand to Mr. Mahi when he's here, so he can carry it back to Iran."

"That's only ten days away. I hope the IBEX team has accomplished a lot while I was gone."

"I checked with your deputy, Tom Bradley, late yesterday afternoon. He said they've made excellent progress. The vendor price quotes should be in by Friday afternoon."

"Good. That means we only have to finish pricing the Associated Aviation part of the job and write in the part about Iran Software's subcontract. I think we can get everything ready for Mr. Mahi by the tenth of February."

"Don't forget, the chairman of the board has to approve a project this large. I'll ask him to be here on the tenth to put his signature on the proposal.

"I'm hoping to have the complete package, including all the details of the whole design, ready to take to the Pentagon and to the State Department by the end of April so they can make out the required licenses. I'll hand carry it to Washington and try to get their OK's in a hurry."

"Remember, *hurry* to the Washington bureaucrats means ninety days."

"Yeah, I know. We design the whole damn system in six weeks and they take ninety days to approve it. But that's the way it works for aerospace exports."

"Brad, you have to understand the point of view of the bureaucrats. Their main interest is following and enforcing the regulations."

"That's a sad commentary. Maybe we need another Boston Tea Party. Only this time the American Revolutionaries can throw the bureaucrats and their regulations into Boston Harbor."

Dr. Morrell laughed and said, "Keep me informed on your progress on IBEX."

"Yes, Sir. I will." Kelly picked up his papers and left. Walking by Helen's desk, he asked her to set up a meeting at 10 with the IBEX team.

She laughed, "I've already done it. I knew you'd want a meeting after being gone a week. By the way, looking over your expense vouchers, it looks like you didn't use the reservations I made for you."

"That's right, I didn't. I went a completely different way. And it's a good thing I did. Terrorists shot and killed someone they thought was me getting off the original flight in London."

"How terrible! Do you want me to keep making reservations for your trips?"

"I sure do. That gives me a better chance of slipping by them while they're concentrating on the scheduled flights."

Hurrying into the conference room, Kelly greeted the IBEX team members. Then he outlined the schedule for the firm proposal in February and the complete package for Washington at the end of April. He explained the adjustments he'd had to agree to in Iran and that the subcontract for the mainframe computers and standard software would go to Iran Software, Ltd.

David Elliott, the team member responsible for the computer hardware and software, interrupted, "But, we already have the prices and delivery schedules for the computer software and standard software from IBM."

"Don't worry, David, IBM will still get the business. Iran Software is their distributor in Iran, so they'll get their money from them instead of from us."

Kelly checked with the other team members to see how much progress they had made while he was gone. They agreed their next meeting would be Friday to discuss the delivery schedules of the equipment vendors and their prices.

Afterwards, Kelly returned to his office and began to plow through his piles of accumulated mail.

At the Friday meeting, Tom Bradley presented a summary of the quotations from the equipment suppliers and the updated cost estimates, with Iran Software Ltd. included.. The total came to $1.15 billion with a profit of 12% or $138 million.

"Wonderful," called out Kelly. "Now we have a $50 million cushion between our estimate and the $1.2 billion the Iranians have budgeted. I want that surplus put in the project manager's contingency fund. If necessary, I'll use it for overruns that may develop."

He continued, "The next step is to give the firm proposal to Mr. Mahi so he can hand carry it back to Iran. Then the Iranian Air Force can issue a firm order for IBEX. We need that order before we can submit the Export License application for approval."

Tom Bradley exclaimed, "That sounds like a *Catch 22*. What if the license isn't approved?"

"You're right, Tom, that's a big problem! We can't control the Washington bureaucrats. However, we do have an Ace-in-the-hole. The CIA Director wants that sixth site so he'll do everything he can to see that we get that license."

The team went over the suppliers and the equipment needed for IBEX. The encryption equipment had to handle two kinds of encryption. First, the communication data from the mountain top collection sites to the central processing station had to be encrypted, or coded, to prevent hostile forces from intercepting the messages and data. On the other hand, any coded communications and data from the unfriendly countries had to be intercepted and deciphered so that information about the strength of their armed forces and their intentions could be gleaned.

Dr. John Vries, the encryption/decryption expert on the team, reported on the status of his specialty. "I believe my decryption algorithms can determine what the *unfriendlies* are saying and what their data means. We'll use eight IBM mainframe computers, each working at a speed of eight million instructions per second, or

IPS. This gives us 64 million IPS's of computation power. Almost as much as the National Security Agency's Cray super computers, and their job is much tougher than ours. I tested the algorithms using simulations on our big corporate computers. We can take encrypted voices and produce clear or understandable voices. The same with data."

"John, that sounds fine. How about the other part of the problem, the encryption of our messages?"

"That part's easy. We just buy the equipment from Datamatic, Inc. in Dallas. Their stuff works on telephone, telex or radio communication systems. We don't have to worry about how it works. We just use it."

"Are you sure it's good?"

"The NSA and the CIA use the same equipment. It must be good."

Kelly stood and addressed the whole group. Gentlemen, it appears our preliminary design is sound. Your equipment and supplier choices seem to be good. Dr. Vries seems to have solved all the encryption problems. I think we have a winning system. Let's meet here next Friday for the final review of the firm proposal, ready to present to Mr. Mahi.

The team did their work thoroughly and the proposal was ready the next Friday morning. Kelly started the long and tortuous path of obtaining sign off signatures from the various echelons of management that had to approve the proposal. The signature list seemed unending: the Vice President of Engineering, the VP of Manufacturing, the VP of Quality Assurance, the VP of Contracts and Pricing, etc. Finally, Kelly was ready to present the proposal for sign-off by his boss, the President of Associated Aviation.

Kelly carried three copies of the proposal - each copy was two inches thick - into Dr. Morrell's office at 9am on Monday, February 10. Kelly was able to answer *Yes* to all Dr. Morrell's questions: "Have all the vice president's signed? Are you satisfied with the equipment selections? Are you happy with the Israeli and Iranian subcontracts? Do you think we'll make the proposed profit?"

"OK; Brad, I'll sign it. But, remember, if you're wrong, you'll be fired!"

"I understand, Sir. That's the chance aerospace project managers have to take."

Morrell signed. Then he said, "Brad, I want you in the meeting of the board at 11 today so you can answer any detailed questions. Also, bring a five viewgraph overview presentation."

"OK, I'll see you at 10 to 11. Now I have to phone Mr. Mahi."

Kelly dialed the Beverly Hills Hotel from his office. The hotel operator answered, "Beverly Hills Hotel," with a rolling lilt in her voice.

"Mr. Abfol Mahi, please."

"I'm sorry, Sir, Mr. Mahi has a *do not disturb* on his phone. He isn't accepting calls until noon today."

"Then please have him call me --."

"I'm sorry, Sir, Mr. Mahi doesn't return calls. You will have to call him back at noon. Goodbye." She hung up.

Kelly frowned. *Here's a man who will be given a $50 million fee and a $75 million subcontract for his company and he won't return a phone call!*

The long board room conference table had been carefully set for the chairman and his six man finance committee with a crystal glass, a china tea cup, a small plate of expensive cookies, a notepad in a leather folder and a copy of the IBEX proposal in front of each place.

At 10:55, Kelly met Dr. Morrell in the board room and described his attempt to phone to Mr. Mahi.

Dr. Morrell pointed out, "We'll be finished by noon. The chairman is never late for lunch."

At 11am sharp, the chairman and the six members of the board's finance committee strode into the board room, each dressed in a conservative dark blue suit, white cuff link shirt and striped tie, like a Harvard alumni re-union.

The Chairman of the Board opened the meeting, "Gentlemen, Dr. Morrell is presenting a proposal for a system called IBEX. It is a one point two billion dollar project. Without this business, our sales and profits next year will be disastrous. With this business, we will have the largest sales and greatest profit in the corporation's history.   Now, John, can you summarize the proposal?"

"Mr. Chairman, Dr. Kelly, our project manager, will present a brief overview of IBEX." He pointed to Kelly and sat down.

Kelly briefly explained his viewgraphs summarizing the IBEX system, the suppliers, and the pricing information."

At the end, the chairman asked, "Dr. Kelly, what are the risks to the IBEX program?"

"There are two: one, that the US government will not approve the export license, and two, that the costs will exceed our estimates."

"And how are you minimizing these risks?"

Kelly explained the sixth site to supply data to the CIA. And about the fixed price subcontract to the Israelis for the site preparation and the antennas, the largest risk area. He finished by revealing the fifty million dollar contingency fund against overruns.

"Good, Dr. Kelly. It looks like you've covered all the bases. OK, Gentlemen, let's sign!"

The chairman handed the signed papers to Dr. Morrell, "Congratulations, John. If you make a success of this, you can expect a big bonus next Christmas. If not, you'll get a salary cut."

Morrell replied, "Thank you, Sir. The success of IBEX is in Dr. Kelly's hands. I'm sure he will perform."

Kelly took the signed proposals back to his office and at 12 noon called the Beverly Hills Hotel and asked for Mr. Mahi.

The hotel operator responded, "I'm sorry, Sir. All three of his lines are busy, but you are first when one line clears. Oh, you're in luck, one of the lines just hung up. I'll ring."

A male voice with a slight Iranian accent answered, "This is Mr. Mahi's bungalow. Can I help you, please?"

Kelly replied, "This is Dr. Kelly. May I speak to Mr. Mahi?"

"I'm sorry, Sir. He is speaking to one of his important clients. Please hold and I'll connect you as soon as he is completed."

"But...." Kelly was on hold. Twenty minutes later, the same voice came on the line, "May I ask who is calling? Mr. Mahi is terribly busy. Are you sure you need to talk to him?"

"Yes, of course I need to talk to him. Why else would I call and wait for twenty minutes? My name is Dr. Kelly."

"Oh, yes, of course, Dr. Kelly. Mr. Mahi has been expecting you to call. Please be at bungalow three at 10am tomorrow. Thank you." He hung up.

Kelly heard the dial tone and thought, "At least we have an appointment." He called Morrell's office and told Helen about the scheduled meeting.

She responded, "But Dr. Morrell usually plays golf on Tuesday mornings with the chairman of the board of directors."

"Helen, we don't have any choice on the time or date. Please confirm with me after lunch."

"OK, Dr. Kelly. I'll do my best."

Helen called Kelly back at 1:30 and said, somewhat sheepishly, "Dr. Morrell said that time was fine. He also wants you to drive him and Mr. Bob Jones of Corporate Legal to the hotel. Pick them up in Dr. Morrell's office at 9:15 tomorrow. They'll have the agent's agreement and you're supposed to bring the proposals."

"Thanks, Helen, I'll be there."

"OK, and good luck. Dr. Morrell said I might not have a job if we don't get this contract."

"It may not be quite that bad, but the corporation needs the business. Otherwise, a lot of us may not be here next Christmas."

Chapter 9.

Approval Snag

Tuesday morning the eleventh of February, Kelly drove his wife's station wagon to work. He picked up Morrell and Jones at the Associated Aviation Corporate Offices on the Van Nuys Airport and headed south on the San Diego Freeway and crossed the Hollywood Hills. The Santa Ana wind was blowing warm air over the Los Angeles basin and the visibility was unlimited. At the summit of the pass the three men exclaimed about being able to see the Palos Verdes Peninsula clearly and beyond that Catalina Island.

Kelly remarked, "John, IBEX has cut into my sailboat racing. I haven't been sailing yet this year. I even missed the Midwinter Regatta last week. Fortunately, my oldest son upheld the family honor. He skippered our boat with the rest of the family as crew and they won first overall in the International Ocean Racing class."

"Brad, I must point out to you, IBEX is more important to your future than yacht racing. But, I understand your pride in your son's abilities. I hear he is a candidate for the 1976 Olympics."

"Yes, he won the Tornado World's Championship in Lugarno last summer and hopes to go to the Montreal Olympic Games this summer. He still has to win the US sail off in May to secure a berth on the team."

Kelly turned off the freeway and headed east on Sunset Boulevard. They drove along the winding street with multi-million dollar homes on either side until they reached the discrete sign on the left announcing the elegant Beverly Hills Hotel. Kelly continued a short way beyond the sign, turned left, and drove up the steep driveway to the hotel entrance.

The Beverly Hills was an older hotel, but quiet and luxurious, featuring guest cottages at premium prices. It was the unofficial headquarters for Hollywood, its producers, actors, and directors. The president of MGM lived just around the corner. It was said that more movie deals were consummated in the Polo Lounge and in the bungalows than in the offices of the major movie studios. The hotel also appealed to the new breed of millionaires: the armament dealers. The Iranians, Saudi Arabians and Israelis all mixed around the palm tree circled swimming pool.

Kelly turned his car over to the hotel doorman and led Morrell and Jones into the lobby. They were the only men there wearing business suits. The *uniform* for movie people, men and women, was faded blue jeans and T shirts. Kelly recognized a well known buxom blonde movie star with her latest escort, a six foot six inch African American football player.

The hotel dining room was straight ahead and the reception desk was to their right. Kelly stopped to ask directions. The clerk pointed out the back door and said to follow the signs.

They walked past the famous Polo Lounge, packed with the movie community, having breakfast and discussing deals and took the winding sidewalk leading to bungalow three. The path was lined with luxuriant tropical trees and plants, almost like walking through a jungle. An Iranian answered the doorbell and when Dr. Kelly introduced himself and his associates, invited them in, saying, "Mr. Mahi is in the next room on the phone with the Shah-an-Shah. He will be with you shortly. In the meantime, please help yourself to the refreshments."

The big, circular table in the center of the sitting room was loaded with tropical fruit, orange juice, coffee, and Danish rolls. Kelly, Morrell and Jones seated themselves on the large couch near the coffee table and helped themselves. About 35 minutes later, Mr. Mahi entered the room, wearing a wine colored silk bathrobe and fur slippers. He said, "Thank you for waiting, Gentlemen. The Shah-an-Shah was reviewing his latest shopping list with me. We need more American armaments, especially the IBEX system, for our company's security. He's worried about the advanced arms the US is shipping to the Saudis. He's afraid they will be turned against Iran."

Kelly replied, "There isn't much I can do about the US selling arms to the Saudis, but I can take care of our mutual business. But first, I'd like to introduce the president of Associated Aviation, Dr.

John Morrell, and this is Mr. Robert Jones, of AAC's corporate legal staff."

"Dr. Morrell, I'm pleased to meet you. I'm sure IBEX is as important to Associated Aviation's financial security as it is to Iran's national security."

"Mr. Mahi, IBEX is just another small program for Associated Aviation. We have a lot of large aerospace programs."

Mr. Mahi grinned wryly, "Dr. Morrell, please! Let's not try to bluff one another. We have performed a financial analysis of Associated Aviation and we know that, without IBEX, your country's financial future looks bleak for next year."

Morrell responded, "OK! We do want the IBEX business very badly. But IBEX is important to you, too, Mr. Mahi, and to your company, Iran Software, Ltd. After all, we are giving you a $50 million fee and your company a $75 million subcontract."

"Of course! That's what the armament business is all about. We all profit."

Kelly interrupted, "Mr. Mahi, first things first. Mr. Jones has the agent's agreement for you to sign. We need to formalize our relationship with you."

"Of course!"

Jones held out two copies of the agreement. Mr. Mahi quickly scanned the multi-page documents. "This looks like standard US aerospace *boilerplate*. It's OK with me." He signed both copies with a flourish. Jones signed one copy and gave it back to Mahi.

Mahi addressed Kelly, curtly, "Now that we have that formality taken care of, I have our firm subcontract proposal from my business, Iran Software, Ltd., prepared by my daughter Fahrina and her technical team. The firm, fixed price is $75 million, as agreed."

Kelly opened the document and looked at the computer prices, "Why, Mr. Mahi, these IBM prices are the same ones they gave us and they told us they were special low prices."

"Of course! I had a meeting with the president of IBM and I told him I wanted the same prices, with our mark up, that he offered you. Otherwise he would never sell another thing in Iran."

Kelly asked, "How long do you think it will take before we receive the firm order?"

"The Shah-an-Shah just told me you will get the order immediately if your price is $1.2 billion or less."

Kelly handed Mahi the AAC IBEX proposal and answered, "It's exactly $1.2 billion -- firm, fixed price. It's spelled out right here."

"Good. General Hatami is at home, waiting for my call immediately after our meeting. He is authorized to send you a telex order tomorrow. And the written confirmation will be sent via DHL, also tomorrow. You should have the signed contract by Thursday. Is that soon enough?"

His face covered with amazement, Dr. Morrell interrupted, "Mr. Mahi, you certainly do good work. Welcome to the AAC family!"

Kelly added, "We needed the order before we could apply for the export license. We had expected to wait two months."

Mr. Mahi came back with, "I know. The Iranian government will not hold up the export license. You can apply for it next week, can't you?"

"Not exactly! We have to prepare a very detailed description of the system for the Pentagon's review and approval."

"But, your proposal is five centimeters thick. It looks complete to me."

"Our final description will be twenty volumes long. It will stand two meters high."

"Mr. Mahi shook his head in disbelief, "You Americans certainly turn out lots of paper. I hope your hardware is as good as your paper is thick!"

"The Pentagon bureaucrats insist on a lot of details."

Mr. Mahi observed, "That's probably the main reason your armaments cost so much. We bought some air-to-air guns from the Soviets. Their price was a fraction of the offer from you Americans and their guns were better and more modern."

He clapped his hands. The well dressed Iranian came back into the room, opened a bottle of Mumm's champagne and poured four chilled glasses.

Mr. Mahi proposed a toast, "Dr. Morrell, Dr. Kelly, and Mr. Jones. May the IBEX project be successful and profitable for your company and mine. And, may the information it produces be useful to the security of Iran and be valuable to your American CIA!"

Dr. Morrell replied, "I'll drink to that!" Then he added, "I'm amazed at how rapidly your country will give us this order. I first heard of IBEX at Christmas time and now we'll have a firm order by the middle of February. Our government could never move so quickly."

Mr. Mahi nodded knowingly, "Dr. Morrell, there are two reasons for the apparent speed on my government's part. First, the Israelis have been working with our air force for over a year to define the concept. Second, your Dr. Kelly, presented a comprehensive briefing to General Hatami and his staff at the end of January which convinced them you understood the project and would be able to finish IBEX professionally."

Mr. Mahi shook hands to say goodbye to his guests and hurried into the other room to his telephone meetings. The Iranian escorted them to the door.

On the way back to Van Nuys in the car, Morrell asked Kelly, "When do you plan to take the IBEX package to Washington?"

"John, the documentation, all six feet high of it, will take until the middle of May. Then I'll go to the Pentagon."

"Brad, that's too late. You'll have to do it by the end of April."

"Well, we can speed it up but that will require overtime pay. I can't ask the team to work every week end on uncompensated overtime."

"OK, You've got authorization. Get humping!"

"Yes, Sir. I'll have the package ready for your approval by Friday, 24 April. I'll leave for Washington the following Monday."

Kelly and his team worked 64 hour weeks for the next nine weeks preparing the massive documentation required by the Pentagon for export license approval. The team asked the company photographer take a picture of the IBEX paperwork piled next to a beautiful, young secretary who was 5 feet 2 inches high. The stack was almost twice her height.

All the company approvals were signed off by late Friday afternoon, April 24, 1976.   The AAC director of security personally escorted the huge package to Washington, DC, in the company Sabreliner, so the papers could be locked up in the huge safe in the company's Washington office over the week end. The security director would deliver the document to the Pentagon on Monday morning in time for Kelly's meetings.

Kelly took the 9am Sunday morning American Airlines flight from Los Angeles non-stop to Washington. For security reasons, he bought his ticket at the airport an hour before flight departure. There was a strong tail wind at their cruise altitude of 39,000 feet and the DC-10 arrived at Dulles early, at 3:50pm, after a 3 hour and 50 minute flight.

A bug-like transporter carried the passengers from the ramp where the DC-10 parked the short distance to the terminal. Kelly took a seat in the front so he would be first off. When he stepped into the building, he was greeted by Christina, Olga, and Yossi. He kissed the girls hello, shook hands with Yossi, and vocalized the question in his mind.

Christina replied, "Someone phoned Amnon a little after noon, our time, and told him you were coming on American flight 2, so we came to meet you. We stopped at the Roslyn Marriott and got a suite for you."

"Wow, what service! The US government never treats me this well in Washington."

Amnon was waiting in an Israeli embassy limousine parked in a no parking zone. An airport cop was glaring at the car, frustrated he couldn't ticket it because of the diplomatic plates. They quickly climbed in so Amnon could pull out of the forbidden area.

Amnon answered Brad's question, "Ralph Hauser told me you were coming to Washington this week with the IBEX descriptions. I knew you would take either the American, TWA or United non-stop morning flight from Los Angeles.   I asked the Israeli consulate in LA to send men to those three terminals early this morning to watch for you. The man at the American terminal phoned me at my hotel just as you entered your flight."

"Amnon, I'm sure glad the terrorists are not as resourceful as you are."

"Don't let down your guard. Yossi and I will watch over you here. But, be careful."

"I will be! Now, on another subject, since AAC has received the $1.2 billion order for IBEX, we have issued an order for the Israeli Aircraft Industries subcontract for $250 million. Here's a copy."

"That's great. I know General Izhack and General Yidron were pleased. Also, Colonel Ladrun sends his regards."

"Tell Colonel Ladrun we expect him to deliver the IBEX antennas in person in early August."

Kelly was so engrossed in his discussions that he was surprised when Amnon pulled up to the Marriott and announced, "Here we are. I'll see you and the girls later. I've got to get back to the embassy to send my evening telexes."

Christina handed Kelly the key to their suite as they rode up in the elevator. The rooms had a view in the late April sunlight of the Potomac basin ringed by cherry trees frosted in very pale pink blossoms. Kelly thought, *Washington is certainly beautiful in the Spring. Those trees were a gift from the Japanese government to the American government. I guess four seasons aren't so bad after all. We miss the change of the seasons in Los Angeles, with our endless summer.*

Kelly turned to the girls, "I vote for having a steak and champagne dinner in the room, then watching the x-rated movies on TV and making love all night!"

Christina and Olga chorused, "That sounds wonderful. Oh, Brad, we've missed you so much." They each kissed him passionately.

Kelly climbed out of bed early the next morning and left the girls sound asleep. He went down to the Marriott coffee shop and had a breakfast of orange juice, poached eggs, ham, and black coffee. He had in his briefcase the export license application and the cover pages, table of contents and unclassified summary of each of the twenty volumes of IBEX technical information. The full volumes would be given to the Munitions Control Desk in the Pentagon for safe keeping. They would be used for the upcoming extensive review by the Pentagon personnel and other interested agencies, such as the NSA and the CIA, which had to take place before an export license could be issued for such sensitive equipment.

Kelly walked over to his 9am meeting nearby in the State Department Office of Munitions Control in Roslyn with Mr. Jack Johnson, Director of OMC. He went through the security procedure and took the elevator to the fifth floor office. He told the receptionist he had a 9am meeting with Mr. Johnson and she told him to go right in.

After the greeting and introduction to Mr. Johnson's staff assistant, Kelly said, "Mr. Johnson, here is the export license application for IBEX and my cover letter explaining the attachments, which include the order from the Iranian Air Force, the summary of the IBEX volumes, and the copies of the subcontracts to Israeli Aircraft Industries and Iran Software, Ltd."

"Do you have an agent for IBEX?"

"Yes, Mr. Abfol Mahi, Iran Software is his company. Mr. Mahi's certification that he's not bribing any officials is also attached."

"Good. It appears you've covered all the points including our requirement to follow the Anti-corruption Act. We see Mr. Mahi's name on a lot of Iranian export license applications. He must be a busy man. Rich, too!"

"He seems to earn his fee. He solved two serious problems we had with IBEX in January by making just one phone call to the Shah. Also, he had the order to us just two weeks after I briefed the Iranian Air Force."

"We just hope he's not using his money to bribe officials in Iran. You understand, if you have such information, you are obligated to say so in the application, don't you? Otherwise, you'll be subject to severe penalties, like prison and fines."

"As far as I know, Mr. Mahi is clean."

"We hope so. You're too nice a man to go to jail."

The veiled threat made Kelly think, *The risk of doing international business is higher than I thought. It's not just financial risk for the company, there's also risk of personal prosecution if you make a mistake, even an innocent one.* He asked Mr. Johnson, "Is there anything else you need that I haven't given you?"

Johnson and his staff assistant carefully looked over the license application and supporting documents. Then Johnson replied, "No, Dr. Kelly. It appears everything we need is here. I assume, of course you are providing the complete technical documents to the Pentagon."

"Yes, our director of security is delivering all ten feet of them to the Pentagon International Operations Office this morning. They are Top Secret!"

"Good, that's the proper way to handle the classified documents. We're not set up to have Top Secret here in this office. We don't have enough staff or a big enough safe."

"Now for the important question, when can we expect to get the license?"

"Within three days after we're notified by the Pentagon that they've approved the case. You'll have to ask them how long it will take. I'll warn you, though, the NSA over at Fort Meade will be a key factor in the approval. And they like to take their own sweet time."

Back in his hotel suite, Kelly found the girls were still fast asleep. He sank into a soft chair in the sitting room and dialed Robert Hack at the Pentagon.

Hack answered the phone with, "How's the world traveler? And how's Olga?"

I'm fine and Olga's fine, too. She's asleep in the next room with Christina."

"You lucky dog. I guess you know your security office just delivered the IBEX documents to my office. They're six feet tall!"

"Wrong! They're ten feet tall."

"We can't fit them in our safe. I'll have to borrow vault space from the joint-chiefs-of-staff down in the basement. They have lots of room."

"I'm glad you've got the paperwork. I'd like to discuss the package with you this afternoon as I said last week."

"Brad, I know you have an appointment with me today, but I'd like to delay it until tomorrow, for two reasons. First, the NSA wants to look it over today and second, General Robertson is arriving late this afternoon from Tehran. He wants to come to the meeting. How about 10am?"

"OK, see you tomorrow at 10."

"Good. Don't wear out Olga. I'd like to take you and the girls out for dinner tomorrow night."

"That sounds great. I'll tell Christina and Olga. Until tomorrow!"

The next morning Kelly caught the Metro to the Pentagon and again took the long walk up to the fourth floor of the huge building, walked around the A ring to corridor 10, walked out to the E ring and turned right to room 1018. It was 10 minutes to 10 went he greeted Hack's secretary, Jeannie, "I have a ten o'clock appointment with your boss."

"I know. We got your huge stack of paperwork yesterday. If you're going to cover all those documents, I'd better reserve the conference room for two weeks, not two hours!"

"Don't worry, I have a one hour briefing that summarizes the ten feet of documents. Two hours will be plenty."

"Mr. Hack has something important to discuss with you. Please go right in."

Kelly found Hack reading the IBEX executive summary report. He looked up and said, "Please close the door. I have a favor to ask you."

"What is it, Bob?"

Well, with the new administration that came in this past January, I have a new boss appointed by President Mahoney's new Secretary of Defense. Since I came in during Nixon's administration, I'm about as welcome around here as a skunk at a dinner party!"

"How long do you have?"

"The new boss said I should plan on moving out by the end of the year. It'll take him that long to find a replacement."

"What can I do for you?"

"I would appreciate it if you would put in a good word with Dr. Morrell. I would like a corporate vice presidency, perhaps VP for International Business Development."

"Bob, you know we have to be very careful to avoid violating the Conflict of Interest laws."

"Don't be naïve. Every executive in the Pentagon packs his *golden parachute* before he leaves office. So let's not get legalistic. Associated Aviation needs help getting the IBEX license approved. I need help finding a new job. It's a fair trade."

"I see what you mean. I'll talk to Dr. Morrell when I get back to LA."

"Thanks, that's better. Now, what time shall I pick up you and the girls for dinner tonight? Is 7 OK? We'll celebrate the IBEX export license and my new job."

"Seven is fine. The celebration may be a bit premature, but I'll do my part if you do yours."

In the large conference room 4D1012 the colonels had distributed the IBEX volumes and were busily reading them. General Robertson was concentrating on the executive summary.

Kelly greeted him, "Welcome back to the States, General. I hope you find our IBEX description interesting."

"Dr. Kelly, it's always a pleasure to return to American after being in one of the third world countries. Iran is a difficult place to get used to. As for IBEX, I'll never find time to read all these technical pages. I'll get the important information from your briefing."

"I'll do my best. It'll take an hour."

"OK, Dr. Kelly, but before you start, I have some opening remarks to give to the Pentagon staff here. Gentlemen, I want you to understand IBEX is a very critical system for the security of the US and for Iran. As the new director of the US Military Assistance Advisory Group in Tehran, I can assure you we need the intelligence product that IBEX will provide, particularly about the Soviet Union. It will fill the gap not provided by our listening stations in Turkey and our *spy satellites*. So, I urge you to review the IBEX documents carefully and give your recommendations for approval, if warranted."

Hack added, "Gentlemen, I second General Robertson's remarks. As a representative of the Secretary of Defense for International Programs, I strongly urge you to approve this license case. Any delay will threaten US security interests in the Mid East and in the whole world."

General Robertson turned the floor over to Kelly who went through his briefing, without mentioning that without the program Associated Aviation Corporation would be a financial disaster next year.

There were a few questions. While Kelly was answering them, the secure red telephone rang. Hack answered it. At the end of a few minutes of intense discussion, he announced, "We have a problem with IBEX. That was the deputy director of the National Security Agency. He said NSA would not approve the export of the Datamatic cryptographic equipment to Iran. Now what?"

A deathly silence fell over the room. Everyone looked at Kelly.

Kelly thought a minute, then responded, "Cryptomatik of Switzerland has some new equipment that would probably work for IBEX. Mr. Hack, can you check back with NSA and see if that would be an acceptable alternative?"

Hack answered, "We have to break for lunch now. I'll phone the deputy director back right after lunch. Dr. Kelly, call me at 2:30, I should know by then."

"I'll call you then. Thank you, Gentlemen, for your attention."

General Robertson added, "Thanks, Dr. Kelly, I understand IBEX much better now. I hope you can resolve your problem with NSA. A no vote by them means *no IBEX.*"

Kelly returned to the Marriott to find Christina and Olga watching a film on TV and drinking champagne from the room refrigerator bar.

Kelly said, "Girls, Bob Hack is picking us up for dinner at 7 this evening. I think we're going to a restaurant specializing in soft-shelled crab. I have the afternoon free except for a 2:30 phone call. What shall we do?"

The girls chorused, "Let's watch movies and make love!"

Right at 2:30 Kelly phoned Bob Hack and asked what the National Science Agency people had decided.

"No problem. They said any foreign equipment was fine. They think they can crack any foreign code, you know. So, revise your volume twelve, the part about crypto equipment and algorithms and we should be in business again."

"That's good. But it'll take at least three weeks to get a revision to you. We have to get with Cryptomatik in Zürich to get their offer and description."

"In the meantime, we'll start *staffing* your export license. I'll add a memo about the changes in volume 12. You see, I'm already on AAC's team."

"Yes, I see. Thanks for the good news, Bob. See you at 7."

Kelly returned to his *afternoon delight* followed by a refreshing nap. They got out of bed at 6 and showered and dressed for their dinner with Bob Hack.

Hack drove them to Annapolis to a restaurant overlooking Chesapeake Bay where they all enjoyed their soft shell crab dinner. Later that night at the Marriott, Hack enjoyed Olga and Kelly enjoyed Christina. As Kelly fell asleep he thought, *Boy, I'm glad I can sleep late tomorrow morning. No meetings. I'll try to catch one of the late afternoon non-stop flights to LA.*

Kelly looked out the window of the United Airlines DC-10 as it descended into the Los Angeles basin for the 8pm arrival. Low April fog had drifted in from the chilly Pacific Ocean and veiled the lights of the city. The captain reported the weather at LAX was 200 foot ceiling with one half mile visibility in fog. He added, "Don't worry, folks. With our automatic flight control system coupled to the instrument landing system, it will be an easy landing. Otherwise, we'd have to divert to Ontario or Las Vegas and then bus you the rest of the way to LAX."

The big jet pulled up to the passenger terminal and was connected to the waiting jetway finger. Kelly, with his carry on bag, was one of the first off . Almost immediately he located his family waving happily at him.

Anna hugged him and said, "I missed you so much."

Kelly whispered in her ear, "I missed you terribly, dear. I can hardly wait to get you into bed."

Kelly's oldest son said, "Dad, we're getting good at interpreting your coded phone messages. We had no problem figuring out you meant you'd be on the United non-stop."

The Kelly family piled into Anna's station wagon and headed for the San Fernando Valley. Kelly let his oldest son drive so he and Anna could cuddle in the back seat during the hour long drive home.

Chapter 10.

Cryptomatik

Kelly explained the crisis of the cryptographic equipment during his early Thursday morning meeting with his boss, Dr. Morrell. "NSA refused to approve the export of the Datamatic crypto equipment to Iran. Apparently, NSA believes US made equipment is far superior to anything made anywhere else in the world and that the US *superiority* should be kept strictly within America's borders. Certainly not shared with Iran, which they consider a third world country."

"Oh, boy! What do we do now, Brad?"

"When I was in Iran, Mr. Mahi's daughter told me about a cryptographic firm in Zürich called Cryptomatik, AG. She developed some algorithms for her PhD at ETH Zürich, the Caltech or MIT of Switzerland, that were licensed by that company. They're called *public key* cryptographic codes."

"Do you think these algorithms will work? And will the NSA go along with Cryptomatik as our IBEX supplier?"

"Fahrina assured me the algorithms work very well. I'll contact her and get the details. And NSA told Bob Hack *any* foreign equipment was OK. They say they can break *any* foreign code with their supercomputers."

"It looks to me like the next step is for you to go to Zürich and find out how much Cryptomatik will charge for their stuff and get a complete description of it."

"OK, Sir. Now, there's one other problem."

"Another one! This one sounds bad enough!"

"I'll put it bluntly. Bob Hack wants a vice presidency with Associated Aviation. He hinted that if AAC promised him a job by the end of the year, he'd make sure our export license was approved in a hurry."

"I see. It doesn't look like we have a lot of choice, does it? I'll have to take it up with our board chairman. The board's

compensation committee has to approve all vice president
appointments. I'll let you know as soon as possible whether or not
to have him come out for job discussions."

"It will help to have someone in the Pentagon pushing for
IBEX during the license approval process."

"I think you're right. I'll go to bat for Bob. You start
planning your trip to Zürich!"

On his way out of Dr. Morrell's office, Kelly stopped at
Helen's desk. "Please send the following encrypted telex to Dr.
Fahrina Mahi at Iran Software, Ltd.:

Attn: Dr. F. Mahi,
Urgent. Please call me as soon as possible.
Regards, Dr. B. Kelly."

Late Monday afternoon, Kelly received a phone call from
Fahrina Mahi. He exclaimed, "Am I glad to hear from you. I have
a problem and I think you can help solve it."

"Since I was coming to LA, I decided to wait to call you until
I got here. My father asked me to check on the IBEX project. I'm
at the Beverly Hills Hotel. Can you come to see me here
tomorrow? I'd have you come over this evening, but I just flew in
from Tehran via London with no rest stop. I'm exhausted and
wouldn't be good company."

"I can be there about one o'clock. Is that OK?"

"That's fine. Plan to have lunch here. Can you find a reason
to take an overnight *business trip* tomorrow so you can spend the
night with me?"

"Well, I'm supposed to go to IBM in San Jose to make sure
they are selling you the right computers. I could make that trip
tomorrow night."

"Great. But I can already tell you we are getting the right
ones. I met with their president in Tehran last week. Brad, I'm in
bungalow three. Can you find it?"

"Of course, that's the same one your father stayed in."

Kelly pulled into the Beverly Hills entrance just after 1pm and
turned the car over to the doorman saying, "I'll be spending the
night."

"OK, Sir. Have a nice stay."

Kelly carried his briefcase containing a change of clothes and toilet articles for his *business trip*. He walked through the lobby and out the back door to the path to bungalow three. It had been a typically foggy Los Angeles May morning, but now the sun was out and the sky was blue. The hotel pool to his left was surrounded by sun tanned patrons, sipping their early afternoon cocktails.

Fahrina answered the door, wearing a pink bikini, which was still wet from the swimming pool. "Brad, darling. Am I glad to see you." She grabbed him and kissed him passionately.

Brad returned the kiss. "Here's my overnight briefcase. But before we get involved in bedroom exercises, we have a business problem I must discuss with you, about IBEX cryptographic equipment."

"And before we discuss business, we'll have the lunch I promised you."

The doorbell rang. Fahrina put on a silk robe and let the waiter in. He set up a table in the middle of the room, with white linen, crystal, and silver and placed a huge platter of cracked crab on ice in the center. Next to it, he placed an enormous bowl of tropical fruit, including mango, papaya and fresh pineapple. He served the spinach salad with hot bacon and mustard dressing and opened a magnum of Mumm's champagne which he poured into two chilled glasses. He handed the bill to Fahrina to sign and then left.

Fahrina raised her glass, "Here's to the IBEX project and to our night of lovemaking!"

Kelly responded, "I'll drink to that! So let's get the business taken care of right away so we can concentrate on other things. The government has rejected our plan to use American crypto equipment, so I want to go to Zürich as soon as possible to talk to Cryptomatik about buying their equipment to use in IBEX. Can you help?"

"Of course. I know all those people. But the earliest I can leave here is Friday."

"Why so long? I had hoped to get there sooner."

"My father gave me some urgent family business to take care of in Los Angeles."

"OK, then. I'll leave Friday. I'll take the non-stop Swiss Air flight - standby."

"Why standby? With the early May tourists to Switzerland, you may have a problem."

"I'm still worried about terrorist attempts on my life. By going standby, they can't follow my route on the airline computers."

"I have a better solution. I'll make two first class reservations in my name and we can fly together."

Fahrina continued, "Great. I'll also make the reservations for a room on the top floor of the Zürich Hotel so we'll have a beautiful view of the Zürichsee. And I'll set up your appointments there." She picked up her phone, dialed a number, and spoke Farsi to someone. Then she explained, "That was my father's travel agent in New York, an Iranian, of course. Our reservations are made and confirmed on Swiss Air and in the hotel. Their Los Angeles office will deliver the tickets to me tomorrow. We leave from LA at 5pm Friday and arrive in Zürich Kloten Airport at 11:30 Saturday, May ninth."

She dialed another number and spoke German for several minutes.

After she hung up, Kelly asked, "Who the devil was that? How many languages do you speak anyway?"

"That was no devil, that was Dr. Heidi Zehnzeit in Zürich. And I speak five languages. Heidi is Professor Halter's assistant. We studied for our PhD's together. She'll meet our flight and will set up the meetings with Cryptomatik. She also suggested you meet with Professor Halter to hear about the latest algorithm research in cryptography. It's after 11pm in Zürich now so she'll have to call us tomorrow to confirm the meetings."

"Fahrina! You work fast!"

"Brad, remember. As an executive in Iran Software, I want IBEX to be a success as much as you do."

"I feel much more relaxed about our cryptographic problem now."

"Good. Then maybe you can relax enough to make love."

Kelly and Fahrina spent an afternoon and evening of lovemaking, interrupted only by an eight o'clock dinner break of steak and lobster in their room. The dinner renewed their passion, which was finally quenched at midnight.

Kelly awoke at 10am to hear Fahrina speaking on the phone in German. She turned and reported Heidi had been working while they were having fun and handed a hand written list of appointments to Kelly.

Kelly looked at the list, "There are no appointments on Monday, but lots on Tuesday and Wednesday."

Fahrina laughed, "That's because Monday is a Swiss holiday. We'll have to go to the beach or climb Utliberg mountain."

"Great! We'll have an extra day to get used to the nine hour time change. I'll probably need it. You really do good work, Fahrina. Since I'm on a *business trip to San Jose* today, what shall we do?"

"Thanks for the compliment. First, I've already ordered breakfast. Then, let's go swimming and sunning at the pool. After lunch, we can go to Rodeo Drive. I need some new jewelry. Don't worry, you don't have to pay for it. My dad gave me ample spending money for this trip."

"I like your plan. I really need the rest. I've been working sixty to seventy hour a week for the last two months."

"You Americans should learn to relax. That sounds like an inhuman work schedule."

"That's the aerospace business, Fahrina."

Kelly returned home from his *business trip* about 7pm. Anna greeted him at the door, "Hello, darling. How was your trip? I'm sure glad you're going to be home for a while!"

"I'm sorry to have to say this, but I've got to go to Zürich to buy some special secret equipment."

"Does that mean you'll be meeting with the *Gnomes* of Zürich?"

"Not exactly, but I understand the bankers, or Gnomes as you called them, use the same equipment to protect Swiss banking secrecy."

When do you leave?"

"Late Friday afternoon."

"Do you need me to take you to the airport?"

"No, I'll take the company chopper. That way we can fly over the horrible Friday afternoon traffic."

"If I didn't know better, I would think you had a secret lover on the flight you didn't want me to meet."

Kelly replied as smooth as oil, "Don't be silly, darling. I couldn't possibly accommodate a secret lover. You keep me too busy making love to you."

The next morning, Kelly went to Morrell's office to explain the plans for his trip to Zürich. Helen greeted him, "Good morning, Dr. Kelly. How was your trip to San Jose? If you'll give me your airline stubs, I'll prepare your expense report."

"The trip was fine, but I drove up there, so I don't have much of an expense report. Just mileage and dinner and lunch."

"That's easy. Is eight hundred miles about right for the mileage?"

"Yes, that's fine. Also, $50 for the meals. Can I see the boss now?"

"Go right in."

Morrell started by asking, "What are you doing to solve the crypto problem?"

"John, I've already got meetings set up with Professor Halter and the Cryptomatik people. I leave Friday afternoon, May eighth."

"Good, that leaves you a little time to make the changes to volume 12 before you leave. Will it be a big change?"

"I'm not sure yet. I have Dr. Vries working on it."

"Good. I'm leaving for Washington, tomorrow and then plan to spend a few days skiing in Sun Valley, providing all the snow hasn't melted, that is."

"I understand there's a late Spring Arctic storm moving down into the Rockies from the Gulf of Alaska. You'll have snow all right, don't worry!"

"I hope you're right. I'll see you when you get back from Zürich. Good luck."

Kelly held a meeting with his IBEX team in the conference room to summarize the changes they'd have to make in volume 12 because of the switch to Swiss equipment. Dr. Vries told Kelly to be sure the Swiss used an RS-232C interface. Kelly had to ask what that was.

Dr. Vries explained, "That's the standard serial data interface that lets computers *talk* to other pieces of equipment like printers and terminals. In our case, the computers will talk to the cryptographic equipment."

"I'll be sure to check on that point. Will that be difficult for Cryptomatik to do?"

"No, not at all. In fact, I would be surprised if they didn't have this interface on their equipment, anyway."

"How will it affect the system if they do use this RS-232C?"

"It'll make everything easy. They won't even need to bring their equipment here to connect with the rest of the system. They can ship their stuff directly to Tehran for integration there."

"That'll help us keep to our schedule. You begin revising volume 12 assuming the standard interface will be used by Cryptomatik. I'll phone from Zürich as soon as I know. Then you can have the revised volume ready by the time I get back."

Kelly boarded the company helicopter on the roof of Associated Aviation headquarters at 4pm on Friday, 8 May, 1976, with his carry on suitcase and his briefcase full of papers. In only a few minutes, the helicopter landed on the ramp at Los Angeles International Airport next to a Swiss Air 747. Kelly ducked under the whirring blades, waved goodbye to the pilot, and scrambled up the stairs to the departure lounge.

Just inside the door, Fahrina threw her arms around him and kissed him hello. She said, "Here are the tickets and boarding passes. They just called pre-boarding and first class so we can go right on the plane."

"Great! Let's go!"

Kelly and Fahrina walked through the departure gate for the Swiss Air flight. Fahrina handed the boarding passes to the gate attendant and they both showed their passports. They walked down the jetway, entered the front cabin door, and turned left to their first class seats. Fahrina had the window seat and Kelly was next to her, seats 4A and 4B, with a perfect view of the movie screen. The pretty Swiss stewardess served them each a glass of champagne and hors d'oeuvres immediately after they were seated. She gave them an elaborate menu so they could contemplate the gastronomic pleasures that awaited them during their journey.

At 5pm sharp, Kelly felt the *push back* from the gate and knew they were on their way. The captain started the four large jet engines and taxied to runway 24 right on the north side of the field. The fog had rolled in and the runway was barely visible. The captain received his take off clearance from the airport tower and turned onto the west facing runway. He added power to the engines and the huge 747 lumbered down the runway, loaded with enough jet fuel to fly eleven and a half hours non-stop to Zürich. The giant aircraft lifted off the runway and was immediately in the fog bank. A few more seconds and the plane broke through the low overcast and climbed out over the Pacific Ocean, then turned right towards the great circle route to Europe. Kelly showed Fahrina the mountain peaks of Catalina Island poking through the dense cloud bank. He told her he missed the annual Ensenada race from Los Angeles to Mexico because of IBEX. His eldest son had skippered their sailboat though, with the family as crew, and had won first in class, third overall. Kelly thought *Such is the aerospace business. Your hobby takes a back seat to the hobby of working all the time.*

Kelly and Fahrina reclined in their luxurious first class seats, preparing for the long polar-route flight. Their relaxation was interrupted by a gourmet dinner and two R-rated movies that Kelly had already seen on other flights.

Kelly woke up over the North Atlantic just as the sun was peeping over the horizon. The efficient stewardess served Kelly and Fahrina a hefty breakfast of omelets, ham, croissants, coffee, fresh fruit, and orange juice. Kelly checked his world time watch and noticed it was 10am, an hour and a half before their scheduled arrival. After breakfast, Kelly went into the first class head to shave before the landing. When he came out, he saw they were crossing the French coast near Calais. Shortly thereafter, the captain started the long descent into Zürich Kloten Airport. The gleaming snow capped Alps were to the south, on the right. He picked out Jungfrau Mountain from the peaks and remembered the winter holiday he spent with his family three years before in Interlaken at the foot of that mountain.

The huge 747 approached Kloten from the northwest. Fahrina pointed to the green wooded hill outside the right window. She poked Kelly and said, "That's Utliberg, a favorite hiking place for Zürichers on weekends." She also pointed out the azure Zürichsee extending some fifty kilometers south from the center of the city. Soon the plane landed and taxied up to the jetway at terminal 2, the International Arrivals Terminal.

Kelly and Fahrina cleared Swiss passport control, retrieved Fahrina's two enormous suitcases, and passed through customs. The were met at the customs exit by a beautiful, blue-eyed, blonde with very long legs, long hair, and firm, round breasts pushing against a tight blue sweater.

Fahrina shrieked, "Heidi!"

Heidi shrieked back, "Fahrina!" The two embraced and kissed each other on the cheeks.

Heidi added, "*Gruezi*, Fahrina. It sure is good to see you again, just like the good old days at ETH grad school."

Fahrina managed to introduce Brad. Kelly and Heidi kissed each other on the cheeks and exchanged *gruezi*'s.

Heidi noticed Fahrina's bags were too heavy to carry to the parking lot so she volunteered to bring her car around to the front of the terminal while Kelly and Fahrina wrestled the bags that far.

Five minutes later Heidi pulled up at the terminal entrance in her bright red, sun roof BMW. The sun was shining brightly, the temperature was warm and the air was dry.

Heidi remarked, "We have a *froehn* wind today. It's the south wind off the Alps that compresses and makes it hot in early May, like Los Angeles' Santa Ana wind. We'll probably have warm weather all weekend. We can go to the beach at Zürichsee and maybe even go in the water. It's still only 18 degrees Celsius."

Fahrina added, "I like the beach at Tiefenbrunnen best. Brad, I'm sure you'll love it there, especially the girls."

"What's so special about the girls at Tiefenbrunnen?"

"You'll see when we get there."

Heidi drove out of the airport and followed the signs toward Zürich centrum. They left the autobahn and headed south until they arrived at a black, high rise building, the Zürich Hotel, near the center of the city. The doorman unloaded Fahrina's huge suitcases and Kelly carried his bag and briefcase into the lobby. While Fahrina was registering for the twentieth floor suite, Kelly invited Heidi to join them for dinner that evening.

"I'd love to. I'll be back about 6pm. You two probably need a nap after your long flight."

Fahrina returned with the key and Kelly explained the dinner plans. Fahrina added, "Heidi, when you come for dinner, bring your overnight bag. I think we should show Brad the *Swiss way*, two girls at once."

Heidi replied, "I'd love that. Are you sure it's OK with Brad?"

Brad answered for himself, "It sounds like ecstasy to me!"

Fahrina added, "We're in suite 2010. *Auf wiedersehen.*"

"*Auf wiedersehen.*"

Kelly and Fahrina headed for the elevators at the back of the large lobby. The lobby was full of foreign visitors, Iranians, Arabs, Japanese, Americans, all with money, some to spend and much more to place in safe keeping in the Zürich banks. The Swiss banks have numbered accounts to give full secrecy for both the individual client and for his money, a safe haven for wealth in a turbulent world. The banks also provide full financial services for their clients: stock trading, long and short term bonds, commodity futures, foreign currency options, etc., - a myriad of ways to protect money and make it grow.

The elevator zipped Kelly and Fahrina to their suite on the top floor. One room faced south, overlooking the picturesque Zürich Stadt (city) and the beautiful Zürichsee, which fed the swift flowing Limmat River, dividing the city. The *left bank* included the stylish shops and banks on Bahnhofstrasse, a fashionable daytime walking street reminiscent of Rodeo Drive in Beverly Hills. The *right bank* included the night walking street, Niederdorfstrasse, lined with night clubs and restaurants for the evening crowds. Fahrina pointed out some of the well known peaks such as Jungfrau and Santis among the fabulous, snow capped Alps some sixty to eighty kilometers to the south.

Nearer by, Kelly admired the Zürichsee, littered with the white sails of many large and small sailboats, cruising and racing on the huge Swiss lake, called a *see* in German.

The other room gave an intimate view of the Limmat River and park with the Landesmuseum where the glacier fed Sihl River converged with the Limmat. Beyond lay the Hauptbahnhof, the main train station for the efficient Swiss railway system that handled thousands of passengers every hour. Brad had an irresistible urge to go walking through the beautiful city.

Fahrina quickly agreed. "I'd love to take a walk down Bahnhofstrasse and look in the jewelry and clothing shops. A dollar goes fifty percent farther here than in Beverly Hills."

Without even unpacking their suitcases, the two changed into informal clothing and headed for the lobby. Brad asked if they should take a taxi.

Fahrina replied, "Heavens, no! Let's take the tram. Number 14 is only half a block from here and it goes straight to the Hauptbahnhof. From there, we can walk south on Bahnhofstrasse and see all the beautiful shops. Saturday afternoon is ideal. The shops stay open until 4:30. Then they close for the weekend."

"How much is the tram?"

"Practically nothing. For the cost of the taxi ride, five Swiss francs, we can buy two Day Passes or *Tageskartes* that let us go anywhere on any tram for twenty four hours."

"How much is five francs?"

"About two dollars"

"Let's go!" They barely had time to buy their Tageskartes before the two-minute-spaced tram came by. As the tram passed the jammed Saturday afternoon automobile traffic, Fahrina remarked, "See! If we had taken a taxi, if would have cost twice as much and taken thirty minutes to get here!"

Brad couldn't help remarking, "The Swiss seem to design their cities for people. We need a public transportation system like this in Los Angeles, but we'll probably never get one. It would cost billions of dollars."

In five minutes they got off at Bahnhofstrasse and started their stroll down the street, lined with elegant shops plus several Zürich banks. There was little automobile traffic on this three or four block stretch, except for several limousines and Mercedes parked in front of each bank - presumably the car passengers were visiting their bankers and their secret bank accounts.

As the pair strolled by the Union Bank, Kelly remarked, "Perhaps I should set up a numbered bank account."

Fahrina looked surprised. "You mean you don't have your money in a Swiss bank? My family has had our money here for as long as I can remember. We'd never trust our wealth anywhere else."

"I'm too busy on this trip. Maybe some other time."

"Brad! You really should. What if there should be a revolution or another financial crash in America?"

"I guess I'd just lose everything."

They stopped in front of a jewelry store window and Fahrina admired a large emerald ring with matching necklace and earrings marked 17,000 Swiss francs. She exclaimed, "Oh, I love it. Would you mind coming inside while I buy it?"

"Of course not."

While Fahrina was busy buying the emerald jewelry, a beautiful red headed Swiss clerk served Brad a demitasse of coffee with brandy. Brad grinned to himself, *This is the way to shop. And I don't have to pay for it.*

After the purchase, they continued their stroll down Bahnhofstrasse to Paradeplatz, the central interchange point for the city trams. They crossed to the east side of the street and started back towards the Hauptbahnhof, still admiring the shop windows. At Saint Petersstrasse, Fahrina suggested turning right to walk through the old city. She pointed out some buildings that dated back to 1400 or even earlier.

"That's fascinating. Nothing is that old in the US except Indian ruins."

On the Rathaus Bridge across the Limmat they stopped to look southeast at the beautiful view of the twin church towers of the Gross Munster. The city hall clock said it was almost 5, and Heidi was due at the hotel at 6.

Brad asked, "How do we get back? Walk?"

"No, that's what we bought the Tageskartes for. We'll catch the number 4 tram back to the train station and then transfer to the 14. We'll be back to the hotel in ten minutes."

Kelly was dressed to go out for dinner and Fahrina was in the bathroom finishing her make up when Heidi rang the room door bell. She was wearing a tight silk dress with a low cut top, displaying her generous bosom. Kelly offered her a drink.

"Champagne, please," Heidi called over her shoulder as she headed for the bedroom to stow her overnight bag.

Kelly found Mumm's and hors d'oeuvres in the room bar refrigerator. Heidi came back into the sitting room just as Fahrina walked in wearing a short, pale green dress with her new emeralds.

Kelly remarked, "Those emeralds look fantastic with that dress."

Fahrina explained she had bought the dress on Rodeo Drive and the emeralds that afternoon.

Heidi exclaimed, "I see you still have *wunderbar* taste in clothing and jewelry."

"I also have *wunderbar* taste for love making, as you know. But first, where shall we go for dinner?"

Heidi replied, "There are many fine restaurants in Zürich but the one here in the hotel is great. If we eat here, dinner won't cut too much into our time for love making."

Brad agreed and made 7pm reservations so they would be though by 8:30, leaving lots of time for fun and games in the bedroom. He said, "I'm looking forward to enjoying two luscious morsels, for dessert, so to speak!"

The trio finished their champagne and hors d'oeuvres and took the hotel elevator to restaurant. They had a special Swiss dish: fondue Bourguignon - pieces of meat cooked on skewers in hot oil in a fondue pot at the table so each diner cooked his or her morsels to his or her own taste.

After dinner, they returned to the suite and quickly undressed. The girls went into one bathroom to wash with the spray douche and Kelly did the same in the other bathroom. When he came back to the bedroom he was surprised to see Heidi and Fahrina had already started the evening's festivities. Fahrina was sucking Heidi's breast and Heidi was licking Fahrina's breast.

Kelly interrupted, "Isn't there room for me?"

Heidi answered, "Of course. We were just getting warmed up. I hope you're not offended by girls playing with each other. "

"Don't worry. Nothing offends me in bed," added Kelly as he joined the girls.

They tried every way they could think of for two girls and one man, then dissolved into a deep sleep with everyone intertwined.

In the morning, Kelly awoke to find Heidi already up and dressed. She said, "That was a wonderful evening. We'll have to try it again. But now I have to hurry to take my mother to church this morning."

Brad replied, "It was wonderful, Heidi. And thanks for setting up my business meetings."

"We still have two more days until you have to worry about work. I'd like you and Fahrina to meet me at the beach at Tiefenbrunnen at noon today."

"OK. *Auf wiedersehen!*"

When Fahrina woke up later, Kelly delivered the message. Fahrina suggested snoozing for another hour, then having breakfast. Kelly agreed and climbed back in bed. Fahrina turned over, grabbed Kelly, kissed him passionately. Their *snooze* turned into an hour and a half of love making before they got up for breakfast.

Then they put on their informal clothes, packed towels and swimsuits in a plastic bag and headed for the beach. They used their Tageskartes to ride the number 4 tram to the end of the line on the east side of the Zürichsee, about two kilometers south of the city center. An underpass took them under the road to the Tiefenbrunnen *bad*, a small green grass park right on the edge of the *see* with large rocks perfect for spreading out towels and lying in the sun.

"Now, where's Heidi?" asked Brad.

Fahrina answered, "She'll be right out on the point, reserving our sunning rocks."

It was only a few moment's walk to the point. There was Heidi, topless, in a tiny pink bikini, lying in the sun. There were several girls and women, some in their fifties, all topless and all with uniform tans on their bodies and breasts. A healthy looking group.

Kelly stared in amazement. "I didn't realize this was a topless beach. We don't have such things in the US."

Heidi laughed. "We Swiss are not ashamed of our bodies. We have long, cold winters so when May and the warm weather arrives, we like to enjoy the sun completely."

Fahrina added, "Brad, get your swimming suit on so we can enjoy the sun, too."

"Where do I change? I don't see a bath house."

Heidi smiled. "There isn't any. Just take off your clothes and put on your suit. Everyone does it. Don't worry!"

By then, Fahrina was completely nude. She stepped into her yellow bikini bottom and said, "See, that's the way. Go ahead!"

Kelly complied with her request while looking around nervously at the other topless girls. They were ignoring him! It was a non-event as far as they were concerned. *Not like the US where nudity was equated to obscenity*, thought Kelly. *And in a moment I'll be having a business discussion on a public beach with two topless, female PhD's*. He lay on his back with Fahrina on one side and Heidi on the other and said, "Heidi, tell me what I can expect in my meeting with Professor Doctor Halter on Tuesday."

"Brad, Professor Rudolph Halter is a brilliant mathematician. He received his undergraduate degree in physics at our Federal Institute of Technology, ETH, here in Zürich. Then he went to graduate school at MIT in Boston where he earned his PhD in mathematics. His dissertation was on cryptography."

Brad asked, "What aspect of cryptology?"

"I've never read it. The US National Security Agency, NSA, found out about his research when he published a paper on it. After they read the paper, they placed a secrecy order on all his research."

"That's a bit unusual, to place a secrecy order on academic research."

"Dr. Halter protested to the US authorities, pointing out he wasn't even an American, but a Swiss. The NSA wouldn't budge.

So he brought his knowledge, but not his notes or his dissertation paper with him when he returned to ETH as a math professor."

Fahrina added, "Heidi and I both wrote our dissertations on cryptology under Professor Doctor Halter."

Heidi interrupted, "By then, Dr. Halter had a new idea for cryptology, the *public key* code. He considered his new idea obsoleted all the old cryptology algorithms, including the ones the NSA declared secret.

Fahrina added, "The *public key* algorithm solved the problem of how to transmit encrypted code safely. Long ago they had to have code books at each end of the line, and the code books were always being stolen, or copied. And it meant a secret messenger had to carry the code book to the destination of the message before the message was sent, which meant there was no such thing as rapid secret communication."

Heidi went on, "In other words, using this *public key* idea, anyone can encrypt a message, but no one can decrypt, or decode, it except the intended recipient of the coded message. He alone holds the decryption key that matches the public encryption key."

Kelly commented, "That's a fantastic idea. For example, on IBEX, we can send the encryption key to Iran by open, un-coded telex. Then, even if the Soviets intercept the encryption key, they still can't un-code the message."

Heidi and Fahrina chorused, "Exactly. Now you've got it!"

Fahrina added, "We estimated it would take a supercomputer, working at a billion instructions a second, a thousand years to decode the message."

"But I think NSA has three supercomputers."

"Then it would take them only 333 and a third years."

"Well girls, I'll be old and decrepit in 333 years, so I guess it doesn't matter."

Heidi said, "Brad, I'll bet you would be fantastic in bed even if you were 333 years old. Remember Methuselah. He was 900."

Fahrina added, "Before we get off on sex again, you can change the code each day or even each hour, if you want to. This makes the decoding job virtually impossible."

"I wonder why the NSA said it would be OK to use any foreign equipment."

"They probably didn't know Professor Halter had licensed his new idea to Cryptomatik. They must think he's still writing academic papers on cryptology and having silly girls like Fahrina and me writing PhD dissertations based on his old ideas."

"How long has Cryptomatik had this capability?"

"Professor Halter has been a consultant to Cryptomatik since 1972. He works for one of his own former PhD students, Dr. Peter Dichter, the technical director."

"We PhD's have to stick together, don't we?" queried Brad.

Heidi said, "You mean like last night?"

"Heidi, let's not get off on sex again. I meant in a professional sense."

Heidi and Fahrina chorused, "Yes, of course! In a professional sense."

Heidi continued, "At any rate, it wasn't until the 16 bit microprocessor and the floating point co-processor became available in 1975 that the public key cryptographic equipment became feasible."

"You mean, like the 8086 and 8087 microprocessor in my home computer?"

"Exactly. Those exact microcircuits are used in the Cryptomatik equipment. They just started production in January of this year."

"How does the Cryptomatik equipment compare with the American Datamatic one."

"We don't know. Your NSA won't allow it to be exported. They want to keep US ideas secret. We think the Swiss equipment is far superior to anything the Americans have. After all, our banks have lined up to buy out the production line and their secrecy is much tighter than your American NSA or the CIA."

"Heidi, what's my business agenda this week?"

"Easy! On Tuesday, you spend the morning hearing about the public key algorithm from Professor Halter at ETH. Your afternoon is free. On Wednesday morning, I'll drive you and Fahrina up to Rengensdorf, about thirty minutes from Zürich. You'll meet Dr. Dichter, tour the Cryptomatik plant and have a demonstration of the equipment. After a typical two hour Swiss business luncheon, you'll return to firm up an order for the equipment. We should be back at the hotel by 4. Then, you're free to go back to Los Angeles."

"That sounds like a lot of information packed into two days, but with your and Fahrina's explanations, I feel I almost understand the public key concept already."

Fahrina said, "OK, enough of business now. Let's go swimming. We'll swim nude. The Zürichsee feels delicious on your bare skin."

Heidi and Fahrina stood up, stepped out of their bikini bottoms, dove into the chilly lake, and yelled, "Come on in, Brad. The water's great."

Kelly dropped his swim suit and checked to see if the other topless girls noticed. They could care less! And dove into the invigorating, blue water.

After an afternoon of sunning and swimming, the trio got dressed and rode back to the hotel in Heidi's red BMW. As Kelly and Fahrina climbed out of the car, Heidi said, "I'm inviting you two to my apartment in Triemli for dinner tonight at 7. Bring your overnight bags. I want a reprise of last night in my big wide bed. Then Monday morning, we'll hike up Utliberg."

Before Kelly could ask, Fahrina told him, "That's the mountain west of town I showed you from the airliner window as we were landing yesterday."

"Oh, is that it. OK, how do we get to your flat?"

Fahrina answered, "We catch the number 14 tram and ride it to the end. That's half a block from Heidi's apartment."

"Heidi added, "And the trail up Utliberg starts about half a block from my apartment."

"Sounds great. *Auf wiedersehen.*"

Kelly and Fahrina arrived at Heidi's one *zimmer* (room) apartment in Triemli, a section of Zürich made famous by the Sheraton Atlantique Hotel (at least with American tourists). Utliberg mountain rose some four hundred meters above it. Her apartment was a typical Swiss efficiency flat, one room that doubled as a living room by day and a bedroom by night by virtue of a hide-a-bed couch. There was a well equipped kitchen and a bathroom with a full sized tub with a hand held douche/shower above it. There was a large balcony off the main room with a spectacular view of Utliberg directly ahead, and of the Zürichsee to the left and in the distance. In the basement of the building there was a laundry room and a storage room for winter ski equipment since almost all Swiss people ski.

Heidi exchanged *Gruezi*s with Kelly and Fahrina and directed them to the small but elegantly set dining table in the main room. A flame heated round pot full of bubbling cheese fondue sat on the table and next to it was a large plate of bread cubes to be used for dipping into the melted cheese mixture. Heidi had also prepared a green lettuce salad with fresh vegetables and slices of large, white mushrooms, topped with a piquant salad dressing. A cold bottle of Spumante, the Italian version of champagne, sat in an ice bucket along with three chilled glasses.

The trio spent a happy dinner hour with convivial conversation about the Swiss way of life that emphasized outdoor activities and fresh, healthy food.

Afterwards, Heidi unfolded the queen size convertible bed and all three climbed in. Indeed, they had a delightful reprise of the love *au trois* of the previous evening, before falling into a deep and restful sleep.

The three arose early and had a refreshing continental breakfast of fresh bread, jellies, fresh fruit, yogurt, and coffee made with hot milk. They put on their hiking clothes and headed up the Triemli trail toward the summit of Utliberg. Three minutes after leaving Heidi's apartment they were deep in a magnificent green forest of evergreen and deciduous trees. The trail was well maintained by city workmen who kept the path covered with fine gravel for easy walking. Kelly had to stop to catch his breath half way up the steep trail that switched back and forth up the east side of the mountain.

Heidi laughed and said, "Brad, you're really out of shape. If you come to Switzerland for a month, I'll build up your body."

"I'd need that, after the way you tear it down in bed at night."

After Brad rested a while, they continued up the scenic trail. At the top there was a restaurant and a lookout point with a view all over Zürich and the Zürichsee. The *froehn* wind was still blowing and cleaning out the air so they could enjoy the panoramic view of the Alps to the south. Heidi suggested they go down by a different trail, one that led to Albisgutli. Then they could take that tram back to Tiefenbrunnen and spend the afternoon sunning and swimming again.

Kelly protested, "But, I didn't bring my swim suit."

Heidi replied, "But you do have on your bikini underwear. So do Fahrina and I. We'll wear that. No one will know the difference."

Heidi picked up Kelly and Fahrina at their hotel on Tuesday morning and drove the short distance to the ETH campus on the right bank of the Limmat River at the foot of Zürichberg, a mountain peak that faced Utliberg across the city of Zürich.

Heidi led the duo to the south wing of the main building. Professor Halter's corner office on the fifth floor had a panoramic view of the city with the lake in the distance. Professor Halter welcomed Fahrina back to Zürich and ETH with a stream of German. He hugged her and kissed her on the cheek, then turned to Kelly and said, "Excuse my rudeness, Dr. Kelly, conversing in German, but I'm so delighted to see my former PhD student return, particularly one as beautiful and intelligent as Fahrina. I'm very pleased to meet you."

"It's a pleasure to meet you, too, Professor Doctor Halter. Also, I'm impressed with Doctors Zehnzeit's and Mahi's beauty and their knowledge of cryptology, which is what I wanted to discuss with you today."

"Yes, I understand you've had some problems with the NSA; they won't let you export that obsolete American cryptographic equipment. Well, they gave me a hard time about security orders while I was at MIT."

"The girls told me. I understand you have a more advanced concept, the public key algorithm."

"Yes, Dr. Kelly, I'm going to give you a little blackboard talk this morning about this algorithm developed by Fahrina in her dissertation. I've improved it a bit since. I hope I don't speak down to you, but it's an explanation I gave recently to the board of directors at Cryptomatik. Since ninety percent of their revenue comes from equipment using this plan, I thought they ought to know what it does."

"I would like hearing your presentation very much. And don't worry about speaking down to me. The field is new to me."

Professor Halter rose, strode to the multiple sliding surface blackboard on the wall of his office and started his lecture. He filled four blackboard spaces with diagrams, equations and mathematical statements. He waved his hands vigorously as he explained each point in a booming, resonant voice, intended to keep students from falling asleep. At the end of the two and a half hour presentation, he said, "Dr. Kelly, I hope I didn't make my explanation too simplistic."

Still dazed by the blackboard of equations and complex explanations, Kelly replied, "No, not at all. However, I do think I understand the concept better now. Just two questions though: does it really work? And is it really secure?"

"By all means, it does work. Dr. Dichter, one of my former PhD students, will give you a demonstration tomorrow at Cryptomatik. As to the second question, it's damn secure! I'll tell you one thing, NSA and all their supercomputers won't be able to crack these codes!"

"Sounds very convincing to me. I'm looking forward to seeing the concept work tomorrow."

And now, since it's almost lunch time, let's retire to the faculty dining room. You and Dr. Mahi will be my guests. Dr. Zehnzeit, you're invited, too."

The next morning, Wednesday, May 13th, Heidi picked up Kelly and Fahrina at the Zürich Hotel at 8:30am and drove them the thirty five minute trip to Regensdorf. Cryptomatik sat at the foot of some spectacular wooded hills, similar to Utliberg and Zürichberg. The clean, modern lines of the building, the utilitarian parking lot, and the green park-like grounds reflected Swiss orderliness. Kelly and the PhD girls walked into the lobby and Heidi explained to the receptionist in the local German/Swiss dialect that they had a meeting with Dr. Peter Dichter, the technical director. Kelly and Fahrina handed over their passports and received red escort badges. Heidi had a picture badge since she was a part time consultant here.

The receptionist said, in good English, "Welcome to Cryptomatik, Dr. Kelly. Dr. Dichter is expecting you. Dr. Zehnzeit, you may escort Doctors Kelly and Mahi to the main conference room, just inside on the right."

They were greeted by Dr. Dichter as they walked into the walnut paneled conference room. It was compete with a viewgraph projection screen at the end of the room. There were three men seated at the large oblong table who rose as Kelly came in.

After Heidi completed the introductions of Kelly and Fahrina to Dr. Dichter, Dr. Dichter said, "Doctors Kelly and Mahi, I would like you to meet the president of Cryptomatik, Herr Maler; the public key cryptographic equipment program manager, Herr Rediess; and the director of marketing, Dr. Ochsner."

Kelly and Fahrina shook the gentlemen's hands and were then seated at the conference table close to the screen.

The president gave a short introductory welcome speech and departed. Dr. Dichter then presented a thorough briefing on the new microprocessor cryptology equipment that implemented Professor Dr. Halter's public key algorithm. At the end of the hour presentation, Dr. Dichter asked, "Are there any questions?"

Kelly asked, "Yes, an important one. We designed our system around the Datamatic equipment. Are your interfaces compatible with theirs?"

"Yes, Dr. Kelly, they are. We use a standard digital interface, the RS-232C, between our equipment and the computer, the same as Datamatic does.

"That's great. We were worried about the change-over from Datamatic equipment to your equipment. Our engineers hoped you used the same interface."

"You merely unplug Datamatic's obsolete equipment and plug in Cryptomatik's latest state-of-the-art equipment."

Dr. Ochsner, the marketing director chuckled, "Dr. Kelly, you can see I'm converting our technical director into a marketing man."

"I agree. He's a darn good salesman. He's convinced me. We want to place an order for ten units."

"Dr. Kelly, we Swiss never do business on an empty stomach. There will be plenty of time to discuss your order and our delivery schedule and prices after lunch. But first, we would like to take you to our laboratory for a thirty minute demonstration of the equipment you need. Then we'll go to lunch."

They trooped down a long hall to a modern electronic laboratory. Kelly was led to a small grey box with a host of cables leading out of it to an array of communication devices: two telephones, a voice radio transmitter / receiver, two telex machines, and two computer terminals. Dr. Dichter explained the grey box was the microprocessor system that implemented the public key crypto algorithms for protecting the array of communications devices against interception of secret voice or data by someone not authorized to do so.

He then demonstrated how the system worked with each communication device. Kelly asked to try out the telex part himself. He entered the daily code as a sequence of letters and numbers on the grey box by setting thumb wheel switches. He typed 'Now is the time for all good men to come to the aid of their party' on the telex. The sending telex printed out an unintelligible jumble of letters and numbers.

Dr. Dichter said, "This is what the unauthorized *interceptor* would see if he tapped your communications line."

Kelly said, "I can't make heads or tails of it!"

"Neither could your adversary."

The receiving telex then printed out the same message Kelly had originally entered.

Dr. Dichter added, "And this is what the authorized receiver gets."

"That same thing I sent."

"Exactly!"

"I can see with my own eyes it really works."

The group retired to the company executive dining room for the two hour lunch Heidi had warned Kelly about. A formally dressed waiter served an exquisite meal of beef tournedos, and fresh steamed vegetables, finishing with a green salad, in the

French order. They had flaming cherries jubilee for dessert. They were served three white wines and three red wines with the main course, followed by Cointreau after dessert. Only then did Dr. Dichter announce, "Now we can return to the conference room to complete our business negotiations."

Kelly opened the meeting, "Our requirements are for ten units plus spares and field service in Tehran for two years. Options for additional spares and services up to five more years are also required. We need delivery by the first of August at the latest."

Dr. Dichter replied, "Dr. Kelly, we anticipated your requirements based on your remarks this morning. While we were lunching, my staff was preparing this firm *Angebot*, or offer, for your consideration. I'm afraid we can't meet your schedule requirements, however. The earliest we can deliver due to our Swiss bankers' backlog, is the first of September. Can you live with that?"

Kelly didn't answer for several minutes as he read the offer carefully. He noted the firm, fixed price was a full 30% less than the Datamatic offer. He realized that added another twenty million dollars to his contingency fund. Finally he responded, "I'll accept your offer, providing you can accelerate your delivery to the last week of August *and* will deliver the equipment directly to Tehran with three engineers to help connect your equipment to our system."

Dr. Dichter conferred in German with Dr. Ochsner for several minutes and then replied in English, "Yes, Dr. Kelly. We can meet your date. It means our factory personnel will have to delay their August vacations until September. I hope we have a warm September or I may be shot by the vacationers and their families. We'll furnish you three engineers at $9,000 per month plus per diem and travel expenses to be negotiated."

Kelly responded, "It's a deal!"

They shook hands to seal the agreement. Kelly thought *I've overstepped my authority by committing to this offer without our vice president of purchasing's approval. But, if I didn't, the whole IBEX project would be down the drain. Then, I'd really be fired. This way, I'll probably just get a reprimand.*

Kelly took the revised offer, after one of the secretaries re-printed the revised schedule on her word processor. He and his Doctor girl friends bade Dichter and his staff goodbye and headed for their hotel.

About 6pm, Kelly put through a direct dial overseas call from his hotel room to Dr. Vries of his IBEX team at AAC in California. It was about 9 in the morning the same day, Wednesday. Kelly told Vries the good news that the digital interface was, as they had hoped, the same as the one they had originally planned to use with the old Datamatic equipment. Dr. Vries happily assured Kelly the revision of volume 12 was coming along nicely and would be ready to take to Washington, DC, the next week.

Kelly and the girls celebrated the successful consummation of the deal with Cryptomatik by another evening of bedroom games in the Zürich Hotel.

The next morning, Kelly got up and found the two girls still sound asleep, exhausted from the previous night's activities. He packed and left a note for Heidi thanking her for all her help. He left one for Fahrina saying he would see her in Tehran next August. Then he left for the airport by taxi.

Kelly caught the non-stop Swiss Air flight to Los Angeles, where he was met by his wife and five children, as usual.

Chapter 11.

The Price of Approval

Friday, 15 May, 1976

Kelly walked into Dr. Morrell's office just before 9am for his meeting to explain the details of the Zürich trip. Morrell's secretary, Helen, greeted him, "Welcome back, Dr. Kelly. Did you visit the Swiss Alps while you were in Switzerland?"

"No, Helen, I was too busy but I did get a beautiful view of them from Utliberg near Zürich. The panorama of the Alpine peaks to the south was truly *wunderbar!*"

"I'd sure like to go there someday for my vacation. Dr. Kelly, if you'll give me your receipts, I'll make out your expense account."

Kelly handed her his envelope full of receipts. She looked them over and said, "I can't seem to find your hotel receipt."

"Er...Oh, Helen, I must have lost it. Just put down $100 per night for the hotel. That's close enough."

"Well, OK. But I'll need to get a letter signed by Dr. Morrell approving your expense account with *lost* hotel receipts. Don't worry. I'll take care of it. Go on in, Dr. Morrell's expecting you."

Dr. Morrell waved Kelly to the large couch and asked, "How was the trip? How was Cryptomatik's equipment?"

"Fine, John. I committed the company to a seventy million dollar order for their equipment to replace the Datamatic equipment."

"*You did what?!* You know you're not authorized to commit the company for that kind of money. The vice president of purchasing is the only one who can do that. Even I can't!"

"I know, John. But I saved the company thirty million dollars. Your VP can confirm the order by telex this week."

"OK. I guess that'll work. But you know I'll have to put a letter in your personnel file reprimanding you for overstepping your authority."

"I understand, John. But that's better than being fired for IBEX failing because of no crypto equipment."

"You have a point there! How did the equipment perform?"

"Beautifully! Their demonstration showed all functions worked perfectly. Professor Halter's public key algorithm is great. It's implemented with microprocessors and really works."

"How about delivery and interface?"

"Delivery is about three weeks later than I would have liked so they'll deliver the units directly to Tehran. And the interface is the really good news. It's *plug compatible*. We just remove the Datamatic equipment, which NSA won't let us get, and plug in the Cryptomatik equipment. It makes the revision of volume 12 very easy. Dr. Vries says it's almost finished."

"When do you go back to the Pentagon to get the export license application squared away?"

"Early next Tuesday. I have a meeting scheduled with Robert Hack first thing Wednesday morning."

"Good, that should get the license approval back on track."

"I'm still hoping the license will be approved by the end of July so we don't have to hold up our IBEX delivery scheduled for early August."

"You do good work, Brad. Just don't overstep your authority again, though."

"I have the message, John. Don't rub it in."

Kelly's meeting with the IBEX team went well. Dr. Vries reported the volume 12 revisions were almost ready and only needed the details from the equipment description Kelly brought back from Zürich. The graphics department and Vries were authorized overtime over the weekend to be sure everything was ready by Monday afternoon.

Tuesday, 19 May 1976

Kelly boarded the American Airlines non-stop flight to Washington, DC, at 8:30am. Twenty minutes later, the captain received the *push-back* clearance from the tower and the DC-10 was on its way. After a typical first class flight to Dulles Airport, to which Kelly was becoming more and more accustomed, the jumbo jet arrived at 4:10pm. Kelly exited the mobile lounge transporter at the terminal and, to his great delight, found Christina and Olga waiting there with Yossi.

Kelly remarked, "I see Amnon's surveillance system is still working."

The girls chorused, "Yep, it sure is."

Kelly turned to Yossi, "I'm glad to see you're still here as *shotgun*."

Yossi nodded and smiled widely.

The girls both hugged and kissed Brad, told him Amnon was waiting outside with the limousine, and handed him the key to his room at the Marriott.

"You two sure take all the effort out of my Washington trips, and *add* a great deal of pleasure."

On the drive from Dulles Airport to the Marriott, Kelly explained to Amnon how he solved the cryptographic equipment problem. Amnon asked, "Can you give me some additional details so I can send them to Colonel Ladrun?"

Kelly dug an unclassified, technical description out of his briefcase.

Amnon said, "I'll get this in the diplomatic pouch that's being flown to Tel Aviv on El Al Airline tonight. He'll have it Wednesday afternoon."

Christina asked, "Did you enjoy your trip to Zürich, Brad?"

"Yes, but it was a bit tiring."

She continued, "Olga and I were going to meet you there, but Amnon suggested you would be quite busy and we might tire you out. I guess he was right."

He replied, "I was very busy. It's probably just as well you didn't come. But I hope you'll meet me in Tehran in August." He thought *Mossad must have known I was traveling with Fahrina.*

Olga replied, "Don't worry, we'll meet you there, but we were planning to come to Los Angeles first. Is that OK?"

"It might be a little awkward, with my family and all. But I'll find some way to keep you busy."

At the Marriott, Amnon whispered to Brad, "Stay alert. Mossad just intercepted a message from the Moslem terrorists in Iran that they're determined to stop IBEX and the *devils* who are building it. They're really upset that the Shah plans to spy on their fellow Moslem brothers."

"OK, I will. And I'll need help in Iran next August."

"You'll have to depend on Shaheen and the Savak there. Mossad and Savak have an agreement: that's their territory."

"I'll try to be careful!"

In the Marriott, Kelly was surprised they had the same suite again. He remarked, "This must be the best suite in this hotel. I guess we're lucky."

Christina explained, "It's more than luck. Olga had to forgo her virtue with the hotel manager last night to get these rooms."

Olga added, "And it was hard work, too. He's an atrocious lover."

"Brad tried to soothe her, "I'll try to make it up to you tonight."

Kelly took the Metro to the Pentagon the next morning, arriving thirty minutes early for his 9 o'clock meeting with Robert Hack, with time to have breakfast in the cafeteria at the top of the ramp on the second floor. It was faster, cheaper, and better than in the Marriott coffee shop.

Hack's secretary told him, "Mr. Hack's aide, Colonel Long, is waiting for you over in D ring, the same conference room as last time. Mr. Hack is on the phone with the *spooks* over at Fort Mead. He'll join you in just a few minutes."

In the conference room, Kelly found Colonel Long and three other colonels. He was surprised to see Ralph Hauser from the CIA there too. After shaking hands with the colonels, Kelly walked over to Hauser, "I didn't expect to see you here."

"I wanted to hear about your new cryptographic equipment. I heard how NSA vetoed the Datamatic stuff. Is the Swiss equipment any good?"

"It looks very good. They're using the public key concept."

"I read about that in *Scientific American Magazine*. The academic community is interested in it, but we don't think there's anything there we can't crack."

Their conversation was interrupted by Hack's arrival. He announced, "Gentlemen, Dr. Kelly is here today to give us a briefing on the change to the IBEX system. At NSA's request, Associated Aviation has deleted the Datamatic equipment and replaced it with some foreign equipment that Dr. Kelly will describe."

Kelly gave a short briefing about the change and ended by saying, "Here's the new volume 12. It should replace the old volume 12 in our export license package."

Hack asked, "How secure is this new foreign equipment?"

Kelly answered, "The Swiss tell me nobody can crack their code. They are so confident that all their banks have ordered the equipment. You know how important secrecy is to the Swiss banks."

Hack continued, "I know, but I just got off the phone with the associate director of NSA. He said using the Cryptomatik equipment is OK. To quote him, *We can break that code with our new Cray supercomputer. We'll set all three to work. They'll decode it in no time.*"

"The inventor of the public key idea claims it would take three Cray supercomputers 333 years to decode his algorithms."

Then Kelly asked Hack point blank, "Are you saying that NSA will remove their veto of the export license because of our change to the Swiss equipment?"

"Yes, that's what the associate director just promised me."

Kelly noticed the colonels whispering to each other. He decided that meant the Pentagon bureaucracy would now inform the Office of Munitions Control at the State Department that IBEX had the green light. But he knew it would still take two or three months to get the official paperwork out of the Pentagon because of the multi-level reviews and approvals required. He thought, *Now Hack has all the ammunition he needs to push the export license through. He wants that Associated Aviation vice presidency but he has to deliver the goods first.*"

Kelly said to Hack, "Bob, I'll deliver the revised export license application to Jack Johnson at OMC tomorrow morning."

"Oh, God, no! Don't do that! We'd have to start all over again. We'd lose a month of staff work. Just give him a cover letter describing the change."

Kelly groaned inwardly, *Oh, the wonderful ways of the Washington bureaucracy! It's a good thing we have an inside advisor!* He responded, "OK, a cover letter it will be. I'll give it to Johnson tomorrow morning during my 9am appointment with him."

"Good, Brad. I think we have IBEX back on track. You've done all the right things."

After the meeting, Kelly was invited inside Hack's office for a closed door, one-on-one session. Hack asked how his vice presidency was coming along and again threatened, "I'd hate to see IBEX delayed because of some *problems* in the Pentagon. You know, I have to sign off on the *position letter* that goes back to Johnson at OMC. When he gets that letter, you get your license in a matter of days."

Kelly explained he hadn't had time to talk to Morrell about how things were going about getting Hack's vice presidency since his return from Switzerland and that Morrell was on vacation this week. He promised to talk to Morrell about it on Monday and then phone Hack right away.

Hack emphasized, "I'm glad you see the importance of solving my problem. Now, on the lighter side, is Olga with you this time?"

"Yes, they both are. How about joining us for dinner Thursday night with a reprise at the Marriott afterwards?"

"That sounds great, but I'm buying dinners. I must consider my integrity. You can't pay for the dinner because you work for the company where I hope to get my next job. That would be a violation of the conflict of interest regulations."

"OK, you win."

"How about Hall's for steak, on the Potomac?"

"I thought that restaurant used to be in the middle of Washington."

"It was, but they had to move to a new location when the government tore down the slums around the restaurant and built new apartments."

"But, I rode through that neighborhood recently and it still looks like a slum."

"You know what they say: You can take the slums out of Washington, but you can't get Washington out of the slums. I'll see you at the Marriott at 7 tomorrow, Thursday."

On the Metro, Kelly mulled over Hack's statement of the well-known joke. *Here I am, living in the most powerful and prosperous country in the world and we can't even eliminate the slums in the capital city. Why? Part of the answer is in the 'puzzle palace,' the Pentagon I just came from. If we could agree with the Soviets to disarm, perhaps we could divert some of those billions being spent on guns and instead spend them on our social problems. Maybe we could eliminate the slums, not only in Washington, DC, but all over America. Well, it's a nice thought anyway.*

He got off at Roslyn and headed for the Associated Aviation Washington Office in a large, brown high rise building about two blocks from the Marriott. In the AAC suite on the fifteenth floor he signed in on the register and showed his AAC ID card and his business card to the receptionist, who was a new, green-eyed, red-headed beauty about 22 years old. He said, "I need to use one of the guest executive offices to draft a letter for the State Department that I need tomorrow. I'll need someone to type it on company stationery."

She looked at his business card and said, "Dr. Kelly, everyone here is out to lunch. Mr. Thompson is on the West Coast this week. Why don't you use his office? It has the best view and those guest offices are so tiny! And, I'd love to type your letter. Just give me the draft when it's ready."

"Thank you very much. What's your name?"

"You can just call me Sandy, everyone does. I think it's so exciting to type letters to the State Department and the Defense Department. It makes me feel so important."

"Sandy, this letter to the State Department is *really* important. We need it to get approval for a billion dollar project."

"Oh, that is exciting! I can't even imagine how much a billion dollars is. It's a lot more than my two hundred dollars a week."

"It would take you about five million weeks to earn it."

"What a long time. I'll be old and decrepit by then."

"Sandy, you'll never be old and decrepit."

"Oh, Dr. Kelly. You say such nice things. I wish you could come over to visit me at my apartment this evening."

"Sandy, I'd love to, but I'm doubly busy tonight, getting ready for my meetings tomorrow and all."

"Well, next time you're in town I won't take no for an answer."

Kelly thought to himself, *This must be the young lady I heard about. She has vowed to sleep with every Associated Aviation executive before she retires. With her approach, she'll probably be successful if she doesn't become prematurely old from the effort!"*

Kelly retired to Thompson's office and wrote out his draft letter, then handed the three page document to Sandy. Fifteen minutes later, she returned with the letter, neatly typed on the letter-quality printer connected to the Wang word processor. Kelly made a few changes in red ink and gave it back to Sandy. She keyed in the changes on the word processor and had it back to Kelly in less than five minutes.

Kelly complimented her, "Not only are you beautiful, Sandy, but you're also terrific on the word processor."

She replied, "I hope this letter helps you get the billion dollar project. And don't forget the open invitation!"

"Thanks, Sandy. I'll remember."

Kelly carefully placed the letter in his briefcase and hurried back to the Marriott. Christina and Olga were watching x-rated movies on the video. They were nude.

Kelly said, "I'm finished with business for the day. My next meeting is tomorrow morning at the OMC. What shall we do this afternoon?"

Christina replied excitedly, "Let's go to bed. These movies make us horny. Besides, it's been so long since we last saw you."

"That sounds like a good plan. I need a nap after a hard morning with the Pentagon bureaucrats. Speaking of bureaucrats, Bob Hack is taking us to a steak dinner tomorrow night. Olga, will you take care of Bob again?"

Olga grinned, "I'd love to. He's so cute and really good in bed."

Christina broke in, "Brad, don't think we're going to let you take a nap. Not for a while anyway."

"I didn't think you would."

All three climbed into the king sized bed for an afternoon of fun and games. And then Kelly finally got his nap.

Thursday, 21 May 1976

Kelly awakened early in the morning. He was surprised to find Christina and Olga already up and dressed. Christina announced, "Get up, sleepy head. We've ordered a hearty breakfast for all three of us: ham, waffles, eggs, coffee and orange juice."

Olga added, "Do you realize we forgot to have dinner last night? After your nap, we had two bottles of champagne, made love again, and fell asleep. We woke up this morning starved!"

Kelly answered, "I'm really hungry myself. It's going to be a novelty, having breakfast with you two. You're usually sound asleep when I leave in the morning."

While Kelly was getting dressed the room service waiter arrived. He set up the breakfast table with a pink linen tablecloth and napkins and a huge bouquet of red roses in the center. A bottle of champagne sat in a bucket of ice. The girls had poured three glasses of half champagne and half orange juice.

Kelly remarked, "What a festive breakfast. Why the roses and champagne?"

Christine replied, "They're compliments of the manager. The note says *Olga, thanks for a fabulous night!*"

Olga pouted, "That creep! At least the roses are beautiful and the champagne is good, but it still wasn't worth it. He's really a lousy lover. But then, compared to Brad, everyone is."

Kelly laughed, "Thanks, Olga. Your service yielded fantastic results for the rest of us."

Later, Kelly reminded the girls about having dinner with Hack that evening and left for his 9am meeting. He walked the few short blocks and went into the Office of Munitions Control (OMC) building on the side close to a Japanese restaurant. He took the public elevator to the second floor, showed his Pentagon pass to the government guard for identification, and then took the special elevator up to the fifth floor. He walked into the OMC reception office and asked for Mr. Johnson.

The receptionist replied, "Mr. Johnson is at a staff meeting over at *Foggy Bottom*, the State Department Headquarters. It's called Foggy Bottom because it's an historical Washington site, not the type of thinking that goes on in the State Department. President Mahoney's new Secretary of State is a real stickler for early morning staff meetings. He thinks Munitions Control is so important he asked Mr. Johnson to summarize all the cases over 100 million dollars at the meetings. Mr. Johnson was supposed to give a summary of your IBEX project this morning."

"When will he be back. Perhaps I should come back later?"

"Oh, no. He should be here soon and his executive assistant is already waiting for you in his office."

As Kelly walked down the hall to Johnson's huge corner office he thought about how IBEX was supposed to have been a very *quiet* program. Now the OMC receptionist and the whole State Department staff knew about it. Aviation Week Magazine would probably have a story about IBEX soon. That would put the information right in the terrorists' hands.

Kelly shook hands with Johnson's executive assistant, a colorless bureaucrat about 59 years old, who never said anything, just took copious notes at all of Johnson's meetings. Those notes were probably typed by the secretarial pool of the OMC and distributed to the *Iran desks* in the State Department and the Pentagon. Another *layer of bureaucrats* with access to the information.

After a twenty minute conversation about Washington weather with the executive assistant, Johnson walked in and announced proudly, "Dr. Kelly, you'll be pleased to know that I just briefed the Secretary of State and his staff on IBEX. The Secretary commented that, although he doesn't approve of electronic spying, he would notify Ambassador Hurd in Tehran to give his full support to IBEX."

Kelly protested, "Mr. Johnson, you promised IBEX security would be carefully protected."

"The Secretary of State and his staff are all cleared for Top Secret."

"But IBEX is SCI, compartmentalized security. That's higher than Top Secret!"

"I only talked about the project name and the broad objectives. The Pentagon has all the detailed documentation."

"You're probably right. I think I'm becoming *hyper* about security. There have been two attempts on my life since I've been working on this project."

"I know. I received a CIA report about the incident on the airliner to Los Angeles and the shoot-out in London. But, don't worry, the FBI and CIA will protect you."

"I haven't seen any evidence of it so far! But anyway, here's the cover letter telling about the changes in IBEX because NSA vetoed using American crypto equipment. I got informal feedback yesterday NSA was withdrawing their veto because we've changed to Swiss made cryptographic equipment from a Zürich company called Cryptomatik."

"Is that all spelled out in your letter?"

"Yes, it is."

"I'm glad you didn't resubmit the license application. We would have had to start all over again and would have lost at least a month."

"Bob Hack told me to use a cover letter instead."

"Oh, yes, the director of international programs, a sharp cookie. He's originally from Lebanon, you know. He has an oriental, Machiavellian mind."

"How long will it take to get the license?"

"When do you need it?"

"If we get the license before the end of July, we'll be right on schedule."

"I can't promise anything. But based on your feedback from NSA and the fact that Bob Hack is behind it, I would say you'll probably get the license by the end of July."

Only a little after 10 in the morning and Kelly had finished all his meetings for the day. He hurried back to the hotel and found the girls watching TV. He told them, "Tear yourselves away from the *idiot box*. Let's go out and do a little sightseeing. Have you ever seen the Museum of Science and Industry?"

Christina replied, "No, but I'd love to get out of this room. I'm going stir crazy."

Olga added, "Let's go. What can we see there?"

Kelly replied, "Lots of interesting things: Lindberg's *Spirit of St. Louis*; the *Apollo* capsule that took the first men to the Moon; and one of the first DC-3 airliners."

The girls chorused, "Let's go."

They took the Metro over to Washington, DC and got off at the Dupont Circle station. They walked over to Constitution Avenue and strolled the short distance to the Museum of Science and Industry, one of the many museums that made up the Smithsonian complex. Kelly pointed out the NASA headquarters building and explained he'd been there many times during his years in the aerospace business, especially when he was an advisor to the associate administrator for aeronautics.

Olga exclaimed, "You've had such an interesting career. I wish you could tell us all about it."

"That's one reason I wanted to take you to this museum. I can show you many of the projects I've worked on over the last twenty five years. I want you two to know I can perform well outside of bed, too!"

Christina replied, "We already know that. Amnon has told us what a fantastic engineer and scientist you are."

Kelly and the girls spent the rest of the day studying the various exhibits. Kelly dwelled on the vehicles and systems he had worked on personally. He explained his contributions in the areas of flight controls, aerodynamics, navigation, avionics, and landing systems. He showed them the first systems he worked on that used airborne digital computers and software to make them perform. They still hadn't seen everything when the museum closed at 5 o'clock.

The Metro quickly transported them back to their hotel with just enough time to dress and watch the evening news before Bob Hack arrived promptly at 7. He put his overnight bag in the bedroom and suggested they leave immediately for their 7:30 reservations. Hall's was such a popular place there was a good chance they'd lose their table if they were late. Since the love making combinations had been decided, everyone trooped out to Hack's car: Olga in the front and Christina in back with Kelly.

Hack drove down the George Washington Parkway and left it to take the Seventeenth Street Bridge from Virginia across to Washington, DC. They continued on the expressway towards Baltimore for a mile or two, then left it to wander through the back streets to the new Hall's Restaurant on the Potomac River. Kelly noticed the restaurant didn't look as run down as it had in the original location. It seemed to have lost some of its authenticity when it moved. He was glad to see the large painting of a nude lady was still displayed prominently on the wall behind the old fashioned mahogany bar.

Kelly found the food as good as ever. They all had large New York cut steaks, the house specialty, with all the trimmings, including French Burgundy wine carefully selected by Hack. When Hack paid the bill with his personal credit card, Kelly noticed the tab was $150, with tip. Kelly thought to himself, *The conflict of interest regulations are expensive for the Pentagon bureaucrats. However, if I had paid, I would have put it on my company credit card. That way, it wouldn't have cost anybody (except the taxpayers) anything. In fact, since most of Associated Aviation's contracts are cost plus, the company would have been fully reimbursed by the Defense Department. Using the current Associated Aviation approved rates (130% overhead, 22% G&A, and 10% profit), the dinner would have cost the US government $462.99, the $312.99 difference going into the company's coffers to pay overhead salaries, executive travel, and a little profit. It's no wonder the Pentagon doesn't want contractors to entertain its employees. They can't afford it, even with the bloated Pentagon budgets.*

After dinner, the quartet returned to the Marriott suite for an active evening of love making. All four were quite intoxicated from the wine and martini's with dinner and the champagne after returning to the room.

Kelly woke up about 9:30am with a terrific hangover. Bed squeaking noises came from the next room. Kelly said to himself, "Hack will call in sick this morning and probably spend the rest of the day with Olga, all at full Pentagon executive's pay."

Kelly turned over and kissed Christina. She sleepily returned his kiss. He continued his soliloquy, "I've finished all my business on this trip and the non-stop flights to LAX don't leave until after 5pm. I might as well sleep off my hangover. I can collect full executive's pay from AAC for having fun with Christina."

Kelly finally got up about 2:30 in the afternoon. He dressed and packed his suitcase. Christina was still asleep. Kelly slipped out of the room quietly, knowing he wouldn't be missed at all. He checked out of the hotel, having to pay an extra day, since it was after the twelve noon check out time. He decided Hack and the girls would probably spend another night in the room anyway. Now, they'd have a free room.

At the airport, Kelly flipped a coin to choose between TWA and American: American won. He went to the counter and bought a first class standby ticket for Los Angeles. The plane was not full and he was given a boarding card. He walked down to the Admiral's Club and checked in. He bought a martini and started watching TV. He realized he needed his wife to pick him up at the airport and she didn't know which flight he'd be on. He picked up the white credit card phone next to his chair and dialed his home number.

Anna answered, and Kelly said, "Hello, darling. I'm arriving this evening on one of the non-stop flights from here. The first letter of the airline is the last letter of your name."

"You're still being mysterious."

"Yes. I have to. Did you understand?"

"Yes, of course. It's obvious. I'll meet you there. I'm warning you though, I missed you this week. And with your sixty to seventy hour work weeks lately, you haven't been properly servicing me."

"Don't worry, darling. This is my last trip until August. Everything's going to be relatively calm for the next couple of months."

"Then maybe we can take a few days off and sail to Cat Harbor and be alone. Do you realize you've missed every single yacht race since Christmas?"

"Hey, that's a good idea. You get the boat ready and we'll go straight to the boat slip and head for Cat Harbor tonight."

"And sail at night?"

"Sure. With our LORAN C navigation receiver with area navigation, it's easy. I've already got all the coordinates for a Cat Harbor trip entered in the memory. We'll know where we are within 100 feet."

"Oh, that sounds like a wonderful idea. I'll load our food for the weekend aboard. I'll include three bottles of Mumm's champagne."

"Great, darling. See you about 7:30 tonight, *without* the kids."

"I love you! Thanks for thinking of our wonderful get away!"

Kelly boarded the mobile lounge at 5:15 for the ride out to the Douglas DC-10 parked on the ramp. The wide-body jet started its engines right on schedule, taxied to the active runway, and took off for Los Angeles, five hours and worlds away from the hectic Washington scene.

Kelly was first off the American jet at LAX and ran to Anna. They kissed and hugged and then headed for their slip at Los Angeles Yacht Club in San Pedro. It was just after 8 when they climbed on board their thirty six foot long, light blue, Cal 36 racing sailboat. As Kelly slipped out of his business suit and into his boating clothes, he noticed Anna had completely prepared the boat for their weekend at Catalina Island. They would anchor in the quiet Catalina Harbor on the backside of Catalina Island, about four and a half hours away.

While Kelly was changing, Anna poured them each a glass of champagne in her special acrylic champagne flutes for use on the boat. Kelly proposed a toast, "To our second honeymoon at Cat Harbor this weekend.!"

"I'll drink to that!"

Kelly started the four cylinder engine and motored out of the harbor, while Anna raised the mainsail to provide stability during the night crossing.

When they exited the Los Angeles Harbor with the rotating green beacon on the light house to their right, they were pleasantly surprised to find a fresh east wind blowing some twelve knots. Anna quickly put up the large Genoa reacher and they sailed on a comfortable port tack reach towards the West End of Catalina Island, some twenty four nautical miles away. They made good a solid eight knots. They passed the West End just after 11pm and dropped anchor at Cat Harbor just after midnight.

Kelly and Anna spent an idyllic weekend far from the worries of IBEX and the international intrigues it implied. There was only one other boat anchored in Cat Harbor since the summer season wouldn't start until school let out in mid June. They went swimming in the crystal clear but cold ocean. They hiked up and down the hills of the 24 mile long island. They got to know each other again. It was like the first years of their marriage all over again!

Chapter 12.

IBEX Finished

On Tuesday, May 26, 1976, Kelly walked into Dr. Morrell's outer office and was greeted by Helen, "Good morning, Dr. Kelly. How was your trip to Washington? It looks like you got a sunburn there."

"My trip was fine, Helen, but I got the sunburn on Catalina Island. Anna and I sailed to Cat Harbor on Friday night. We came back Monday afternoon on the Memorial Day holiday."

"You look more relaxed than you have in months. You've been working so hard on this new program. Go on in, Dr. Morrell's expecting you."

Dr. Morrell greeted Brad with, "Welcome back from the *Puzzle Palace*. How'd things go in Washington?"

"They went fine, John. And everything here seems to be on schedule. Most of the hardware comes in next week. The software is coming along well, too. Everything should be ready by the end of July."

"And the license?"

"That should be no problem either, provided you get the job offer out to Bob Hack."

"What?"

"All the hurdles for the export license have been removed. With our change to Cryptomatik for the cryptology equipment, NSA removed their veto. We'll have the license three days after the Pentagon sends their position letter to the OMC, (the Office of Munitions Control). Bob Hack is the key to the Pentagon's letter."

"You mean, if we don't make Hack an offer, we won't get the license?"

"We'd eventually get it, but without Hack pushing the paper work through, there could be long, bureaucratic delays."

"We need the IBEX sales on the books this year, not next. We can't book the sales until we get the license."

"If we deliver the system to Iran during August, we can book at least 80% of the 1.2 billion dollars. If there's a delay, delivery might slip into next year."

Morrell reached for his phone and dialed the five digits to reach the *hot line* of the chairman of the board of directors.

When Morrell hung up, he told Brad, "You can tell Hack he'll get the formal job offer before the end of the week: vice president of international business development with a salary of $100 thousand a year. The chairman pointed out that's only 0.1% of the profit this year from IBEX. He also said the extra 100 million profit from IBEX will make the earnings per share go up enough to make the company's stock worth $2 more per share. Considering the ten million shares outstanding, that's a $20 million increase in the value of the corporation's stock."

"John, from a personal point of view, that means my 25,000 shares will be worth $50 thousand more."

Kelly hurried back to his office. His mail baskets were overflowing as a result of his week away. He ignored the piles of paper and dialed Bob Hack's Pentagon number on the Wats line.

Hack asked, "How's it going, Brad? You missed a fantastic Friday night in your hotel. The hotel people said the suite was paid for through an extra night. Olga and Christina really kept me busy all night."

"I sailed to Catalina Friday night with my wife and had a fabulous three day weekend."

"You Californians really have it made. We had thunderstorms all week end here. Any news regarding the matter we discussed?"

"Yes, that's why I called. They're offering you VP of International Business Development and one hundred grand a year. You should get a telegraphic offer to your home by Friday. And a formal letter will be mailed later this week."

"Fabulous, Brad. What a great Memorial Day present."

"And how's the license coming?"

"Now that the *air is clear*, I'll call a meeting of the colonels this afternoon to make sure the paper is moving through the system."

"Bob, the thirty first of July is a *drop dead* date for us. We have to have the license by then."

"Don't worry, Brad. You'll have it!"

Kelly then called Helen and asked her to set up a 1:30 meeting of the IBEX team in the large conference room.

Helen replied, "It's already done. I assumed you'd want a meeting after being gone all week."

"You're really efficient, Helen. You can even read my mind."

"Not on everything. I was going over your expense report for Washington and I noticed you paid for your hotel for Friday night. Didn't you come home Friday?"

"Yes, I did, but I slept late Friday past checkout time so I got charged an extra day."

"Oh, you poor dear. You must have worked terribly hard in Washington."

Kelly laughed, "Yes, Helen, Washington is always hard work. I spent a late night with Mr. Hack of the Pentagon Thursday night. I'm just not used to these late hours the Washingtonians keep."

"That's quite a coincidence. Dr. Morrell just gave me a letter to type to Mr. Hack, offering him a vice presidency. Do you think he'll accept?"

"He should make a valuable contribution to the company with all his Pentagon experience on international programs. I'm sure he'll accept. He likes California and Associated Aviation."

When Kelly walked into the IBEX meeting, Tom Bradley, his deputy program manager, announced, "Welcome back, Chief. We have an up-to-date status briefing for you. But the best news is - all the hardware is here now. Now we can start integration and test of the system."

"Good, because it's absolutely imperative that we deliver the system to Iran the first week in August so AAC can book a billion dollars in sales and a hundred million in profit from IBEX this year."

Tom drawled, "Well, Brad, we got the message about the schedule. We all want our jobs, don't we, fellows?"

The IBEX team chorused, "Yes, Sir!"

Kelly responded, "Then, roll the briefing charts."

First, Tom Bradley gave an overview of the total system integration and test status. The each team member presented five to ten viewgraphs covering his part of the system: the communications equipment, the controls and display consoles, the computer connections, the cabling and interface equipment and, finally, Dr. John Vries explained the software.

Kelly interrupted, "Are you sure you can get all that software working by August? You have almost a million words of code."

Vries replied, "We've taken a low risk approach to the software. We're using *reusable* software, except for the cryptographic software and we're getting that in firmware from Cryptomatik."

"Hold on there, Dr. Vries. You're getting too technical for me. Remember, I went to engineering school before they had computers. What's *reusable* software?"

"It's software we've used on other projects. Instead of writing all new software, we take some existing software, add a little new software, and re-use it."

"And what's firmware?"

"That's software that's stored on *read only memory* chips, called ROM's by the computer types. Cryptomatik stores their software on ROM's built into their hardware. They make sure it works. We don't have to add anything."

"That sounds good, John. When do we know if your reusable software works?"

"We'll load the software into the computers and start checking it out. The testing will take about 6 weeks, until the middle of July. Now that we know our jobs depend on delivering the system in early August, I'll make sure it works by then. I've become addicted to my salary here!"

Tom Bradley finished the briefing by listing the detailed schedule for IBEX. "So, we should be ready to start the final acceptance test for IBEX on the fourth of August."

Kelly checked his calendar, "That's a Tuesday. That means Colonel Fahi should be here by Monday of the week to observe the acceptance tests."

"Yes, Sir. That would be good timing. The tests will take four days."

"And we'll be able to ship on Friday night, the seventh of August."

"Yes, assuming Colonel Fahi signs off that IBEX passed the tests."

Brad answered, "I'll worry about Colonel Fahi signing. You just make sure it all works!" He smiled to himself, *I'll ask Christina and Olga to help get Colonel Fahi in the right mood to sign off for the tests. After those two work their magic, he'd sign even if the system didn't work.*

On Monday 27 July, Kelly received a telephone call from Bob Hack. Hack said, "How are things coming along there? I've got good news for you."

Kelly answered, "The system integration and test are almost finished. We're only waiting for the export license."

"That's the good news. Jeannie just hand carried the Pentagon position paper to Jack Johnston at OMC. You should have the license this week."

"You really did come through! I was beginning to worry about the license."

"I told you not to worry. I'm almost one of you now. I've already notified the director of the Defense Department research and engineering section that I'm leaving the government the end of November. Thanks for pushing the job offer through so quickly." And Hack hung up.

Kelly immediately placed another call. A cheery voice answered, "Associated Aviation Washington office. Sandy speaking."

Kelly responded, "Hello, Sandy. This is Brad Kelly. I'm trying to reach Mr. Thompson."

"Oh, Dr. Kelly, it's nice to hear from you again. I'm afraid I'm the only one in the office. It's lunch time here in Washington, you know. Is this something connected with the letter to the State Department I typed for you?"

"Yes. What a good memory you have."

"I always remember the executives I like. Don't forget my invitation!"

"Don't worry, I'll remember, but I'll be in Iran for a few months before I return to Washington. Right now, you can help me."

"I'll be glad to."

"Our export license will be ready to pick up next Thursday morning at the Office of Munitions Control close to you in Roslyn. Could you please pick it up and put it on Federal Express so we can have it by Friday?"

"I'd rather bring it to you in California personally, Dr. Kelly, but yes, of course, I'll do that for you."

"I'm afraid we'll have to depend on Federal Express this time. Please phone me with the waybill number as soon as you get it from Fed Ex."

"I certainly will, Dr. Kelly. Oh, I feel so important getting to help on such an important project as IBEX."

"Thanks a lot, Sandy, and have a nice day."

"You, too."

Late Wednesday morning, his time, Kelly received a phone call from Sandy, "Oh, Dr. Kelly. I have good news. I called OMC this morning to check on the IBEX license. Mr. Johnson's secretary said the license was approved and ready to pick up. So I rushed over there and then took it to Federal Express. You should have it by noon tomorrow, your time. The waybill number is 031-45569."

"That's great news, Sandy. Thanks. I really appreciate your efficiency."

"You're welcome, Dr. Kelly. And have a nice trip to Iran. Don't forget to visit me when you return."

"Thanks, Sandy. Don't worry, I'll remember."

On Thursday, 30 July, Kelly called a meeting of the IBEX team. He asked Tom Bradley, "Are we going to be ready for the acceptance test next week?"

Tom replied, "Yes, Brad, we're wrapping up the *in-house* tests this afternoon. We'll be ready for Colonel Fahi's inspection next Tuesday. But, what about the export license?"

Before Brad could answer, Helen rushed into the conference room and exclaimed, "Here it is, Dr. Kelly! Fed Ex just delivered the export license!"

The team chorused, "That's great!"

Kelly told Helen to telex Colonel Fahi to confirm the acceptance test would begin the next Tuesday and to ask for his arrival flight number and time so we can meet him at the airport. Send a similar telex to Colonel Ladrun in Israel."

"Anything else, Dr. Kelly?"

"Yes, please set up a party for Friday night, 7 August, to celebrate passing the acceptance test."

"But what if Colonel Fahi *flunks* the system?"

"Don't worry, Helen. We'll pass."

"I love your confidence. I'll try to set it up at the Squadron 29 Restaurant on the airport. Are wives invited?"

"No, company personnel only. Be sure to invite Dr. Morrell. And make sure he'll pick up the tab for the party. I'd hate to have to pass the hat among the IBEX team after all the uncompensated overtime they've put in this year."

"Don't worry. He'll foot the bill. He already authorized me to arrange a party. He's even arranged for the company Sabreliner to fly Mr. Thompson and his secretary, Sandy, from the Washington office, to help celebrate. Mr. Hack will be on board, too. It's his pre-hire visit here to meet all the brass!"

That's going to be quite a party. I assume you'll be there too?"

"I wouldn't miss it for anything," Helen exclaimed.

Tom broke in with his Oklahoma drawl, "Well, Brad, now that you've got the license and all our social affairs arranged, maybe we should give you the briefing so you can find out if the system will be ready for the party."

"Sorry I held you up, Tom. Yes, let's get the briefing started."

Tom and the rest of the IBEX team reported on their parts of the effort. Each was optimistic the system was ready for the final acceptance test. Kelly happily congratulated them for their outstanding efforts. Just then the phone rang. It was Ralph Hauser, looking for Brad.

"Hi, Ralph. How goes it at the *Spook Farm*?"

Hauser replied, "Everything at CIA Headquarters in Langley is fine. I understand from the grapevine you're going to ship IBEX on Friday, 7 August."

"Your *spooks* are good, Ralph. I just found out for sure myself."

"Well, don't ship it!" Ralph said loudly.

Kelly's face went white and his heart sank. His throat tightened up so much he could hardly get the words out. He croaked, "What do you mean, don't ship it?"

"I just had a meeting with the CIA Director. He has arranged for a C-141 to pick up the system there at Van Nuys Airport on that Friday afternoon. They'll have it in Tehran late Saturday evening. I've been directed to go with it to see that everything arrives OK. Ambassador Hurd and General Robertson will meet the plane at Doshen Toeppeh Air Force Base. Brad, IBEX is real popular!"

Brad's voice returned to normal. "What great service! That will save me $100 thousand in shipment costs. It sounds like the CIA is helping improve my profit picture."

"Believe me, Brad, the Agency has its self interests at heart. The Director just wants to make sure nothing happens to the stuff in transit. He's hot to get the *product* from IBEX."

"It's too bad you can't wait to leave until Saturday morning. There's a big completion party Friday night."

"Thanks, Brad. I'll have to take a rain check on the party. A lowly agent like me doesn't keep an ambassador and a three star general waiting at the airport!"

"I guess not. Thanks for the help. I'll see you Friday."

"OK, I'll be there about 1:30pm, with two hours to load the equipment. We figure it will fill the C-141. We'll only have four passenger seats for the flight: myself and three USAF armed guards."

After he hung up, Kelly thought *Three armed guards for the equipment, which could be replaced, and no guards at all for me. What does that say about my value to my country?*

Monday, 3 August 1976

Kelly arrived at his office early. This was going to be a big week for the IBEX project. Kelly and his team were ready for their customer, Colonel Abe Fahi of the Royal Iranian Air Force, to witness the formal acceptance test.

Big money was riding on passing the test. The Shah's government had deposited 80% of the contract price with Citibank in New York with instructions to release these funds, nine hundred sixty million dollars, to Associated Aviation upon certification by a *designated representative* of the Iranian government that the acceptance tests had been successfully completed. Colonel Fahi was the designated representative.

As soon as Colonel Fahi signed the *completion certificate*, the treasurer of Associated Aviation would present it to an officer of Citibank and the $960 million would be electronically transferred to Associated Aviation's bank account. At an interest rate of 12%, Associated Aviation would earn $316,484 per day on these funds! Or $13,187 an hour!

The company treasurer had arranged for an officer of Citibank to be at the signing of the *completion certificate*. The bank officer would telephone the Citibank home office, using a special code to authorize the electronic transfer of the funds from the government of Iran's account to Associated Aviation Corporation's account. By making the transfer Friday instead of Monday, which would have been the transfer date without these special arrangements, Associated Aviation would earn an extra $949,450! Well worth the $3000 in travel expenses Associated Aviation had paid to Citibank so the bank officer could be present.

Per the terms and conditions of the contract, the government of Iran would later deposit the remaining 20% of the contract funds, $240 million, in Citibank with instructions to transfer that amount to Associated Aviation upon receiving a *final acceptance certificate* after the IBEX project was completely installed in Iran. Colonel Fahi was also the *designated representative* of the Iranian government for signing the final acceptance certificate.

For these financial reasons, it was very important that Colonel Fahi should be completely happy during his stay in the Los Angeles area. Since Kelly already knew Fahi liked sex with Olga, Kelly had made sure the girls were in LA during Fahi's visit. The girls had arrived yesterday afternoon from Israel with Colonel Ladrun and were staying at the Beverly Hills Hotel. Kelly had reserved a bungalow there for Colonel Fahi, to facilitate the social interchange.

Kelly phoned Colonel Ladrun. "Shalom, Joseph. Welcome to Los Angeles. Did you enjoy your first night here?"

Ladrun answered, "Shalom, Brad. Yes, the Beverly Hills is a fabulous hotel. The weather in Los Angeles is similar to Tel Aviv. It always makes me feel at home to visit here."

"How are the girls?"

"I haven't seen them yet this morning. I think they're still sleeping. They're in bungalow three and I'm in room 204 in the main building. That was a long flight yesterday. We took off at 7am Tel Aviv time and arrived here at 7pm your time. That's twenty two hours of travel time. I think they were exhausted. We rented a Hertz car and drove straight to the hotel."

"That's good. Colonel Fahi is coming in on TWA flight 761 from London at 3pm today. Could you and the girls join me as a welcoming party? He'll be staying in bungalow two."

Ladrun laughed, "I see you've got plans to keep him happy! Sure, we'll be glad to meet you at the TWA Ambassador lounge. Is 2:30 OK?"

"That's perfect. See you then."

Next, Kelly and Tom Bradley checked on the IBEX laboratory complex, a whole building near the flight line. The roof of the building bristled with the array of antennas furnished by the Elta division of Israeli Aircraft Industries. Inside the building the listening equipment had been laid out in six separate areas to show the equipment that would be installed at the six mountain-top sites in Iran. A special room had been set up to duplicate the central processing station to be set up at the Iran Software, Ltd., headquarters building in Tehran

Kelly stopped at each of the emulated remote sites and asked questions of the operators to be sure they were ready for the acceptance test. At the end of the walk through, Kelly remarked, "Tom, it looks like we're ready for Colonel Fahi now. The hardware looks professional. The engineers answered all my questions quickly and thoroughly."

Tom drawled, "Well, Brad, we're as ready as we'll ever be. Now all you've got to do is get that *Ai-ranian* fellow to sign off."

"I think he will. Now, about loading the C-141 to go to Iran. How long do you think it will take to get everything on board after the plane arrives at 1:30 Friday afternoon?"

"Well, we should finish the last of the acceptance tests by 10am Friday. By working through the lunch hour, we should have everything in crates by the time the C-141 arrives. We can use the three fork lifts to load the crates."

Kelly asked, "How will you get the crates from the fork lifts into the airplane?"

"Oh, hell, Brad! That C-141 is a big as the barn on my daddy's farm in Oklahoma. We'll just drive the fork lifts up the ramp and unload them inside. We'll be done in about two hours. Those boys know the party starts at 5 and they want time to clean up for boozing. I hope there'll be some good chicks at the party."

"Don't worry, Tom. There will be lots there. I'll tell Ralph Hauser they can plan on a 1600 departure for the C-141."

Kelly went back to his office and phoned Ralph Hauser in Langley, Virginia. "How goes it at the *Spook Farm*, Ralph? Everything's coming along fine here. We expect the sign off to be at 10am Friday."

"I just got through calling MAC, the Military Airlift Command, to reconfirm our ETA, Estimated Time of Arrival, at Van Nuys in the C-141. We get there at 1315 and should be at the Associated Aviation ramp at 1325. How long will it take to load the equipment?"

"We expect to have everything crated up by 1330 and then we'll load the crates within two hours, using three fork lifts."

"Good. Our load-master will supervise the loading and check the weight and balance. I'll tell the flight commander to plan on a 1600 departure, local time. We're flying to Tehran non-stop, with two airborne refuelings. I've got two pilots who are trained for that procedure. We should get to Tehran by Saturday evening. Sorry I can't stay for your party, but duty calls."

Brad added, "By the way, Ralph, Colonel Ladrun is in LA this week for this acceptance test. He'll be responsible for the installations at the remote sites."

"I expect to spend a lot of time with him in Iran. The Director has instructed me to *straw boss* the installation to make sure the antennas are optimally pointed so we get the right *product* from the folks *up north*."

"You mean, Russia?"

"Careful, Brad. I'm not using the scrambler! But, yes, you understand."

"Good. I'll be arriving in Iran the first of October for the final tuning and initial operation of the system."

"Hey, Brad, that's when we can really have a party. I know this great resort hotel on the Caspian Sea."

"Sounds great! See you Friday."

Kelly parked his car in the LAX lot across from the TWA terminal at 2:15 and walked inside. He went through the security check and headed down the long corridor toward the escalators leading to the departure level. He turned right and took the big elevator used by the crews to go to the planes. He got off at the third level and walked to the entrance of the TWA Ambassador lounge. It was 2:25. He pressed the entry button and the attendant buzzed the door lock, allowing Kelly to open the door. He walked a few steps toward the check in desk when he hear a loud chorus, "Oh, Brad! Here we are!"

Christina, Olga and Colonel Ladrun hurried toward Kelly. The girls kissed him and Ladrun offered him a drink, paid for by the Israeli government. Kelly chose a double Tanqueray on the rocks with a twist. The girls ordered splits of champagne. Ladrun told them to choose a table where they might see Fahi's plane land while he gave the order to the waiter.

Kelly said to the girls, "I'm going to ask you a big favor. As you know, this is my home town and I won't be able to stay with you while you're here. However, Colonel Abe Fahi is here and...."

Olga interrupted, "Don't be sorry, Brad. I really enjoyed my night with him in Tehran. I'm sure Christina will think he's great, too."

Christina put in, "You're doing us a favor by letting us have that beautiful hunk. But, we'll sure miss you, Brad. You're the best!"

"Thanks girls. You know we have so much riding on Colonel Fahi's approval of this acceptance test."

Christina said, "Is that all you need from Abe? Don't worry, you'll get it. We'll see to that. When's he supposed to sign?"

"Friday morning. It means a lot of money to Associated Aviation for him to sign then instead of sometime later."

Christina replied, "Brad, Thursday night Olga and I will extract an iron clad promise from Abe that he'll sign the papers on Friday morning. We have our ways."

"I know you do," he grinned lasciviously.

Ladrun returned, carrying their tray of drinks. "There was only one bartender on duty and he was really busy so I brought our drinks."

Kelly proposed, "Let's drink to a successful completion of the acceptance test Friday morning."

Ladrun replied, "I'll drink to that!"

The girls chorused, "To Fahi's signature!"

A TWA 747 touched down on runway 24 north as they made their toast. Kelly said, "That could be Fahi's plane. If it taxis over to the International Arrivals Terminal, that's it. If it comes here, it's not."

The plane rolled down the runway, turned around and taxied back east toward the cluster of terminal buildings. When it came to the TWA terminal, it kept right on going toward the International Terminal. Kelly checked his watch. 10 past 3. He observed, "It'll take Fahi at least 30 minutes to get off the plane, clear passport control, retrieve his bag, and clear customs. If we leave here in 20 minutes we'll be at the door to greet him as he comes out of the customs area and heads for the main terminal."

They strolled over and had been waiting less than five minutes when they spotted Colonel Fahi, carrying a huge suitcase and fighting his way through the crowd jamming the exit doors. Kelly rushed over, "Welcome to the US, Abe. What have you got in that big suitcase?"

"Selamat, Brad, It's great to get into the country. The way those *Nazis* in your immigration service treated me, I thought they were going to send me back to Tehran."

"Don't feel discriminated against, Abe. They even treat returning Americans that way. Apparently their philosophy is: everyone is a crook and it's our job to catch them."

"Anyway, it's good to be here. My suitcase is almost empty. My wife wants me to fill it up with presents from Rodeo Drive in Beverly Hills. Do you know where that is?"

"I sure do. And I have two assistants to help you with the shopping. Christina and Olga have fantastic taste and know Rodeo Drive like the inside of a bed."

"Good. My wife gave me a long list, but I'm really poor at picking out things."

"Abe, you're going to be pretty busy witnessing the acceptance test. You just give the list to the girls and they'll do the shopping while you're working."

"But, how much money shall I give them?"

"Don't worry about paying for the gifts. Associated Aviation will take care of that."

The girls hugged and kissed Fahi. Fahi and Ladrun embraced each other and kissed on each cheek in the universal Mid East fashion.

Ladrun said, "It's good to see you, Colonel Fahi. We'll be together a lot this week, going through the acceptance test. We plan to send the equipment to Iran on Friday afternoon. Then I'll see you in Iran next Tuesday to start installing everything in your country."

Fahi replied, "The shipping depends entirely upon my approval of the tests. The Royal Iranian Air Force requirements are very severe. Nobody ever passed the acceptance test the first time through. I'm planning on being here at least three week so Associated Aviation can correct the deficiencies I shall find."

Olga noticed the disappointment on Brad's face and whispered in his ear, "Don't worry. We promised he'd sign, and we'll see that he does."

Kelly whispered back, "I certainly hope so. He sounds a lot tougher than I expected."

Kelly said to Fahi, "I'll drive you to your hotel. The others are staying there, too, but they came in a separate car. We'll meet them there."

During the drive, Brad asked Fahi, "We've reserved a bungalow at the Beverly Hills Hotel for you, but Olga and Christina already have a large bungalow. I know they'd love you to stay with them. Which do you prefer?"

"That's no choice at all! Of course, I'd prefer to stay with the girls. You're sure it's OK?"

"Yes, I'm sure. Olga is in love with you after the night you spent with her in Tehran. Christina finds you very attractive, too. They specialize in two girls in bed games."

"Sounds great. Theoretically, we Moslems can take four wives. But in today's Iran it's only one wife. We couldn't afford more than one with Tehran's living costs. My grandfather had four wives, but he only slept with them one at a time. Imagine - two at a time! It sounds like paradise."

Because of the heavy afternoon traffic on the San Diego Freeway, it was after 5 when Kelly parked on a street behind the Beverly Hills Hotel, near bungalow three. Kelly helped Fahi carry his huge suitcase and briefcase to the cottage. As they walked along the path, Fahi remarked, "What a lovely, tropical garden. This doesn't seem like a hotel at all, no lobby, no check in."

"The Beverly Hills has a lobby and check in like all hotels, but it's more discrete. A lot of movie people stay here and they like their privacy. So, if you're staying in one of the bungalows, you can enter from the back of the hotel and never go through the lobby if you don't want to."

"I thought movie people liked to be seen."

"Sometimes they do. The hotel has the famous Polo Lounge for the residents to use when they want to be seen."

"I'd like to see a movie star."

"We can have dinner in the Polo Lounge this evening. Maybe we'll see some movie stars."

"I'd like that very much."

They walked up the stairs to the porch and Brad opened the door using Olga's key. Kelly pointed to a bedroom, "Put your things in there. I believe the girls left you an empty closet."

Christina and Olga walked in at that moment. Olga said excitedly, "Guess who we saw in the lobby, Brad?"

"I can't imagine. Who?"

"Richard Dreyfuss. He looks just like he does in the movies, except he has a beard now."

"He's probably growing it for his next role. I read something in the LA Times about his next movie, but I can't remember what it was."

Christina added, "I just love his movies. He's so cute!"

Fahi overheard the conversation from the bedroom and said, "A real movie star! Brad says we'll have dinner in the Polo Lounge this evening and maybe we'll see some movie stars then."

Christina replied, "Abe, you can be sure there will be at least one star at dinner time. The movie people use the Polo Lounge to transact business. I must tell you, Colonel Ladrun said he can't have dinner with us tonight. He's visiting a cousin who lives in Beverly Hills."

Olga broke in, "The sun's still high. Let's go down to the pool before dinner."

Kelly asked if Fahi had an extra swim suit. He did, and remarked, "I need a swim to relax after my long flight from London."

After their swim, they stretched out on the lounge chairs to dry off in the hot California August sun. Over a round of drinks, Fahi enjoyed the view of the *beautiful people* around the pool, especially the girls in their tiny bikinis.

During their meal in the Polo Lounge, Christina pointed out two well known actresses. Olga identified three actors who had appeared in recent films. Fahi savored this opportunity to *rub elbows* with the stars. During dinner Brad managed to squeeze in the information Fahi needed about the schedule for the next day, "The acceptance test will begin at 9:30 and there'll be a short briefing beforehand at 9. An Associated Aviation chauffeur will pick you up at 8am. You'll be coming in style. For you, he's using the Cadillac limousine of the Chairman of the Board." After telling the girls to *take good care of Abe,* he headed for home.

That night in bungalow three, Christina and Olga treated Fahi to a long series of sexual delights. All three, satiated, fell into a deep sleep. Fahi spent the night dreaming of the sexual exploits he would experience this week with the beautiful girls.

On Tuesday, 4 August 1976, Colonel Fahi arrived at the huge entrance lobby of the Associated Aviation corporate headquarters at 8:50 in the long, black limousine. Kelly opened the limousine door and escorted Fahi into the lobby where he was given a royal welcome by President Morrell and the vice president of finance. He was led to the doorway of the private office of the Chairman of the Board who greeted him with a warm, "Welcome to Associated Aviation, Colonel Fahi. Come in and be seated."

The chairman's office looked more like a living room than a business office. There was no desk, just a round marble table with a telephone that the chairman used to communicate with the outside world. There was a comfortable sitting area with two large leather couches and three leather chairs and a huge coffee table, laden with an array of pastries plus a large silver coffee pot with china tea cups and saucers next to it. There was a crystal pitcher filled with fresh orange juice. A beautiful young secretary dressed in high fashion clothing was present to serve the coffee and other refreshments.

During the conversation the chairman remarked, "Colonel Fahi, I hope you have a profitable visit to Associated Aviation. I'm sure our president, Dr. Morrell, and our IBEX project director, Dr. Kelly, will take care of your needs and concerns."

Fahi replied, "Sir, everything has been perfect so far. I must warn you, however, the Shah-an-Shah's government has placed very severe requirements on the IBEX system. It is my duty to see that these requirements are met completely."

The chairman responded, "I know the Shah very well. My wife and I spent a week skiing with his majesty and the queen at St. Moritz last January. After you approve the acceptance test Friday morning, I plan to call the Shah and explain what an outstanding job you have done in fulfilling his duties."

Next Kelly led Fahi to the large conference room where Tom Bradley gave a twenty minute explanation of the IBEX system and outlined the steps in the acceptance test along with a schedule, showing completion early Friday morning."

Fahi responded, "Dr. Kelly, it looks like your team has done an excellent job of integrating the IBEX system. I truly hope you finish on Friday. But, if so, it would be the first time I've witnessed an acceptance test that didn't have to be re-run at least once to eliminate the discrepancies I discovered."

Kelly answered, "Colonel Fahi, we think you'll be pleasantly surprised."

Tom added, "Let's get over to the *secure* IBEX building and get started on the almost 100 tests planned for today."

At the end of the day, the company chauffeur drove Fahi back to the Beverly Hills Hotel and to Christina and Olga. The strenuous testing schedule continued from 9 to 5 on Wednesday and Thursday. Each evening at the bungalow, Christina and Olga showed Fahi the regal gifts they had chosen for his wife from her long list. Then each night, the girls showed Fahi a fabulous time in bed.

As Fahi prepared for bed Thursday night, Olga and Christina confronted him, completely nude. Olga said, "Abe, we need to discuss something with you."

"What is it, Olga? A new sex position?"

"No, it's a serious matter, Abe. Brad called this afternoon and he's worried to death you're not going to sign the completion certificate tomorrow morning. He says you've found several discrepancies that need to be fixed."

"That's true. I did find four discrepancies, but they were minor. None the less, they must be fixed before I sign the completion certificate."

"Brad says the discrepancies are software changes that can be fixed easily. He has a proposal to make to you, but he didn't want to discuss it at Associated Aviation. He doesn't want to embarrass or compromise you in front of others."

"I'm willing to listen."

"He's waiting at this number to hear from you." Olga handed Fahi a slip of paper with Kelly's home phone number on it.

Fahi dialed the number and said, "Good evening, Brad, I understand you want to talk to me."

"Yes, Abe. I'd like you to sign the completion certificate tomorrow morning and I'll promise you that within two weeks, you'll have the software changes to fix the discrepancies you found."

"How can you do that? The hardware would be in Iran by then."

"I discussed it by phone today with Dr. Fahrina Mahi at Iran Software, Limited, and she told me she can do it."

Fahi had his mind on the two nude bodies in front of him. He told Brad, "I'll have to sleep on your proposal. I'll give you my answer in the morning. Good night." Fahi hung up the phone and said to the girls, "I listened to Brad's offer. Now let's get to bed. I'm horny as hell tonight."

Christina replied, icily, "Then, Colonel Fahi, you better go to bed and *Jack-off*. Olga and I are not going to bed with anyone who would treat a friend like you just treated Brad."

"What do you mean? I told him I'd sleep on it. Now, let's go to bed."

Olga said, "No, Abe. Brad made you a fair proposal with no risk to you. If you want Christina and me in bed tonight, you better call Brad back and say you'll sign tomorrow."

"Well, I don't know…."

Christina interrupted, "How would you like your dear wife to know who picked out all those presents for her?"

"Ah... ah…" sputtered Fahi. He took a deep breath and answered, "Your logic is impeccable. There isn't any risk to me if Iran Software is fixing the software. OK, I'll call him back right now and accept his idea."

Olga said, "That's better! You can phone him from bed."

Fahi flopped flat on his back in the middle of the big bed. Christina dialed Brad's number and handed the phone to Fahi while Olga cuddled up beside him.

Kelly answered the phone and heard Fahi say, "Ahhh, that's good."

Kelly asked, "What's good? Is that you, Abe?"

"Oh... ah... The proposal is good. Brad, I thought over your plan to fix the software. I accept it. I'll sign the certificate in the morning. Have a good night!"

"You too, Abe." Kelly thought to himself, *I was really sweating. I see the girls' magic worked after all."*

Fahi, Christina, and Olga had another exciting night at the Beverly Hills Hotel, completely fulfilling Abe's wildest expectations.

On Friday, 7 August 1976, Kelly met Fahi's limousine at the lobby entrance. "Abe, the final test is scheduled from 9 to 9:30. Then the signing of the completion certificate will be in the chairman's office at 10."

Fahi picked up his security badge in the lobby and they strode over to the IBEX building. The final few acceptance test steps were quickly completed and the two returned to the headquarters building. The completion certificate was sitting on the chairman's large round marble table. Surrounding the table were the five corporate vice presidents and the president, Dr. Morrell, with the chairman of the board in the center, holding a flashing gold pen. A company photographer stood to one side with a flash camera to document the signing. A TV camera had also been set up to put the signing on video tape. Fahi appeared dumbfounded by the reception.

Kelly whispered, "Don't get nervous, Abe. The chairman just likes a show."

The chairman pointed to the document of the table, "General Fahi, if you'll step forward, here is the golden souvenir pen for your signing of the completion certificate. This is a milestone in Associated Aviation's great history and we want it recorded for posterity. I hope you don't mind the photographers."

"No, Sir, I don't mind. But, Sir, I'm only a Colonel, not a General.

The chairman replied, "Not any more, General Fahi. I just talked to the Shah this morning and told him what a great job you've done here in fulfilling your duties on IBEX. At my suggestion, he awarded you a star. He said he would personally arrange a ceremony to present your commission and star on Sunday when you return to Teheran."

Smiling broadly, Fahi replied, "Sir, I'm astounded. Thank you for the good news." He walked forward, took the pen and, to the flashing of bulbs and the whir of the TV cameras, he signed the completion certificate.

The vice president of finance immediately reached over, grabbed the certificate and handed it to the Citibank officer who witnesses the signing. The Citibank officer took the document, hurried to a telephone in the back of the chairman's office and called the Citibank home office. Exactly 85 seconds after General Fahi signed the certificate, nine hundred sixty million dollars were transferred to the Associated Aviation bank account. Before General Fahi and Dr. Kelly sat down for lunch in the executive dining room, the funds had earned over twenty thousand dollars in interest.

After lunch, Fahi, Ladrun, and Kelly walked over to the Associated Aviation flight line. On the concrete apron of the huge hanger sat three slick jet fighters, just off the production line, receiving their final ground checks. The production test pilot was sitting in the cockpit of one of the fighters, checking the sophisticated weapon delivery and navigation electronics for which Kelly supervised the design in the early 1970's.

Kelly looked up and down the long north-south Van Nuys Airport runway. He looked south towards the Santa Monica mountains stretching westward from the San Diego Freeway. The sides of the mountains were studded with expensive hillside homes, each with an azure-blue swimming pool. The bare rock mountains west of the airport hid the Rocketdyne test facility where the enormous rocket engines had been tested before they carried man to the Moon on the Apollo space vehicle. Kelly had helped design the inertial guidance system that put the Apollo into orbit around the moon.

A large military jet transport with four jet engine pods under its wings flew into his field of view. It was entering the landing pattern for Van Nuys Airport. Kelly exclaimed, "There's what we're waiting for, the C-141 that will take IBEX to Tehran today."

Kelly, General Fahi, and Colonel Ladrun watched the plane turn from base leg onto final approach, heading south. The huge transport set down within the first one hundred feet of the runway. The pilot applied reverse thrust on the four engines and he was able to turn off the runway in less than a thousand feet.

Ladrun remarked, "Your American MAC, Military Airlift Command, pilots are always practicing short field landings and take offs. They act like every landing is an urgent exercise of national security. Our Israeli pilots are just as good. They are driven by the pressures of the threat surrounding our country."

Kelly responded, "Joseph, our MAC pilots face pressures like your Israeli pilots. Our strategic threat from the Soviet Union is just as real and just as great as your tactical threat. Those big military air transports like the C-141 and C-5 will be sitting ducks in case of a war with the Soviet Union. And Europe's survival depends on the MAC airlift from America if the Soviets ever attack Western Europe."

The huge C-141 taxied up to the Associated Aviation ramp, dwarfing the three new jet fighters sitting there. They would fit inside the cargo hold if their wings were removed.

The engines shut down and the door on the left side opened. Ralph Hauser waved to the three men. The Associated Aviation ramp chief, who was responsible for loading the IBEX equipment crates into the C-141, hurried with his electric cart to the exit door and began a conference with the loadmaster. Before Kelly and his companions could get to Hauser, the huge loading ramp in the tail of the C-141 had been opened and the three yellow fork lift trucks from Associated Aviation were queuing up to load the first crates.

Kelly introduced the two men with him to Ralph Hauser, who said he remembered them from Iran, when Kelly gave his briefings to the Air Force people. When Kelly explained how Colonel Fahi became a general, Hauser congratulated him warmly.

"Thank you, Ralph. I'm really excited about becoming a general. I really thought I would retire as a colonel."

Ladrun added, "Abe, a general in the Iranian Air Force with your technical knowledge is a rare bird. You deserve your commission."

Kelly said, "Ralph, you're going to see a lot of these two during the next two months. Colonel Ladrun is responsible for the site construction and installation of the electronic equipment and antennas. General Fahi will oversee the whole operation." Then Kelly explained Ralph would be responsible for the US government's part of IBEX.

Fahi interrupted, "You mean Ralph is going to make sure we collect good intelligence information from the sites overlooking the Soviet Union."

Hauser responded, "I can't confirm that officially, but I'm sure you know why IBEX was allowed to go to Iran."

"Yes, I know, and I also know it cost my government an additional $200 million for site six so you can spy on the Soviets."

"Abe, let's just say we're going to provide *surveillance* of the Soviets to insure the security of the Western World, of which Iran is an important part!"

"Enough of this *flag waving!* Let's make sure the airplane gets loaded so all this stuff can be on its way to Iran."

Tom Bradley, the deputy project director, walked up to Hauser and the others. Kelly asked if they had finished crating everything. Tom answered, "We were ready thirty minutes before the C-141 got here."

Kelly explained Tom and three other engineers would be flying to Tehran on Sunday to supervise the installation from Associated Aviation's point of view as prime contractor.

Ralph Hauser responded, "Tom, you and your engineers, and Joseph, Abe and I are going to spend a lot of time together during the next two months. We'll be out in the remote sites three nights out of the week. I hope you can play Poker."

Tom's face lit up. "I sure can. When I was just a kid, I learned how from my grandfather in Oklahoma. He was a professional card shark.."

The loading crew worked feverishly until the last crate was loaded at 3:30 and the huge tail gate was closed. The loadmaster and the AA ramp chief checked that all the paper work was in order. Hauser waved goodbye as the exit door closed. The ATC, Air Traffic Control, gave out the clearance for a non-stop flight to the Doshen Toeppeh Air Force Base in Tehran, Iran.

Over the ramp loudspeaker, Kelly heard the Air Traffic Controller exclaim, "Are you sure you have enough fuel to fly non-stop to Tehran?"

Back came the answer from the C-141 flight commander," Yes, Sir. We have two airborne refueling rendezvous scheduled at checkpoints Alpha and Bravo."

"So that's how you do it. We don't get many C-141's here. Have a good trip!"

"Roger, Sir, and you have a good day!"

Kelly and the others watched the huge plane lumber along the taxiway to the north end of the runway. They heard over the loudspeaker, "This is Heavy Eagle, ready for take off."

"Heavy Eagle, " responded the tower, "you're cleared for take off."

The engines roared as the flight commander pushed the four throttles forward. The C-141 lifted off half way down the runway and leapt into the air. The landing gears retracted. The spectators heard, "Heavy Eagle, contact departure control on 127 point 35 now. So long."

"Roger, so long!"

Tom hollered, "Yippee! IBEX is on its way!"

The onlookers added a loud chorus of "Hooray!"

Tom added, "Let's head for *Squadron 29!* It's party time!"

The whole Squadron 29 Restaurant had been reserved for the IBEX party. The restaurant, a copy of a French farmhouse used as the World War I headquarters of Squadron 29 fighter airplanes, overlooked the Van Nuys Airport runways. Helen was checking that the huge buffet table was loaded with the variety of hors d'oeuvres she had specified: stuffed hard boiled eggs with red and black caviar, barbecued spare ribs, hot and cold cheese dips, and an array of fresh cut vegetables to use with the dips. There were also bowls of guacamole with tortilla tostados for dipping. Guests were already queued up for drinks at the two *open* bars at each end of the room.

All the executive secretaries, dressed in tight fitting slacks and blouses that exposed their bosoms, were there. So was the entire IBEX team.

Tom Bradley remarked to Kelly, "Boss, this is quite a spread you've put on for us. It makes all that hard work worthwhile. Where's that notorious Sandy from the Washington office? I'm looking forward to meeting that little lady."

"Look out there on the runway. She's on the Associated Aviation Sabreliner taxiing toward the company ramp, along with

Mr. Thompson and Mr. Hack. I'll introduce you as soon as she gets here."

"If you don't mind, Brad, I'll mosey over to meet her coming off the plane. I don't want to take any chances on her being intercepted by someone else. I hear she's pretty hot stuff!"

"Sandy does have a reputation for liking sex."

"I'm just the one to help her out!"

Kelly caught sight of a blonde and a red head coming in the door. "Excuse me, Tom. I've got to greet someone."

Kelly rushed over to the two girls and kissed each one on the cheek, "Welcome to the IBEX party. It's really due to your *magic* that we're having this celebration today."

Christina remarked, "You know we were glad to help, and we had a fabulous time doing it. Wow, what a spread. The food looks fabulous. Here goes my diet."

Olga added, "So many handsome men. Are we going to have dancing?"

Kelly answered, "There'll be a small combo here in about an hour. We can dance as late as we want."

Tom Bradley came back into the restaurant with the Washington group in tow. He held Sandy's hand possessively.

Bob Hack spotted Christina and Olga and embraced each in turn, saying, "Fancy meeting you here!"

Sandy gushed, "Oh, Dr. Kelly, you're a dear to invite me to the IBEX party. And thanks for Tom here. He's a darling. I understand he's your deputy." She kissed Kelly on the cheek.

Kelly responded, "Sandy, we appreciate your help with the export license. Without that, we couldn't have this party!"

The party continued on until the wee hours of the morning. General Fahi and Bob Hack made an agreement. Hack got Olga and Fahi got Christina. Ladrun found a big-breasted red headed Jewish girl who *just loved Israel and Israeli officers!* Tom Bradley invited Sandy to bed and she accepted. No one missed Kelly when he left for home at ten.

Chapter 13.

Return to Tehran

Thursday, 1 October, 1976

In the two months since Kelly's deputy project director, Tom Bradley, and his three engineers went to Iran, they had worked hard to install the IBEX system in Tehran and in the surrounding mountains. From Los Angeles, Kelly kept in almost daily contact by secure telephone.

Sandy had been transferred to the Tehran office of Associated Aviation to be Tom's executive secretary. She and Tom had set up housekeeping in a large two bedroom flat in a high rise apartment building in east Tehran, about one kilometer from the Hilton Hotel. The corporation had a rule against husband and wife working together. However, there was no rule about live-in couples. So they kept their marriage secret. Sandy had given up on her plans to sleep with every Associated Aviation executive. She recognized the advantages of fidelity to a single, outstanding executive who was her very own.

Tom's base salary was $30,000 and Sandy's was $15,000 a year. Each of the pair received a per diem allowance of $75 a day, plus a 25% overseas salary bonus, so they had an income of $9,187.50 a month. That was enough to live very well in expensive Tehran and to put away $5000 a month into a joint Swiss account they'd opened in Zürich. After their three year stint in Tehran, Tom had estimated they would have more than $200,000 in their Swiss bank account, enough to make them financially independent, particularly if they lived in a low cost area like Lisbon, Portugal, where the living costs were less than half those in expensive Los Angeles. Tom planned to take early retirement from Associated Aviation after his Tehran assignment. He figured with his $800 a month retirement pay from AAC and the $1700 a month interest from their Zürich nest egg, they could live like royalty in Lisbon.

Sandy liked the idea of living in Europe. She recognized the advantages of the European culture: operas, concerts, travel to beautiful and historic cities where Western Civilization had its roots. She noticed almost immediately from the many Europeans she met in Tehran that not everyone thought the US was the best place in the world to live.

Three other Associated Aviation engineers had flats in the same apartment building. One of them, David Elliott, brought his wife, but after a month in Tehran, the cultural shock got the best of her and she returned to California alone. The other two engineers, Dr. John Vries and Jack Nishamoto, were confirmed bachelors and shared a two bedroom apartment.

Each morning, Sandy and Tom and the three engineers shared a ride in a company car with an Iranian driver to Doshen Toeppeh Air Force Base, where the IBEX central control station was being set up.

The men flew from Doshen Toeppeh to the remote sites almost every week in an Iranian Air Force C-130 with an HH-60 helicopter in the cargo bay. When they reached an airfield near one of the sites, they rolled the chopper out the tail of the big plane and flew the short distance to the mountain top where Colonel Ladrun and his Iranian crew of laborers had constructed the buildings needed for the listening post equipment including the antennas.

Tom and the three engineers were away from Tehran almost every Sunday night through Tuesday night. They stayed in dormitories at the various sites. They returned to Tehran Wednesday afternoon, all ready for the two day weekend: Thursday and Friday, the Moslem Sabbath. Their work week was Saturday through Wednesday, like all the other residents of Tehran. They acquired the *mind set* that Wednesday night was like Friday night at home, the night to start celebrating the coming weekend.

There were several reasons why Colonel Ladrun was a special asset to the IBEX project. He was born in Tbilisi, in the Soviet Republic of Georgia in southern Russia at the foot of the Caucus Mountains. His father was a party official in Tbilisi and his mother was Jewish. Ladrun went to engineering school at the University of Moscow where he met and fell in love with a beautiful Jewish girl, Ilona, with a similar background. She pointed out that he was a Jew by Jewish law since he had a Jewish mother. The two began attending clandestine services in a tiny synagogue operated by a Rabbi who was an *underground* Jew also. After graduation, Joseph went to work in Moscow as an electrical engineer on military communication systems. Ilona worked for the same agency developing software for digital communication systems. Unknown to the Western intelligence community, the Soviet invested heavily in this technology and developed advanced spread spectrum communications systems for secure military use.

When Joseph and Ilona decided to immigrate to Israel, Joseph appealed to his father for help. After getting over his initial shock, Joseph's father agreed. He approached a boyhood friend, a key official in the Moscow immigration office, and asked that Joseph and Ilona's permission be granted quickly.   Joseph's father willingly paid from his large bank savings account the equivalent of two years' salary in bribes required to pull the right strings. When the couple applied for permission to leave Russia, they were in Israel within the record time of two months. Joseph took with him not only his technical education but also a knowledge of how Russians think and react.

Kelly went to his office before 7:30 Thursday morning to receive a scrambler telephone call from Tom Bradley.

"Good evening, Boss. I guess it's still morning in Los Angeles. This eleven and a half hour time difference gets confusing. It's almost as confusing as the weekend starting Wednesday evening instead of Friday. Sandy and I are getting used to it and really love it here."

"That's good. Too bad David's wife didn't like it. How's he holding up?"

"He's doing OK, spends a lot of time and money in the girly bars, dancing with those expensive European whores."

"How's the project coming?"

"All of the six remote sites are working now. We just sent the first data from each site to the central processing center this week.

Everything worked great. Joseph Ladrun's a genius when it comes to communications. He really knows how to make it *play*! I wish I could say as much for your favorite *spook*. Ralph Hauser's a real pain in the ass. Always worrying about the wrong things!"

"We need Ralph's help, though. He gives us entry to a lot of information we need to do our job. Tom, I'm leaving for Tel Aviv today and I've got a meeting there with Ladrun on Sunday. We'll be getting to Tehran about 1pm Monday. We don't need to be picked up but I wanted you to know when to expect us"

"Great. Have a good trip."

Kelly finished packing papers into his briefcase and carefully tucked his courier permit for the hand carrying of classified papers overseas into his jacket pocket. None of his papers were US classified, but they were classified *Iran Secret*. By contractual agreement, Associated Aviation handled Iran Secret using the same procedures as US Secret. The only thing that would be US classified was the *product*, the electronic spying data from IBEX. Ralph Hauser and his CIA colleagues would take the *product in-country* so Kelly didn't have to worry about that. That was an *agency* problem.

Kelly took the elevator down to the lobby and headed for the parking lot where his wife and five children were waiting in the family station wagon to take him to the airport. He'd be gone for six weeks, getting back in time for Thanksgiving, but missing the La Paz sail boat race starting October 31st. His son planned to skipper the *Orion* on the 1100 nautical mile race, with Kelly's wife and other children as crew, augmented by Kelly's friend, Brian Cabot, as navigator.

At the Los Angeles Airport, Kelly bought a standby ticket on the TWA flight that stopped in New York, Rome, Athens, and finally reached Tel Aviv about 3:30 in the afternoon of the next day, Friday. Kelly and his family had time for coffee and sweet rolls in the Ambassador Lounge and then walked together to departure gate 38. Kelly wished his eldest son *Good luck* on the La Paz Race, and told his wife, "Anna darling, I'm going to miss you. Have a good race to La Paz. When I come back the Friday before Thanksgiving, that will be the end of my traveling for this year."

"It's been so nice having you home all summer. It's hard to get used to your traveling again. At least, I'll be busy thinking about the race instead of missing you during the week of the La Paz Race. I'll fly back to LA so I'll be here when you get back."

Kelly kissed Anna goodbye, hugged the kids, and rushed onto the Lockheed Tristar wide body jet. He settled down into his window seat in first class. He was surprised to find he knew the passenger who took the seat next to him: Christina! Olga took the seat just across the aisle in the center section.

Astounded, Kelly exclaimed, "What in the world are you doing on this flight?"

Christina answered, "Olga and I came to Los Angeles with Amnon this week. He had business at the Israeli consulate. He asked us to watch over you during your flight."

"How did you know I'd be on this flight? I didn't even tell my wife which airline I planned to use until we got to the airport."

"I don't know but Mossad has it's ways. Amnon got a call just before 9 this morning. We had to rush to get tickets."

Kelly thought to himself, *The only person who knew what flight I was taking was the girl in the TWA Ambassador Lounge who gave me my boarding passes. She must have called Amnon.*

"I'm delighted to see you both. Now I won't have to search for you in the big crowd that always meets the Friday afternoon arrivals at Ben Gurion Airport."

Kelly and the girls had a festive flight. During the long overnight leg from New York to Rome they were served roast beef with all the trimmings from a warming cart. After the third after dinner drink, Christina reached under the blanket covering Kelly and grabbed his member.

She whispered into his ear, "Brad, please meet me in the left head. I want you so much. It's been so long!"

"You've got my dander up. I'll be right there!"

Kelly and Christina passed an amorous thirty minutes in the head.

Then Christina said, "Brad, don't leave. Olga and I flipped coins and I won first. Let her in when she knocks."

Christina left and Olga came in and had her turn with a repeat performance.

Afterwards, the three stretched out in their big first class sleeper seats and didn't stir until the stewardess awakened them to serve a sumptuous breakfast before the landing Rome.

After the short stops in Rome and Athens, they arrived at Ben Gurion just after 4. Colonel Ladrun met them at the passport control and escorted them through the crew clearance line. Within twenty minutes after the landing they were in General Yidron's staff car, driving towards the Tel Aviv Hilton. Ladrun announced, "Here's the key to your suite. I've already checked you in. You're on your own until 8 Sunday morning when I'll pick you up. I'm spending the Sabbath with my family because I've been in Iran so much since I last saw you."

"Joseph, I'm sure with Christina and Olga as companions I'll make it until Sunday morning without you. Have a good visit with your family. What's our schedule?"

"A meeting with General Izhack first thing Sunday morning at the Ministry of Defense. Then the Elta briefing in the director general's conference room at 10. We should be finished by noon. Then you're free until we leave for Tehran Monday morning at 9. I've got our tickets on the El Al flight from Ben Gurion to Mehrabad in Tehran."

"As usual, Joseph, you've got everything well organized."

After putting their things away in the suite, Kelly and the girls hurried down to the pool to take advantage of the last hour of Israeli sunshine. They picked up their towels from the pool attendant and chose lounge chairs on the sunny east side of the pool. Kelly challenged the girls to a two lap race up and down the length of the pool. He was barely able to beat them. They rested in the warm sea water at the north or deep end and watched the orange sun sinking in the western sky over the Mediterranean. The Jewish Sabbath started at sundown. Most businesses closed at noon on Friday and the people crowded the markets and shops before the Sabbath closing, eager to be home with their families at sundown. A solemn quiet descended on the city as the Sabbath approached.

At six, on the way back to their suite, Kelly asked, "Where would you like to have dinner tonight? How about the Alhambra in Jaffa?"

Christina replied, "I've had my fill of expensive restaurants. Why don't we walk down to Dizengoff Street and eat in the sidewalk cafes?"

Olga added, "That's a good idea. We can have appetizers in one, a meat course in another, and dessert in a third one."

"Sounds like fun," agreed Kelly.

They quickly changed out of their swim gear and into street clothes. Another few moments and they were walking down the Hilton entry/exit driveway to Arlozoroff and then along the two short blocks to Dizengoff, the tree lined walking street of Tel Aviv. Both sides of the street were lined with shops and a multitude of sidewalk cafes selling a variety of goodies. They chose one and Kelly ordered three fried pastries filled with melted cheese and three large glasses of fresh orange juice, as cocktails and hors d'oeuvres. The bill came to 20 shekels, a little over $1.50 at the exchange rate of 12 shekels to a dollar. While seated at the little table, Kelly admired the long legged Israeli girls walking by in their tight jeans that showed off every curve.

They continued along Dizengoff to the corner of Keren Kavemet where they chose a table on the sidewalk at the corner cafe. Here they ordered shashlik (charcoal broiled lamb kebabs) and french fries as their main course with Orangiata (orange soda) to drink. This bill was 60 shekels.

Strolling further along Dizengoff they came to a small café serving soft ice cream and pastries. They had chocolate éclairs filled with whipped cream for dessert. This bill was 15 shekels. Kelly computed the total was 95 shekels, less than $8. A lot less than the 1800 shekels he would have paid in one of the restaurants frequented by the businessmen and tourists.

The group decided to continue walking to Frishman, where they turned right and walked to Hayarkon, which ran north and south along the beach. They strolled along admiring the lights reflecting in the dark Mediterranean Sea, until they reached their hotel. In the lobby they collected their three free drinks, using vouchers found in their suite. They had Sabra on the rocks, an

Israeli coffee-orange liquor and returned to their room about 9. After Brad made love with Christina (since it was her turn), they fell asleep. The quarter moon shone soft light into their room.

Saturday morning the group decided to drive to Jerusalem. They rented a Hertz car in the Hilton lobby and reached the city just after 9. They drove around the Old City on Maale Ha Shalom to just west of the Dung Gate. Kelly found a parking spot on a steep hill next to the old city wall. They walked down the hill to the Dung Gate, turned left into the Old City. Kelly noticed the contrasts here: new Mercedes cars entering along with donkeys and the usual hordes of tourists who had just disgorged from a tour bus. On the way to the *Wailing Wall* they paused to look at the excavations on the right that the Israeli government was sponsoring: ancient ruins, remains of a long ago Jewish building. The *Wailing Wall* is the holy remains of the destroyed Jewish Temple of King Solomon. Being the Jewish Sabbath, there were large groups on the men's side, the left, and on the women's side, the right – all praying. The bearded Jews' heads were nodding as they prayed, the sounds of their incantations drifted back to where Kelly, Christina and Olga stood gazing at the wall.

Kelly remarked, "This is quite a sight. And to think, before the 1967 war, when the Old City was under Jordanian control, Israeli Jews were not permitted at the *Wailing Wall*."

Olga nodded in agreement, "With the Old City under Israeli control, there is religious freedom in all four religious quarters: Moslem, Christian, Jewish, and Armenian."

Christina added, "The Israeli archeologists are intent on discovering their Jewish roots around the old temple. They have excavated tunnels under the old wall and found a number of religious rooms there. The entrance is just left of the *Wailing Wall*."

Kelly replied excitedly, "Let's go and explore the tunnels."

"I'm sorry, Brad, but visitors are not allowed on the Sabbath. You'll have to do your exploring some other day."

"Too bad, but I'm sure there are many other things we can see on Saturday, aren't there?"

Olga answered enthusiastically, "Of course. We can visit the *Dome of the Rock*, which is the second most religious place for

Moslems. And we can follow the path of Jesus on the day of the Crucifixion as he passed the *Stations of the Cross*."

"Let's do both!"

Leaving the *Wailing Wall* area, the trio headed north towards the Moslem Quarter, wandering through the narrow streets, more like alleyways, of the Old City. They turned right up a street to the entrance to *Haram esh Sharif*, the plateau where stood both the golden *Dome of the Rock* and the *El Aqsa Mosque*, built on the ruins of the destroyed Jewish temple. They paid the Moslem attendants the 15 shekel fee and walked into the *Dome of the Rock* where they found the enshrined Rock which is supposed to be the place from which Mohammed ascended to Heaven. The inside of the building was very beautifully decorated with colored geometric designs.

They left through the same gate and headed towards the Via Dolorosa where they searched out the signs marking the *Stations of the Cross*, ending at the *Holy Sepulcher*, the Christian shrine where Christ's body was supposed to have been entombed after the Crucifixion. Armed 2-man Israeli patrols, in charge of keeping the security of the Old City, reminded them of the constant threat of violence that hung over this holy place of three of the world's great religions.

Next they wandered through the Old City markets. There was a vast array of goods to buy: everything from oriental carpets to water pipes. There were also many oriental foods for sale: the aromas of spices and cooking food surrounded the visitors. They settled for having lunch in a tiny restaurant where they chose lamb kebabs and Turkish coffee with paklava for dessert.

On Sunday morning, Kelly got up early enough to have a leisurely breakfast in the Tel Aviv Hilton coffee shop. He reached the lobby at 8am, just in time to see Ladrun arrive at the Hilton entrance in General Izhack's staff car. Kelly exchanged *Shalom*s with Ladrun who was in the back seat. Kelly sat in the front right seat, the honored guest seat, next to the general's driver during the fifteen minute drive to the Ministry of Defense and through the guarded entrance gate.

A mini skirted private met them at the entrance to General Izhack's building, and escorted them to his office where the general greeted them with a loud *Shalom*.

Kelly answered, "Shalom, General Izhack. It's a pleasure to be back in Israel after such a long time. My man in Tehran tells me Colonel Ladrun is performing yeoman's service with his site construction and installation."

"Dr. Kelly, IBEX is lucky to have Colonel Ladrun. But his real talent will show when you start collecting intelligence information. He has a real talent for interpreting what the enemy's intentions are from intercepted **ELINT** (ELectronics INTelligence) and **COMINT** (COMmunications INTelligence). He turned the Yom Kippur War from an early disaster into a resounding success by figuring out what the Egyptians and Syrians were up to."

Kelly responded, "We are impressed with him, too."

The general added, "We hope you will approve the release of the first 80% payment, $160 million, on Israeli Aircraft Industry's subcontract to Associated Aviation soon."

"I should be able to sign the *completion certificate* to authorize that money by the middle of the month. I have to visit all six sites first. Now, I'd like to give you a short status briefing on IBEX."

At the end, Kelly said, "Colonel Ladrun and I plan to begin operations of site six on Takht-i-Suleyman Peak, overlooking the Soviets, on Saturday 17 October. The US intelligence community is really eager to get information from this particular site."

"And Mossad is interested in the information from the sites overlooking some of the Shah's neighbors, particularly Iraq. We're still at war with them."

Ladrun interrupted, "It's time to head for the conference room for the Elta briefing."

The general requested, "Wait a moment. I want to ask General Yidron of Mossad if he wants to hear the briefing." Izhack dialed Yidron on his scrambler phone and talked with him in Hebrew. Kelly heard the phrases *IBEX system* and *intelligence product* and also the names *Christina, Olga,* and *Amnon*. After hanging up, General Izhack turned to Kelly, "Apparently the general is well informed about IBEX. Mossad has its ways of getting information, you know."

Kelly said goodbye to the general and he and Ladrun went to the MOD director general's conference room for the briefing by the Elta section of Israeli Aircraft Industry on their work on IBEX. Kelly realized *If we'd given this subcontract to a US construction company and a US antenna company it would have cost at least $600 million because of the per diem and other special costs, instead of the $200 million we're paying IAI.*

The IAI vice president of finance asked, "Dr. Kelly, we have the *completion certificate* here. We'd greatly appreciate it if you would sign it now, rather than the middle of the month. The interest we'd lose in fifteen days would be $1.25 million. To us Israelis, that's a lot of money."

Ladrun added, "Don't worry, Brad. I'll give you my personal guarantee the work's been done right."

Kelly remembered how important it had been for Fahi to sign for Associated Aviation. "After all, Tom Bradley said everything is going well. OK, I'll sign now." He took the certificate, scanned it, and signed.

Ladrun left Kelly at the Hilton entrance saying, "I want to spend this last night in Tel Aviv with my family. I'll pick you up here tomorrow at 7am. That will give us plenty of time to catch our 9am flight. I have a special assistant from Mossad to get us through the formalities quickly."

Kelly returned to his suite and found Christina and Olga ready and willing. They had dinner in the room and watched an R rated movie before retiring to their bed time games.

Kelly got up at 6am, packed, and kissed Christina and Olga goodbye. He went down to the cashier in the lobby and checked out, then snacked on coffee and a sweet roll while waiting for Ladrun. He arrived promptly at 7am and Amnon was with him.

Kelly said, "I thought you were still in LA. You must be going to walk us through the airport security."

It only took them until 7:30 to get to the airport. Amnon by-passed the extensive security checks the other passengers had to go through and they were in the departure lounge by quarter to eight. Kelly used the time to exchange his shekels back to dollars and to buy gifts for his family in the various shops.

The boarding call for the El Al flight to Tehran came at 8:30. Kelly and Ladrun went to the departure gate, descended to the ground level and boarded the bus to their Boeing 707. They took their seats on the crowded plane. There was no first class. Kelly had a window seat on the left side in row 4.

After take off, the plane climbed out over the Mediterranean and turned northerly. They crossed Nicosia, Cypress, at 9:25 and turned right toward Adana, Turkey, flying over it at 9:45. This course avoided flying over Israel's enemies, Syria and Iraq. They headed further right on an easterly heading to Tabriz in Iran, arriving an hour and ten minutes later. They made another turn farther right on a southeasterly heading, reaching their destination at Mehrabad Airport at 1pm Tehran time, some two and a half hours flying time.

Kelly and Ladrun had no trouble clearing passport control and customs at Mehrabad. Fahrina was waiting just outside the customs area. She rushed up and hugged and kissed Kelly, "Welcome to Tehran. Have I ever missed you!"

"It's great to see you, too. How did you know I was coming on this flight?"

"Easy. Shaheen Mouhoud called my office just before lunch."

Kelly, Ladrun and Fahrina fought their way through the unruly crowds in the terminal and found Fahrina's car parked right by the exit steps, guarded by a parking attendant. Fahrina gave him a 100 rial note and they loaded in. After passing the modernistic monument marking the beginning of Eisenhower Boulevard, they soon came to Shimron Road, the freeway leading easterly to the Tehran Hilton.

Kelly and Ladrun checked in while Fahrina had her car parked. She met Kelly at the front desk, carrying her overnight bag. "I hope you don't mind if I spend the night with you."

"Of course not. I'd be disappointed if you didn't."

Ladrun headed for his room while Kelly and Fahrina took the elevator to Kelly's rooms on the eighteenth floor. He again had a corner suite with one room facing the snow capped Elburz

Mountains to the north and one facing towards eastern Tehran with a view to the south as well.

Just as Kelly and Fahrina finished putting their things away, the phone rang. Tom Bradley said, "Welcome to Tehran, Brad. I thought Sandy and I would drop by and see you. We ought to talk about the schedule for tomorrow. I just got back from site six last night."

"Good idea, Tom. Come on over and by all means bring Sandy. You two can plan on having dinner with Fahrina and me and Colonel Ladrun. Why don't you invite the other three fellows to meet us at 7. We don't want them to feel left out."

"Thanks, Brad. I'm sure they'd love to come. Sandy and I'll be over in twenty minutes."

Kelly phoned Ladrun's room and asked him to come up. Then he told Fahrina about the group dinner that evening. She suggested an authentic Iranian Night Club called Shahad that had stage shows as well as dinner. And also single girls who loved to dance with foreigners between the performances. She added, "Since the Shahad is owned by a friend of mine, Nasser Nahim, we'll get a good table near the stage even without reservations."

Shortly, Tom and Sandy arrived and were greeted warmly. Tom had words of high praise for Fahrina's professional crew at Iran Software, Limited, and for some American expatriates she'd hired to work with them.

Kelly told Tom, "I've got a meeting with General Hatami and General Fahi at ten in the morning to give them a briefing on IBEX."

"Fahi knows as much about IBEX as I do!"

"I know, Tom, but this is a protocol briefing. It gives me a chance to touch base with the commander-in-chief for their air force, General Hatami."

"I understand. Hey, I've got an idea. Why don't you ride out to Doshen Toeppeh with Sandy and me and the other engineers in the morning? We go right by here every day. That way we can show you the IBEX control station before your meeting."

"Good idea. What time do we leave?"

We'll pick you up here at 7:30, just a little after the rest of us get picked up at the apartment. We leave about 7:10 every morning."

Tom explained the inspection scheduled. Kelly would visit each site starting Saturday morning using the same C-130 with HH-60 inside as Tom and his crew. They usually used Iranian pilots, but Tom knew there would be American pilots for Kelly's tour.

Colonel Ladrun arrived at Kelly's room and agreed the C-130 was a good way to get around the sites. He added to Kelly, "You and I are scheduled to begin operations at site six beginning a week from next Saturday."

"I suppose Ralph Hauser will be there, too. The CIA is hot to get their first real *product* from the Soviets. Your command of Russian will be a big help there."

"Yes, I'm sure Ralph will be at site six for that occasion. General Fahi and Shaheen will be there, too. Ralph has to report in to the US embassy twice a week so we'll be there without him about half the time."

Fahrina added, "Brad, I'll be operating the central control station at Doshen Toeppeh, receiving and processing any raw data you send over the secure communications links."

Kelly exclaimed, "It looks like IBEX is almost operational. I think we should break out the champagne and drink a toast to IBEX." He strode over to the large refrigerator bar and took out a magnum of Cordon Rouge, opened it with a loud bang, and poured five glasses.

Joseph raised his glass and toasted, "Here's to the IBEX project and the hard working team members who have made it work! L'Chaim!"

The others chorused, "L'Chaim!" and drank the toast.

Tom said, "Sandy and I will be leaving now to get dressed for our evening out. We'll come in the company car with the three engineers and meet you at the Shahad Restaurant at seven, OK?"

"Good. Joseph and I will ride over with Fahrina in her car. See you at seven."

The IBEX group arrived at the Shahad Restaurant just after 7. Kelly greeted the other three AAC engineers, Dr. John Vries, Jack Nishamoto, and David Elliott. The owner, Nasser Nahim, was happy to see Fahrina and, as she had predicted, gave them a choice table in the front-center of the stage. Fahrina asked her friend for a feast of typical Iranian dishes and they dined with enthusiasm as Fahrina explained the Farsi name of each dish.

During and after dinner, the group was treated to a lavish show of Iranian songs and dances performed by a troupe of about twenty dancers, singers, and musicians. Later four beautiful Iranian girls appeared at their table and Nasser placed four additional chairs next to the four unaccompanied men. Everyone had a dance partner so the six couples danced to the live band music until midnight. The two unmarried men negotiated for their two girls to spend the night with them. The two married men passed up the offered pleasure. Kelly, Fahrina, and Ladrun returned to the Hilton in Fahrina's car and the others went back to their apartment in the company car with the Iranian driver.

Kelly woke up about 5am with a severe case of *Traveler's Disease*. He took a dose of anti-diarrhea medicine from his pill bag, but it didn't help. Reluctantly, about 6am, he woke Fahrina up and explained his gastro-intestinal problem.

Fahrina exclaimed, "You Americans just can't accommodate our Iranian bugs. I've got some medicine that I guarantee will work. But you'll have to stay in bed until nine. It takes about three hours to fix you up."

Kelly downed the medicine with a glass of water and groaned, "Thanks, Fahrina. It tastes awful enough to work!"

"You'll be OK for your 10 o'clock meeting with General Hatami, but you can't ride in with Tom at 7:30. I'll call and tell him to go on to Doshen Toeppeh without you. I'll drive you there later."

When Fahrina explained the problem, Tom responded, "Yeah, Brad has the *Iranian Trots*. I used to get that 'til I got accustomed to the food here. You tell him we'll see him later at the base."

Fahrina called Ladrun and explained the change in plans to him and then went back to the bedroom to hold Brad's hand until he felt better.

Tom and Sandy and the three engineers left for the base in the company car at 7:10, as usual. They told the driver not to go by the Hilton, but just to drive them to work as he always did. The Americans then began to talk about the good time they'd had the night before. David Elliott teased Tom about being married to Sandy and keeping it a secret all this time. Sandy laughed and said she was glad their marriage was finally out in the open. She leaned over and gave Tom a kiss on the cheek.

The driver wove through the heavy morning Tehran traffic. By 7:30 they were in the south-eastern part of the city, stalled in heavy traffic. Tom and Sandy were sitting in the middle seat of the station-wagon with Vries, Elliott, and Nishamoto in the back seat. Suddenly Sandy's eyes widened in terror and she started to scream. She had seen two men carrying machine guns rushing up to their car. The Moslem fundamentalists yelled in Farsi for the driver to lie down. They sprayed the inside of the station wagon with bullets, horribly mutilating the bodies of the five Associated Aviation employees. The terrorists dashed away and disappeared in the early morning crowds. The Iranian driver raised himself up after they were gone, saw the five bleeding bodies, and started screaming, immobilized!

Soon a police car arrived. One officer got out to view the carnage while the other called for an ambulance. The policemen waited until the ambulance arrived to carry the bodies away to the city morgue for autopsies before they could be released later in the week. A tow truck came to drag the bullet riddled car to the police garage. The policemen took the driver back to the police station. He couldn't shed any light on who performed the brutal act, but he knew the five victims were Americans who worked at Doshen Toeppeh Air Force Base. He mentioned there should have been a sixth American, an executive who had just arrived in Tehran, but he hadn't come with them because he was sick.

The police phoned the air base and explained the tragedy to one of General Hatami's administrative aides, who immediately informed Generals Hatami and Fahi.

General Fahi called the Hilton Hotel, but there was no answer in Kelly's room. He had already left with Fahrina and Ladrun

Fahrina drove up to the air force base at 9:50 and used her pass to drive onto the base. She continued to General Hatami's building where the trio went to his outer reception office on the second floor. They were met by an ashen faced General Fahi, who blurted out, "I've got terrible news for you. Your five AAC employees were assassinated by terrorists on the way to the base this morning."

Tears welled up in Fahrina's eyes. She exclaimed, "Brad! If you hadn't been sick this morning you would have been in that car, too!"

She broke down into uncontrolled sobbing. Brad put his arms around her to comfort her while he tried to collect the details from Fahi who told him the policeman had said it was the bloodiest mess he had ever seen.

Kelly shook his head in confusion. "I don't know what to say. I guess I'd better call Dr. Morrell and break the bad news to him."

It was 9.30 at night in Los Angeles so Kelly phoned Dr. Morrell at his home to tell him of the tragedy and how he'd been lucky not to be killed too. He explained how Ambassador Hurd and General Robertson would probably have the bodies flown home on a MAC flight, maybe on Wednesday.

As soon as he could organize his shattered feelings, Dr. Morrell asked if he should send replacement engineers.

"No, no," Brad answered emphatically, "I don't want anyone else in danger. Their job here was almost finished. They would have been ready to go home next week. No, I'll finish up alone."

Fahi asked Kelly if he would like to cancel or postpone his briefing to General Hatami.

Brad thought a minute, then decided he'd rather continue on schedule, saying it would help keep his mind off the catastrophe.

Kelly, Ladrun and Fahi walked into General Hatami's office. After the general offered his condolences, Kelly gave his briefing.

Then General Hatami said, "We certainly picked the right company to implement the IBEX system. General Fahi tells me you've done an outstanding job. May the intelligence we receive through IBEX be a monument to the five brave Americans assassinated today."

"Thank you very much, General Hatami. IBEX will begin operating officially a week from Saturday. I'll be at site six along with Colonel Ladrun, where my government will collect information about the Soviets."

Kelly spent the rest of the day at the IBEX control center at a special location on Doshen Toeppeh Air Force Base. Fahrina explained the operation of the software she and the Iran Software, Ltd., personnel had installed on the IBM main frame computers. Colonel Ladrun explained the functions of the array of antennas installed by Elta on the roof of the control center. General Fahi pointed out the seven different operator-manned stations in the center. Three operators were dedicated to *gisting* the information pouring in from the six sites. Three other operators examined radar signals intercepted at the remote sites. The seventh operator was the supervisor who decided priorities of which data to analyze.

The control center was inside a specially shielded room in order to prevent emanations from leaking outside where they could, in return, be intercepted by enemy intelligence agents using their own sensitive receivers.

Kelly surveyed the extensive array of computer consoles, whirring tape recorders, flashing lights, and operators with head sets listening to the multiple signals collected by the vast IBEX system. He thought to himself, *Think of the fantastic resources expended on this electronic spying layout. Multitudes of hungry people could be fed with the money spent on this dirty business!*

About the middle of the afternoon, Ralph Hauser showed up at the control center. He told Brad, "We just heard from the police about the murders. Be assured the CIA knows the group responsible for this atrocious act!"

Kelly responded, angrily, "If you guys knew who did it, why couldn't you prevent it?"

"Brad, we don't have the resources to protect every American overseas. You know that!"

"I don't want you to protect *every* American overseas, just the few working on projects that are crucial to your own agency's intelligence collection!"

"Protection of people is outside our charter, Brad."

"Well, whose charter is it in?"

"Really, nobody's."

"In other words, when you're an American traveling overseas, even in the service of your country, you're pretty much on your own?"

"I guess you're right, Brad. I'm sorry, but that's about it."

Then Ralph explained Ambassador Hurd had checked with the Iranian Foreign Minister and had been given a commitment to take delivery of the bodies on Wednesday afternoon after the autopsies were completed. They would be flown to Frankfurt where they would be transferred to a C-5 flying non-stop to Southern California. Ralph had already sent a telex to Dr. Morrell with the ETA (estimated time of arrival) at March Air Force Base.

Brad sighed, "I must say the US government is really efficient at handling the bodies after Americans have been killed. Too bad they couldn't do something to prevent the killings in the first place." He continued to himself, in utter frustration, *The US government spends many billions of dollars a year on strategic defense, preparing for an all-out nuclear war that's never gong to happen because it's too dangerous for either side, the American or Soviet, to start. If they did, the populations of both countries would be largely destroyed, not to speak of the other populations in the northern hemisphere that would die from fall-out and the effects of nuclear winter. Too bad these billions can't be spent on eliminating the root causes of terrorism. There must be a way.*

Chapter 14.

The Six Sites

When Kelly finished his inspection of the control center about four, General Fahi reminded him there would be a meeting in the control center conference room in the morning at 10. All the key Americans and Iranians involved in IBEX had been invited to hear Kelly explain the plan for starting up the initial operations.

Kelly and Fahrina returned to the Hilton without Colonel Ladrun, who went to the Israeli embassy for a late afternoon meeting. In their room, Kelly declared, "Do you mind if we have dinner in the room and go to bed early? I'm emotionally drained from the horror of the massacre this morning."

"I was going to suggest the same thing. I hope you're not too exhausted to make love?"

"No! I think that would be the right way to get our minds off the day's tragedy."

After a dinner accompanied by several double Martinis, they danced to radio music in the room and went to bed just after 8pm. They removed themselves from their all-encompassing world of worry by enjoying the feel of each other's bodies and finished in a frenzy of exotic feelings. Kelly fell asleep with the tragic events of the day somewhat erased from his mind.

The next morning, they were awakened by a loud knock on the door. Kelly asked who it was. Someone made a loud, gruff reply in Farsi. Fahrina told Brad, "It's OK. My father was quite disturbed when I called him yesterday and told him of the multiple assassinations. He said, 'I should have provided protection for them! Don't worry! I'll send Shahan to watch you and Dr. Kelly around the clock from now on.'"

Kelly opened the door and was confronted by a giant of a man, well over 6 feet 6 inches tall and weighing at least 250 pounds. It was clear he slept just outside their door in a sleeping bag that was now rolled up and under his arm. He was carrying an Uzi machine gun in his left hand. Kelly could see the handle of a large caliber automatic pistol protruding from his jacket. Shahan strode into the room and spoke to Fahrina in Farsi.

Kelly asked, "What did he say?"

Fahrina replied, "Shahan said, 'Don't worry. No harm will come to you or Dr. Kelly. I'll make sure of that!' He doesn't speak English but he certainly knows how to make guns speak. My father pays him one hundred thousand dollars a year plus expenses for armament to protect Mahi family members. There are three more people on his guard team. We're going to have his protection full time while you're in Iran. He'll even go to the remote sites with you. He has the highest security clearance granted by Savak. He is also well known and trusted by your CIA."

Kelly looked Shahan up and down. "I sure feel a lot safer now!"

During breakfast in the room, Shahan carefully screened the waiter who brought the food. Shahan carried his Uzi in his left hand at all times. The waiter glanced nervously at the gun as he served the breakfast and left hurriedly.

During the drive to Doshen Toeppeh in Fahrina's car, Shahan sat in the back seat with his Uzi resting on his lap. Every time Kelly glanced back at Shahan and the Uzi he felt a warm glow of security.

Fahrina drove up to the guard gate at Doshen Toeppeh, they showed their badges, and continued on to the special area for the IBEX control center. Fahrina led them into the plush conference room. Already in the room were Ambassador Hurd, General Robertson, chief of the US MAAG (Military Advisory Assistance Group) in Tehran, General Fahi, General Doshenshah, and the three intelligence agents assigned to IBEX: Ralph Hauser of the CIA, Amnon Milchbucher of Mossad, and Shaheen Mouhoud of Savak.

Ralph Hauser looked at Shahan and his Uzi and said to Kelly, "I see you arranged for your own protection after our discussion yesterday."

"No, Fahrina's father, Mr. Mahi, arranged the protection for both of us while I'm in Iran."

Hauser replied, "Shahan is one of the best *protectors* in the business. Your personal security is well taken care of now!"

In his briefing, Kelly explained the prime contractor, Associated Aviation, would be responsible for the start up operations and after that, operations would be turned over to the Iranian governments and US government agencies responsible for the actual use of the system. Next Kelly met separately with Colonel Ladrun and General Fahi to go over the details of their visits to the six remote sites during the next week. They planned to start with site one, near Kermanshah, and then go on to the new installations ringing the borders of Iran in a counter-clockwise fashion, finishing with site six near the Caspian Sea.

Then Kelly and Fahrina, with Shahan as their constant companion, left for the Hilton to get started on the Iranian week end that began Wednesday evening and included Thursday and Friday.

Fahrina suggested they spend the weekend in the mountains northwest of Tehran. She explained her family belonged to a water ski club there and owned a five bedroom chalet overlooking the lake. Kelly agreed heartily. They reached the chalet just as it was getting dark. Kelly and Fahrina chose a room with a view of the lake and the family dock with their speedboat moored alongside. Shahan and his Uzi were assigned to one of the other bedrooms. They passed two relaxing days dining at the nearby water skiing club and sunning on the large balcony overhanging the lake. They water-skied behind the speedboat driven by Shahan, with his Uzi sitting on the seat next to him. With reluctance they left late Friday evening to return to the Tehran Hilton.

Early Saturday morning, Fahrina drove Kelly to the base, with Shahan in the back seat with his Uzi protector. The C-130 was waiting on the ramp with the pilot sitting in the left side of the cockpit, ready to start the four big turbine engines. Hauser, Ladrun, Fahi, and Shaheen, along with the young USAF captain who would serve as copilot and the staff sergeant load master were all standing at the front, left entrance, right in front of the huge turbo propeller. Kelly kissed Fahrina goodbye and strode over to the plane, followed closely by Shahan and his Uzi. The USAF captain copilot looked questioningly at the Uzi.

Hauser reassured him, "This is Dr. Kelly's bodyguard. The terrorists got five of his people last week."

The captain replied, "I read about that in the *International Herald Tribune*. Dr. Kelly, I understand from Mr. Hauser you're a good navigator. You may sit in the jump seat in the cockpit, if you wish."

"Thank you, Captain. I would love to."

Hauser, Shaheen, Ladrun and Shahan took passenger seats on the cockpit side of the hull. Behind them sat the HH-60 helicopter and other items of cargo being taken to the sites. The inside of the plane was stark and functional, with hydraulic lines and electrical cabling visible. The toilet was in the back, connected to a boxy aluminum structure, with a curtain providing a minimum of privacy.

Kelly climbed the aluminum steps to the *green house* cockpit with windows going to the floor, 180 degrees around the pilots and strapped himself into the jump seat midway between and behind the two pilot seats. A master sergeant was seated on the right in front of a panel with all the engine and other aircraft utilities instrumentation.

A second master sergeant was seated at the electronic navigation console on the left. This console had an inertial navigation set that read out the location of the aircraft to the nearest hundredth of a minute of latitude or longitude, or 100 feet. It also had forward looking radar which let the plane hug the terrain and fly along below the enemy's radar line-of-sight. There were special sensors to permit the crew to look ahead at night and *see* the terrain features ahead on a TV screen.

The pilot introduced himself, "I'm Major Wells. Captain Bradock and I will be your pilot and copilot for your tour of the IBEX sites. We'll be taking you up to the peaks in the helicopter, as well. Here's a copy of our flight plan for today."

Kelly thanked the major and studied the flight plan. They were scheduled to leave at 0755 and the trip to Kermanshah would take one hour and five minutes. The plan allowed 15 minutes to get the helicopter out of the C-130 and ten minutes to reach the first remote site, a mountain peak called Kuh-e-Peran, some 3357 meters or 10,994 feet high.

The crew started the four big turbo props, called the control tower and were given clearance to taxi to the active north-south runway. Once there, the tower gave clearance for take off and the pilot pushed the four throttles forward. Kelly felt himself pushed back into his seat and the big, four bladed props bit into the cool morning air. After a short take off run, the huge craft leapt off the runway. Through the glass nose bubble ahead, Kelly watched the ground receding rapidly as the C-130 climbed to its cruise altitude of 20,000 feet. The plane turned left and headed south westerly toward Kermanshah, 240 nautical miles away. There was a thick yellow pall of smog over Tehran but beyond in the distance over the desert-like terrain, the sky was blue and the air was crystal clear, with over one hundred miles visibility.   Within thirty minutes, Kelly could see the Zagros Mountains in the distance.

The copilot turned around and spoke over the intercom to Kelly, who was wearing headphones, "See that big peak straight ahead?"

Kelly nodded affirmatively.

"That's Kuh-e-Peran, where Site One is located."

Soon the C-130 began its descent into Kermanshah, landing at the airport right on schedule. They taxied to a remote area of the field. A troop carrier parked there immediately disgorged about fifteen Iranian soldiers with their weapons who formed a circle around the C-130 to guard it.

The sergeant load master and his crew of three opened the big clam shell cargo doors at the rear of the plane. Using a fork lift truck carried inside the plane, they towed the HH-60 helicopter outside.

Major Wells and Captain Bradock emerged from the C-130 and climbed into the cockpit of the HH-60. The master sergeant load master motioned the passengers inside the helicopter, gave them flight helmets with earphones and also belts with lanyards to connect to safety points inside the barn-like cavity packed with electronic boxes and electric and hydraulic cabling. The pilot cockpit was accessible by three steps up from the cargo area.

Captain Bradock motioned to Kelly to stand on the steps. "You can watch out through the cockpit from here, if you want to."

"Thanks, Captain. That will be interesting."

The two pilots went through their preflight checklist. The pilot taxied a short distance from the C-130, revved up the twin turbines to 95% power, applied the collective pitch lever. The big helicopter leapt off the ground and headed north easterly toward the high peak, Kuh-e-Peran. Within ten minutes they landed on a cement helicopter pad constructed by the Israelis and their Iranian laborers. About twenty meters away stood a stark, windowless building, 20 meters square, its roof bristling with antennas of every type imaginable. Colonel Ladrun led the group into the structure. The control area was packed with electronic consoles similar to those in the control center at Doshen Toeppeh. There were crew quarters, a small kitchen, a wardroom for dining and watching TV, and a bunk room.

Colonel Ladrun explained, "The other five sites are essentially carbon copies of this one. The only difference is *what* they can see, electronically speaking that is. This one can see Baghdad and northern Iraq, about 160 nautical miles south west."

Hauser added, "One bonus of Site One that interests my agency is that, if we rotated the antennas a little, we could pick up communication signals from three Soviet cities north of here: Jerevan, the capital of Armenia, Azerbydan, and Baku on the Caspian Sea. They're between 325 and 370 nautical miles away."

Kelly asked, "What can we learn today?"

Ladrun switched on a communications console and entered a code on the keyboard. The loud speakers blared out an unintelligible, to Kelly, babble of Arabic voices.

Ladrun explained, "This is a small Iraqi task force near the western border of Iran under attack from some Kurds who roam around both Iraq and Iran. The Iraqis are asking Baghdad to send air support. They had better hurry. It sounds like the Kurds are winning."

General Fahi broke in, "We can't let the Iraqis send an air strike against the Kurds. They're our allies!" He grabbed for the phone, called Doshen Toeppeh and ordered a flight of six F-14's to give fighter cover to the Kurds. He read out the coordinates from the IBEX console. The Iranian major at Doshen Toeppeh accepted the request.

About 25 minutes later the group in Site One heard an Iranian F-14 exclaim, "Sir, we turned the Iraqi MIG-23's back towards Baghdad. The Kurds are safe!"

General Fahi exclaimed, excitedly, "IBEX is really going to do the job! General Hatami will be really pleased!"

Colonel Ladrun spent another two hours explaining the features of the site to the group, finishing just before lunch. An Iranian corporal served a meal of lamb, rice and vegetables. By 12:30 they were ready to head for the next site. They climbed into the HH-60 and flew back to Kermanshah airport, stowed the helicopter into the bay of the C-130, and took off for Site Two on Kuh-e-Karun, a peak near Ahvaz. They landed at Ahvaz within an hour. The forty minute helicopter ride placed them on the 3609 meter (11,819 foot) peak overlooking Al Basrah, Iraq, and Kuwait, some 150 nautical miles away. As Colonel Ladrun had pointed out, Site Two looked pretty much like Site One.

Kelly asked, "What can the Iranians learn from this site?"

Colonel Ladrun explained, "The Shah can keep track of oil tanker traffic in and out of the southern Iraqi oil ports and from the port of Kuwait. He can also monitor Iraqi troop movements and military aircraft flights in the southern sector of Iraq."

By operating the electronic consoles, the group heard communications from Iraqi military aircraft and from the Iraqi army on maneuvers between Al Basrah and Almarah, Iraq. By listening carefully, they determined there were ten tanks and twenty armored troop carriers in the exercise. They estimated there were about 500 troops involved. General Fahi again phoned the major on duty at Doshen Toeppeh. This time he ordered a surveillance aircraft to take aerial photos of the Iraqi forces.

General Fahi remarked, "We probably know more about what's happening in southern Iraq than the army commander in Baghdad!"

By now it was after 5. They decided to RON (remain over night) at Site Two. Kelly and the others stayed up until almost midnight, playing with their new *toy*, IBEX. They became adept at using the consoles. They could ask for all radar signals of a certain type and the screen would display them and give their geographic location. They could ask to hear all Iraqi air force or army communications and the system would determine the location of the transmitter, the frequencies used, and record the voice or data on tape. Ladrun's language skills let him understand the *gist* of what the communications were about. There was so much data being collected that the on-site operators had to be trained to decide what was important and only record that information. Otherwise the IBEX analysis facilities at the control center in Tehran would become saturated with a lot of irrelevant data.

The next morning the group got up at 6:30, had breakfast, and headed for the next site at Kuh-e-Hormoz, a 2804 meter (9,183 foot) peak overlooking the strategic Strait of Hormuz, through which passed all the oil from the countries on the Persian Gulf: Iraq, Iran, Kuwait, the Arab Emirates, and Saudi Arabia. The huge C-130 landed at the Bandar Abbas airport just after 10 local time. The helicopter soon reached the mountain peak, a flight of some 25 minutes.

Kelly, Fahi, Ladrun, Shaheen and Hauser spent a couple of hours operating the IBEX consoles. They identified a squadron of F-5's flying over the Persian Gulf.

Ladrun announced, "We can even identify American planes sold to the Arabs. That squadron of F-5's are at 27°30' north by 51°22' east, just over the Karan off shore oil rig. They are traveling southerly at 512 knots."

Again, General Fahi called the major at Doshen Toeppeh and told him a flight of Saudi F-5's was approaching Iranian air space. He gave the coordinates from the IBEX console and ordered four F-14's to discourage them from intruding.

Hauser added, "The CIA is always interested in what our client states do with the arms we sell them. This site will let us know what the Saudi's do with the F-5's we sold them."

Kelly asked, "You mean we electronically spy on our friends as well as on our enemies?"

Hauser smiled wryly and replied, "Brad, you never know when our friends are going to turn into enemies."

When they finished checking out Site Three the Iranian cook gave them box lunches to eat during the twenty five minute flight back to the C-130. They soon took off from Bandar Abbas and turned north easterly toward Zahedan, an hour and ten minutes away. Site Four was on top of the peak called Kuh-e-Taftan, towering 4043 meters (13,214 feet) above sea level. It was near the tri-country border of Iran, Pakistan, and Afghanistan, and was reached by a thirty minute helicopter ride from Zahedan.

Kelly remarked, "I wouldn't think that either Afghanistan or Pakistan would represent a great threat to Iran."

Hauser replied, "Brad, that isn't necessarily so. Pakistan has a huge and poor population. They've built up a powerful military force to oppose the Indians to their east. There is strong evidence they are trying to build a nuclear weapon to counter the nuclear device exploded by India. They could very easily turn their power westward and grab part of Iran."

Ladrun added, "Afghanistan doesn't have nearly as large a population as Pakistan, but they have a Marxist government supported by the Soviets. I think there's going to be trouble ahead in Afghanistan. It could easily spill over into eastern Iran."

Kelly responded, "In other words, any country in this region could become a *hot spot* that would *burn* Iran."

Hauser answered, "Exactly, Brad. The Shah may be wise to worry about external threats but he probably should worry about internal threats as well. The agency believes the Tudah or Communist Party is a real danger to the Shah's government."

General Fahi interrupted, "Ralph, the Shah-an-Shah knows his problems better than you Americans. Believe me, the Tudah Party is not a threat. The fundamentalist Moslems are!"

Kelly thought to himself, *The US government thinks Communists everywhere are a threat. From what Fahrina has told me, it looks like General Fahi is right! The fundamentalist Moslems could be the real threat to the Shah. She thinks it was the fundamentalists that killed my people, not the Communists. However, it's best not to voice these concerns to a CIA agent. I might get the reputation of being soft on Communism and lose my security clearance! I'm glad General Fahi spoke up."*

During their check out of the area covered by Site Four, they heard communications from a fleet of Pakistani helicopters practicing simulated air to ground combat near Yamach, Pakistan.

Ladrun was able to interpret the conversations. He commented, "These Pakistani helicopter pilots and their gunnery crews are lousy. The army commander is raising hell with them because they're not hitting their simulated ground targets."

Again Fahi used the *real time* information from IBEX to respond to a perceived foreign threat. He called the air base in Tehran to send a surveillance aircraft to get high altitude aerial photos of the Pakistani operations.

Kelly changed the subject, "The Cryptomatik equipment is working really well. I was switching the decryption switch on and off while listening to the Pakistani communications. In the off position, it sounded like complete gibberish. In the on position, it sounded like human language. I could even understand some English words embedded in the communications."

Ladrun replied, "Your engineers, God bless their souls, performed the integration and check out in less than a week. Without this equipment, we wouldn't be able to understand any of the *scrambled* or *encrypted* communications we're receiving from those Pakistani pilots."

He continued, "Your comment about the imbedded English words is certainly true. All the ancient languages, such as Hebrew, Arabic, and Farsi, are thousands of years old. They are good for expressing body functions, eating, making love, and everyday living, things that humans have been doing for millennia, but they are completely inadequate for describing modern warfare techniques. These languages borrow English words to express modern concepts."

Kelly and the others spent the rest of the day and evening operating the electronic spy consoles, stopping only to enjoy the typical Iranian meal the resident cook prepared for them. There was a full time Iranian tea server at this site who made sure no one ever had an empty tea glass.

The traveling contingent returned to Zahedan airport in the morning and climbed into the waiting C-130, which had been carefully watched over by Iranian army guards. Kelly's armed guard, Shahan, watched everyone at the airport, including the army guards.

The flight from Zahedan to Mashhad flew over one of the major trade routes of the Middle East. Many centuries ago traders had to cover vast distances through this desert area which was dominated by fierce warrior tribes.

Kelly sat in the cockpit jump seat and watched the latitude-longitude read out from the inertial navigation set on the C-130. The numbers constantly told where they were within sixty feet, and their ground speed in knots, and how far it was and how long it would take to reach their destination. He thought, *What a contrast inertial navigation is to the celestial navigation we used on Orion when we raced from Los Angeles to Honolulu in the TransPac Race. All we had was a watch, a sextant, and the star tables in a book. It was hard work to figure out where we were.*

They landed at Mashhad after an hour and fifty minute flight, arriving about 9:40am. The helicopter flight took twenty five minutes to Kuh-e-Sorkh, some 3019 meters (9,887 feet) high, overlooking Western Afghanistan and the southern USSR Republic of Turkmen. They spent several hours listening to communications of the air and ground traffic in Afghanistan. Kelly was surprised at the number of Soviet military planes operating in and out of the country.

Ladrun explained, "The Russians helped set up a Marxist government in Afghanistan by supporting the local Communist party. They supply military and economic aid now that their boys are running the country."

"Why are the Soviets so interested in a desolate country like Afghanistan?"

"Brad, the Russians have long wished for a warm water port, an ice free opening to the world's oceans. As it is, they have to pass through the Bosporus Straits under the watchful eyes of the Turks if they want to get out of the Black Sea into the warm Mediterranean. If they could take part of Afghanistan and part of Iran, or Pakistan, they would have direct access to the Indian Ocean."

Hauser interrupted, "Nonsense, Joseph, the Russians know the US would never permit them to take over a country like

Afghanistan or Iran. That would start a nuclear war. The CIA is watching the situation over here very closely. There's no danger of Soviet intervention here."

Ladrun replied, "Ralph, I know how Russians think. They set long term objectives and pursue them relentlessly and patiently. They have a continuity of government and leaders unknown to you Americans. Believe me, one way or another they'll get their port by patiently chipping away, while your democrats and republicans are fighting each other in Washington."

Kelly interrupted, "Enough of this geopolitical philosophizing. You said on this site we could turn the antennas northward and intercept Soviet radar signals and communications. Can we do that now?"

Joseph replied, "Sure. Using this antenna console, let's point the antennas toward Tashkent, a large eastern Soviet city 600 nautical miles northeast of here. I'll tune in a local state radio station there. Can you hear it?"

Hauser replied, "Yes, it sounds like a news broadcast."

"Right. Now look at the ADF (automatic direction finding) needle on this console. Push the button *Align-to-ADF* and *Voilà!* All the antennas are now pointing toward Tashkent."

Kelly said, "That was easy. You Israelis did a great job on the IBEX antennas."

A short while later Kelly asked with a concerned note in his voice, "Joseph, I'm picking up some communications and some strange radar signals off to the left of the ADF line to Tashkent. What do you think it is?"

Ladrun came over to Kelly's console and clicked a few keys, "I read 220 nautical miles at a bearing of 037° to the north-north-east. The only thing there, according to the data base read out, is a small Russian Moslem village called Césme-oj. But these signals mean there's some fancy radar and communications gear there now. The only access is by a dirt road, an old donkey trail."

Hauser came over to Kelly's console, "Very interesting! I went over our latest spy satellite photos just last Thursday and I saw nothing in that area. I remember thinking the desert was extremely desolate and empty there."

Joseph answered, "Well, Ralph, there's sure something there now! The communications and the radar signals indicate it's a big and expensive installation. Surely it would show up on your satellite photos."

Kelly interjected, "Maybe it's new. Maybe the Soviets flew the gear in by helicopter since last Thursday. This is Monday. Could they have moved that much equipment and set it up in three days?"

Yes, Brad, the Soviets have specialized in transportable equipment, including big radars. They can move a major ground to air missile site and have everything set up and working in 24 hours."

Ladrun examined the radar signals coming in and observed, "I've never seen radar signals like these. They're not like anything the Soviets supplied to the Egyptians and Syrians, and those countries get some of the latest types of Soviet gear. There is something strange going on here!"

Kelly asked Hauser, "When can you get new satellite photos of the Césme region?"

"The next regular photos will be at the US Embassy in Tehran next Thursday. I could ask for a *special* on that area, but by the time my request gets processed and they realign the sensors on the satellite, it would take three days anyway. So Thursday's the soonest."

Kelly said earnestly, "Fellows, here's what I think we should do. Spend the rest of today here studying the signals from Afghanistan that this station was expected to listen to. Tomorrow, we'll go to Site Six and spend Tuesday and Wednesday there, listening to Césme. And, Ralph, you'll fly back to Tehran on Wednesday evening as originally planned and get the newest satellite photos. How long will it take you to get back?"

"The Moslem weekend on Thursday and Friday will make it difficult to schedule a flight but I'm sure I can come back with the Site Six crew when they fly back to work Saturday."

"OK. We'll plan to spend the weekend on the Caspian Sea so we'll meet you at the site on Saturday."

Ladrun said, "Maybe by that time I'll have had a chance to analyze the data and figure out what my former countrymen are up to."

Fahi added, "Since this appears to be an American problem rather than an Iranian one, you won't need Shaheen and me. We'll go back to Tehran on Tuesday from Rashit and we'll see you in Tehran when you return."

On Tuesday, 13 October, 1976, Kelly's group left Site Five to fly to Site Six. Their route from Mashhad to Rashit took them over the southern part of the Caspian Sea. During the two hour flight the C-130 pilot pointed out their destination, Takht-i-Suleyman, 4,819 meters or 15,782 feet high.

Kelly remarked, "That's higher than Mount Whitney in California, the highest point in the continental United States."

The pilot continued, "You'll have a beautiful view of the Caspian Sea from there."

Kelly agreed, "We'll have a fantastic view of the Soviet Union from up there, too."

"Yes, Sir. We're less than twenty miles from Soviet air space right here. We have to be careful not to stray over the line. See those contrails over to the right?"

"Yes. It looks like four aircraft flying in formation."

"Those are MIG-23's from Baku, about 150 nautical miles inside Russia on the west coast of the Caspian. We have to be careful not to become an *international incident!* Our inertial navigation set keeps us from making a navigation error, though."

Shortly afterwards, the C-130 descended into Rashit where the C-130 was immediately ringed with an Iranian guard. The HH-60 was quickly unloaded and the reduced size group flew to the mountain top where they arrived exactly at 9:30 just as their flight plan had said.

The view was breathtaking. Far in the distance to the north, Kelly could just make out the peninsula where Baku jutted into the Caspian Sea. Much closer and to the south, the city of Tehran was coated in smog. The Soviet Republic of Armenia was to the northwest. The Soviet Republic of Turkmen and the mysterious Césme was to the northeast.

Kelly, Ladrun, and Hauser spent the next two days at Site Six using the complex electronic spy equipment to study the signals from Césme. The Israeli furnished antennas captured the signals and directed them to the sophisticated receivers inside the building full of millions of dollars worth of electronic equipment. Sitting at the master control console, Kelly narrowed the wide area surveillance beam to zoom in on Césme.

Ladrun sat at the communications console scanning the voice channels and deciding which were worth listening to. He was assisted by three communication specialists who understood Russian. They had been trained to listen to one channel in the right ear and a different channel in the left ear, and still make sense out of the babble.

Hauser sat at the radar signal console, assisted by three signal analysis specialists who derived all kinds of information from the incoming signals.

All day Tuesday and Wednesday, they collected an enormous amount of data from the mysterious Russian site, but they were unable to answer the question, *What is really going on at Césme?*

Shortly after 5pm on Wednesday, Kelly said to Ladrun and Hauser, "Well, Fellows, that's about all we can do this week. Let's take the chopper back to Rashit. Ralph, you go on back to Tehran for the satellite photos. Joseph and I'll spend the weekend at a hotel in Tonkabon recommended by the flight crew. We'll let our subconscious minds work while we're relaxing. Maybe we'll have some theories about Césme by the time we get back together Saturday."

Hauser remarked, "I've never seen radar signals like these. With the satellite photos we'll know exactly what the installation looks like. Without IBEX, we never would have thought to examine the Césme area."

The HH-60 had a nearly full load for its 30 minute flight to Rashit. Hauser and most of the regular mountain top crew returned to Tehran for the weekend in the C-130. Kelly and Ladrun, plus Shahan and his ever-present Uzi, reboarded the HH-60 for the flight to Tonkabon on the blue Caspian Sea and within thirty minutes Captain Bradock announced they were approaching the helicopter pad adjacent to the Royal Caspian Hotel. Green lawns and trees surrounded the beautiful hotel and its swimming pool and Jacuzzi and Kelly could even see a beach behind the hotel on the Caspian Sea.

As Kelly climbed out of the helicopter, Christina and Olga rushed up to hug and kiss him. Kelly asked the usual question.

Christina replied, "Oh, Brad, you always ask how we know. We were with Amnon in Tehran and he told us."

Kelly and the two girls spent the next two nights in bed and recovered during the days lying in the warm sun. Ladrun and Shahan had their meals with the trio and joined them in their sun sessions. Kelly and Ladrun did not mention IBEX or Césme.

Saturday morning, Kelly woke up at 6am, with Christina on his left side and Olga on his right. He kissed them in turn and climbed out of bed. After dressing and packing his small bag, he wished the girls goodbye. They answered sleepily with matching goodbyes.

In the coffee shop the flight crew of the HH-60 were already eating their hearty breakfast of bacon, eggs, and toast, at a large round table. Kelly, Ladrun and Shahan joined them. The waiter appeared immediately to take their orders. Kelly and Ladrun both ordered scrambled eggs and ham. It had been impossible for Kelly to have ham or bacon for breakfast in Israel because of the dietary laws strictly enforced at the Israeli tourist hotels. The waiter returned shortly and served Kelly poached eggs with ham and served Ladrun fried eggs with bacon. Kelly protested to the waiter who said something in Farsi and disappeared.

Kelly asked Ladrun, "What did he say?"

"He said you got what you ordered. He then muttered some obscenity about Americans as he walked away. I think we better eat what we got."

Chapter 15.

Surprise at Césme

A short helicopter ride returned the group to Site Six atop Takht-i-Suleyman. Kelly and Ladrun took a few moments to admire the view from the 15,000 foot peak and then went into the concrete building.

Kelly asked Ladrun, "Have you some thoughts on the Césme facility?"

"Before I left Russia, I heard of some work done by a Russian scientist named Leontief on special radar signal processing called *spread spectrum*. Maybe they have built some *spread spectrum* radars."

"How would they be different?"

"It could be very accurate. You can take an ordinary radar and make it very accurate to about 200 feet by making the pulse width very short, like two tenths of a microsecond."

Kelly exclaimed, "That's really short. Light only travels about 400 feet in that amount of time."

"Exactly, and since radar signals have to travel out and back, that's equivalent to a 200 foot long radar pulse in space. That's how accurate it would be, the length of the radar pulse."

"So what can *spread spectrum* radar do?"

"By using Leontief's method, the equivalent pulse width can be reduced to about one nanosecond. That's an accuracy of between two and ten feet. And the effective power would be much higher than with ordinary radar."

"That means the radar could see objects much farther away and have that high accuracy over a very long distance."

Ladrun answered, "Right Brad. And before he left, Ralph told me he found there were three radars at Césme. When somebody sets up multiple radars, they are usually used for guiding a rocket or missile. And what I'm thinking is that the Russians may have a new radar guided long range missile with unbelievable accuracy."

Kelly exclaimed, "With an accuracy of two to ten feet, that means they could destroy a car, or an airplane, or an office building from a long distance away. But why would the Russians need such an accurate weapon when they could just explode a nuclear warhead and destroy everything for miles around?"

"Think about it, Brad. If the Russians launched a nuclear weapon, they would invite immediate retaliation against their motherland. But if they used a conventional warhead against a military target like an airplane, Washington probably wouldn't get stirred up enough to retaliate with a nuclear war."

Kelly agreed, "You're right. No one can win a nuclear war. That's the concept of MAD: mutually assured destruction. No leader is MAD enough to risk nuclear war. So it's the side with extremely accurate conventional weapons that can win the kind of wars that may actually be fought."

Kelly and Ladrun spent the rest of the morning collecting additional data from Césme. They confirmed there were three radars and noticed their transmissions had greatly increased since last Wednesday.

Just before noon, Ladrun jumped up from his radar signal console and exclaimed, "Brad, it looks like the three radars are looking right at site six. Their radars are in a narrow angle scan of five degrees. I have been monitoring the signal strength fluctuations. The center of the beam is on a bearing of 259°, pointed right at Takht-i-Suleyman!"

"Why would they be watching us?"

"They probably aren't. We're too close. They wouldn't need long range radar to look at us. It's more likely they're lined up on something much farther away. Is there a map here showing the Middle East area?"

Kelly found one and spread it on a table. They drew a long line from Césme on a bearing of 259°. It crossed Iran, Iraq, Jordan, and Israel.

Ladrun exclaimed, "It goes through our big military air base at Mizpe Ramon, south of Be'er Sheba!"

Kelly measured the distance. "That's almost 1400 nautical miles from Césme. Surely the Russian radars can't see that far away. The curvature of the Earth would prevent that."

"That's true, Brad. They couldn't see the ground in Israel, but they could see a missile in the air headed for an Israeli target!"

"Do you think that's what they're up to? Planning to attack Israeli targets?"

"I don't know. We need more data."

They were interrupted by the noise of a helicopter landing outside. Hauser rushed in and exclaimed, "Brad, we have a real crisis on our hands!"

Kelly assumed Hauser meant he had looked at the satellite photos and somehow confirmed Ladrun's suspicions. Kelly said, "Yes, we know. Did it show on the satellite photos?"

"No. I mean a *real* crisis! NSA has intercepted some of our IBEX communications that were encrypted by the Cryptomatik equipment and they can't decode them!"

Brad retorted, "So what! We're not their enemies. We're all on the same side!"

Hauser continued, "They tried for two weeks using all of their Cray supercomputers and they still can't decode it. They threaten to shut down the IBEX operations if we don't give them the decoding keys we are using!"

Kelly turned red in the face and replied angrily, "Ralph, here we are trying to figure out what the Russians are up to at this strange facility they have at Césme, something that could be a real threat to the free world, and you come up here telling us about some ridiculous bureaucratic tempest-in-a-teapot!"

"Brad, you have to understand! From NSA's point of view, the fact that they can't decode these IBEX communications is a threat to national security! Besides, the fact that IBEX is using Swiss crypto technology, not US technology, because NSA itself had required you to use it, makes the situation doubly embarrassing. You better comply with their request!"

"Bullshit!" he yelled. "They forced us to use the Swiss equipment! They deserve to be embarrassed!"

Then as he calmed down a little, Kelly said, "OK. If it will keep the dimwitted bureaucrats happy, here's the decode key. But, it must be transmitted with the utmost security. If it falls into the Soviet's hands, then everything we do here is public knowledge."

"Don't worry! I've got that all set up," answered Hauser. "There's a fellow from the embassy waiting in the chopper to hand carry the key back to Washington to give to the NSA man who called me yesterday. The courier has the highest security clearances, so you don't need to worry about compromising IBEX secrets."

"OK, Ralph, give the courier the key and send him on his way."

When Ralph returned without the key, Kelly asked, "Can we turn our attention to more important things now? Let's see the photos."

Ralph answered, "They're sure different from a week ago." And spread them on a table.

An expanded view of Césme showed a large block house bristling with communication antennas. Nearby sat three radar antennas and in front of them were ten triangular concrete pads with missile launchers on them. The grid lines on the photo showed the center of the complex was at latitude north 38° 40' 00" and longitude east 63° 45' 00".

Ladrun drew a line from Site Six to Césme.

Hauser asked skeptically, "You mean the Russians have installed this elaborate facility to wipe out Site Six?"

"No, no, Ralph. Look at this map of the Mid East. If we extend the line from Césme to Takht-i-Suleyman, it passes right through the biggest Israeli Air Force Base, just south of Be'er Sheba at Mizpe Ramon."

"You mean the Russians are planning to attack Israel?"

"It's certainly beginning to look that way. Brad and I figured out this morning those missiles at Césme would have an accuracy of two to ten feet if the Russians are using *spread spectrum* radars for guidance."

"Wow! They could choose an individual airplane to hit. But wouldn't it take a thousand missiles to destroy a thousand military planes?"

"Not if they use missiles with multiple independently targeted warheads."

"Do you mean nuclear warheads?"

"No. I figure the Russians could use depleted uranium warheads as penetrators. These warheads would weigh, say, two pounds each. As they strike the airplane they become exothermic and would burn the metal of the plane!"

"Wouldn't using uranium be very expensive?"

"Not really, Ralph. Depleted uranium is a waste product of nuclear reactors that generate electric power. It's basically worthless. The only cost would be making the warheads."

"Joseph, that's quite a theory you have. How do we find out if it's true?"

"Actually, your satellite photos confirm many parts of the theory. The three antennas are pointing toward site six. The ten missile launchers show the Russians have enough weapons for a massive attack on a small country like Israel. That leaves two unknowns right now."

Hauser questioned, "And what are they?"

"First, we need to run a computer simulation to find out if the missiles really could deliver multiple warheads against targets 1400 nautical miles away, with an accuracy of less than ten feet. Then, second, we need to find out if the Russians really intend to do that."

Kelly added, "Joseph, the only way I know how to get a simulation of the Césme missiles' capability is to take the tapes we have been recording here, which have the radar and missile characteristics on them, and run a simulation on the computers at AAC in Van Nuys, California. We can't do such a complex simulation at the IBEX control center in Tehran because they don't have the capability. NSA has the computers, but not the people with training in running simulations."

Ladrun said, "Then, Brad, you may have to go and run that simulation. You certainly can't send any of your engineers. They're all dead."

Hauser interrupted, "I can have Ambassador Hurd arrange for MAC to fly you back to March Air Force Base by C-5. There's one leaving at midnight tonight. If it went non-stop, you'd be at March about 7 Sunday morning. How long would it take to run the simulation?"

Kelly thought a moment, "I could probably get it finished by Thursday night."

"Then I'll ask Ambassador Hurd to arrange for MAC to fly you back from March, leaving 8am Friday. That would get you back to Tehran at midnight Saturday. You could be back up here by mid morning Sunday, a week from tomorrow."

Kelly replied, "I'm willing to fly back to California to run the simulation. But how about the second part? How can we confirm what the Soviet's intentions are?"

Hauser said, "If we had a well placed CIA agent buried in the right Soviet agency, we could find out easily. But we don't have one."

Ladrun added, "We need to continue listening to the communications from Césme. We need the good Lord's help to intercept a message that confirms the Russian intentions. But then, God has helped us Jews before. Maybe he'll help us again this time! However, Ralph, one advantage of having so many Jews in Russia is that Mossad *does* have an agent in the right Soviet agency. Brad, you'll be interested to know that agent is controlled by your good friend, Amnon. I'll get Amnon working this *HUMINT*, *HUMan INTelligence*, problem."

Hauser added, "Brad, if you're going to get back to California tonight, I better get on the phone to Ambassador Hurd right now."

Kelly answered in a sarcastic tone, "OK, call him, but use the IBEX crypto system. I wouldn't want NSA to know about my plans!"

Hauser answered angrily, "Brad, you shouldn't joke about the National Security Agency. You could lose your security clearance for loose talk like that!"

"You're right, Ralph. I was only kidding!"

Ralph headed for the phone while Kelly and Ladrun collected the papers and tape recordings Kelly would need to take with him, then spent the remainder of the day monitoring the signals from Césme, looking for a message that would tell them what the Russians really intended to do. At 11pm, Kelly left site six on the HH-60 helicopter and twenty minutes later it landed next to a C-5 transport at Doshen Toeppeh Air Force Base. He climbed aboard and the load master assigned him three seats in a row, so he could sleep during the non-stop flight. The rear of the airplane was loaded with cargo on pallets. There were six rows of back facing passenger seats, six seats in each row, with an aisle down the center. All the other seats were filled. Kelly was a little embarrassed to take up three seats, but he was so tired he was not about to volunteer to give up his spaces. He noticed that, except for a few military personnel, most of the passengers were elderly civilians.

In a conversation before take off with one of the civilian men, a retired air force master sergeant, Kelly discovered that all military retirees and their families could travel anywhere in the world on Military Air Command flights by going to a MAC air terminal and asking for a standby seat. If there were empty seats, they could fly wherever the aircraft was going. The ex-sergeant explained that he traveled around the world almost continuously, staying here for a month, and there for a month or two. He said he and his wife had been in Tehran for six weeks, staying in USAF visitors' quarters. The six week round trip from California had cost only $250 total, and most of that had been for Christmas gifts for his family in the US. He said his monthly retirement pay was $1300 a month, so he had banked $1700 while he was on this six week trip.

Kelly thought to himself, *We American taxpayers are really generous to our retired military personnel. This man put in twenty five years in the army, retired at age fifty, and has a life time income of $1300 a month, with automatic increases whenever the cost of living index goes up. He also gets to shop in the military base exchanges where he can buy subsidized food and clothes at about half the price in civilian stores. He and his family get free medical care for the rest of their lives. By using the 'perks' in the military system, he can live well while traveling around the world, free. His benefits are paid for by the US defense budget. No wonder the defense part of the US budget is so high!*

The C-5 took off, its huge engines roaring, right at midnight. It climbed steeply to 41,000 feet, or flight level four-one-zero, as the air traffic controllers referred to the cruise altitude. The load master announced over the intercom the passengers could unfasten their safety belts. Kelly spread out over the three seats and fell asleep immediately. He woke up ten hours later, very hungry, and headed for the galley area in the back of the plane. The load master gave him a hot cup of coffee and a box lunch which he carried back to his seat. He found several pieces of fried chicken, fresh fruit, canned juice, and a big piece of chocolate cake for dessert. Since Kelly was a *choc-o-holic*, he ate the cake first and then devoured the rest of his meal. He then asked for permission to enter the cockpit, which was granted.

He climbed up the stairs, sat in the jump seat behind the two pilots, and introduced himself. The pilot, a young captain, motioned for Kelly to put on a set of earphones.

The captain said, "See this beacon target on the radar?"

"Yes. It seems to be headed right for us."

"It is. We are rendezvousing with a tanker aircraft. We're going to feed this monster another gulp of fuel. See this pattern on the radar scope? It's the rendezvous template that we fly relative to the tanker. When the tanker reaches this spot, he makes a standard turn to the left, which will put him right in front of us. We then line up using the rendezvous lights on his tail. We couple up with the fuel probe and then transfer the jet fuel."

"A pretty complex operation!"

"It is. Only about 20% of the MAC pilots are qualified for airborne refueling. We usually stop at Frankfurt on the way home from Tehran, but on this flight we had some VIP who had to get to March in a hurry."

"Captain, I think I'm the VIP."

"I thought you might be. In that suit and tie, you don't look like our typical passenger."

"You must have to fly very precisely while you're hooked up to the tanker."

"Yes, Sir. We have to stay in a cube about ten feet on a side. It requires precise speed and position control. After 45 minutes of that kind of flying, which is about what it takes to refuel this baby, I'm ready for a nap. Watch the tanker on the scope. He's beginning his standard turn."

When the blip of the tanker was lined up with the center of the scope, Kelly looked out the windshield and saw the huge tanker less than a thousand feet in front of them. The C-5 pilot adjusted his speed so the distance gradually reduced. Soon Kelly saw the lights on the fuel probe that would connect with the C-5's fuel socket. The color coded lights tell the pilot to fly up or down, right or left, speed up or slow down. With a thump, the probe connected with the fuel socket and the fuel began flowing aboard.

Afterwards, Kelly asked what the estimated arrival time was for March Air Force Base. The pilot responded that if the winds continued as forecast, they would land at 0727 Sunday morning. He added the helping winds had put them ten minutes ahead of schedule already.

Kelly returned to his seat and fell asleep again and didn't wake up until the load master announced all passengers should fasten their seat belt for approach to March Air Force Base. Kelly had sent an encrypted telex to Dr. Morrell asking to be met at March with a company helicopter. The plane landed at 7:26am, one minute ahead of the ETA the pilot had given Kelly the night before over the dark Atlantic Ocean. Out the window, Kelly saw a red and blue Bell helicopter with the AAC logo on it parked on the ramp. He was surprised to see Dr. Morrell himself standing next to the Associated Aviation pilot, Bob Anderson

The load master told the other passengers to wait until Kelly had left the plane. The March base commander, a one star general, met Kelly at the airplane door and welcomed him to the base. The general added, "With your protocol rank of three star general because of your service on the Secretary of Defense's Science Advisory Council, you are welcome to use any of the officer's facilities here at March."

Kelly told him thanks and hurried toward the helicopter, meeting Dr. Morrell halfway.

Dr. Morrell shook Kelly's hand warmly, "Welcome back to California, Brad. I got a call from Ambassador Hurd as well as your telex. It sounds like you've found a real *gem* of information. I organized your simulation team for round-the-clock work this week. They're waiting in the conference room now."

Kelly and Morrell climbed into the back seat of the helicopter and Kelly greeted the pilot, "Hi, Bob. Thanks for the lift."

"You're welcome. We already have our take off clearance from the tower. We'll be at the plant in thirty five minutes."

Anderson applied power to the turbine engine, pulled back on the collective pitch, and the chopper lifted off the ramp. Kelly looked back at the huge C-5 and watched it growing smaller as the helicopter climbed into the crisp, blue October sky. The Los Angeles basin unfolded beneath the chopper as they flew at 4,500 feet, below the tops of the Sierra Madre Mountains on the right. Mount Baldy's snow cap shone in the morning sun. They flew over Glendale and entered the San Fernando Valley with the Hollywood Hills on the left. Kelly picked out the Van Nuys Airport in the distance and the sprawling complex of buildings that housed Associated Aviation. As they got closer, Kelly looked to the right and made out the hill where his home was located.

Kelly mentally mapped out his activities for the next few days: In a couple of hours, after his kick off meeting at AAC, he would be able to go home and spend the rest of Sunday with his family. By then, his team would be working hard to program the Russian missile and guidance system into the big simulation computer. Kelly knew he'd have to spend sixteen hours a day at the plant until he left Thursday at midnight to go back to Iran.

His mental planning was interrupted by the deceleration as Anderson brought the chopper in for a landing on the pad on top the Associated Aviation headquarters building. Kelly and Morrell hurried down the stairs to the top floor and into the large conference room. The twelve waiting engineers, including one lady engineer, rose from their chairs. Kelly recognized the best and most talented simulation engineers at Associated Aviation. He turned to Dr. Morrell, "John, I really appreciate your organizing this blue ribbon team. Now I'm sure we can finish before I have to leave Thursday night."

Dr. Morrell answered, "Brad, because this is such an important project, you have carte blanche for any resources you need."

Morrell strode to the front of the conference room and said, "Lady and Gentlemen, thank you for coming in on a Sunday morning. First, I've authorized unlimited overtime pay for all of you this week. You will all report directly to Dr. Kelly. This urgent project has been placed under Special Compartmentalized Security. You are to discuss the project with no one except the people in this room. Now, Dr. Kelly will explain the task and schedule."

Kelly told the engineers, "First, I would like to add my thanks for your meeting here this morning. As you may have overheard, I'm scheduled to return to Iran on Thursday night. I have to take the results back with me. That means we have to go on a round-the-clock schedule to finish on time. We'll divide into two six person *watches* and use the *Swedish watch system...*"

One of the engineers, Bill Wilson, interrupted to ask, "What's a *watch system?*"

Kelly explained, "It's a scheduling system we used on long distance sail boat races. Watch One works from 6am to noon, takes six hours off, and then works from 6pm to 10 pm, takes four hours off, and returns to work from 2am to 6am, and then takes six hours off, etc. Watch Two works whenever Watch One is off."

Wilson interrupted again, "Oh, I see. The day schedule and night schedule reverse each day, so no one has to work two night shifts on two consecutive days."

"That's right. Bill, you write the names on the board so we can divide into two watches and then break each watch into three subgroups. Subgroup 1 will simulate a missile with about 1500 nautical miles range and a radar system to track it. Subgroup 2 will simulate the guidance and control of the main missile, using radar tracking data, to a point where the missile dispenses terminally guided sub-missiles. Subgroup 3 will be responsible for guidance and control of the terminally guided sub-missiles from the point of dispensing to hitting a ground target. Again radar tracking will be used for guidance."

Wilson asked, "How many sub-missiles are on each missile?"

"That's a good question. We know there are ten missiles. You can see them on the satellite photo. But we will have to assume the number of sub-missiles. Begin with assuming 100 per missile. But set up the simulation so we can vary the number from 50 to 200."

"What's the accuracy of these sub-missiles?"

Kelly replied, "That's the 64 billion dollar question that the simulation must answer. Colonel Ladrun, whom some of you have met, believes the accuracy will be between two to ten feet."

"Wow! We don't have any missiles with a range over 1500 nautical miles with accuracy like that."

"I know, but it looks like our adversary does!"

Bill Wilson had written the twelve names on the board. Various people volunteered for Watch One and Watch Two and for the three subgroups in each watch. After about twenty minutes of discussion, negotiation, and arguing, the list was complete. Watch One would start immediately and Watch Two would take over at noon today. There would be daily noon meetings to review progress. Kelly displayed the satellite photos showing the new Russian installation. He explained the radar signal data collected on the IBEX computer tapes. He also covered the geography of Césme, the Sixth Site, and the Israeli air base. And answered a variety of questions about various details of the project.

Finally Kelly was able to call his wife, "Darling, I'm at the office. Will you pick me up now?"

"Dr. Morrell phoned me you were coming home. I thought you'd have to work all day. I'll be there in thirty minutes. I have really missed you. I didn't think I'd see you until after the La Paz yacht race."

"I missed you too. Hurry up and get here!"

Just as Kelly hung up, his red telephone connected to the IBEX encrypted line to Iran, rang.

Ralph Hauser was on the line. "Brad, I'm here with Ladrun. We have some information to crack into your simulations."

"Good timing, Ralph. The first team is just starting to put information into the computers."

"First, let me put Joseph on the phone. He has something hot!"

Ladrun's voice came over the red phone, "Brad, one of Amnon's agents in Russia has been working on the Césme missiles. He's a guidance and control engineer and knows the whole system."

"That's great, Joseph. Can he tell us how many sub-missiles are carried in each main missile?"

"105. They're deployed at 100,000 feet over the target."

"But, Joseph, that means the sub-missiles would be deployed beyond the line-of-sight of the Césme radar because of the curvature of the Earth at a distance of 1400 to 1500 nautical miles. The sub-missiles couldn't receive guidance commands from the Césme radar."

"Wrong. Our agent says they get around the line-of sight problem by using a satellite to bounce the radar signals to the target area. So the sub-missiles get radar guidance commands all the way to their impact point. Also, he said the maximum range is 1600 nautical miles."

Kelly asked, "How do they get enough *channel capacity* to control that many sub-missiles? They can't violate *Shannon's Law* of information rate."

"Since it's a spread spectrum radar, they use a separate coded signal for each sub-missile. Your American satellite navigation system, the Global Positioning System (GPS), uses a similar concept because they need very high accuracy and have to communicate with a large numbers of objects over the same frequency channel without interference."

Kelly responded, "Thanks for the information. That removes a lot of the uncertainty in our simulation. I still have a question: How do the Russians get their satellite in the right spot to bounce the radar signals off it?"

Ladrun turned the phone over to Hauser. "Brad, our satellite tracking facility has just identified a new Soviet satellite that was launched just last Friday. They've got the orbits pinned down really well now. Guess what?"

Kelly came back with the appropriate response, "What?"

"Twice a day, the satellite passes over Césme on a true bearing of 259° . Does that ring a bell?"

"It sure does. That's the bearing from Césme to Site Six and on to the largest air base in Israel."

Hauser continued, "Right! Joseph and I have computed for that orbit the Russians have two six-minute windows per day when they could attack Israel."

Kelly cautioned, "All these numbers about the orbit and so forth could be just coincidental. How about Amnon's agent. Doesn't he know what the system is to be used for?"

"Ladrun asked Amnon the same question. His agent is just an engineer who knows how the system works but not what it's going to be used for. The Russians use compartmentalized clearances like we do. That way, no one person knows too much about what's going on. To find out what the Russians intend to do, we'll just have to keep listening and hope we intercept the right information."

Kelly thanked his friends for the information and said he'd see them Friday night. They said they'd meet his flight at the Tehran airport and then they'd all take the chopper straight to Site Six.

As Kelly hung up he remembered Anna would be in the lobby by this time. He called the lobby and one of the guards answered, "Dr. Kelly, there's a beautiful woman waiting for you down here. Want to speak to her?"

"Yes, thanks, officer."

Anna's voice came through the phone, "Oh, Brad, you're going to have to work all day after all, aren't you?"

"No, Anna, but I just got an overseas call and now I have to spend about thirty minutes talking to my simulation team. Hope you don't mind."

"Brad, I've been the wife of an aerospace engineer for over twenty five years. I don't mind at all. I have my knitting with me. Have a good meeting!"

"Darling, you're wonderful to understand. See you soon."

Brad walked back to the conference room and found Watch One working at the black board. Bill Wilson said, "Brad, am I glad to see you. We figured out the sub-missiles would be in the shadow of the Earth before they reached their target. The Césme radar couldn't send them control messages."

Kelly responded, "I just got new information about that. There's a satellite midway between Césme and the target area that can bounce radar signals to the target. Also, now we know there are 105 sub-missiles on each main missile. The Russians are using an orthogonal coded system like our GPS to communicate with all those sub-missiles on the same communications channel without running into interference problems. Bill, I want you to approach the simulation from a *war games* point of view. Try to simulate a system that would destroy all Israeli aircraft at that field."

"OK, Brad. I'll make sure Watch Two members get the latest word when they come in at noon today."

Kelly said goodbye with "Thanks, Bill. I want to see both Watches at noon tomorrow for a status report," and headed down to the lobby and his waiting wife.

On the drive home, Kelly gave Anna a summary of his round trip to Iran, but told her nothing of the international drama unfolding under the electronic *eyes* of IBEX. They spent several hours lying in the warm October sun alongside their swimming pool, then took a mid afternoon nap, enjoying the feel of each other's bodies. Later Anna prepared a lavish dinner for the whole family letting Kelly catch up on all his family members' diverse activities. He found this family get together very relaxing. But he couldn't completely eliminate the nagging thoughts, *What do the Russians intend to do with the Césme missiles?* and *Can we really find out using IBEX?* He fell asleep that night with those questions running endlessly through his mind. He couldn't shut them off.

For the next four days, Kelly spent sixteen hours a day at the Associated Aviation plant. Every day at noon the team discussed their findings over sandwiches and soft drinks brought in by the company caterer. The simulation unfolded slowly but surely, revealing the awesome destructive capability of the new Césme missile system. During the Thursday noon meeting, Bob Wilson told Kelly the results would be ready by 6pm for Kelly to take back to Iran. He then proceeded to tell Kelly what the Russians could do with their Césme system:

"One. They can launch all ten missiles simultaneously towards Israel."

"Two. Each missile can be assigned a separate target for a total of ten targets. For the study, we selected nine Israeli air force bases, including Ben Gurion Airport, plus the Israeli nuclear facility at Dimona."

"Three. The system can control each of the 1050 sub-missiles to an accuracy of three feet. Each sub-missile can be assigned a different Israeli aircraft at one of the target air bases."

"Four. From time of launch, it takes five minutes and 49 seconds for the first missile with its 105 sub-missiles to wipe out the aircraft at Rosh Pinna, north of the Sea of Galilee. It takes six minutes and 40 seconds for the last missile to destroy all the aircraft at Sharm el Sheikh at the tip of the Sinai peninsula."

Kelly asked, "You mean all Israeli aircraft on the ground would be obliterated in only 51 seconds?"

"Exactly. We figure the Russians could pick a time, say 3am, when virtually all the Israeli aircraft are on the ground. Then, in 51 seconds, pouf! They're all gone. Burned up by the depleted uranium warheads. Those things don't explode. They just burn."

Kelly gasped, "Wow! That would completely destabilized the Middle East. The Israeli Air Force is the most powerful in the whole area. Hard to believe!"

"Brad, simulations don't lie. They just report the results of the inexorable laws of nature. That's what the Césme missiles can do!"

Shortly before midnight, Thursday night, Kelly stepped out of the AAC helicopter onto the tarmac at March Air Force Base and hurried the few steps to the C-5 transport. The load master quickly closed the entry door behind Kelly and the pilot started the huge plane's four engines. Within five minutes, they were on their way to Tehran.

The load master helped Kelly stow his briefcases and packages, the results of the simulations, including the computer print outs of the trajectories and destructive results of a simulated missile raid on the Israeli airfields. In addition, Bill Wilson had prepared a twenty five view graph briefing summarizing the results with pictures, figures, and words for Kelly to give to the decision makers in Tehran, if he, Ladrun, and Hauser could confirm that the Russians were, in fact, planning to wipe out the Israeli air force with a devastating attack. Kelly knew he couldn't give the report to Admiral Hurd, General Robertson, and the other leaders before he had conclusive evidence of the Soviet intent. Otherwise, the decisions makers would say, *Just another war games simulation! It doesn't mean anything!* Kelly fell asleep wondering when and if IBEX would confirm the Russian plans.

Kelly slept right through the rising and setting of the sun, accelerated by the C-5's polar route fight path at subsonic speeds. When Kelly woke up he looked at his watch. It was almost midnight, Tehran time. The load master noticed Kelly was awake and said, "The aircraft commander just told me we would be landing at Doshen Toeppeh in about an hour. Would you like something to eat before landing?"

Kelly, groggy from his long sleep, mumbled, "Yes, a cup of coffee and one of your outstanding C-5 box lunches would be great."

While eating, Kelly felt the plane begin its descent from cruise altitude. After finishing the box lunch, he went up into the cockpit to observe the landing approach. At first the lights of Tehran glowed in the distance and then gradually expanded. On final approach, the runway lights appeared to grow bigger. Kelly heard the control tower operator say, in perfect American English, "Grey Fox, you're cleared to land, runway two-one, wind calm."

Kelly remarked, "That tower operator speaks perfect English."

"He should. He's one of our own controllers. We don't trust the Iranian air traffic controllers when we're bringing in one of our big birds. Their English is almost un-understandable."

Kelly thought to himself, *The US has created a Little America here in Tehran. The Americans stationed here are effectively isolated from the Iranian culture, language, and economy by living in a US enclave. I suppose it's the same at all US bases around the world. Maybe there's a little bit of truth to foreigners' strident accusations that we Americans are imperialists. We bring our ways to foreign countries and try to get them to emulate us.*

Kelly's thoughts were interrupted when the C-5 taxied up to the ramp and the exit door opened. There were Hauser and Ladrun waiting for him. The three climbed on the waiting HH-60 and twenty five minutes later, they were in the Site Six control center. In spite of the hour, they immediately went through the simulation results.

Ladrun gasped, "Three foot accuracy with 1050 sub-missiles with depleted uranium warheads!"

Kelly replied, "Now our job is to intercept a message from the Russians with proof of their intentions. Joseph, that's your job since Russian is your native language."

Hauser added, "That's right. We need to intercept a message."

Ladrun replied, "I know one thing for sure. The Soviets intend a major operation soon. I can tell by the increase in communications and the tenor of their clear (un-coded) messages."

The three spent long hours for the next several weeks, studying intently the messages and radar signals from Césme. The electronic eyes and ears of IBEX were as busy as the operators. They stopped taking weekends. One day ran into the next. Tuesday, 24 November, two days before the American Thanksgiving holiday arrived before Brad knew it.

Late in the afternoon, Ladrun screamed, "This is it! The missing link! I just intercepted the following message from Moscow: *Commander Ivanov, you are ordered and authorized to destroy the Israeli Air Force at 0200 GMT 27 November!*"

Kelly exclaimed, "That's 4am local time in Israel when the whole air force will be on the ground. And that's 11pm Thanksgiving Day in Washington. The Americans will be falling asleep from eating too much turkey. Perfect timing!"

Chapter 16.

Crisis

Wednesday, 25 November, 1976.

Amnon Milchbucher arrived at Takht-i-Suleyman by USAF HH-60 at 7am in response to Ladrun's urgent request to help decide what Kelly should say in his 6pm meeting with Ambassador Hurd and General Robertson.

Hauser immediately interjected, "General Robertson is planning to invite General Fahi. He thinks it's important to keep the Iranians tied into this problem since it's the Shah's pet project."

Milchbucher added, "General Yidron wants to be there, too. He'll have to fly back to Israel afterwards to explain the problem to the Knesset."

Hauser added, "Amnon, I've already got the CIA Director's permission for General Yidron to be present. Also, Shaheen Mouhoud from Savak has been invited. The Director thinks our three countries' intelligence services must cooperate fully during this crisis."

The four decided the briefing should include the *HUMINT* (*HUM*an *INT*elligence) that Amnon learned from his Mossad agent in Russia, the satellite photo intelligence Ralph collected about Césme, the simulation results from California, and the *SIGINT* and *COMINT* (*SIG*nal and *COM*munication *INT*elligence) collected at Site Six, particularly the message Joseph intercepted the evening before. They busily collected the necessary view graphs, print outs and photos.

At about 5pm, the four carried the materials to the HH-60 and flew straight to Doshen Toeppeh air base in Tehran, landing near the IBEX control center. They headed straight for the conference room and while Kelly was focusing his introductory chart on the projector, Ambassador Hurd and the three generals walked in. During Kelly's presentation, he was interrupted frequently by the

Americans who asked clarifying questions. Generals Yidron and Fahi listened intently but asked no questions.

At the end of the presentation, General Robertson rose and said, "Ambassador Hurd, this is a grave situation. IBEX, together with the fine intelligence work of the CIA and Mossad, has uncovered a dangerous and diabolical plot of the USSR. I am obligated, Sir, to inform the US Joint Chiefs of Staff of this development so the American military can be placed on red alert."

Hurd replied coldly, "General Robertson, I greatly respect the Pentagon's military might, but a military solution is not the answer to this problem. It's going to take delicate political maneuvering to convince the Russians their plan is folly."

General Yidron broke in, "Gentlemen, it's Israel that has the problem. We are a sovereign nation and will take whatever action we have to. Israel can't survive without its air force. We don't need President Mahoney's help or the help of the US Joint Chiefs of Staff. I plan to recommend to the Knesset that we take out these Césme missiles, immediately!"

Ambassador Hurd turned red in the face and announced firmly, "General Yidron, we don't need a US or Israeli military response to this problem. That could precipitate an unthinkable catastrophe: thermonuclear war between the US and the Soviet Union. It must be solved through high level diplomacy. It's 11am in Washington now. Please let me call President Mahoney now, before he leaves on Air Force One to spend the Thanksgiving holiday in Plains, Georgia."

Both Robertson and Yidron nodded their assent.

Ambassador Hurd said, "I must return immediately to the US Embassy to use the red phone to call Washington."

Hauser interrupted, "We have a secure red phone here."

"Are you sure it's secure enough? I have to be sure the line is not tapped?"

"Sir, the NSA couldn't break the code after trying for two weeks with their supercomputers. The CIA Director has authorized its use for very sensitive matters."

General Fahi added helpfully, "Mr. Ambassador, use my private office. There's a red phone there."

Hauser instructed, "Phone straight to the US Embassy. Our resident CIA man there has a properly matched IBEX phone. That's how I called you from Site Six. He can patch you in to the President's red phone. That will be a secure communication routing."

Ambassador Hurd went into Fahi's office and dialed the embassy number connected to the IBEX phone there. The CIA man answered. Hurd gave his special code to identify himself to the CIA agent and requested an immediate connection with President Mahoney. Ten minutes later, Ambassador Hurd was speaking to the President.

"Mr. President, speaking as one Georgian to another, we have a real crisis on our hands." He spent the next five minutes summarizing the situation.

After a moment of silence, the President responded, "Richard, are you telling me the Soviet Union has a weapon system that can completely wipe out the Israeli Air Force in fifty one seconds? That would destabilize the whole Middle East. Does General Robertson agree with your assessment?"

Hurd answered, "He's here with me. Would you like to speak with him directly?"

"Yes, Richard. He's another Georgian I trust."

General Robertson hurried to the phone, "Mr. President, this is General Robertson, Chief of the US MAAG in Tehran."

The President inquired, "Is the situation really as grim as the Ambassador says it is?"

"Yes, Mr. President, I'm afraid it is. I personally looked at the data and heard the recordings. And they plan to do it on Thanksgiving night when our resources are reduced for the holiday."

"Those Russians are diabolical. If they believed in God, like us, they wouldn't do such horrible things."

"Yes, Mr. President, you're probably right. But what are we going to do?"

"We must stop this mad Russian plan. Put the ambassador back on the phone."

Robertson handed the phone to Hurd and the President continued, "Richard, I'm going to call an emergency meeting of my Security Council right away before everyone leaves for the Thanksgiving holiday. I want them to hear the problem first hand from you and General Robertson. Call me right after 5pm today, Washington DC time."

"I'll do that, Mr. President. Goodbye for now."

Hurd returned to the conference room and explained to Kelly and Robertson about the phone call during the meeting of the National Security Council. The ambassador asked Kelly to provide a ten minute oral summary of the situation over the red phone and to show him the summary before the meeting. Because the meeting would be at 12:30 midnight, Tehran time, he asked Kelly and Robertson stay in the US Embassy VIP quarters that night.

The ambassador continued, "By the way, General Robertson, the President said the chairman of the Joint Chiefs of Staff would be in the meeting."

Robertson responded, "Thank God. The President has enough sense to invite the top military to the meeting."

Kelly and the Ambassador rode back to the US Embassy in the ambassador's special bullet proof limousine, followed by General Robertson's limousine. The ambassador's limousine had an American flag flying in the breeze on its right fender. The general's limousine had a blue flag with two stars, showing the general's rank, waving on its right fender. They were protected by two cars filled with armed security men, one car leading the parade and the other bringing up the rear. Shahan, Kelly's bodyguard, rode in the front car with his Uzi resting on his lap. The procession was led by two military policemen on motorcycles with sirens on and blue lights flashing. Kelly couldn't help thinking, *What an advertisement to the terrorists that some important Americans are passing by!*

What little traffic there was moved out of the way to allow the procession to pass so they reached the embassy in about twenty minutes. Marine guards opened the gates and saluted as they drove into the huge American compound.

On the way, Hurd said to Kelly, "You and General Robertson will be my guests for dinner this evening in my private dining room. It will give us a chance to discuss the Césme situation in a more relaxed atmosphere. Dinner will be at 10. That will allow you time to dress for dinner."

The limousine pulled into the driveway in front of the building housing the ambassador's office and living quarters. Hurd climbed out saying, "Remain in the limousine. My driver will take you to your quarters. See you at 10."

The big, black, Cadillac limousine carried Kelly a short distance to the building with the VIP living quarters for guests of the US Embassy. General Robertson's more modest Chevrolet limousine was already there and he was standing on the steps talking to an air force colonel who quickly introduced himself to Kelly, "I'm Colonel Bennett, Ambassador Hurd's aide. If you will come with me, Sir, I'll show you and General Robertson your suites. You will be in the presidential suite where President Nixon stayed when he was here in 1973."

Kelly responded, "Thank you, Colonel Bennett, but shouldn't General Robertson get the presidential suite?"

"No, Sir. You outrank him because of your protocol rank of a three star general."

Colonel Bennett led Kelly and Robertson up to the second floor. Kelly's suite was at the end of the hall, with three large bedrooms, a paneled study, an enormous living room with a well equipped wet bar and a refrigerator stocked with delicacies, and two bathrooms, one connected to the master bedroom. The furnishings were elaborate with silk bed spreads and velvet drapes. Of course, there were Persian carpets on the floor. The picture window overlooked the embassy gardens. General Robertson's suite next door had only two bedrooms and one bathroom. His living room had a bar and refrigerator as well stocked as Kelly's. Colonel Bennett told them he would pick them up at five minutes to ten for dinner.

Kelly was unpacking his small bag when there was a knock at the door. It was Colonel Bennett carrying part of a word processor. He said, "I'll be back in a minute with the rest of this and with a secretary. Ambassador Hurd told me to set this up so you could prepare a written copy of your report and bring it to dinner. Then if he or General Robertson suggest changes, they can be made immediately on the word processor and a revised copy printed right away."

Soon Colonel Bennett returned with the rest of the word processing equipment and a beautiful young lady, whom he introduced as "Joanne Curtis, Ambassador Hurd's executive secretary." And then he asked, "Where shall I set this up?"

Kelly looked at him blankly for a minute and then said, "I'm sorry, but I was thrown off balance by this beautiful young lady's entrance. I've been in the field at an all male compound for the last four weeks. Put it in the study, please."

Joanne turned to Kelly, smiled sweetly, and said, "Dr. Kelly, I'll bet you flatter all the girls like that. Please call me Joanne."

Kelly replied, brightly, "Joanne, I wasn't trying to flatter you. I've come down from a month on a mountain side surrounded by dirty old men and I find a beautiful young American girl sent to my room. It's a fantastic treat, believe me!"

Joanne responded, "I understand from the ambassador that you and the *dirty old men* have been doing a really great job. Let's get started on the report."

Joanne was a whiz on the word processor. Kelly dictated, she typed, they rechecked, and soon the short presentation was ready.

Kelly asked, "Will you be at the dinner?"

She answered, "Yes, of course. They will go over this report at dinner. I will probably need to come back up to your room to rework something before the midnight phone call."

"How about after the midnight phone call? Do you think you might need to come back to my room to get your notebook or something?"

"Or something, what?"

"Oh, Joanne, please spend the night here. I want you!"

Joanne smiled broadly, "I was afraid you'd never ask! I'll see you after the phone call" and she walked out of the room.

Kelly dressed for dinner by putting on the most formal clothes he had with him: his dark blue suit, the aerospace executive's uniform. He put on his cuff links and tie clasp with the presidential seal on them. They had been given to him in recognition of his large financial contribution to the last presidential election campaign. Kelly found it amusing that tonight he would be speaking to the winner of that election, however, not the one he had supported.

A knock at the door announced Colonel Bennett, "Dr. Kelly, the ambassador is awaiting your pleasure in the dining room. It's a beautiful evening out, so we will walk over to the ambassador's quarters."

Kelly, Robertson and Bennett walked along the pathway through the softly lit and beautifully kept embassy grounds. In the ambassador's building, Bennett led them to the second floor dining room where a black waiter in a smart formal white uniform greeted them at the doorway and asked for their drink orders.

Before they could answer, Joanne walked in, saying, "Good evening, Gentlemen. The ambassador included me in your dinner tonight to partially balance out the sexes. It's a pleasure to see you both again."

Colonel Bennett added, "Gentlemen, you are in good hands now. Good evening, Sirs."

They chorused *goodbye*, then turned to the waiter, Benjamin. Kelly ordered Tanqueray on the rocks with a twist, Joanne chose champagne cocktail, and Robertson picked Jack Daniels on the rocks.

Joanne explained she'd phoned President Mahoney's secretary so she could dig out Kelly's résumé. The President likes to know the background of key people he talks to, you know."

Kelly thanked her and said he was flattered to get such high level attention and asked her to call him Brad.

Joanne answered, "I'm sorry, Dr. Kelly. I can't do that. If Ambassador Hurd caught me calling an important person like you by your first name, I'd be fired on the spot."

"OK, call me Dr. Kelly here, but if we ever meet elsewhere, please call me Brad."

"I promise, Dr. Kelly."

At that point Ambassador and Mrs. Hurd entered the dining room. After introductions, Mrs. Hurd pointed to the beautifully set round table and said, "Richard, you sit here. Dr. Kelly, you sit on the ambassador's right. Joanne, you sit between our two guests, and I will take my place at the ambassador's left." She motioned to Benjamin.

Benjamin then announced, "Ladies and Gentlemen, I am serving Chateaubriand this evening, with wild rice and French cut fresh green beans. How would you like your meat, Dr. Kelly and General Robertson? I already know the other's preferences."

Kelly replied, "I'll take an end cut, if available."

Robertson said, "Very rare, please."

After Benjamin retired to the kitchen, the ambassador brought up Kelly's report.

Kelly remarked, "I'm afraid I may have made it too technical."

"Good, good, Dr. Kelly. Don't worry about too many technical details with the President. He likes to become involved in detail. In fact, he was a nuclear engineer with the Navy during his early career, you know."

"I'm glad to hear that, Mr. Ambassador. It's difficult to explain about the crisis without some technical detail. The whole concept depends on *spread spectrum* technology."

"Dr. Kelly, I don't know anything about that technology, but don't worry about covering that kind of detail with the President. If he doesn't know about it now, he'll find out quickly from his Science Advisor who will be in the meeting! Now, what are the points you're going to cover?"

Kelly started reading from his report:

First, we detected some strange signals coming from the Turkmen Republic of the USSR at a place called Césme-oj. Analysis of these signals showed they came from a very sophisticated Russian radar that used spread spectrum wave forms.

Second, we found a new Soviet installation at Césme. The satellite photos from the week before showed a small rural village. Then the next week's photos showed three radar dishes, ten missiles on pads, and a command and control center building bristling with communication antennas.

Third, an Israeli Mossad agent who works on missiles like those at Césme told us each of the ten missiles carries 105 sub-missiles, each of which could be individually guided against ground targets up to 1600 nautical miles away with an accuracy of three feet.

The ambassador interrupted to exclaim, "Dr. Kelly, I heard you say that in the briefing this afternoon and could hardly believe it. As I remember from the newspapers, our missiles with that kind of range have an accuracy of only a few hundred feet. How do the Russians do it?"

"That brings me to the next point," said Kelly and continued reading:

Fourth, the Mossad agent told us, and the CIA confirmed, the Soviets have a satellite that bounces radar signals from Césme to the sub-missiles so they can be individually guided to their targets. So each of those 1050 sub-missiles can be aimed to destroy a different Israel aircraft on the ground.

Fifth, we conducted a simulation that showed the missiles can be programmed to hit the nine Israeli Air Force Bases and their Dimona nuclear facility, and that the entire Israeli Air Force can be destroyed in a period of 51 seconds, just six minutes and forty seconds after the simultaneous launches of the ten missiles.

The ambassador interjected excitedly, "And if the Israeli Air Force is destroyed, they are open to attacks from their Arab neighbors. It would completely destabilize the Middle East. That could be the beginning of World War III."

"Right, Sir. And that brings me to my final point."

Sixth, yesterday afternoon we intercepted an encrypted message from Moscow to the Russian commander at Césme authorizing and ordering the destruction of the Israeli Air Force at 0200 GMT on 27 November, Friday morning at 4am Israeli time. All their planes would be on the ground, vulnerable.

The ambassador added, "That will be 11pm Thanksgiving night in Washington. Everyone will be sleepy after their turkey feast. Most of the military and civilian decision makers will be scattered around the country, home for the holiday!"

"Exactly, Mr. Ambassador. President Mahoney doesn't have much time to solve the problem."

"Dr. Kelly, I don't know how he will do it, but, somehow, President Mahoney will solve the problem, and peacefully. I've known the President for almost forty years, since we were boys together in Georgia. He's a problem solver and he doesn't believe in using military power except as a last resort."

General Robertson interrupted, "Mr. Ambassador, with all due deference to Mr. Mahoney and his peaceful means, damn it! Sometimes military action is called for, and I think this is it. I can order six of my crack fighter pilots, who are advisors to the Iranians at Doshen Toeppeh, to fly a strike mission against Césme. At Mach 2, it would take the F-14's only twenty two minutes to reach there from Tehran, and only thirty seconds to destroy those radars and missiles."

Ambassador Hurd responded angrily, "And what then, General Robertson? Do you think the Russians would sit on their hands after a military attack on Soviet territory by American fighter bombers flown by American pilots?"

"Well, they might.   And anyway, we've got Minuteman missiles targeted on all Russian targets. We'd decapitate them!"

"General Robertson, it sounds like you are advocating we start World War III. I think we better let President Mahoney solve the problem by peaceful means."

General Robertson glanced down sheepishly and mumbled, "Perhaps you're right, Mr. Ambassador." Then he looked up and said defiantly, "But, if the President gives the word, I'll take out those missiles and radars at Césme. I've already asked my deputy to make the attack plan, just in case."

"General, the President will never ask you to do that. Mark my words!"

At that moment, Benjamin arrived with the large silver serving cart and announced happily, Ladies and Gentlemen, dinner is served!" In no time, everyone had their plates in front of them. Benjamin poured champagne for all five.

Kelly raised his glass, "Mr. Ambassador, I would like to propose a toast. Here's to President Mahoney's peaceful solution, whatever it may be!"

General Robertson added grimly, "I'll drink to that, even though I doubt he can do it."

Everyone drank to Kelly's toast.

General Robertson said to Kelly, "You made all the important points in your summary. After the phone call tonight, the ball will be in the President's court."

Kelly asked, "How do you suggest we conduct the actual phone call, Mr. Ambassador?"

"First, I plan to provide some brief introductory comments explaining the gravity of the situation. Next, I will introduce you, Dr. Kelly, and you should read your notes. Then I will introduce General Robertson and he will present his contingency plan. Finally I'll get back on the phone to sign off."

"What if President Mahoney or one of the members of the Security Council asks a question?"

"In that case, Dr. Kelly, do your best to answer the question, of course."

After the delicious meal, Mrs. Hurd excused herself and the others moved to the conference room. As the hour grew close to midnight, Joanne went into the next room to place the call, using the secure red phone, to be sure there was an open line ready at 12:30. Soon she came back into the conference room and announced, "Mr. Ambassador, the President's executive secretary is holding on the flashing line. She says the President is ready to receive your call. Just push the button on the speaker and you can all hear."

Hurd picked up the phone, "Good afternoon, Elizabeth. I have Dr. Kelly and General Robertson here with me. We're ready to be put through."

There was a momentary silence, some clicking noises, and then President Mahoney's voice came over the speaker phone, "Ambassador Hurd, this is Jimmy Mahoney in Washington. I've got the whole Security Council here in the room with me. Please go ahead and explain this dreadful situation so all of us can hear."

Hurd responded, "Mr. President, members of the National Security Council, we have a grave crisis on our hands. Our US-built IBEX system installed here in Iran has detected a significant new USSR threat to world peace. Dr. Kelly is the program director of IBEX. He will give you the details."

Kelly started, "Mr. President, members of the Security Council. I would like to present six points that describe this crisis:" He read his written statement clearly and with verbal emphasis. No one interrupted him.

At the end, President Mahoney asked, "Dr. Kelly, you've been intimately involved in this Césme missile problem from the beginning. Do you really believe the Russians can destroy the Israeli Air Force?"

"Yes, Sir, I do! However, the fact that we have discovered their secret plan will allow the Israelis to take counter measures to reduce the damage, like moving the airplanes just before the attack. But then the planes will have no place to land, because the strike will have blown up their airfields. However, our knowledge of the Soviet plan gives us a definite advantage."

The President responded, "That is an excellent point, Dr. Kelly. We do have a psychological advantage now, knowing their diabolical intentions." He asked the Security Council if any of them had any questions but no one did.

Hurd interjected, "Mr. President, General Robertson would like to present a contingency plan for a military strike he and his staff here at Doshen Toeppeh have prepared."

The President responded, "OK, put him on. The Chairman of the Joint Chiefs of Staff has been agitating for a military solution also. But, I'd like to make my position crystal clear on that issue. I think a military strike would precipitate a catastrophe. None-the-less, it's important that we hear his plan."

Robertson said, "Mr. President, members of the Security Council, the United States has assembled here in Tehran a powerful military force as military advisors to the Shah's forces. Here under my command is a group of six crack combat pilots, seasoned from over 100 missions each in Vietnam. We can launch an attack from here in Tehran and twenty two minutes later the missiles and radars at Césme will be wiped out."

The President interrupted, "And thirty minutes later, every American city will be wiped out by the Russian thermonuclear intercontinental ballistic missiles!"

A voice in the background interrupted and General Robertson whispered to the others, "That's the Chairman of the Joint Chiefs of Staff."

"Mr. President, the Russians wouldn't necessarily launch a ballistic missile strike against the United States. I think we should hear General Robertson's contingency plan. The Security Council needs to examine all options available to us."

"That's right," agreed President Mahoney. "General Robertson, forgive my interruption. Go ahead with the details."

General Robertson presented his plan. At the end he said, "We would be using F-14's with Iranian markings. The Russians would think they were being attacked by the Shah's Royal Iranian Air Force."

"Maybe, unless they shot down one of the planes. Then your charade wouldn't work. But we do need to examine all our options."

Hurd said with concern in his voice, "There is one other thing, Mr. President. You should call Prime Minister Begin and make sure the Israelis don't try to take out the Césme missiles on their own. The Israelis know all about this situation."

"Good point. I'll call him."

Ambassador Hurd added, "Mr. President, that's our presentation of the facts to you. I pray to God you find a peaceful solution."

President Mahoney responded, "Amen, Brother Richard, amen. Thank you all for your fine reports. Before we hang up, I have a message for Dr. Kelly. Please plan to stop by the White House as soon as you can after you return from Iran. I want to give you a medal. Goodbye."

President Mahoney asked his Security Council members to prepare a list of options based on the telephoned information and to present them to him at 10am Thanksgiving Day. He reminded them thirteen hours after the start of that meeting, the Soviet Union planned to launch an attack against Israel.

Joanne came back into the conference room, "Dr. Kelly, a Dr. Morrell is holding for you. He was very insistent that I interrupt your telephonic meeting until I told him you were speaking to President Mahoney."

Kelly followed Joanne into her office and picked up the flashing phone.

Morrell blurted excitedly, "Brad, what in the world were you discussing with the President?"

"I'm sorry, John, I can't tell you over this phone."

"That's right, this isn't a secure line. Now, my problem. We have a real cash crisis here at Associated Aviation. We need the last twenty percent payment from the Iranians for IBEX. That's $240 million. Can you get General Fahi to transfer payment before Thanksgiving?"

"I'll speak to him today. I'm sure he'll agree IBEX is operational."

"Pressure him for an immediate payment. Don't take no for an answer!"

"OK, John. I'll do what I can. Have a good Thanksgiving."

"I'll have a lousy Thanksgiving if you don't call back to say the cash is on the way. The chairman's after my neck!"

"I'll call you back as soon as I have any news. Where can I reach you?"

"I'm home for the Thanksgiving weekend. Call me at home no matter what time it is."

"OK, John, I'll do my best. Goodbye."

Kelly rejoined the ambassador and the general, who were rehashing the overseas call. Kelly said, "If it's not one thing, it's another. The home office wants the final payment for IBEX immediately. I'll have to call General Fahi first thing in the morning. Let's call it a night. I don't think we can do anything else to take care of the Césme crisis right now."

Shortly after Kelly got back to his suite, he heard Joanne tap at the door.

She said, "Brad, honey, please pour me a glass of white wine."

"It didn't take you long to switch from Dr. Kelly to Brad!"

"Just complying with your request."

"It could be dangerous, complying with my requests. There's no telling what request I may make after you finish your wine."

They hurriedly ran for the bed. They engaged in sexual games until they were both sexually satiated. Kelly fell asleep thinking, *I've had more than enough excitement, political and sexual, for one day!"* He hardly stirred when Joanne left early in the morning.

The next tap on the door was Colonel Bennett with Kelly's breakfast on a tray. He asked Kelly's plans for the day.

Kelly answered, "I really don't have any. I've been concentrating so heavily on getting the information about the crisis to the President that I haven't made any plans."

"Of course, you may join our Thanksgiving celebration here at the embassy if you wish."

"Thank you. I may decide to do that. I'll let you know later. First, I must phone Doshen Toeppeh. May I use this room phone?"

"Of course, Sir. I'll check with you later," said Bennett as he left, carrying the word processor back to the office where it belonged.

Kelly decided he might as well get the phone call over with. He poured himself a cup of coffee from his breakfast tray and dialed General Fahi at the IBEX control center.

"Abe, this is Brad. Dr. Morrell called last night about our final twenty percent payment for IBEX. It totals $240 million dollars. It's due and payable after demonstration to you that IBEX is operational. Surely, with all the information we have collected about your neighbors, you do agree that IBEX is operational now."

Fahi agreed, "Yes, it is operational, and I've started the steps toward final payment. But that's a time consuming bureaucratic process. Many different people have to sign the documents. There's no way we can transfer the money before the first of the year. You can plan on receiving the funds by the fifteenth of January 1977."

"Isn't there any way you can speed up payment?"

"No, even Christina and Olga couldn't help expedite this process."

"Dr. Morrell wanted payment by tomorrow."

"Brad, I don't know of any way, unless your President called the Shah."

Kelly answered with desperation in his voice, "Abe, the President of the United States won't intervene on behalf of a private company for payment."

"Then I guess you'll have to wait until January fifteenth."

"OK, thanks for the information anyway."

Kelly dialed again, this time Dr. Morrell's home number. Morrell answered, "Brad, I didn't expect to hear back so soon. You work quickly."

"John, I'm afraid I have bad news for you. The soonest we can expect payment is the fifteenth of January." He recounted his conversation with Fahi.

"Brad, I may lose my job because of this cash flow problem. I want you to get back here right away and explain this payment situation to the chairman. Be in the office Monday. That's an order."

OK, but I have to go to Washington shortly afterwards. President Mahoney said he's going to give me a medal."

"Congratulations. I'll be glad to hear the details later. You'll be super busy here. You'll probably have to meet with the whole board of directors. They're all up in arms about this cash flow disaster, and they've decided to blame IBEX."

"I'll try to think of what to say to them between now and Monday."

"Oh, Brad, I almost forget. Someone from the US Customs Department stopped by here yesterday. Something about an illegal export."

"I wonder what that's about. Something else to take care of while I'm in LA. See you soon. Goodbye."

26 November, Thanksgiving Day

President Mahoney started the emergency meeting of his National Security Council by announcing, "Gentlemen, we simply cannot permit the Soviet Union to launch their Césme missiles. It could very well be the start of World War III. It's up to us to stop this mad Russian plan, *now, today!* What are the options you have for me?"

The President's National Security Advisor responded, "Mr. President, your National Security Council fully appreciates the gravity of the Césme crisis and agrees with your general assessment. We continued our meeting last night until well past midnight. We took a short break to sleep and reconvened very early this morning. I must say honestly there were many heated discussions; however the options we have prepared for your consideration represent a consensus of the complete NSC membership, including the Director of the CIA, the Secretaries of State and Defense, and the Chairman of the Joint Chiefs of Staff. We recognize time is very short and therefore recommend you take action immediately to avoid this impending disaster."

The President grew impatient with this long, elegant preamble and said, sharply, "OK, OK. Please give me the options."

"Yes, of course, Mr. President, and please understand, we do not wish in any way to inhibit your decision making prerogatives, but...."

As the President grew more irritated his face became red, "For God's sake! But, what?"

"But we strongly recommend you select Option One!"

"Please, -- the options!"

"Mr. President, we have carefully ordered these options in descending order of preference."

The President's patience vanished. He yelled, "What are they?"

"Option One is to exercise General Robertson's contingency plan to surgically remove the Césme missiles and radars."

The President looked directly at the Secretary of State and asked sharply, "And, Mr. Secretary, did you agree to this option as being the best?"

Mine was the only dissenting vote. If you select this option, I believe you must call Premier Brezhnev and inform him of the action. Otherwise, we risk an ICBM attack against the US. That is my opinion."

The President exploded, "In my opinion, we risk such an attack whether we warn the Premier or not. We are talking about a US military strike against Mother Russia. The Russians won't put up with it. This option is insane! What's the next option, Mr. Chairman?"

Option Two is to put the US military on Red Alert and to threaten the USSR with an ICBM retaliatory attack if they carry out their planned attack."

Highly agitated, the President shouted, "That really is the start of World War III. If we launch Minute Man missiles against the Soviet Union, they will retaliate in kind. Besides that violates the

US policy against being the first to use nuclear weapons, you know this as well as I do. It's a toothless threat!"

The Secretary of Defense spoke up, "Mr. President, I should remind you that the US policy does permit a first nuclear strike if the Soviets should attack Western Europe with conventional forces."

The President replied with disdain, "Mr. Secretary, Israel is not Western Europe. I'm not going to be the President that violates this long standing bilateral policy of both Democrats and Republicans. No, Gentlemen, Option Two is completely unacceptable to me."

"Option Three is to request the Israelis move all their military aircraft to one of our NATO Air Force Bases in Greece. Then the Russian attack will be against empty air force bases."

The President's agitation increased again, "You should know the problems we are having already with the Greeks, trying to keep them in NATO. The Greek government would go crazy if we should suddenly have a thousand Israeli warplanes land at our air force bases there. There's a lot of agitation to close those bases now. Besides the Greeks have very close relations with the Arab countries, particularly Libya. Colonel Gadafi hates Israel and the US with a passion. He would immediately cut off all trade with Greece, including oil products. That would destroy the Greek economy overnight. Option Three is unacceptable. What is your next option?"

The Chairman responded, "We only had time to come up with three options."

The President yelled again, "You know as well as I do that we are out of time. We must do something now!"

"Yes, I know, Mr. President. What do you think we should do?"

The President calmed down perceptibly and said, "Mr. Chairman, we should do what any good Christian would do. Let's tell the truth. Let's phone Premier Brezhnev and tell him we know what he is planning. We will tell him he must kill the plan, that it's an uncivilized way to behave!"

The Secretary of State responded, "Mr. President, your approach is so simple it might just work. Telling Brezhnev we know about his plan will put him off guard. Then you simply ask him not to do it, without any explicit threat. Now, that is real diplomacy, not saber rattling!"

The Secretary of Defense added, "And the Premier will know you command a whole range of retaliatory options, without your mentioning them. Yes, I agree, it may very well work."

The Chairman of the Security Council added his endorsement and cautioned, "Let me warn you, you're going to have to give these Russians something in return. And, it may hurt! I know how the Slavic mind works, I'm Slavic myself you know."

The President answered, "Mr. Chairman, I know very well I may have to give something, but whatever it may be, it will be better than World War III. Now, let's put the phone call through to Premier Brezhnev. We'll need a Russian interpreter."

The Secretary of State responded, Mr. President, in anticipation of your need to call the Premier, I took the liberty of bringing in the best Russian interpreter in the State Department. He's in the next room, ready to serve you."

"Mr. Secretary, you really did think ahead. Please have him get Premier Brezhnev on the phone for me. In addition to the interpreter, I would like the following four individuals present during my call: the Secretaries of State and Defense, the Chairmen of the Joint Chiefs of Staff and of the National Security council. The rest of you may leave for your Thanksgiving dinners. God bless you all for your advice."

Ten minutes later, President Mahoney was talking to Premier Brezhnev, each using the best interpreters in the world to aid in this crucial discussion.

After an hour and a half of intense telephonic negotiation, President Mahoney announced, with a broad grin on his face, "Gentlemen, the forces of peace have prevailed today. Premier Brezhnev has agreed to cancel the strike against the Israelis. In return, I had to agree to three conditions. Before you all leave this room, I want your solemn promise that none of you will ever reveal this discussion or the conditions I agreed to, even when you publish your memoirs."

The President then explained that as the three conditions were implemented, they would appear as normal world events and would never be connected with the Césme missile crisis by the President or by any of the government executives in the room. The President pointed out the Premier had also agreed never to reveal the agreements. In return, the US government would never reveal the existence of the Césme missile crisis.

On Thursday the third of December 1976 in a private ceremony, Dr. Brad Kelly was awarded a medal by President Mahoney for *Meritorious Civilian Service to the United States Government*. There was no public announcement of the award.

Chapter 17.

Césme Accords

Air Force One began its descent into Mehrabad Airport in the late afternoon of December 31st, 1976. The President and his wife were going to be guests of honor at the gala New Year's Eve party tonight in the Pahlano Palace. President Mahoney looked out the window of the Boeing 707 and picked out the snow capped mountain peak of Takht-i-Suleyman, gleaming in the last rays of the setting sun. He thought it was ironic that the information from the electronic spy system on top of that peak, a system sponsored by the Shah himself and paid for by his own government, was the cause of the message, in fact the order, the President would give to the Shah during their business meeting scheduled for New Year's Day afternoon.

Air Force One taxied up to the special arrival area. The red carpet was rolled out and the Shah and his queen, the US Ambassador to Iran, and the Shah's trusted General Hatami, flanked by a smartly dressed honor guard, were ready to welcome the visitors. In the airplane, the President's wife stood beside him. The President's Security Advisor and his wife were also ready.

Shaheen Mouhoud had worked closely with Ralph Hauser to assure proper coordination between the large Iranian Security Force and the US Secret Service agents assigned to protect the US President. The security arrangements made it virtually impossible for anyone to harm either the Shah or the President or members of their party.

The Shah had banned the press from the welcoming ceremonies, for security reasons. Instead, there were official photographers and video cameramen who would later release official photos and videos tapes for the newspapers and TV news broadcasts. The US news services and TV networks had protested this ban to the President's press secretary. But President Mahoney decided to allow the Shah to have his way in this matter, almost as if it were his *last wish*. A press release was issued stating the US government could not interfere with the sovereignty of the independent nation of Iran.

The President and his party descended the stairs to the red carpet. The President grinned broadly for the cameramen as he shook the Shah's hand and kissed the queen on her cheek. He shook Ambassador Hurd's hand and whispered, "Richard, tomorrow's meeting is going to be painful for me!"

The ambassador whispered back, "Not nearly as painful as it will be for the Shah!"

The President made a statement to the video cameras to be broadcast on Iranian TV, translated into Farsi, and also released to the western news media. He pledged continued friendship between the two nations and US support of the Shah's government. The Shah made a short speech citing the long friendship between the Royal Iranian government and the US government and gave his official welcome to the President, his wife, and the officials accompanying the President. The Shah remembered well how the CIA helped him return to Iran and the Peacock throne in the early 1950's. He was truly grateful for the continued support from the Americans.

The royal and presidential parties boarded the black, bullet-proof limousines parked on the ramp. The procession was led by six heavily armed policemen on motorcycles with flashing blue lights. There were three car loads of heavily armed guards interspersed among the officials' cars. However, the probability of a terrorist attack had been greatly reduced since Savak had arrested almost 200 people in the last two days, people who were suspected of having possible motives for attacking the procession. The parade moved from Mehrabad Airport onto Eisenhower Boulevard, transitioned to the Shimron Road Expressway, and continued to Avenue Pahlano, where they turned north toward the Royal Palace. The President and his wife and their secret service guards were assigned guest quarters in the palace. The other government officials pealed off the procession as it passed the Tehran Hilton Hotel and proceeded to their rooms on a heavily guarded floor reserved for them. All the travelers had time for naps, to help shake off their jet lag.

At 10:30, the President and his wife joined the Shah and his queen to welcome the almost one hundred guests to the New Year's Eve celebration. All the top level officials of the Iranian and US governments invited to the party passed though the Royal/Presidential reception line on the way to the bountiful tables stacked with a dazzling array of hors d'oeuvres. A large contingent of waiters in crisp white uniforms circulated through the guests making sure their glasses and plates were never empty.

Just before midnight, all the guests were seated at beautifully decorated tables set with linen, crystal, bone china and gold flatware. At midnight, the President offered a toast to the Shah, the queen, and the Peacock Throne. He wished the Shah and the Iranian nation continued happiness, success, and peace during the coming year. The Shah offered a toast to the President, his wife, and the American people. He wished for the continued friendship and cooperation of the two nations against the forces of evil in the world. Then the Shah gave the royal order to all the guests to enjoy the sumptuous feast served by the horde of waiters. The dining continued until 3am when the guests disappeared quickly, leaving the Shah and his queen and the President and his wife in the palace to retire for the night.

The Peacock Throne overlooked the conference table in the royal throne room of the Pahlano Palace. The US President was seated at one end of the table with Ambassador Hurd seated at his right. The Shah was seated at the other end of the table with his foreign affairs advisor seated at his right. Since the discussions were to be in English, no interpreters were present, just the four men.

After exchanging pleasantries and the Presidential thanks for the royal New Year's Eve party, the President opened the business meeting by saying, "Your Majesty, my government is deeply concerned about the unrest in your nation. We believe the Communist Party is poised to overthrow your government. Our nation can not let that happen. It would be a disaster for the Free World and would inevitably lead to a Soviet take over of Iran, thus giving them a strangle hold on Western oil supplies."

The Shah interrupted, "But, Mr. President, the Savak has effectively combated this Communist menace and has eliminated the threat."

"That may be your opinion, Your Majesty, but our CIA believes the threat is there and must still be eliminated. My government is going to get rid of that threat once and for all."

The Shah interrupted again, "We do not agree there is such a threat, but, of course, we welcome your government's assistance in eliminating any danger to my government. How do you plan to get rid of the threat?"

"Your Majesty, our CIA is in contact with one of the exiled religious leaders of your country, Khomeini. We plan to bring him back to Iran from France. Khomeini believes in the same God as we Christians. He will destroy this Godless Communist threat."

"He and his fundamentalist followers will also destroy Iran and my government. That is why I banned him from Iran in the first place. He is a crazy madman who uses religion as an excuse for getting rid of all those that oppose him."

"Your Majesty, my government doesn't agree with your assessment of Khomeini. We believe he can bring the stability to Iran that is required by the Free World. Of course, you will have to leave Iran. My government will help you find a country in which you can live out your remaining years in peace and tranquility."

The Shah was shocked speechless. He could hardly believe his ears. He had no idea the President was implementing the first accord of the Césme agreement with the Soviet Premier. Finally he regained his composure and said, resignedly, "And when do you want me to leave, Mr. President? Right away?"

"No, Your Majesty. I do not want your departure to appear in any way connected with my visit here. Khomeini's return must appear to be a natural result of the Iranian people's desire for a religious government. You must leave within a year."

"And if I refuse?"

"Then my government will withdraw all our military advisors immediately and shut off your arms supplies. Your government would fall immediately. What I offer you today is time to put your affairs in order and to make it appear you are leaving voluntarily."

"Mr. President, it appears I do not have a free choice in this matter. May I come to live in the United States?"

"No, Your Majesty, that would not have the appearance of propriety. The American people would not understand. I'll advise you shortly of a friendly, third world country that will give you political asylum. Ambassador Hurd will give you my solution next week."

"Mr. President, I am very upset by your message today. I really felt that after twenty five years of close and friendly relations between my government and the Americans that I could depend upon America. I can see I was terribly wrong."

"I assure you, friendly relations will continue between our two nations."

"I know Khomeini much better than you or your CIA. Mark my words! You will live to see you have made a grave error in judgment. Khomeini really is a blood thirsty monster who kills in the name of God!"

Ambassador Hurd took a silent cue from the President and broke up the meeting by saying, "Mr. President, we must leave now. Air Force One is scheduled to take off at 5pm."

The President took leave of the deeply shocked Shah of Iran and headed for the airport.

The words of the all-powerful American President had shattered the Shah's world. He was appalled and shaken by thoughts of what would happen to his country when this madman, Khomeini, took over. His years of labor to bring Iran into the twentieth century, to modernize the country's economy and life style, and to give freedom and equality to women, would all be eliminated after he departed. True, he would still have wealth, but his power would be gone forever. His only hope for Iran was that his son might return someday to reassume the Peacock Throne and to rebuild the country.

Air Force One climbed to altitude and headed for its first refueling stop: Cairo, Egypt. The President's Security Advisor closed the door of the Presidential compartment for a private conversation with the President. He asked, "Mr. President, how does it feel to have set in action the implementation of the first accord to the Césme agreement?"

"Frankly, I feel greatly relieved. It was personally painful for me and, of course, the Shah took the news with shock. He was very derogatory in his attitude towards Khomeini, the Man of God. The Shah called Khomeini a blood thirsty monster! That's really sacrilegious!"

"Just sour grapes, Mr. President. In time he will see that what we are doing is in the best interest of the Iranian people. It is much better for a religious leader to take power than to have the Communists, and then later the Soviet Union, take over Iran."

"Yes, I tried to explain that to him but, of course, he didn't have the global view of the world that you and I have. He was just thinking of his local kingdom."

"Mr. President, your secret meeting with President Sadim during our *fuel stop* in Egypt is confirmed. He and his closest advisor will board Air Force One disguised as security guards. I will escort them into your compartment here so the meeting will be known only to the four of us."

"Good. When are we scheduled to arrive?"

"In a little less than three hours from now. About 6:30 local time. We'll be on the ground two hours. That should give you plenty of time to give Sadim the word."

The President broke into a broad grin, "Excellent! Excellent! This has been a very fruitful trip so far!"

"Yes, Mr. President, while the rest of the world has been celebrating the New Year, we have been taking positive steps to assure world peace and tranquility. Believe me, what we are accomplishing will assure your election to a second term."

The President welcomed the Egyptian President Sadim and his foreign affairs advisor aboard and exclaimed with a broad grin, "Thank you for agreeing to meet with me, President Sadim. I have an important new peace initiative to discuss with you. My government is well aware of the economic difficulties Egypt has been experiencing, since you had the foresight, as a great leader, to expel the large number of Soviet foreign advisors from your nation."

Yes, Mr. President, it has been difficult for us, but I felt it was the right thing to do, so I did it. We Egyptians discovered the cost of doing business with the Soviets was too dear. They expected too much in return for their aid."

"President Sadim, we are both religious men and believe in the same God. And our God is the same as the Jewish God. In fact, we Christians, Moslems, and Jews share many of the same prophets and religious beliefs. I am going to ask you, as a good Moslem, to perform a very brave act."

"And what is that, Mr. President?"

"I want you to take the initiative to make peace with the Israelis. You must go to Jerusalem and meet with the Israeli Knesset and declare that it is time for your two nations to sign a comprehensive peace treaty and to re-establish diplomatic relations."

President Sadim's expression became one of horror. He exclaimed, "Ridiculous! Mr. President, the Israelis are our mortal enemies. They have taken the Sinai and its oil fields from us. They completely destroyed our air force during the Yom Kippur War and except for Richard Nixon's intervention, they might have occupied Cairo. They were on their way here. I would be an outcast in the eyes of the Arab world!"

"But, President Sadim, you are overlooking the advantages of the peace agreement. I will see that the Israelis give you back the Sinai. Also, the US will grant Egypt new economic and military aid. We'll supply your air force with new F-16 fighters, just like the Israeli Air Force is getting."

"But the Israelis would never give back the Sinai. They have built new tourist hotels, new air force bases, and new settlement communities there. They have increased the number and productivity of the oil wells there and are collecting considerable revenue from that oil."

"The Israelis have no choice in the matter. Without US aid, their economy would collapse. The US supplies the funds and military equipment that make Israel a viable nation. If the Israelis won't give back the Sinai -- no more American aid! They'll agree to give it back. Don't worry."

"What an excellent idea, Mr. President. I'll do it. I'll become a man of peace in the eyes of the world. Perhaps the extremist Arabs will sever relations with Egypt, but the conservative Arab nations will respect me for regaining the Sinai."

"And you might even win the Nobel Peace Prize for taking such a giant step toward Middle East peace!"

"Mr. President, are there any other strings attached? You have emphasized the benefits. What other price must we pay?"

"President Sadim, there is something else. The US is concerned about threats to the Free World's oil supply in the Middle East and in the Persian Gulf region in particular. I have asked my Secretary of Defense to establish a mobile, special force to act quickly to protect those oil supplies in case of hostile action against the oil wells or supply routes. We would like Egyptian bases for assembling and training these forces. We would, of course, pay your nation for their use. We would also be willing to provide Egypt with AWAC (Airborne Warning And Control) aircraft to provide surveillance of Libya and Colonel Gadafi's forces, operated by American crews, of course."

Sadim and his advisor nodded to each other in agreement. Sadim exclaimed, "We would be willing to grant the US use of Egyptian bases for that purpose, providing we receive adequate compensation. After all, your objective is to protect Arab oil. And, so far as Libya is concerned, we certainly need to keep a watchful eye on Colonel Gadafi. We want to keep him out of Egypt."

"President Sadim, there is one more thing I must ask of you."

"And what is that?"

The Shah of Iran is planning to leave Iran for exile later this year. He just revealed his secret to me today. Will you accept him in exile here in Egypt?"

"Why, of course we will accept the Shah!"

"President Sadim, thank you very much. The world will admire you for what you are going to do. I want you and Prime Minister Begin to come to the US for peace negotiations. I will act as an honest broker in those discussions."

"Mr. President, I'll have my foreign minister contact the Israeli foreign minister in the near future to arrange for my historic trip to Jerusalem. My country will welcome the return of the Sinai."

The two leaders sealed their secret agreement with a warm hug and a handshake. Both men agreed never to reveal this secret meeting. The Israeli/Egyptian peace agreement would appear as a natural world development, uncoupled to the Césme missile crisis.

After Air Force One took off from the Cairo airport, the President said to his Security Advisor, "I want you to make a secret trip to Israel next week as my personal envoy to Prime Minister Begin. Explain the *facts of life* to him about the Sinai. Also, arrange a time for him to meet with me and Sadim in Washington for the peace negotiations at Camp David."

"And what shall I tell Mr. Begin is he refuses to give up the Sinai?"

"You heard what I said to Sadim. Tell Begin all US aid will cease immediately and that all orders for aircraft and military supplies from the US will be canceled at once. That will melt his resistance."

"I'm sure it will, Mr. President. But, how can you do that? Congress may not go along."

"Simple. By Executive Order. The President of the US has extraordinary powers if he chooses to exercise them. In this case, I would do that. The Israelis understand the workings of the US government better than most Americans. Begin will agree to give up the Sinai when he understands the consequences of not agreeing."

During the Christmas holidays of 1979, the Soviets invaded Afghanistan. The Soviet Premier explained to the Politburo that he had negotiated this agreement with the US President as the third Césme accord on November 26, 1976. Part of the agreement was that he delay the invasion as long as possible.

The dour faced Soviet Foreign Minister Gromyko asked, "And, Mr. Premier, what price must we pay to invade Afghanistan without counter military action by the United States? I'm sure the Americans are not fools. They must have made you pay dearly for Afghanistan."

"You are right, Andrei Andrejevich. The US President did insist on some stringent conditions. First, he is going to cancel all American grain sales to the Soviet Union. Second, he is going to refuse to send American athletes to Moscow for the 1980 Olympic Games."

"Surely, Leonid Ilyich, you jest! We can buy grain from the Argentineans much cheaper than from the Americans. And if the Americans don't come to the Moscow Olympic Games, then our Soviet athletes will win more gold medals. That seems like no price at all!"

"None-the-less, Andrei Andrejevich, that was the agreement with the President."

"Perhaps I was wrong then, Leonid Ilyich. The Americans *are* fools!"

The President met with his Security Advisor after announcing his sanctions against the Soviet Union for the Afghanistan invasion. He said with his characteristic broad grin, "Mr. Chairman, my secret agreements with Premier Brezhnev are now completed. The world will never know how close we came to World War III. Now, if I can only convince Khomeini to release our American hostages in the US Embassy in Tehran, my first term as President will be considered successful in the history books."

"You haven't been able to negotiate logically with Khomeini so far. Maybe the Shah was right. Maybe Khomeini is a madman!"

Epilogue

In early 1977, the Tehran newspapers were filled with reports about businessmen who were being persecuted by the Shah's eclipsing government. It almost seemed as though the Shah was trying to declare to the Iranian people, "My regime is not corrupt. Look! I'm putting all these outstanding businessmen in jail for profiteering. See! I'm not so bad after all."

Mr. Abfol Mahi was at his villa on the Côte d'Azur of southern France between Nice and Monaco when he read the news of his indictment for corruption in the *International Herald Tribune.* He had just returned to his French home the night before after hand carrying an hundred million dollar deposit to his Swiss bank account in Zürich, which brought his liquid assets up to $500 million. Even though his paper assets were well over one billion dollars, he only counted the liquid assets in the Swiss bank as *real.* After reading the newspaper article, he realized his other non-liquid assets – airplanes, office buildings, company net worth, and his residence with its gold leaf ceiling in the study – all in Tehran – were gone forever. Fortunately, his daughter, Fahrina, was still visiting her friend, Heidi, in Zürich. The rest of his family were with him. Iran and France did not have an extradition treaty that covered the crime he'd been charged with. He was glad he had a passport for Monaco where he was registered as a resident. He would never use his Iranian passport again.

Mr. Mahi dialed Heidi's number in Zürich to warn Fahrina about the article in the *Herald Tribune* and to warn her not to go back to Tehran, since she had been an executive in Iran Software, Ltd. She told him not to worry. She planned to go to Athens and buy a house there overlooking the Aegean Sea. She thought maybe she'd buy a software company there to keep her mind busy. She signed off with, "Iran is finished! Good luck, Papa."

In January 1977, Dr. Kelly had a meeting with the Los Angeles US Attorney about the *illegal export matter* Dr. Morrell had mentioned during his November call to Kelly in Iran. The US

Attorney had advised Kelly to bring his attorney to the meeting. US Customs Agents had obtained a court order and had picked up all Kelly's papers having to do with the export of the Swiss Cryptomatik equipment to Iran. The Customs Agent cited an obscure section of the complex US export laws that gave the US export people control over items of foreign manufacture if they were integrated with US manufactured equipment. Kelly discovered the US Attorney was considering bringing the case to the Federal Grand Jury to get a felony indictment against him. Kelly was surprised the investigation was directed against him personally, not AAC.

Driving back from his meeting, Kelly heard on his car radio, "General Hatami, chief of the Iranian Air Force, was killed today in an accident in Iran. Details are sketchy but reports are that General Hatami was engaged in his favorite sport of hang gliding on a mountain peak north of Tehran called Takht-i-Suleyman. His body has been recovered and his funeral will be Friday. Over two hundred people are expected to view the funeral parade of the popular Iranian military leader."

Kelly said to himself, *And I thought I was having troubles because of IBEX! That was no accident. General Hatami was assassinated, either by the Shah's enemies or by the Shah's Savak. We'll probably never know which it was.*

In the months after Kelly's return from Iran, he spent many hours meeting with the Associated Aviation board of directors to try to explain why the last $240 million of the IBEX contract had not been paid on January 15th as promised. Of course, Kelly didn't know the furious Shah, after his meeting with the US President, had ordered that no more Iranian money would go to the United States. The cash flow problems at AAC were very bad and there had to be a scapegoat. It was Dr. Morrell.

Two months after Robert Hack joined AAC as executive vice president, Kelly noticed that Hack was involved in almost all decision making processes. One day, Kelly went to Dr. Morrell's office to get an important decision about a new proposal. Dr. Morrell referred Kelly to Hack instead and added, "Brad, apparently you don't understand how top executives are fired in the aerospace business. I still have the title, the office, my salary, and my executive secretary but I don't make corporate decisions any more. I'm spending full time looking for a new job."

Kelly mumbled his apologies and left quickly. He'd been around the aerospace business long enough to understand the basic concept: it wasn't healthy to appear too friendly with a fired executive.

A short time later, an announcement appeared in the *Los Angeles Times* financial section: Mr. Robert Hack has been elected president of Associated Aviation Corporation, the giant aerospace firm in Van Nuys. He replaces Dr. John Morrell, who held the post for six years. Dr. Morrell is becoming a management consultant. Mr. Hack was formerly an executive with the Defense Department in the Pentagon.

The Shah left Iran in October 1977 and was given political asylum by President Sadim of Egypt. The Shah and his family had comfortable quarters in a large villa overlooking the majestic Nile River.

In January 1978, Kelly read in the *Los Angeles Times* about the beginning of the Khomeini revolution and the associated fighting in the streets of Tehran. He was growing more relaxed about the illegal export problem since he hadn't heard anything about it in almost a year. He was working long hours at AAC trying to bring in a new contract connected with the new US Space Station project. He hadn't thought about IBEX for a long time. As he read the back pages of the article a paragraph caught his eye: "General Fahi of the Iranian Air Force was captured by a horde of Homofahrs (non-commissioned officers) at the Doshen Toeppeh Air Force Base. He was tortured and beaten by the Homofahrs, whom Khomeini is using to bring Moslem Ideals back to the Iranian armed forces. General Fahi's badly mutilated body was turned over to relatives for burial." Kelly suddenly realized General Fahi was killed because he had been promoted from colonel to general by the Shah. He read farther in the same article, "General Doshenshah of the Iranian Air Force was convicted of *corrupt practices* by the Iranian Revolutionary Council, which announced, 'His body was hung in the streets of Tehran so all citizens could show their contempt for this evil criminal'."

Like all other loyal Americans, Kelly followed the story of the US hostages very closely in the newspapers. The reports made him think of the time in November 1976 when he talked to the President from that same US Embassy. He thought of his night there with the secretary, Joanne, and it pained him to realize she was one of the hostages. He hoped President Mahoney would take some heroic action to get them released, since nothing seemed to be happening in the endless negotiations. The cruel parading of these American victims in front of the TV cameras kept going on and on. Kelly wondered what the Khomeini revolutionaries hoped to achieve by the kidnapping.

Then he answered his own question, *They want to show the world the supposedly all-powerful US government can do nothing. If they try to rescue the hostages, the captives may be killed. If they don't, the world will think American is weak and doesn't care about its citizens being held hostage.*

Kelly was glad to read about the abortive attempt to rescue the hostages. Even though it was unsuccessful, it showed President Mahoney was trying. From information he gathered at some of the scientific study groups he attended, Kelly knew the President had not used his Special Forces. He had used elements of the air force, the navy, and the marines so they could all share equally in the glory. Kelly felt the operation had failed because too many people were involved and because the President had tried to control the operation from Washington. Then Kelly remembered Ambassador Hurd's comment about his telephone briefing for President Mahoney, *Don't worry about too many technical details with the President. He likes to become involved in detail!* Kelly concluded Mahoney was defeated in the November 1980 election because of the Iranian hostage problem.

In the same issue of the *Los Angeles Times* carrying the election results, the headline of an article buried inside the paper

caught Kelly's eye: ISRAELI AGENT AND TWO
COMPANIONS MURDERED IN PARIS.

With grave foreboding, Kelly read the text: "An agent of the
Israeli Mossad was found murdered in his plush Paris apartment
along with two female companions. The Israeli Embassy
identified the male victim as Amnon Milchbucher, formerly of Tel
Aviv, who had been residing in Paris with the two female victims
for the last three years. The Swedish Embassy identified the
female victims as Christina Rimsen and Olga Sonnensohn. The
Paris police suspect the victims were killed by PLO agents. The
bodies were horribly mutilated."

Just before Christmas 1980, Kelly received a call from the US
Attorney's office, asking him to come with his attorney to sign
some *routine papers*. At the meeting, the US Attorney asked Kelly
to sign a letter stating that he waived his rights under the statute of
limitations regarding the illegal export matter. The US Attorney
said Kelly's cooperation *would be appreciated* by the courts. At
first Kelly refused to sign, but his attorney advised him in private,
"If you don't, the US Attorney will go for an immediate indictment
because the statue of limitations will be running out soon. This
way, maybe we can convince him to drop the case."

Kelly reluctantly agreed to waive his rights, since he couldn't
conceive that the US government would really act to indict a loyal
citizen, especially one who held the medal for meritorious civilian
service.

Later, after further discussions with the US Attorney, Kelly's
attorney became worried an indictment would result. He explained
to Kelly, "The Federal Grand Jury is a *rubber stamp* for the US
Attorney. They give him whatever he asks for."

Kelly was incredulous. Like most Americans, he believed the
Federal Grand Jury system protected citizens from overzealous US
Attorneys, not just act as their helpers.

In February 1981, Kelly heard two news items on his car
radio:

ITEM 1: "It was announced in Athens today that the
fabulously wealthy shipping magnate, Agnos Spiro, has taken as

his bride Miss Fahrina Mahi, formerly of Iran, daughter of Mr. Abfol Mahi, now residing in Nice, France. The union brings together two of the wealthiest families in the world."

ITEM 2: "Paris police reported another terrorist shooting on the streets of Paris. A spokesman for the deceased Shah of Iran's family reported the victim, Mr. Shaheen Mouhoud, a nephew of the Shah, had been responsible for the exiled Shah's security. Mr. Mouhoud had gone with the Shah on his tragic exile in Egypt, accompanied him to the US for medical treatment, and remained with him until his death in Panama. The police suspect supporters of Khomeini committed the assassination, using an Uzi submachine gun."

Kelly again relaxed into his ritual of work. He worried, *The Statute of Limitations for my case would have run out by now if I hadn't signed that letter waiving my rights. But, I guess they are going to drop the case since I haven't heard from them for a while.*

A few months later Kelly read in the *Los Angeles Times*, "Fahrina Mahi Spiro was named the recipient of $750 million in the will of her late husband, Agnos Spiro, the 75 year old shipping magnate who died of a heart attack in bed last month. His son, 50 year old, Aristotle Spiro, was furious at the settlement. He exclaimed to reporters, "This bitch killed my father by sexual overexertion. My sister and I plan to contest the will." Analysts estimate this inheritance makes Fahrina wealthier than her father, Abfol Mahi, the reputed bastard brother of the late Shah of Iran.

In the summer of 1981, Kelly was indicted by a Federal Grand Jury for US export law violations. The US Attorney, Robert Boniface, who presented the case to the Grand Jury, charged, "Dr. Bradford R. Kelly illegally exported high technology cryptographic equipment. Even though he obtained a Swiss export license, he should have known he needed a US export license, since the Swiss equipment was integrated with sensitive US equipment. The NSA and Pentagon would never have permitted the export of such high technology cryptographic equipment as that which Bradford R. Kelly blatantly exported.

Kelly was charged with seven counts of export law violation, one for each of the six IBEX sites and one for the central processing site. Each charge carried ten years in prison and $100,000 fine.

In the press conference following the Grand Jury indictment, US Attorney Boniface declared to a battery of TV cameras, "Bradford R. Kelly was responsible for the export of high technology cryptographic equipment as part of the IBEX project in Iran." No one seemed to notice that the attorney was revealing SCI (secret compartmentalized information) to the general public.

Associated Aviation Corporation laid Kelly off the day the news of the indictment was announced and claimed they were prohibited by law from contributing anything to his defense fund. In spite of spending his life savings hiring a famous, expensive Century City attorney to defend him, Kelly was convicted by a jury in Los Angeles Federal Court.

In sentencing him, Judge Pamela Rinehardt said, "I should have given you the full 70 years for this major crime, but, in view of the meritorious civilian award you received from the former President for your work on the IBEX project, I am sentencing you to only ten years in prison plus five years on parole plus a fine of $350,000."

Judge Rinehardt was later appointed to the Supreme Court by President Reagan and confirmed by Congress. Her firm record against *White Collar Criminals* was cited in her Presidential recommendation.

Dr. Jon Schiller

www.ingramcontent.com/pod-product-compliance
Lightning Source LLC
Chambersburg PA
CBHW051137030726
47504CB00004B/918

9 780977 430529